Erica James
PARADISE HOUSE

ORION

First published in Great Britain in 2003
by Orion Books
This paperback edition published in 2022
by Orion Fiction,
Carmelite House, 50 Victoria Embankment
London EC4Y 0DZ

An Hachette UK company

1 3 5 7 9 10 8 6 4 2

Copyright © Erica James 2003

A CIP catalogue record for this book is
available from the British Library.

ISBN (Paperback) 978 1 3987 1072 6
ISBN (eBook) 978 1 4091 0749 1

Typeset by Deltatype Ltd, Birkenhead, Merseyside

Printed and bound in Great Britain by Clays Ltd, Elcograf S.p.A.

MIX
Paper from
responsible sources
FSC® C104740

www.orionbooks.co.uk

To Edward and Samuel, with love and respect

PART I

Chapter One

When Genevieve Baxter was eleven years old, her family played a trick on her father; they organised a surprise fortieth birthday party for him. Nineteen years later, Genevieve and her sisters were planning to surprise him again.

The plan, once they'd given him his cards and presents after breakfast, was to make him think that they were all far too busy to spend the day with him (or be up to anything behind his back) and to hint that perhaps he ought to take himself off for a long walk. To underline this, Genevieve had told him that she had a thrilling day of ironing and bookkeeping ahead, Polly had said that she had lessons to teach in St David's, and Nattie had kicked up a fuss that she would have to put in an appearance at the wine bar where, reputedly, she worked. This was perhaps the least convincing fib as Nattie rarely worked if she could help it. She claimed a job wasn't compatible with being a single mother. Truth was, despite being all of twenty-eight, she still believed that money grew on trees. The rest of the family lived in hope that one day Lily-Rose, a sweet-natured four-year-old, would teach her mother the ways of the world. No one else had managed to.

Genevieve carried her tea and toast to her favourite spot in the garden (the private area, away from their guests) and thought of the one person who might give the game away: Granny Baxter, Daddy Dean's mother. The name Daddy Dean had been Gran's invention. She had started calling him this when Genevieve was born. The name had stuck and his daughters had subsequently followed their grandmother's example, as had Lily-Rose. Gran had always been a one-off, but these days she alternated between blithe confusion and sparkling lucidity, which made her as unpredictable as the weather.

Yesterday had been a typical example of the fickleness of the Pembrokeshire weather, an area known for having its own climate. The morning had started out pleasantly enough but by the afternoon the wind had gusted in from the Atlantic and rattled the windows of Paradise House. Driving rain had sent all but the hardiest of coastal walkers fleeing for cover – straight into the teashops of Angel Sands and the only public house, the Salvation Arms. This morning, though, the wind and rain had passed and a golden sun shone in a sky of misty apricot: it was a beautiful May morning.

At eight o'clock, in an hour's time, Genevieve would be cooking and serving breakfast. Three couples and a single man were staying with them – all first-timers, which was unusual; a lot of their bed and breakfast guests had been coming for years.

Before moving to Angel Sands, Genevieve and her family had been regular visitors to this part of Pembrokeshire, spending every summer holiday in a cottage a mile out of the village. It had become a second home to them, somewhere Genevieve longed to be the moment she was back at school for the start of the autumn term. But there again, whenever she was at school she longed to be anywhere else. Then their father had decided to sell their home, Brook House Farm, a 450-acre dairy farm that had belonged to his father and his father before him. Genevieve knew that he had never forgiven himself for this bold step. 'It's a new beginning,' he'd told the family, when he finally accepted an offer that was too good to turn down from the builder who had pestered him to sell

4

up for more than three years. It was an offer that would give them financial security.

The New Beginning had been Mum's idea. Serena Baxter had never really taken to the role of farmer's wife. 'Whoever came up with the design for a cow deserves to be one,' she used to say. 'Anyone with an ounce of sense can see those legs at the back aren't made right. That's why they walk in that peculiarly stiff way.'

Genevieve's parents had met at a church barn dance. It had been love at first sight when Serena had tripped over a bale of hay and fallen into the arms of an anxious-looking man five years older than her. The spirited youngest daughter of the local vicar was an unlikely match for the stolid only son of a farmer, but they were wed within the year and settled into married life without a backward glance.

The years passed. Genevieve arrived, her sisters following shortly after, and their father took on the running of Brook House Farm, his own parents deciding it was time to take it easy. He threw himself into updating the milking parlour for greater efficiency and acquiring extra land from neighbouring farms to grow more of his own animal feed, while Serena began to dream of another life – a life that didn't include five o'clock milking or smelly overalls that needed washing every day. She imagined an idyll by the sea, a picturesque guest house with breeze-filled bedrooms decorated in pastel shades, with borders of stencilled flowers; bowls of pot-pourri placed on polished antique furniture that she and Daddy Dean had lovingly restored together; scented bags of lavender tucked under guests' pillows; linen as white and fresh as snow. And because their father was crazy about Serena, her dream became his.

The day they heard that a sizeable property with ten bedrooms in Angel Sands had come onto the market, he made an offer for it. They knew exactly which house it was, didn't need to view it to know that it was just what they wanted. Paradise House, with its whitewashed walls and pantiled roof, was well known to anyone who had ever visited Angel Sands – it even featured on local postcards. It stood imposingly alone on the hillside with magnificent views of the pretty bay and out to sea. The previous owners had let the Edwardian house go. Water poured in through missing roof tiles, broken windows were boarded up and gutters hanging off, and the lantern roof of the original conservatory leaked like a sieve. It was going for a song, and was just the opportunity her parents needed. Although more than ten years had passed, Genevieve could still recall the family's excitement the day they moved in. She suspected the removal men could remember it, too. The drive to the house was too steep and narrow for the large van to negotiate and the men had nearly killed themselves lugging furniture up to the house in the sweltering heat of an August afternoon.

And so The Dream became reality and they all lived happily ever after.

Except it didn't quite work out that way.

Selling Brook House Farm had been the hardest thing their father had ever done, and his conscience told him he'd sold out. Not that he said as much – he was a man of few words and rarely expressed himself – but as the years went by and Serena eventually guessed what was on his mind, she too fell victim to a guilty conscience, for hadn't she been the one to instigate the change in their lives? Yet instead of sitting down to discuss it – talking things through wasn't a Baxter trait, as Genevieve knew better than anyone – Serena turned the problem into an even bigger drama by running away from it. Literally.

'We need some time apart,' she told their father, as the taxi waited at the front door to take her to the station. 'I still love you, but I can't bear to see what I've done to

6

you. Forgive me, please, and let me go.'

Unbelievably, he did just that, and Serena went to stay with her sister in Lincoln. 'I had to do as she said,' he told Genevieve and her sisters. 'She'll be home soon. When she's ready. I know she will.' This apparent benign acceptance of the situation was so typical of their father. Many times Genevieve had seen him wrong-footed by the complexities of life, but rarely had she witnessed him lose his temper or act impetuously. He was a stoic to the last. Genevieve was frequently maddened and frustrated by his behaviour, but she was too much like him to hope that he would ever change. Neither could cope well with confrontation.

Serena had been gone six months now and he was still patiently waiting for her to come home. Initially she phoned every other week and chatted about nothing in particular, but the calls petered out and were replaced by letters. At the end of March, Genevieve and her sisters, plus little Lily-Rose, went to see Serena in secret, to try to persuade her to come back. Lily-Rose was their trump card, or so they thought. But no. Serena had Plans.

An old school friend, living in New Zealand, had invited her to stay. The so-called friend ran a winery in Hawkes Bay and was, of all things . . . a *man!* She swore blind that there was nothing to read into the situation, but Genevieve and her sisters had been so appalled that they left early, Nattie driving like a lunatic and swearing she would never speak to their mother again. To leave their father temporarily to go off and find herself was excusable, but to travel to the other side of the world and take up with some New World man was unthinkable! Until then, they had been patient and believed that their mother was just going through another of her phases. Like the time she had insisted there was no need for them to wash their hair, that once their scalps were allowed to behave as nature had intended their hair would adapt and acquire a healthy sheen. The phase came to an abrupt end when Polly caught nits from the girl she sat next to on the school bus; consequently every known chemical was vigorously applied to their heads.

They never told their father about the visit, nor said anything when Serena wrote to him with the news that she was going to New Zealand to visit a friend. They pretended it was the first they'd heard of it and, by way of distraction, Genevieve suggested that he threw himself into getting Paradise House into better shape. Things had been allowed to slip – the bags of lavender had certainly lost their scent – and some of the comments in the Visitor's Book were less than kind.

Another father in another family might have been able to rely upon his grown-up children for practical help, but sadly this was not to be. Polly, the baby of the family and the only one still living at home, was undeniably the cleverest and the prettiest, but she was dreamily vague and languid. She went in for what Genevieve called a 'vintage' look, wearing long Forties style flowery dresses she picked up from charity shops or jumble sales, and it wasn't unheard of for her to be seen leaving the house in shoes that didn't match. She was a brilliant musician, though. She could play the flute, violin and piano, and could have played in any number of orchestras if she'd put her mind to it, but she opted to work as a peripatetic music teacher. She loved her subject and she loved children, probably because, though twenty-six, she still possessed a wide-eyed innocence and an endearing ability to think well of others. The boys she taught, big or small, were always having crushes on her.

But her practical skills rated a big zero. Only the other day Genevieve had asked her to keep an eye on the bacon while she went to take another breakfast order: when Genevieve returned from the dining room, smoke was billowing from the grill. Glancing up from the book she was reading – *Charlotte's Web* – she had looked at Genevieve with an expression of mild curiosity, as if wondering why her sister was throwing open the back door and hurling the smoking grill pan through it. She was exasperating, but Genevieve knew it was pointless getting angry with Polly, she meant no harm. You just had to grit your teeth and accept that she inhabited a different world from the one in which everyone else lived.

As for Nattie, well, it was difficult to know where to start. She was the middle sister and lived in Tenby in a grotty bedsit in a house of giro-claiming slackers. There was a tenuous boyfriend on the scene, but he wasn't Lily-Rose's father. Which was just as well because he was totally unsuitable, a feckless beach bum who spent his every waking moment riding the breaking waves at nearby Manorbier, thinking he could surf his way through life with nothing more to his name than a pair of baggy shorts and flip-flops.

If Nattie excelled at picking appalling boyfriends, she also excelled at being rebellious and stubborn. As a child she had driven their parents mad with her constant tantrums – nobody, even now, could slam a door quite like Nattie. She was a loving mother to Lily-Rose, but perhaps wasn't as consistent as she ought to be. She thought nothing of arriving at Paradise House and expecting someone to take care of Lily-Rose while she went off on some crusade or other. Life for Nattie was one long fight against those who would abuse or exploit others. It never occurred to her that she did her own share of exploiting. No one at Paradise House rebuked her for her lack of consideration, for luckily they enjoyed looking after Lily-Rose. Blue-eyed and strikingly blonde with corkscrew curls, Lily was adorable and a delight to have around.

It was partly because her sisters were so impractical that Genevieve had, over the Easter break, made the decision to come home to Paradise House during her mother's absence. She'd held off from doing so, knowing that like her mother she was running away, but it would only be for a while, until life had steadied for her and she knew what she wanted to do next. It wasn't just Paradise House that needed a firm hand to steer its course; she did too.

Top of Genevieve's list of Things To Be Done at Paradise House had been to advertise for a cleaner – the last woman had left shortly before Serena departed and no one had thought to replace her. But finding a replacement hadn't been straightforward. The only applicants were drifters, male and female, wanting to fund their surfing habits – did she have any idea how expensive decent boards and wet suits were? Well, yes actually, she did; Nattie's boyfriend constantly bored them all to death on the subject.

She advertised again. The only candidate to come forward this time was Donna Morgan, a cousin of Debs who ran Debonhair, the local hair salon. Donna had recently moved from Caerphilly to Angel Sands to escape her bully of an ex husband. She was in her mid-fifties with a touch of the Bonnie Tyler about her – lots of back-combed dyed blonde hair, husky voice, faded denim and high heels, and a heavy hand when it came to eye make-up. Donna worked part-time behind the bar at the Salvation Arms and had already made a name for herself on karaoke night with her rendition of 'Lost in France'. She had only been in Angel Sands for three weeks, but was already a fixture.

Genevieve had offered her the job but couldn't deny how uneasy she felt. Had it been her imagination, or had Donna looked at her father with more than passing friendliness when they had discussed the work involved? Since Serena had gone and tongues had begun to wag, there had been a surprising number of female callers at

Paradise House. They came bearing offers of help – did her father want his ironing done? Or maybe a casserole or two cooked? It would be no trouble. It was difficult for Genevieve to view Daddy Dean as a sexual being, but there was clearly something about him that was drawing attention from the widowed and divorced. Gran said it was a biological fact that once a single woman got a whiff of a helpless and bewildered man, there was no stopping her. 'Heaven help him, but they'll keep banging on that door until Serena comes home.'

Helpless and bewildered described her father perfectly. Like so many men who have lost their partner, he'd suddenly become inept at the simplest tasks. Just finding his socks and underpants required all his attention.

But any female attention lavished on him was in vain and invariably had him running in the opposite direction, usually to his workshop in the garden. If things got really bad, he shimmied up a conveniently placed ladder and hid on the roof, claiming the lead flashing or a broken tile needed fixing. Essentially he was a shy man who hated to be the focus of attention, but he was also a man who loved his wife as much as the day she'd tripped and fallen into his arms more than thirty years ago. Genevieve knew he had built an exclusion zone around himself so he could go on living in the hope that Serena would simply turn up one day and say, 'Surprise! I'm back!' If Genevieve was honest, she thought this was exactly what her annoyingly, capriciously inconsiderate mother would do. It would be typical of Mum, to behave as though there were no consequences to her actions.

Her tea and toast finished, Genevieve walked back up to the house. She had seven breakfasts to cook, a birthday cake to ice and a surprise party to arrange. Donna would also be arriving for her first day at Paradise

House, which meant her father would make himself conveniently scarce and perhaps go for that long walk she had suggested.

Chapter Two

Genevieve rang Granny Baxter's doorbell. Waited. Then rang it several more times. Not because her grandmother was hard of hearing, but because the television would be on and the volume turned up. Ten minutes to three wasn't the best time to come – Dick Van Dyke would be in the final stages of uncovering the guilty party in *Diagnosis Murder*. Gran was an avid follower of daytime telly. She was no slouch when it came to late-night viewing either. At eighty-two years old, she was embarrassingly up to date with all the latest trends. She drew the line at Graham Norton though, saying he was too saucy by half.

There had never been any question of leaving Gran behind in Cheshire when the family moved to Angel Sands. But she had surprised everyone by insisting that she didn't want to live with them at Paradise House. 'I want my own little place,' she'd said, 'like I have here.' For years Gran (and Grandad before he'd died) had lived in a specially built bungalow on the farm: she had kept herself to herself and expected others to do the same. As luck would have it, a month after they'd moved into Paradise House a cottage had become available. Perfectly situated in the main street of the village, it was fifty yards from the nearest shops and, in Gran's own words, within shouting distance of the rest of the Baxters up on the hill. It meant she still had her independence, but help would be on hand should she need it.

Genevieve had a key to let herself in at Angel Cottage,

but she had promised her grandmother to use it only in an emergency. 'And what constitutes an emergency?' the old lady had demanded.

'Knowing what a telly addict you are, Gran, losing the remote control for the TV.'

At last the duck-egg blue door was opened. 'I knew all along who the murderer was,' Gran said. 'It was that smart piece of work with the shoulder pads. She had spurned lover stamped all over her face. You'd think they'd make it harder, wouldn't you?'

Genevieve followed her through to the sitting room. It was low-ceilinged and appeared even smaller than it was due to the quantity of furniture and ornaments squeezed into it. Hundreds of framed photographs adorned every surface – faded ones of long-dead relatives; any number of her father growing up; myriad ones of Genevieve and her sisters doing the same and, of course, snaps of Lily-Rose repeating the process. In pride of place on the television was a black and white picture of Gran and Grandad on their wedding day, the pair of them staring poker-faced into the camera. But for all the clutter in the room, it was spotless. Gran, an early riser, was usually dusting, polishing and running her ancient Ewbank over the carpets before most people were up. Invariably she was snoozing in the armchair by nine but was awake in time for elevenses and then *Bargain Hunt*.

In the last year Dad had banned her from washing the windows and the outside paintwork. But after a neighbour told him she had spotted her polishing the windows with a ball of scrunched up newspaper, he confiscated the small pair of stepladders she kept in the under-stairs cupboard. Outraged, she'd said, 'Daddy Dean, I'll thank you to keep your nose out of my affairs!'

'I will when I can trust you to do as you're told,' he'd said quietly but firmly. He rarely raised his voice.

'You always were a cussed little boy, Dean Baxter!'

From then on, Dad had cleaned Gran's windows. Of course, they never shone as brightly as when Gran did them.

'I was about to make myself a snack,' Gran said to Genevieve. 'Do you want anything?'

'No thanks. You haven't forgotten the party, have you? There'll be plenty to eat then.'

Her grandmother clicked her tongue. 'Of course I haven't forgotten!' She moved a cushion on the sofa and revealed a carefully wrapped present. 'I hid it there in case your father popped in.' She repositioned the cushion and said, 'If we're going to be drinking this afternoon, we ought to line our stomachs. I'll make us a quick sandwich.'

'Really, it's okay. I don't need anything.'

The tiny kitchen was just as cluttered as the sitting room. Genevieve's hands always itched to tidy it. The ironing board was out and the iron was hissing gently, sending little puffs of steam into the air. Goodness knows how long it had been left there.

'Shall I put this away for you, Gran?'

'Better still, finish those odds and ends for me.' With a flash of steel that made Genevieve step back, Gran used the bread knife to point to a pile of undergarments and dishcloths. Granny Baxter was famous for ironing absolutely everything. 'The day she stops ironing her knickers, we'll know it's time to worry,' Nattie often said.

While Gran hacked at the wholemeal loaf, Genevieve pushed the nose of the iron into places other irons dare not go. She was conscious that if she didn't keep an eye on the time, and the reason she was here – to fetch Gran and take her up to Paradise House – her father's party would never happen. Being with Granny Baxter wasn't dissimilar to being sucked into a black hole.

The sandwich made (Genevieve having taken a sur-reptitious glance at the best-before date on the pot of crab paste), Gran sat at the postage-stamp-sized table the other side of the ironing board. 'So how are you, Genevieve?'

Genevieve had wondered how long it would be before Gran seized her opportunity. She kept her eyes on the iron. 'I'm fine,' she said.

'Sleeping?'

'Better.'

'Still taking the pills?'

'No.'

'That's good. Any more nightmares?'

'A few.'

'Eating properly?'

'Of course.'

'Mm . . .'

Seconds passed.

'You should talk about it more, Genevieve. Bottling's for fruit, not people.'

Obviously Gran was in one of her more lucid frames of mind. 'Coming from a Baxter, that's nothing short of pioneering stuff,' Genevieve said.

'We should learn from our mistakes. It's time you and your parents did the same. You're not depressed, are you?'

'No. I told you, I'm fine.'

Gran went to change for the party, her sandwich scarcely touched. Genevieve knew the last fifteen minutes had been nothing but a ruse to ensure some time alone. Listening to her grandmother moving about upstairs, Genevieve tidied the kitchen, or tidied what she could without incurring Gran's fury at being interfered with. She put the loaf back in the bread bin, butter in the fridge, knife, plate and empty paste pot in the sink. She knew better than to throw it away. Glass bottles of any size were always washed and stored in the pantry, ready for jam-making, pickling and bottling.

The interrogation hadn't been as bad as it could have been. Considering her grandmother's nickname of Gestapo Gran, she had let Genevieve off lightly. She was right, though; Genevieve *should* talk about it more. But each time she did, she ended up reliving the experience and for days afterwards felt anxious and unable to sleep at night. She had been told that she would have to be patient with herself, that it would be two steps forward and one back.

Telling herself that today wasn't a day for taking a step backwards – there was her father's party to enjoy – she pushed the memories away and put the iron on the window sill to cool. She went through to the sitting room to wait for Gran.

The local paper was on the coffee table. She picked it up and read the lead story slowly. It wasn't until she was twelve that she had been diagnosed as dyslexic. Up until then, while she'd been at primary school, she had learned to keep quiet during lessons, to blend into the background and hope the teacher wouldn't ask her to read anything out – by this time she'd realised that she couldn't read as fast as everyone else. By the age of twelve it was getting harder to cover up her embarrassment at never being able to copy correctly from the blackboard. Embarrassment then turned to shame as she was classed as a 'slow learner'. Finally, an English teacher, long exasperated with the muddled mess of her homework, suggested to her parents that Genevieve be professionally tested for dyslexia. Tests showed that while the language part of her brain didn't work properly, her IQ was surprisingly high. This, Genevieve and her parents were told, explained why she'd managed to cover her tracks so successfully. If her coping strategies had been less effective, the disorder might have been picked up sooner.

No matter how sympathetically she and her disorder were treated from then on, the harm had been done: the label of 'lazy and thick' had been applied to her for so many years, subconsciously it would never leave her. Even now, at the age of thirty, she felt the need to prove she wasn't stupid.

One of her biggest regrets was that when she was seventeen, due to what became known as That Time When She Wasn't Well, she'd dropped out of school and taken a variety of jobs – cinema usherette, shop assistant, even a stint as a kennel maid. Then from nowhere she got the idea to become a cook, and found a part-time job in a restaurant as little more than a skivvy – washing, chopping and stirring. Before long, by attending the local technical college twice a week, she proved herself both competent and quick to learn. But just as things seemed to be coming together for her, her father sold the farm in Cheshire and they moved down to Pembrokeshire. For the next nine months she helped her parents run Paradise House, but inevitably she soon felt the need to widen her horizons. She applied for a post at a hotel in Cardiff, where Nattie was doing a Media Arts degree at the university. The two of them shared a poky one-bedroomed flat.

It was a disaster. Genevieve would stagger home from a twelve-hour day on her feet in a sweltering understaffed kitchen, while Nattie, not long out of bed, would be in party mode. Genevieve seldom had the energy to do more than collapse exhausted on the sofa. She lasted ten months working in the kitchen from hell, putting up with ridiculous hours and a foul-mouthed, hard-drinking chef who knew less than she did, before she decided enough was enough. She found another job in an upmarket restaurant specialising in overpriced nouvelle cuisine, but soon realised she was out of the frying pan and into the fire. Her new boss was an arrogant Gallic chef from Marseille. He had a fiery temper – euphemistically referred to as an artistic temperament – and clammy, groping hands. She gave in her notice after three months. When the owner of the restaurant, the groping Gallic's wife, asked her why she was leaving, Genevieve told her. 'Because your sleazy husband can't keep his hands to himself. If I had the energy, I'd have him for sexual harassment. Oh, and you might like to check the cold store; I locked him in there five minutes ago.' That had been Nattie's inspired idea.

She walked out of the restaurant, head held high, in search of a change of direction. She was only twenty-two, but felt more like ninety-two. Trainee chefs, she had come to realise, were treated as little more than cannon fodder, to be used and abused by egotistical maniacs in a male-dominated environment. It wasn't for her.

A spate of jobs followed, as diverse as the ones she'd tried on leaving school. Then clever old Gran came up with a novel career move for her. 'Why don't you keep house for some la-di-da family? I bet there's plenty of folk willing to pay through the nose for someone who can cook as well as you do and keep them organised.'

As daft as it sounded, Genevieve pursued the suggestion and found to her astonishment that there was quite a market for housekeepers – and not the scary fictional ones dressed in black with keys hanging from a belt! So long as she was prepared to be flexible and take anything on, plenty of opportunities were on offer.

Having been bitten before, she started as she meant to go on and chose her employers with care: no more egotistical maniacs, and no potential gropers. The work was varied and not badly paid. It also came with live-in accommodation and occasionally the opportunity to travel, when the families took her on holiday with them, claiming it wouldn't be the same without her. The only downside was that she had so little time off, it was difficult to make friends outside the family. And sometimes she grew too fond of the people she worked for, and they of her, so when the time came to move on, the wrench was hard.

The sweetest of all the people she'd worked for had been George and Cecily Randolph, an elderly couple who had treated her more as a granddaughter than an employee. But just thinking of them brought on a stab of pain, and she was glad to hear Gran coming down the stairs singing 'Mine Eyes Have Seen the Glory'.

Good old Gran. She could always be relied upon to chase away a maudlin thought.

Chapter Three

To Genevieve's relief, everything had gone according to plan and the surprise party was well into its stride. A quick glance round the garden told her that the guests were having a good time and mixing happily. Even her father looked as though he was enjoying himself. It was good to see him smiling.

Their friends were mostly what the born-and-bred locals referred to as Newcomers, but when it came down to it, there were very few in the village who could lay claim to being a true local. Stan and Gwen Norman, who'd taken over the mini-market in the village five years ago, were laughing and chatting with Huw and Jane Davies who, a short while after the Baxters had moved to Angel Sands, had given up the rat race in Cardiff, bought the former blacksmith's cottage and workshop and converted it into a pottery and art gallery. Jane was a noted artist in the area and Huw (a former Inland Revenue inspector) produced whimsical mugs, jugs and teapots in the shape of dragons. Clichéd stuff, he'd be the first to admit, but it was instant bread and butter on the table. As a sideline, he helped them all with their tax returns.

Over by the conservatory and sitting in the shade, Ruth Llewellyn was nodding her head to whatever Gran was saying. Ruth and her husband ran Angel Crafts, a gift shop in the centre of the village – William was currently holding the fort with their two teenage daughters. They were recent arrivals in the village, having bought the shop last year when it had been a ramshackle angling supplier.

One of the facts of life in Angel Sands was that running any business off the back of tourism was harder than people thought, and shop premises changed hands almost as regularly as the tide came and went. The Lloyd-Morris brothers, on the other hand, had stood the test of time. Roy and David had been butchers in Angel Sands for as long as anyone could remember and, once tasted, their Welsh spring lamb and homemade sausages could never be forgotten. There was talk that with the help of their wives, Ann and Megan, they might set up a mail order side to the business. Sadly only Roy and Ann had been able to come to the party as David had drawn the short straw and was back at the shop.

Genevieve had thought about holding the party in the evening, but then Huw and Jane wouldn't have been able to make it, along with Tubby Evans – his real name was Robert. So late afternoon it had to be. The only other guest was Adam Kellar. Everyone knew that Adam had an enormous crush on Nattie, and predictably the object of his desire was ignoring him. She stood barefoot, wearing a pair of enormous dungarees rolled up to her knees, nothing underneath, and was lecturing Tubby on the perils of pesticides, flinging her hands about to emphasise the seriousness of her message. Genevieve suspected that Tubby was only letting her rant on because there was every likelihood that a small pink breast would peep out from behind the bib of her dungarees.

Tubby – so called because of his short legs and rotund shape – drove the local mobile fruit and veg van and was very much the man in the know. He had access to anything newsworthy in the area; houses had been bought and sold via him in a single afternoon. It was Tubby who had nicknamed Genevieve and her sisters the Sisters of Whimsy. He claimed they were the strangest collection of girls he'd ever come across. But as their father commented wryly, Tubby had never had a family and experienced the hair-raising roller coaster of bringing up three daughters.

A flash of white across the lawn caught Genevieve's attention. It was Polly, dressed in an ankle-length white cotton dress that was practically see-through, and looking like a girl from a Timotei shampoo advert. She was drifting absently through the orchard in the dappled sunlight, clutching a bunch of bluebells. Lily-Rose was following closely in her footsteps, quite a feat in the long grass, given that she was wearing her mother's multi-coloured clogs. She trailed behind her a cardboard box containing a collection of favourite dolls and teddy bears.

Seeing that Adam was standing on his own, Genevieve carried a tray of canapés over to him. 'How's it going?' she asked. She was fond of Adam and couldn't help but feel sorry for him. Ever since he'd arrived in Angel Sands, he'd been hopelessly smitten with Nattie. But Nattie refused steadfastly to have anything to do with him. Genevieve thought her sister was a fool. Adam was warm-hearted and endlessly generous. Endlessly forgiving, too, especially with Nattie.

'But how could I consider him as a potential date?' she would say. 'I mean, for pity's sake, he wears a gold bracelet! And worse, he holds a knife like a pencil!'

As children, the Baxter girls had been repeatedly warned by their mother of this heinous crime. 'The way you eat says a lot about the person you are,' she would tell them. That Nattie should ever think her manners were better than anyone else's was, of course, laughable.

Adam helped himself to a miniature Yorkshire pudding topped with a sliver of rare beef and horseradish sauce, the movement causing the offending piece of jewellery to slide down his tanned forearm. 'Everything's just cracking,' he said. 'Couldn't be better.' Adam was always upbeat. 'I've bought another caravan park. At Nolton Haven. I signed the contract yesterday.'

'So I hear.' Genevieve had already heard the news, from Tubby, of course.

'I got it cheap as buttons. It needs wads of cash throwing at it, but by the time I've finished, I'll have turned it into another of my premier sites.'

This was how Adam had made his money, buying rundown caravan parks and turning them around. He owned five in Pembrokeshire, three in Devon, five in Cornwall and another two near Blackpool. He was thirty-five but had been a bona fide millionaire since the age of twenty-six, after selling everything he had and borrowing heavily to buy his first site in Tenby. He'd cashed in on a changing market, he'd once explained to Genevieve. He'd seen how caravan sites were being remarketed – nowadays no one referred to static caravans; they were called Executive Holiday Homes and their owners included football players, retired bookies and well-off car dealers as well as ordinary holidaymakers wanting a bolt-hole by the sea. According to Adam, some of these people were so image-conscious they competed with each other over who had the biggest balconied decking, the best exterior lighting, or the best boat. 'What's a man to do,' Adam would say, 'but pander to them shamelessly?' He did this by providing excellent on-site facilities in the form of clubhouses, swimming pools, play areas, gyms, spa centres and evening entertainment.

Genevieve admired him for his enterprise and sheer hard work. He'd left school in Wolverhampton when he was sixteen and had worked tirelessly ever since, although these days he reckoned he'd earned the right to work the hours he chose. 'What's the point in slogging my guts out,' he'd say, 'if I can't sit back and enjoy it occasionally?' He had a lot to enjoy: a beautiful house in Angel Sands he'd had built eighteen months ago, a choice of flashy cars to drive, and an apartment in Barbados. All that was missing was the right person to share it. The only one he wanted was Nattie but, sadly, she despised him.

'He represents everything wrong in this world,' she complained. 'He's slowly destroying the natural beauty of where we live with his bloody awful shack parks. If he ever tries to build one near here, I'll personally burn it down.'

She would, too.

'Your sister's looking well,' Adam said. His gaze was fixed on Nattie across the lawn, where Tubby was still allowing her to berate him.

Genevieve offered Adam another canapé. 'She's not worth it, Adam. You're better off without her.'

He smiled and for a split second looked almost handsome. He had what Genevieve thought of as a solid, dependable face, the sort that wouldn't get him noticed, but would slowly grow on a person. 'I'm no oil-painting,' he once joked, 'but you should have seen me before I had the surgery!' He also joked that it was okay for Tom Cruise to be a short-arse, but for an ugly devil like him, it was no laughing matter.

Still staring at Nattie, he said, 'She's unique, Gen, and I'm a patient man.'

Genevieve knew this wasn't arrogance, it was his unshakeable belief that if you wanted something badly enough, it would eventually be yours. He chewed on the miniature Yorkshire pudding. 'You know, these aren't bad. Ever thought of setting up your own catering business? You could do really well; small business functions, wedding parties, anniversaries, you know the kind of thing. People today can't be arsed to cook like they used to. Sure, they all watch the cookery programmes on telly, but that's *all* they do. They watch someone else cook then say they haven't got the time to do it themselves.'

She laughed. 'You hate anyone to be idle, don't you, Adam?'

'Not true. I want people to be idle. That's how I make my living. You should try it.'

'What? Sit twiddling my thumbs? I don't think so.'

'No. Start your own catering business. That's if you're going to stick around Angel Sands.'

'On top of running Paradise House for Dad?'

'You can do it, Gen. You know you can. It's a matter of organisation, which I know you're good at. All you have to do is decide what you want, then go for it.'

'Is that what keeps you from giving up on Nattie?'

He ignored her question. 'If capital's a problem, I could fund you initially. You know, just to get you up and running. You'd need a small van. I could probably find you a second-hand one. I know a bloke who – '

'Adam Kellar, you are the sweetest man alive. But I'm okay for money. For the time being, anyway.'

The theme tune from *The Great Escape* had him reaching into his jacket pocket for his mobile phone. Leaving him to answer his call, Genevieve wandered over to Polly. She was sitting on the old rope swing in the orchard, her bunch of bluebells carefully laid to one side. She was humming softly and looking out to sea, her long, baby-fine blonde hair lifting on the warm breeze.

'Everything okay, Poll?'

Her sister turned; her face both beautiful and sad. 'I was just thinking of Mum. She should be here.'

Genevieve sat on the grass beside the swing and gazed at the turquoise sea glittering in the bright sunshine. A lone seagull wheeled overhead, its cry adding a poignant echo to the moment.

She should be here.

It was a simple but true statement. Their mother's absence was the only thing wrong with the party. Serena hadn't forgotten their father's birthday – she had sent a card and a small present all the way from New Zealand – but she was very much the missing guest.

It was when they had finished singing 'Happy Birthday' and Daddy Dean was holding Lily-Rose aloft so she could help him blow out the candles on the cake, all fifty-nine of them, and Tubby had teased him for being a whole two and a half years older than him, that a surprise guest appeared.

'I hope it's not too late for me to wish you a happy birthday,' said a vision in faded denim and sparkly rhinestone gems.

Chapter Four

Donna Morgan looked very much as though she'd turned up at the wrong party, in her phenomenally tight jeans, fringed and bejewelled jacket and white cowboy boots.

'I don't want to intrude, but I wanted to give you a little something,' she said. With her strong Caerphilly accent and husky voice, the words directed at Daddy Dean came out loaded with sing-songy innuendo.

You had to admire the woman's cheek, thought Genevieve. She had only mentioned in passing, while Donna was helping her clean the guests' rooms that morning, that it was her father's birthday, and here she was dressed for action as the Rhinestone Cowgirl, ready to lasso her man. Genevieve watched her father's reaction as Donna advanced towards him. Holding Lily-Rose as though she were a human shield, he took a step backwards.

Right onto Gran's foot. She let out a yelp and spilled her glass of Madeira down the front of her dress. Adam was instantly on hand with a paper napkin, but Gran was more worried about her empty glass. 'I hadn't even had a sip of it!' she muttered. Once it was refilled and Donna had apologised, calm and order were restored. Donna looked around for the intended recipient of her present, but there was no sign of him. He had fled.

Genevieve had to bite back a smile. 'I'll go and see if I can find him,' she said, picturing her father locked in the loo, refusing to come out. Thank goodness he had Lily-

Rose with him and couldn't hide on the roof.

Nattie caught up with her in the conservatory. 'The bloody nerve of that woman! Just who does she think she is, coming onto Dad like that? Tell me you didn't invite her, Gen.'

'Of course I didn't.'

'So how did she know it was his birthday?'

'I let it slip this morning.'

'Well, she'll have to go.'

Annoyed, Genevieve said, 'Perhaps you'd like to pull your weight around here and take her place.'

Nattie dismissed the comment. 'Don't be stupid, you know I can't do that. Not with Lily-Rose. But did you see how tight her jeans were?' She tutted. 'Women of a certain age. They should know better.'

'This from the girl who's been flashing her nipples at Tubby all afternoon?'

'Yeah, but for a good cause. I'm trying to convert him. A bit more persuasion and I'll have him stocking only organic produce on his van.'

'And there was me convinced you were only doing it to wind up poor Adam.'

Her sister feigned innocence. 'Oh, is he here?'

'You really are awful. One of these days you're going to regret treating him so badly. He's a great guy.'

Nattie gave her a withering look. 'Then why don't *you* go out with Mr Wonderful?'

'Because a, he's never asked me, and b, he's mad about *you.*'

They found their father upstairs in his and Mum's bedroom. He was sitting in the rocking chair he'd bought and restored for their mother when Polly was born. Lily-Rose was bouncing on the bed, beaming happily because no one was stopping her, but Dad was staring wretchedly at the card in his hands; it was the one Serena had sent him.

Genevieve and Nattie knelt on the floor, one either side of the chair. Neither spoke. What could they say? Every time a woman showed the slightest interest in him, it made him think of Serena and how much he longed for her to come home.

'I'm sorry,' he said, his words catching in his throat. 'Silly of me, I know.'

'Not silly at all,' said Genevieve, stroking his hand.

'Absolutely not,' agreed Nattie. She took his other hand. 'I'd be the same if that woman turned up at my party. Do you want me to get rid of her?'

He shook his head miserably. He was about to speak when Lily-Rose, breathless from all the bouncing, came to a wobbly stop and said, 'Don't be sad on your birthday. Come and bounce on the bed with me. Look!' She continued to demonstrate.

Their father's face instantly brightened. He got up from the chair and went to his granddaughter. He was just swinging her off the bed when they heard the sound of a car, its exhaust pipe blowing loudly. Nattie went to the window.

'Damn! It's Rupe with his brother Jules. I told them not to come till later.'

Genevieve joined her sister at the window. She didn't think she'd ever get over the fact that Nattie was going out with someone called Rupert Axworthy-Smythe. Worse, he was a useless waste of space, not yet old enough to shave on a regular basis – attached to his chin was a straggly tassel that would have looked more at home on Donna's denim jacket. All he talked about was surfing and catching the wave. His greatest responsibility in life was to own a Volkswagen camper van that was more than twice his age. When he wasn't posing on the beach with his brother and pals – more over-privileged refugees from Gloucestershire – he was painting naked women onto the psychedelic bodywork of his precious van. What Nattie saw in him was beyond Genevieve.

But then Nattie had never had much taste in boyfriends. Lily-Rose's father had been another example of her poor judgement. The moment he'd learned Nattie was pregnant he'd vanished faster than a ten-pound note during happy hour at the wine bar he worked in. There had been no question of Nattie not having the baby or giving it up for adoption. Neither of those options would have sat comfortably with her crusading instinct.

By the time they made it down to the garden, their father having recovered himself and promised not to do a runner again, Rupert and Jules had helped themselves to a drink and were eyeing up the untouched birthday cake. The other guests were keeping their distance, watching them suspiciously, especially Adam, who looked ready to grab Rupert by his goatee and toss him out to sea.

Genevieve soon realised why. Rupert was drunk.

Catching sight of Nattie, he smiled lopsidedly. 'Hiya, Nat.' He staggered towards her, came to a stop and looked her up and down. 'Ah, so that's where my dungarees went. I wondered why I couldn't find them.' He leaned in for a kiss, but she pushed him away.

'Rupe, are you drunk again?' She sounded bored more than cross, as though it was a question she'd asked him once too often.

'And what if I am? What's it to you? You, who didn't want me to come to your dad's party.'

She folded her arms across her chest. 'You're pathetic, Rupe. I don't know why I bother with you.'

'And I don't know why I bother with *you*.' He jabbed a threatening finger at her shoulder.

Genevieve sensed the other men draw themselves up to their full height, including her father. He said, 'How about something to eat, Rupert?' He'd had years of experience with Nattie's unsuitable boyfriends.

The threatening manner gave way instantly, and was replaced by the boyish grin that Genevieve suspected usually got Rupert exactly what he wanted. 'Yeah, some cake would be nice. Cheers.'

But Nattie wasn't having it. 'No, Dad,' she snapped. 'He's drunk and I don't want him here.' She looked Rupert straight in the eye. 'Please leave, Rupe. I'll see you tomorrow, when you're sober.' She turned to his brother, who had the grace to look sheepish. 'Take him home, Jules.' She walked away, her resolute manner telling them that as far as she was concerned, the matter was dealt with.

It wasn't, though. Rupert swayed on his feet, then moved after her. 'Hey! Nobody speaks to me like that. I'm not a child.'

'Then perhaps you should stop acting like one.' This was from Donna. And any trace of sing-songy innuendo was gone from her voice. In its place was a low, full-throated, assertive tone that brooked no argument. Everyone stared at her, including Rupert.

He looked her over and sneered, 'You're that tart from the pub, aren't you? The one who thinks she can sing.'

'That's enough, young man! You've gone too far now.' Dad's voice was as firm as Genevieve had ever heard it. 'I suggest you apologise to Mrs Morgan and go. You're not welcome here in this state.'

'It's okay, Mr Baxter,' said Donna. 'I can handle myself. I'm more than used to boys still wet behind the ears who can't hold their drink.'

Rupert laughed. 'I'm not apologising to anyone, least of all an old tart from the valleys. What d'yer think, Jules, should we ask her to sing just to give us a good laugh?'

Rupert was so full of himself, he didn't see the punch coming: it landed square on his nose with a squish of bone, followed by a spurt of blood. There was a collective gasp. He reeled backwards, a hand clamped to his face. Then he realised who had thumped him and that she was coming at him again. He took a swing at Nattie. It was his biggest mistake of the day.

Adam grabbed his arm, swung him round and head-butted him. His legs crumpled and he would have fallen to the ground if Adam hadn't had his hands gripped around his throat.

'Now, why don't you put your Home Counties vowels to good use and apologise to everyone here? And when you've done that, get your scrawny body out of my sight before I really lose my temper.'

The apology never came. But Jules did the decent thing and dragged his brother away. 'I never liked that boy,' Gran told Nattie, who now had her hand jammed in a bucket of ice. 'Eyes too close to-gether. Shifty as a cock-roach.'

'His eyes won't feel so close when that nose swells up,' laughed Stan Norman. 'When did you learn to box, Nattie?'

'Kick-boxing classes last year,' she said, removing her hand from the bucket and checking it over. 'I'm a firm believer in women learning self-defence. In my opinion it should be taught as a matter of course in schools. Far more useful than freezing to death on a hockey pitch.'

They were sitting on the terrace, plates of birthday cake on their laps. Genevieve knew that while her sister was making light of what had happened, she would be furious that Rupert's appalling behaviour had been witnessed by Adam. She hoped he would have the sense not to try to capitalise on it.

'How's your head, Adam?' she asked him, her voice lowered so her sister wouldn't hear. It was a miracle that Nattie hadn't castigated him for stepping in to help, when she'd thought she had the situation under control.

'It's fine,' he muttered, touching the red patch on his forehead. 'It'd take more than a prat like that to do any real damage. Honestly, Gen, what does she see in him? What's he got that I haven't?'

'I don't have a clue, Adam. And I'm not sure she knows either.'

From across the terrace came the sound of husky laughter – Donna was deep in conversation with Tubby. Funny how things had changed in the last hour, thought Genevieve. One minute Donna Morgan was the enemy and had their father running for cover, and the next he was defending her honour. Not that she'd given the impression of needing it. Like Nattie, she appeared more than capable of taking care of herself.

Genevieve wanted to believe it was progress, her father doing the gentlemanly thing, but something told her it might make matters worse. What if it gave Donna the green light to make further overtures?

Chapter Five

'But would it really be so bad if Donna did fancy Daddy?' asked Polly later that night.

They were alone in her bedroom at the top of the house where they'd always slept in what had been the attic rooms, while their parents and guests slept on the floor below. Nattie and Lily-Rose were stopping over. Genevieve and her sisters were sitting cross-legged on Polly's double bed with a tray of leftovers between them. An empty bottle of wine stood on the bedside table. Polly's question had taken Genevieve by surprise. Surely it mattered. He was their father.

Nattie said, 'Poll, I'm warning you, don't you dare go all Pollyanna on me, imagining good in everyone. Donna Morgan is bad news.'

'But how do we know that?'

'Because it's obvious. She just is.'

Polly tilted her head and frowned. 'So why did you rush to her defence when Rupert was so rude to her?'

'It's no big deal. He was annoying me and I felt like laying one on him.'

Polly let it go, but Genevieve said, 'You're such a liar, Nattie. You lashed out at Rupert because what he said was unspeakably vile and for a split second you saw Donna as a victim and not a threat.'

Nattie grunted and stuffed a piece of pizza into her mouth.

'It's true,' Genevieve said, 'and what really upsets me is that we've acted no better than Rupert. We took one look at the way Donna dresses and decided against her.'

'And with good reason! The woman is clearly after husband number two and sees Dad as a sitting target. She'd have him for breakfast.'

'You have no way of knowing that,' persisted Genevieve. 'But it strikes me the only crime she's committed so far is to overdress and wear too much make-up. Who are we to talk? We're hardly the epitome of sartorial elegance, are we?'

They looked at each other – Polly in their father's old paisley pyjamas, Nattie in a vest top and a pair of boxer shorts that had belonged to some long-forgotten boyfriend, and Genevieve in her knickers and a faded tee-shirt that seemed to grow each time it was washed.

They fell silent until Nattie said, 'But what you're both losing sight of is that Dad won't ever be interested in her. Or any other woman for that matter. It's Mum he wants.'

'In that case, what are we worrying about?' Genevieve said. 'Donna will soon get the message and leave him alone.'

Not even Nattie disagreed with this piece of logic.

'What are you going to do about Rupert, Nattie?' Genevieve said, 'You're surely not going to carry on seeing him, are you?'

'Oh, don't you worry, I know exactly what I'm going to do. Axworthy-Smythe is for the chop good and proper.' She laughed. 'Get it? Axworthy. Chop. Oh, never mind. Anyway, I was beginning to get bored of him. I reckon it's time for a change.'

'You could try abstinence.'

Nattie looked at Polly and laughed again. 'You two might want to take a vow of chastity, but this girl doesn't. I don't know how you do it.'

Polly blushed. Being so pretty, she was never short of offers, but she was a very particular girl. 'I've told you before,' she murmured, 'I'm more interested in a meeting of minds than meaningless sex.'

'And I've told you before, don't criticise what you haven't tried.'

'We could say the same to you,' said Genevieve. 'Why don't you try a new kind of relationship, one that might lead to love? Or are you afraid to?'

Nattie groaned. 'Oh, please!'

'You think love doesn't exist, then?'

'It's a myth, Polly. You know that, I know that. Deep down, everyone in the whole wide world knows it too, except they're too busy buying into the hype.'

Polly got off the bed and went to stand by the open window. She let out a long, wistful sigh. Even in Daddy Dean's tatty old pyjamas, she still managed to look like a princess worth rescuing from the castle tower. She turned from the window. 'Have you *never* been in love, Nats?' she asked.

Nattie frowned. 'Of course I have. I love you and Gen, Mum, Dad, Gran and Lily-Rose. Most of all Lily-Rose.'

'That's not what I asked. I'm talking about being *in* love. Like Dad still is with Mum.' She came and sat on the bed again. 'When I fall in love I want it to be the real thing. And by that, I mean even if the relationship came to an end, I'd still want the best for him. I'd hate to unravel all that had been good in the relationship.'

Nattie looked sceptically at Polly. 'Cloud cuckoo land, that's where you are, girl.'

Later, lying in her own bed and listening to the sound of the sea lapping on the rocks in the bay, Genevieve thought of what Polly had said. And what Nattie had scorned.

She couldn't claim a wealth of experience on the subject, but the few relationships she'd been in had taught her that love, *real* love, was infinitely better than the inferior version one usually made do with.

She was just nodding off when there was a soft tap at the door.

'It's me, Gen, can I come in?' Polly closed the door quietly behind her and slipped into bed with Genevieve.

'What is it, Poll? Can't you sleep?'

'I've been thinking. About Dad.'

'And?'

'We need to find him a girlfriend.'

'Uh?'

'Only a temporary one. I don't think he deliberately neglected Mum, but he might have overlooked her needs. You know, her emotional needs.'

'Are you talking about romance?'

'Yes. He has to learn how to make her feel special again. And to do that he needs to practise with another woman. Maybe more than one.'

Genevieve put her arms round her sister. Suppressing a yawn and conscious that she was tired and only humouring her, Genevieve said, 'So, how do you suggest we go about finding a suitable woman he can learn from? Assuming, of course, that Donna doesn't fit the bill?'

'We advertise. I've been checking out the Lost and Found pages in the local paper.'

Genevieve hugged her sister. Just as you began to worry that she was behaving too rationally, she put you right. 'I think you mean the Kindred Spirits pages.'

'Is there a difference?'

And there she went again. Absent-minded romantic to incisive genius in one small step.

Chapter Six

A week had passed since her father's birthday. After hanging out the washing – sheets, pillowcases, duvet covers, towels and bath mats – and leaving a bowl of bread dough to rise, Genevieve decided to go for a walk. Dad was down at Gran's fixing a leaky tap and Polly was playing the piano in the guest sitting room as she waited for the piano tuner to arrive.

Not wanting to disturb her sister, Genevieve wrote a brief note saying when she would be back. If she'd been writing a note for anyone else she would have laboured over it, but as it was for her family, who knew how to interpret her unorthodox spellings, she dashed it off in seconds flat. She propped the piece of paper against the jug of wild flowers on the table and listened to her sister belting out a piece of explosive music. To look at Polly you'd never expect her to play with such energy. Hidden depths, thought Genevieve as she shut the door behind her and stepped outside into the sunshine.

Instead of going round to the front of the house, then down the hill into the village, the way she often went, she walked the length of the garden and climbed over the low wall to join the coastal path in an easterly direction. The path was steep and narrow to begin with, lined either side with golden yellow gorse bushes, but after a while it levelled out and widened. She paused to catch her breath and looked back the way she had come, to Angel Sands, where the houses looked as though any minute they would tumble down the hillside and slide into the water.

It was a funny little community, close-knit and traditional with its roots in limestone quarrying. But the quarrying had stopped a long time ago; nowadays tourism was the staple. When she and her family first started coming here, people called Pembrokeshire the poor man's Cornwall, and for no good reason she could think of, it was still overlooked in favour of Devon and Cornwall. But once discovered, it was a gem of a place that drew one back again and again. Visitors relished the peace and quiet and beauty of the coastline, as well as the genuine warmth of those who welcomed them here. Considered as Little England Beyond Wales, South Pembrokeshire had a reputation for being a happy melting pot of all things Welsh and English. In some of the neighbouring villages and towns, Welsh was often spoken. Genevieve particularly enjoyed hearing it, but despite Tubby's efforts to teach her – he'd been brought up in Llanelli and had the most marvellous 'Valley's Welsh' accent – she had never mastered more than a few basic words. But then for a dyslexic, one language was more than enough.

But it would always be the rhythmic ebb and flow of the sea and the invigorating walks that Genevieve loved most about being here. There were plenty of stories, some even true, about the rugged coastline; many a tale of ships that had run aground and of locals descending upon the beach to gather in the booty washed up on the shore. One tale told that the timber used in the building of some of the older cottages in Angel Sands had come from a ship that had been smashed on the rocks in the neighbouring bay, aptly named Hell's Gate.

Angel Sands had acquired its name because of these treacherous rocks. Centuries ago, if a storm blew up and an unfortunate ship found itself being pushed towards the mouth of Hell's Gate, the sailors knew their only chance of escape was to hold fast against the wind and hope to sail into the calmer waters of the bay around the headland. Unsurprisingly, given the superstitious nature of sailors, a myth was soon established, that the bay was guarded by an angel and it would only come to your aid if you prayed hard enough and loud enough. There were a few fanciful people in the village who believed that if you listened carefully on a wild and stormy night you could hear, rising up from the swelling waters, the agonised cries of those whose prayers hadn't been answered.

Genevieve started walking again, enjoying the warm, salty breeze against her face: it was good to be out in the fresh air. It had been a hectic morning. The guests had been down early for breakfast, eager to make the most of the glorious weather. They were keen walkers and she'd made packed lunches for them all, something she often did. She liked to think that running a successful bed and breakfast was down to being flexible and offering the guests these little extras.

If she stayed – and she might have to if her mother didn't come back – she would want to make some changes at Paradise House. It would be nice to offer an evening meal to those guests who couldn't be bothered to make the short walk down into the village where the Salvation Arms provided basic, unimaginative food. Only yesterday, Donna had been less than flattering about the meals there and had suggested that Genevieve could easily outclass the pub's kitchen staff. Genevieve loved to cook, and the daily round of egg and bacon hardly satisfied her creative flair. Something else she'd thought of doing was setting out tables and chairs in the garden and providing cream teas. But she would have to go carefully. There were already two teashops in Angel Sands and she wouldn't like to step on anyone's toes.

It was working well, having Donna helping with the

cleaning. Better than Genevieve could have hoped for. She wasn't one of those sloppy cleaners who rushed through the job, missing hairs in basins and only hoovering the bits of the carpets and rugs that showed. But for all her efficiency, there was still the problem of her and Dad. Whenever she was around, he would instantly make himself scarce. Gran was seeing a lot more of him these days, much to her irritation – with every visit, he claimed to find something else wrong with her little house, something that required his immediate attention.

'What's got into him?' Gran had asked Genevieve and her sisters. 'Just as I'm settling down to watch the telly, he knocks on the door wanting to fiddle with my plumbing.'

'I bet that's the best offer you've had in years, Gran,' Nattie had smirked.

They hadn't told Gran what was going on, that Dad was hiding from Donna, because the last thing they needed was her involvement. It was possible that she'd stir things up just to spite Serena. No, that wasn't true. Gran wasn't spiteful, but she might like to teach her irresponsible daughter-in-law (which was how she currently viewed Serena) a lesson she wouldn't forget.

At two o'clock in the morning, Polly's idea to find their father a woman on whom he could hone his courting technique hadn't seemed too daft, but in the light of day, it had been revealed as the ill-thought out plan it was. 'A typical Polly plan,' Nattie had said, 'okay on paper, but not in practice. That's what comes of being too smart up top. Just how would we have ever got him to go along with it? And how about the small matter of him being married? He would have come across as a right nasty bastard trying to pass himself off as a single man.'

In fairness to Donna, she was showing no sign of intensifying her attack on their father. Maybe she was smarter than they'd given her credit for and knew when she was backing a loser. Nattie wasn't convinced, though, and was sure she was just changing her tactics. 'When we're least prepared for it, she'll strike,' was her opinion.

'Perhaps it's Donna we should be finding a partner for,' Polly had suggested.

'Now why didn't I think of that?' Genevieve had said. 'We could run a dating agency as well as a bed and breakfast.'

But no matter how negative Nattie was, Genevieve wasn't prepared to lose Donna. Especially if she was going to start cooking evening meals. Then, of course, there was Adam's suggestion that she start a catering business.

Goodness, so many options.

So many decisions.

It was good having so much to think about. It gave her less time to dwell on the real reason she had come back home, to the place where she had always felt safe. In all the times she had walked this path, even alone as she was today, she had never once felt in danger. Perhaps it was because death out here wouldn't seem so bad. A small push off the cliff and it would be all over.

Despite the warmth of the day, she shivered at the thought and walked faster. It wasn't good to be gloomy. No one knew better than she did that it was the easiest thing in the world to slip into a downward spiral. But real fear was difficult to shake off, and since that dreadful night when two masked men had broken into George and Cecily's home, she had known exactly what fear was.

It had been a perfectly ordinary evening. She had cooked George and Cecily their supper, and after she'd cleared away, they had all settled down to watch the television together. She didn't always do this, but the elderly couple often invited her to join them. 'We don't like the thought of you upstairs on your own,' they had said when she first went to work for them as their house-keeper. 'Please sit with us. Unless, of course, you'd rather not.' She had agreed all too readily. They had travelled the world and were a fascinating couple to talk to. Right away she felt at home with them and nothing she did was out of a sense of duty. It was a happy time. They lived in a beautiful sixteenth century manor house in Surrey. It was far too big for them, but it had been their home for nearly forty years and they couldn't imagine living any-where else. They had other help, besides Genevieve; a gardener-cum handyman and a cleaner, both of whom only came once a week.

The two masked men had got in through a French door in the library and crept into the drawing room while Genevieve was making George and Cecily a cup of tea during an advert break. It was only when she was carrying the tray back to the drawing room that she realised something was wrong. In the short time she had been out of the room, the robbers had tied up the couple and were threatening George with what looked like a hunting knife, its jagged edge pressed against his throat.

Genevieve dropped the tray and tried to make a run for the door, to lock it and call the police from the tele-phone in the hallway. But the men were too fast for her. They grabbed her by the hair and dragged her back into the room, the knife now pressed against the side of her neck. As they had with George and Cecily, they pushed her to the floor, covered her mouth with tape, strapped her hands behind her back and then tied her ankles. While the men ransacked the house, she willed her employers to cooperate with the men – she knew instinct-ively that they wouldn't survive unless they did. When the robbers demanded George give them the code to open the safe in the main bedroom upstairs, and he refused, they went mad and seized Cecily . . .

Genevieve sat down on the grass; she was shaking and her heart was pounding. It was too much. The memory of the terror in Cecily's eyes would never leave her. Or the look on George's face when he realised what he'd allowed the men to do to his beloved wife. Never had Genevieve felt so helpless. Or so frightened.

The robbers were never caught. If they had been, they'd be charged with murder; both George and Cecily died as a result of the attack. Three months later, Genevieve was still having nightmares and couldn't face being on her own at night. That was why she'd come home to Paradise House and her family. She knew that once she was back, she would feel safe again and recovery would kick in. So far it was working. The nightmares were fewer and further between and her nerves were less strung-out.

Only Gran had an inkling of what she'd gone through – she'd deliberately underplayed it with the rest of her family, especially her parents, not wanting them to over-react. But Gran had a nose for these things.

There was one inescapable truth about life at Paradise House. Nothing stood still; the moment your back was turned, things happened. When Genevieve returned home after her walk, she found that Nattie and Lily-Rose had moved in, bringing with them a wealth of clutter that filled the hall and stairs. They'd also brought a donkey, and it was tethered to a wooden stake on the front lawn. While the donkey honked and brayed and Lily-Rose went berserk with delight at the prospect of riding him as soon as she'd had lunch, Tubby's van rolled up the drive. Genevieve could tell from the cursory glance he gave the donkey – but there again, he was used to odd goings-on at Paradise House – that he had important news to deliver and nothing was going to stop him.

'Well, look you see, you'll never guess what,' he said, stepping down from the van, his Llanelli accent as bright and jolly as his face. 'At long last, Ralph Griffiths's got planning permission for that dilapidated old barn of his and has agreed to sell it.'

This *was* Big News. The sale of any property in the area caused ears to flap and tongues to wag.

'Who, what, when and how? And name your source,' demanded Nattie.

Tubby wiped his hands on the front of his apron. 'Well, *cariad*, I just heard it down at Debonhair, so it's got to be on the button.'

Both Nattie and Genevieve nodded. The gospel according to St Debs was always to be believed.

'But the bit you girls are going to like is who Ralph's selling to. He's selling to an eligible young man.'

'Anyone we know?' asked Genevieve.

Nattie scowled at her. 'Get real, Gen, how many eligible young men do we know round here?'

'He's not from round here,' Tubby informed them. 'He lives in Buckinghamshire and the barn's to be a holiday home for him. Debs says his name's Jonjo Fitzwilliam and he's only thirty-three but has made a bundle of money out of health and fitness centres. He runs a sort of franchise from what I can gather. So just think, girls. Available totty with cash to flash! How lucky are you three?' He grinned. 'Question is; who would he be brave enough to choose out of the Sisters of Whimsy? Hey, I know! How about you fight for him, and he wins the victor? A mud wrestling session at The Arms would go down a treat.'

While Nattie looked ready to give him the same treatment she'd given Rupert last week, Genevieve said, 'So why's he coming here? If he's got money, why isn't he buying a holiday home somewhere more glamorous?'

'Perhaps he's a man of discernment. Debs also said

he's bringing his own architect to turn the barn into something really special.'

Nattie tutted and put her hands on her hips. 'Some fancy architect from London, who's going to turn the barn into a hideous eyesore, no doubt. Well, I certainly hope no one's going to turn a blind eye to the fact that the barn's probably a listed building.'

Tubby smiled. 'Apparently this young architect boyo spent part of his childhood here. His parents owned a house nearby. So with a bit of luck, he'll do a sympathetic job of the conversion.' Then, rubbing his hands on his apron again and bringing the gossip session to an end, he said, 'Now then girls, what can I get you from the van?' He chuckled and glanced over towards the donkey. 'How about some carrots for your hairy friend?'

'Are they organic?'

But Genevieve wasn't listening. She walked away, back into the house, up the two flights of stairs to her bedroom. Only when she had closed the door behind her and leant against it, did she let her brain receive the information her heart had registered the moment Tubby had described the man who would be coming to Angel Sands with Jonjo Fitzwilliam . . . *this young architect boyo spent part of his childhood here . . . His parents owned a house nearby . . .*

It had to be Christian.

Chapter Seven

There were questions that needed answering.

Why had a donkey taken up residence at Paradise House? Why had Nattie and Lily-Rose upped sticks from Tenby? And more importantly, how was Genevieve going to find out if Jonjo Fitzwilliam's architect was indeed who she thought he was?

Although it was this last question that dominated her thoughts, it seemed the donkey was destined to be the focus of conversation while she prepared lunch for everyone, including Gran, whom Dad had brought back with him after fixing a loose stair rod – a stair rod that Gran said had been perfectly secure until he'd got his wretched hands on it.

'In case you were wondering,' announced Nattie as she put Lily-Rose onto her booster seat, 'his name's Henry.'

'That's a nice name,' said Gran. 'Very solid and reliable. What does he do?'

'The usual kind of thing, I guess, if he's given the chance; a romp in the sun, plenty of juicy green stuff to nibble on and a regular supply of carrots. That's why I had to rescue him. I just had to give him the opportunity of a better life.'

'I should think you did. Vegetarianism is all very well, but he won't last two minutes with a girl like you unless he gets some good red meat down him.'

Everyone stared at Gran and laughed.

Genevieve said, 'Gran, Henry's a donkey.'

Realizing her mistake, but utterly unfazed, Gran said, 'Well, I still think Henry's a good name. Even for a donkey. After all, they're solid and reliable, aren't they? Certainly more reliable than any of the young men you've dallied with in the past, Natalie.'

'So how did you come by him?' asked Genevieve. She had a sudden picture of Jack and the Beanstalk in reverse – Nattie going out with a handful of precious magic beans and coming home with the pathetic-looking animal currently grazing in the orchard.

'Huw and Jane told me about him. He'd been horribly neglected by a miserable old bloke who died at the weekend. And good riddance I say. He had poor Henry in a filthy back yard with nothing but a bucket of dirty water and a bag of mouldy hay.'

Dad glanced up from his paper, an eyebrow raised. 'And where's he going to stay, love?'

Nattie turned on the charm. 'Well, I was rather hoping you might like to have him here. He wouldn't be any trouble.'

'Isn't there a proper donkey sanctuary somewhere he could go to?'

'But Daddy, you'd love having him at Paradise House. Just think, you wouldn't have to bother mowing the grass any more. And there'd be an endless supply of organic fertilizer for the garden. Go on, what do you say? Please can Henry stay?'

Her father folded his newspaper and put it down. He helped himself to some chicken and two slabs of Genevieve's homemade bread, and after he'd made himself an enormous sandwich, mayonnaise leaking out through the crusts, he said, 'I suppose there's a chance he might redress the balance around here. It'll be two males to five females if he stays.'

Nattie jumped up from her chair and went to hug him. Genevieve smiled. As if there'd be any doubt of Henry staying. Their father was incapable of turning anyone or anything away. 'So what about you and Lily-Rose?' she asked, sounding worryingly like the only responsible adult at the table. 'Why have you decided to move back?'

'Call it a run of bad luck. They don't want me at the wine bar any more and the tenancy on the bedsit's come to an end, leaving your wee niece and penniless sister without a home.'

'What will you do?' Again the boring, responsible adult.

'Do?' echoed Nattie, with just a hint of sarcasm, 'Why, stay here of course. Home sweet home. There's nothing like it.' She paused, as if sensing there had been more to Genevieve's question than at first appeared. Which there was. Genevieve knew her sister of old – Nattie wouldn't lift a finger to help at Paradise House. She would actually make more work for everyone. 'If coming home's good enough for you, Gen,' Nattie added, 'it's certainly good enough for me.'

Genevieve wasn't averse to taking Nattie on, but she knew when to back off. She wasn't in the mood for an argument over her sister's legendary slothfulness.

Daddy Dean took up his paper again and Polly, who hadn't yet uttered a word, chewed slowly on a piece of bread and cheese, her attention absorbed in the book she was reading: *Little Women*. Every now and then, Polly reread all her favourite classic children's novels. Very likely it would be *The Secret Garden* next week, followed by her namesake, *Pollyanna*.

All three Baxter girls had been named by their mother and it had been no random affair. Serena had chosen the name Genevieve because of the movie starring Kenneth More, who had reminded Serena of her father; Natalie had been named after Natalie Wood for the simple reason she was the luckiest woman alive being married to Robert Wagner; and Polly was so named because when she was born, Gran said she looked like an angel who would never see bad in another person.

While Polly continued to turn the pages of her book, Nattie and Gran egged on Lily-Rose's noisy farmyard impressions. But a dispute broke out when Gran started encouraging her to hiss like a snake. Challenged by Natalie about the likelihood of such a species being found in a farmyard, Gran retaliated, 'It's well known that there were adders in Pembrokeshire. Everyone knows that.'

'Okay,' conceded Nattie. 'Now I come to think of it, there are plenty of snakes in the grass hereabouts. Adam and Rupert to name but two.'

Dad rattled his throat from behind his paper, registering his disapproval. He had a soft spot for Adam and wouldn't have a word said against him.

'And I bet any money you like,' Nattie went on, 'that this Jonjo Fitzwilliam will turn out to be just as awful. More money than sense and with terrible taste. He'll ruin Ralph's barn, make it chocolate-box twee with poxy coach lamps and a rusting old plough posing on the front lawn. Or worse, he'll try and turn it into a pseudo loft apartment with – '

Looking up from her book, Polly interrupted, 'Gen, have you thought who the architect might be?'

All eyes suddenly turned on Genevieve, apart from Lily-Rose's – she was carefully unwrapping a triangle of Dairylea and mooing.

'It's crossed my mind that it could be Christian,' said Genevieve.

No one said anything.

'It's only a wild guess,' she said, in the awkward hush. 'I could be wrong, of course. I probably am. After all, there have to be any number of architects who holidayed here when they were children. What's more, we don't know for sure he went on to become an architect.'

Daddy Dean looked at her, concerned. 'And if it is him?'

'Then . . . then I'll look forward to meeting him again. Think how much we'll have to catch up on.'

Nattie leant back in her seat and snorted. 'Yeah, I can picture the two of you. "How are you, Genevieve?" "Oh, not so bad. How about you, broken anyone else's heart recently?"'

'For goodness' sake, all that's in the dim and distant past. I put it behind me years ago. I suggest you do the same.'

Nice try, she told herself later that afternoon as she walked Gran home.

'Come in for a cup of tea,' Gran said, putting her key in the lock and pushing against the door. It had begun to swell in the warmer weather.

Genevieve edged away, afraid to cross the threshold. It wasn't PG Tips Gran was offering, but another of her open-heart-surgery-minus-the-anaesthetic sessions.

'I ought to be getting back,' Genevieve murmured. 'You know what it's like, new guests arriving. A pile of paperwork to do as well.'

Granny Baxter reached out to touch her arm. 'Just a quick cup. I want to show you something.'

Liar, liar, pants on fire! Run for it Genevieve!

'Sorry, Gran, another time.'

It was rude and cowardly of her, but she kissed the old lady's cheek and turned to leave. Instead of going back up the hill to Paradise House – the new guests wouldn't be arriving for another two hours – she headed for the small beach where families with young children were making sandcastles before the tide came in. A frisky dog with a deflated ball in its mouth danced briefly around her ankles, but she ignored it and carried on, taking the footpath that led up the hillside and out west along the coastal path towards the next headland.

Her destination was Tawelfan beach. Tawelfan was Welsh for quiet place, and it was where she and Christian had met. It was also where they had done a lot of other things.

They say you never forget your first kiss. Well, amen to that! She could still remember hers quite vividly – it was nothing like the sweaty disco fumble that Nattie could lay claim to – and as the path dropped down the grassy slope towards the sandy bay where Christian had first kissed her, she pictured the scene. She had been fifteen (laughably old by Nattie's standards) and Christian seventeen. They had been sitting in the shelter of the sand dunes, warming themselves after a swim and eating hamburgers from the kiosk in the car park at the back of the beach. There was a smear of ketchup on her lip, so he later claimed, and he'd tilted his head towards hers and kissed it away.

He was from Ludlow in Shropshire and his family had been coming on holiday to Pembrokeshire for years. But whereas her family stayed in the same rented cottage in Angel Sands every summer, his owned a pretty, stone-built house in the next village. She'd met him when she was twelve. She'd been standing at the water's edge, letting the waves swoosh and swirl around her feet, enjoying the sensation of the pebbles and sand shifting beneath her. She was just thinking how funny it would be if the sand gave way and she fell deep into the centre of the earth, when a voice cut through the squeals of other children playing nearby in the rock pools.

'You're not afraid to go in, are you?' The voice had a strange, almost unconnected tone. She turned to see who had spoken, thinking that perhaps he was foreign. A tall, angular boy in cut-off denim shorts was smiling at her. Or was he taunting her? His question had implied as much.

'I'm not afraid of anything,' she retorted, turning

away and running into the shallow water, trying not to gasp at its numbing coldness. She kept going until it was deep enough to fling herself in and swim. There, that would show him! She looked back to the shore to see if he was watching. She was surprised to see him no more than a couple of yards behind her.

'You're a good swimmer,' he said, coming alongside. Again, that peculiar awkward tone to his voice. Definitely foreign.

'I've got badges,' she said. Immediately she was annoyed with herself; it was such a childish boast, the type of thing her best friend, Rachel, would never say. 'I also swim for my school,' she said, not meeting his gaze.

He frowned. 'What did you say?'

'I said I swim for my school.'

The frown was replaced with a wide smile. 'Me too.'

It was the first thing they found they had in common and it set the tone of their friendship.

But the kiss, coming several years later, changed all that.

Chapter Eight

A light, drizzly rain was falling and the churning sea was as grey as the sky. It was a chilly and inhospitable day for the end of May. Inside the cosy kitchen at Paradise House, Genevieve was doing what she liked best, spending the afternoon baking. The comforting smell of syrup and allspice filled the kitchen – a fruitcake was in the oven, a treacle tart cooling on the wire rack – and now she was trying out a new recipe for meringues, carefully whisking glossy egg whites and icing sugar over a pan of simmering water.

When the mixture was the right texture, she switched off the electric whisk and turned to check on her niece, who earlier had been sitting at the table playing with some leftover pastry. The circle of leathery pastry had been abandoned and Lily-Rose was now under the table, her face daubed with flour as she 'read' to her collection of dolls and teddies. They were neatly lined up, legs extended at ninety degrees, and were being told to listen carefully. This was a favourite game. She couldn't read yet, but she had a wonderful memory and a scary fondness for being in charge. With a book of Bible stories on her lap and a floury finger pointing to the words that didn't match her spoken words, she began.

'So the king told his men to throw Daniel into the den with the lions.' She glanced up from the book and growled for extra effect, then said to the attentive toys, 'And what do you think happened next? Don't you know? Then I'll tell you. In the morning, the king ran to the den and called to Daniel, and Daniel shouted back that God had sent a special angel to stop the lions hurting him.' She shut the book slowly. 'And they all lived happily ever after. Except for the bad men. The king threw them into the den and their bones were crushed.' Unaware that she was being watched, she asked the toys if they'd like to hear another story.

Genevieve smiled and left her to it. If you discounted the tantrums brought on by tiredness and the daily arguments over what she wanted to wear, her niece was easy to look after; a confident little girl who enjoyed her own company and was quite happy devising games to keep herself amused. She had never attended a playgroup or nursery school on a regular basis – getting her there each day would have proved too much of a commitment on her mother's part. But at Gran's insistence, Lily-Rose often went to church with her in Angel Sands and was a keen member of Sunday School. The vicar's wife at St Non's, where Polly occasionally played the organ, was in charge of entertaining the handful of children who attended, and she had instilled in Lily-Rose an active interest in the Lord Jesus. The Christmas before last had been Lily-Rose's first acquaintance with Christ and, for months afterwards, whenever she saw a baby, she would smile and say, 'Ah, look, baby Jesus.'

Nattie was far from pleased. 'People will think I'm some kind of religious crank,' she complained. But perversely she never stopped Lily-Rose from attending church with Gran. 'I'm not going to be one of those censorious parents,' she would say. 'She'll learn for herself soon enough what to believe in.'

Back with her meringues, Genevieve removed the bowl from the pan of water, placed it on a tea towel and whisked the mixture some more. According to the recipe, which as usual she'd rewritten to get it firmly into her head, she should keep doing this until it cooled. When it had, she reached for the piping bag.

'It's time to do the piping now,' she told Lily-Rose. 'Do you still want to help me?'

Lily-Rose shot out from under the table. 'Where's my pinny?'

'Here. But first we'd better wash your hands.'

Lily-Rose was in the process of dragging a chair across to the sink when there was a knock at the back door.

It was Adam, and by the look of him he'd recently had his hair cut. He was smartly dressed in a dark blue suit with a cream shirt. He would have looked great if it hadn't been for the novelty tie. One day, thought Genevieve, someone would have to tell him to keep the comedy away from his wardrobe.

'If it's Dad or Nattie you're looking for, you're out of luck. They're not here. It's just Lily-Rose and me.'

'That's okay. It was you I wanted to see anyway.'

'I'll be with you in a minute, when I've done this. Sit down and make yourself at home.' Looking at the amount of flour her niece had got everywhere, she said, 'You'd better be careful where you put yourself. I don't want you ruining that classy suit. Where've you been, dressed like the cat's whiskers?'

Instead of answering her, he closed his eyes and breathed in deeply.

'You haven't taken up some weird form of meditation have you?' she asked him.

He opened his eyes and laughed. 'No. For a moment there, I was a small boy. My mum was a great cook just like you. There was always something cooking. Something to look forward to.'

Adam freely admitted that part of his success was attributable to his upbringing. His father left home when he was a baby and when he was sixteen his mother was killed in a car crash: he learned from an early age to stand on his own two feet. After leaving school he went to work in a garage as a trainee mechanic. His employers soon realised that he was a natural salesman, so they took him out of his overalls and put him in a suit. In no time he was easily outperforming the other salesman. From cars he turned to caravans, and then to caravan parks. What would come next for him? Genevieve wondered.

'Genvy, will you help me wash my hands?' Lily-Rose was standing on the chair at the sink, her arms outstretched towards the taps.

'Of course, darling.'

Lily-Rose smiled shyly at Adam. 'You could help us make the cakes.'

'I don't think he's wearing the right kind of clothes,' Genevieve said.

'If you gave him a pinny he'd stay clean.'

'That's all right, Rosy-Posy, I'm just fine watching you two.'

While Lily-Rose giggled at the pet name he used for her behind Nattie's back, he removed his jacket, hung it on the cleanest chair and made himself at home by putting the kettle on. Genevieve liked that about him; he was easy to have around. There was never any standing on ceremony. By the time he'd made a pot of tea and found some juice for Lily, she had two trays of bite-sized meringues ready for the oven, along with a special one of Lily-Rose's oddly shaped efforts. She took out the fruitcake, lowered the oven temperature and slid in the trays.

'So what did you want to see me about?'

But her question went unanswered. From the garden came an unearthly groaning.

'What the dickens is that noise?' Adam joined them at the window above the sink, where Genevieve was once again helping Lily-Rose to wash her hands.

Genevieve pointed towards the orchard and explained

about Henry. 'He's been with us for two weeks now, another of Nattie's crusades. Recently he's started braying like a thing possessed. Once he gets going, nothing will stop him.'

'He's lonely,' Adam said knowledgeably.

'How do you know?'

He went back to the teapot and poured out their tea. 'When I was little, the local neighbourhood nutter kept a pair. Then when one of them died we were kept awake all night. The din was horrendous. But as soon as a replacement was found, the lovesick donkey perked up.'

Genevieve groaned. 'As if I didn't have enough to do. Now I have to find Henry a soulmate.' Since being back at Paradise House it seemed each day brought her yet another responsibility.

He passed her a mug. 'I could help you if you like. I know a bloke over in Saundersfoot –'

She interrupted him with a laugh. 'Just how many *blokes* do you know, Adam? You seem to have one for every occasion.'

He shrugged. 'I'm just a fixer. A go-between. Which leads me nicely on to the reason I'm here.'

'Oh? And there was me thinking it was my irresistible company, that you were seeing me behind Nattie's back to make her jealous.'

A faint hue of red appeared on Adam's face. He could take any amount of teasing about his professional life, or the trace of his Brummie accent that crept in now and then, or even his gold bracelet, but Genevieve knew his feelings for Nattie were not to be made fun of. Hiding his discomfort by helping Lily-Rose off the chair, he said, 'I've got a proposition for you. A business proposition,' he added hastily, letting Lily-Rose climb onto his lap as he sat down.

Genevieve took a chair opposite him. 'Go on, I'm listening.'

'I've just had lunch with my accountant and his daughter's getting married next weekend. The thing is, they've been let down by the hotel where they were going to have the reception. Well, actually the hotel's been closed by Health and Safety; mice were found in the kitchen and a dead rat in one of the water tanks.'

Genevieve cringed. 'And you want to know if we've any spare rooms that weekend.' She went to fetch the bookings diary she kept by the phone.

'No. Accommodation isn't the problem; everyone's more or less local. It's the buffet that's giving Gareth and his wife palpitations. And no doubt their daughter, too.'

She sat down again. 'Oh, I get it; I've just become one of your magical *blokes*, haven't I?'

'All I said was that I'd have a word with you. Nothing more than that.'

'And how many would I be cooking for? Twenty? Twenty-five?'

He looked down at Lily-Rose, whose large blue eyes were fixed intently on his tie. 'Um . . . the guest list is quite big.'

'How big?'

'Eighty-odd.'

'*What!*'

'You can do it, Gen. I know you can. It'll be nothing but a loaves and fishes exercise for you.'

'Yeah, a flipping miracle! Feeding eighty hungry people, that's a lot of cooking. And a lot of stuff to ferry about.'

'That's where the second part of my proposition comes in. Is there any chance the reception could be held at Paradise House? You have to admit, if the weather's good, it's a great spot. The views are the best in the area. Great backdrop for the photos.'

She had to admire his gall. 'And if the weather is like it is today?'

They both turned and looked out at the garden; the drizzle had become a downpour.

'To be on the safe side, I'll tell Gareth and Gwenda to organise a marquee and tables and chairs. That way all bases will be covered and you won't have to worry about transporting food back and forth.'

'You've put an awful lot of thought into this,' she said, amused he'd taken her consent as a foregone conclusion.

'No more than any problem I'm confronted with.'

'Okay,' she conceded. 'I'll do it. Although I'll have to check with Dad. It's his house, after all.'

Again Adam lowered his gaze to the top of Lily-Rose's curly blonde hair. 'Don't be cross, but I've already done that. He said it was your decision.'

Genevieve rolled her eyes. 'I've been stitched up good and proper, haven't I?'

'Not a bit of it. I merely saved time by having a quick word with your father earlier on.' He smiled. 'Your dad's getting the hang of using that mobile now, isn't he? He answered straight off. No sweat.'

After years of saying he didn't need one, and that the local reception was too variable, Adam had finally persuaded her father that a mobile phone would come in handy. Genevieve was now the only member of her family to buck the trend.

'Don't push it, Adam Kellar,' she warned, 'or I might change my mind about feeding the five thousand.'

Sliding off Adam's lap, Lily-Rose said, 'Can I have another drink, please?'

Adam reached for the carton before Genevieve had put down her mug of tea.

'If you're not careful, you're going to make yourself indispensable where that girl's concerned,' she joked. The look on his face told her he wished the same could be said of the child's mother. Regretting her clumsiness, she said, 'So how much am I going to be paid for stepping into the breach?'

From his jacket pocket, he produced a phone number and a cheque. 'Gareth hoped you'd say yes, so he wrote this out in advance. When the job's done, there'll be that much again coming to you.'

'Trust an accountant to be so organised.' Genevieve said absently. But when she took the cheque, she did a double-take. 'Good grief, what's he expecting me to serve? Truffles and pâté de foie gras?'

'I couldn't say, but I suggest you ring Gwenda asap and get the lowdown on what she has in mind.'

Genevieve looked at him doubtfully. 'You haven't billed me too high, have you? Made out I'm better than I am.'

'All I've done is tell Gareth the truth. I reckon if you do exactly what you did for your father's birthday party, you'll be a huge success. And once word goes round, I guarantee you'll have more offers of work.'

Genevieve turned from tucking the cheque into her bag. 'Adam,' she said slowly, 'it sounds suspiciously like you've engineered this. Are you trying to organise me?' He was the only person outside the family who knew the reasons behind her return, but the last thing she wanted was him thinking she couldn't cope by herself.

He put a hand to his chest. 'Hand on heart, there's been no skulduggery; this has fallen right into your lap. So, if I were you, I'd grab the opportunity.' Then switching his attention from her to Lily-Rose, he said, 'Your auntie isn't very trusting, is she? I wonder why that is, Rosy-Posy.'

Lily-Rose giggled, put down her plastic mug and wandered out of the kitchen. As Genevieve eased the fruitcake out of its tin and onto a wire cooling rack, she reflected how every inch of her trust had been turned to cold-hearted suspicion a long time ago. As a result her instinct was always to question, even if it meant doubting the kindest of people, like Adam.

Her thoughts were interrupted by Adam saying, 'Gen, there's talk down in the village.'

'There's always talk down in the village.' She was only half-listening as she peeled away the greaseproof paper from the base of the cake.

'But this time it's about . . . well, and you know I never listen to gossip –'

She laughed. 'That's because quite often you're the focus of it. You're much too interesting and successful to go unnoticed. So who's the latest victim?'

He hesitated. 'It's you, Gen,' he said. 'And I heard it from Debs while she was doing my hair this morning.'

He had her fullest attention now. 'But what on earth has anyone to say about boring old me?'

'Quite a lot, actually. It's about this Jonjo Fitzwilliam character who's bought Ralph's barn. Or more precisely, about the architect who'll be doing the conversion work. Is it true you used to be childhood sweethearts?'

Thwack! There it was. Exactly what she'd known all along. She plonked herself with a heavy thump in the chair opposite. 'What else are the good folk of Angel Sands saying?'

'That he broke your heart. That you've never got over it. That you've decided to die a spinster of this parish having loved only the one man.'

She stared open-mouthed at him. 'You're kidding!'

He shook his head.

'But that's rubbish. Why, I've . . . I've had plenty of boyfriends. And it's nonsense that I've decided to live out my life as a lonely old spinster.'

'They didn't say lonely. And if it makes you feel any better, there are plenty of men in the village of the opinion they could put you on the road to sexual fulfilment.'

'Put me on the road straight out of here, you mean!' Shock had now turned to anger. How dare people talk about her like that! What right did they have to say such things?

'You can always tell me to mind my own business, but did he really break your heart?'

She nodded. 'And some.'

'Does it bother you to talk about it?'

'I don't know. It's not a subject that crops up much these days.'

'But now that it has, do you want to discuss it?'

'So that I can satisfy your curiosity?'

'No,' he said firmly. 'To put us on an equal footing. You know everything there is to know about me, but you're unusually guarded about yourself. I figured out a while ago that you operate on a need-to-know basis. Much like your father.'

He was right, of course. She *was* guarded, and preferred to keep things to herself. But how to tell Adam what had gone on? Where should she start?

She decided to go right back to the beginning, to that first day, when she met Christian and wanted to prove she wasn't scared of anything. Least of all a taunting boy with a strange voice.

PART II

Chapter Nine

They swam in silence, away from the splashing and squealing children who were all much younger than them. The tide was going out and Genevieve knew they had to be careful. Her father had lectured her many times on the dangers of being swept out to sea, of children, even grown-ups, drifting away on flimsy lilos and having to be rescued by the air-sea rescue helicopter.

'We better not go too far,' she said. She didn't add that she was supposed to stay within eyeshot of her parents, who were on the beach with her younger sisters.

He nodded and pointed to the nearest rocks, which formed the right-hand spur of the bay. For a few seconds he swam on ahead, his arms cutting through the water cleanly, effortlessly, his body tilting to the side as he came up for air. Most boys she knew made a clumsy hash of front crawl – hands slapping the water, feet thrashing wildly – but this one did it properly, even the breathing. She followed suit and was soon level with him. Neither was out of breath when they climbed up onto the smooth, flat rocks that were warm from the sun. For a moment they both stood and stared at the sea, shading their eyes from the dazzling glare.

'I love it here,' she said, 'it's the best place in the world.'

When he didn't respond she wished she hadn't said anything. He probably thought it was a silly thing to say. Childish and gushing. She squeezed the water from her ponytail and sat down.

He sat down too, and looked directly at her. 'It's great here, isn't it? It's my favourite place,' he said, in his strange, off-key voice.

She frowned, wondering why he'd as good as repeated what she'd just said. 'Yes,' she agreed. 'My family and I come here every year. How about you?'

There was a pause before he answered, during which she realised he was making her feel uncomfortable.

'We've been coming since I was eight,' he said. 'How old are you?'

'Twelve. And you?'

Another gap in the conversation, followed by the same feeling of discomfort.

'Fourteen,' he replied.

And then she understood why he was making her feel so weird. He was staring at her too closely, his gaze too penetrating. She shifted away from him and turned her head to look back towards the beach and her parents. Dad was scanning the water's edge looking for her while her mother was helping Nattie perform the Towel Dance. This entailed a lot of self-conscious wriggling behind a towel before finally emerging – *ta-daa!* – dressed in a swimsuit.

Genevieve stood up and waved to her father. When eventually he caught sight of her and waved back, she sat down again, although part of her didn't want to. This strange boy might be an excellent swimmer, but he wasn't the easiest person to talk to. She'd have to be careful. This was only the first day of the holiday and she didn't want to get saddled with him for the rest of the time they were here, not if he was always going to be so odd. She dangled her feet into the water and felt the tickly touch of the swaying fronds of seaweed attached to the rocks. 'Do you have any brothers or sisters?' she said.

Once again he ignored her question. That's it, she thought. I'm not having anything more to do with him.

She turned her head. 'Don't you know it's bad manners to ignore people?' She was about to slip back into the water and swim away when he laid a hand on her forearm.

'You have to look straight at me when you speak. If you don't, I can't read your lips. I'm deaf.'

Never had Genevieve felt so rude or cruel. Or so ignorant. Why hadn't she realised that that was why he spoke in that odd way? And that he had looked at her so intently because he was trying to read her lips. Mortified, she thought in an instant of all the things he was denied: music, television, laughter, birdsong. How awful for him. Head down, she murmured an apology.

He tapped her on the leg. 'What did you say?'

'I'm sorry,' she repeated, this time looking straight at him and stupidly raising her voice.

His mouth curved into a soft smile. 'Why are you sorry I'm deaf?'

'I'm not. I mean . . . well, I *am* sorry you're deaf, but what I meant was, I'm . . . I'm sorry I was so horrible to you.'

'And if I could hear properly, would you be so apologetic?'

He was twisting her words, just like Nattie did sometimes. Holding her ground, she said, 'If you weren't deaf I wouldn't have needed to apologise because I wouldn't have been so nasty.'

He paused, as though he wasn't sure what she'd said. 'I said – '

He stopped her with a hand. 'It's okay. I got it. So what you're saying is that you make a special case of being rude to the deaf. Or do blind people get the same treatment?'

Shocked that he could accuse her of something so awful, she opened her mouth to defend herself but then saw he was laughing at her. He'd been making fun of her all the time! Annoyed, she shoved him hard. She caught him off balance and with great satisfaction, watched him topple into the water.

When he surfaced, he slicked back his wet hair and rubbed his face. 'What was that for?'

'For being a pig and teasing me!' she shouted.

'You'll have to speak up,' he yelled with a grin, 'I can't hear you.'

His name was Christian May and they arranged to meet for a swim the following day, same place, same time. But the weather wasn't so nice, so they went for a walk along the coastal path instead. Her parents were happy for her to go off with her new friend, having met him briefly the day before and concluded that he was 'a well brought up young man who could be trusted to take good care of her'.

They walked for nearly an hour, stopping only to refer to the map and compass he'd brought. This was a new phenomenon to Genevieve; she wasn't used to being with someone so organised. No one in her family would have thought of bringing a map. Mum was always saying life should be a spontaneous adventure, which was her way of covering up for her oversights, like not making a note of dental appointments, losing her keys, going out and leaving the oven switched on or, one afternoon, forgetting to collect Polly from nursery school. 'I wondered where she was,' Serena said when Polly's teacher phoned.

But it was obvious from looking at the contents of Christian's tidily packed rucksack – map, compass, cagoule, camera, can of Coke and Mars bars – that he was as thorough as he was talkative. Now that she'd got the hang of remembering to look at him when she spoke, and to give him time to take in the shapes her mouth made, there was no stopping the flow of chatter between them. He told terrible jokes too. 'What do you call a crab when he's in a bad mood? . . . Crabby! And what was Hitler's first name? . . . Heil!'

To her surprise, she shared things with him that she wouldn't ordinarily discuss. She told him she had recently been diagnosed as dyslexic, something she preferred to keep quiet for fear of people automatically classing her as stupid.

'Does that mean you have fits?'

Thinking he must have misread her lips, she exaggerated her pronunciation to help him. 'Dyslexic, not epileptic.' The slight twist to his own lips told her that once again he'd caught her out. 'You're too sharp for your own good,' she muttered.

'At least you're cottoning on to the fact that just because I can't hear properly it doesn't necessarily mean I'm thick.'

And that was the bond between them. In their different ways, they were both striving to convince the world they were as capable as the next person.

'I hate it when people talk down to me,' Christian told her. 'I get it all the time. Once they realise I have a hearing problem, they halve my age. What they don't realise is that when you have one sense taken away, the others take up the slack.'

'Do you ever wear a hearing aid?'

'Sometimes, but I don't like to. What little I can hear gets drowned out or distorted by background noise being over-amplified.'

'And what about sign language? Can you do all that complicated hand stuff?'

'A bit, but I prefer lip-reading.'

'Could you teach me?'

'I could, but it's not easy. It's not something you can teach exactly; you have to practise it over and over. Like with most things, some make better learners than others.'

She soon realised just how difficult it was when he

explained how certain letters looked the same when spoken. 'P, b and m are pretty tricky,' he said. He showed her how hard it was to tell the difference between pat and bat.

'So how do you tell the difference?' she asked, beginning to think he was some kind of genius.

He shrugged. 'You just have to fit the pieces of the jigsaw together by figuring out the context. It's the same with learning any new language. And remember, I've been doing this for years.'

'How many years?'

'Since for ever.'

'You were born deaf?'

'Partially. But I'll tell you about that another time. It's all very boring.'

But there was nothing boring about him or anything he said, and three days into the summer holiday they were inseparable.

And insufferable, if Nattie was to be believed. 'You never want to do anything with me any more,' she complained bitterly at breakfast one morning when Genevieve reminded her mother that she was spending the day with Christian again and would need a packed lunch. 'You're always off with that *boy*.' Nattie spat out the word 'boy' with as much disgust as she could muster. At ten years of age, she was of the opinion that boys, weedy and inferior beings, were like doing the washing up or anything else helpful around the house; to be avoided at all costs.

'But you've got Polly to play with,' Genevieve said, hurriedly buttering her toast and deciding to make her own sandwiches – Mum was miles away, drinking her cup of tea and staring out of the window. 'It's not as if you'll be on your own.'

'As good as. Polly's no fun. All she wants to do is read. Just look at her!'

Though only eight years old, Polly was never without a book. She was reading now at the breakfast table, her cereal bowl untouched, completely oblivious to the conversation going on around her.

Genevieve felt a pang of guilt. Maybe she was being selfish by going off with Christian yet again. 'I suppose you could come with us,' she offered. 'I'm sure Christian wouldn't mind.'

But the invitation was thrown back at her. 'I'd rather eat a plate of maggoty cabbage.'

'Who wants a plate of maggots?' asked Daddy Dean, glancing up from the newspaper he'd fetched at the crack of dawn that morning. Newspapers were his holiday treat. At home the farm kept him so busy he rarely had time for such a luxury. It was a wonder he could spare the time to come away at all. But that was Mum's doing. She insisted every summer that he left Grandad and the relief milkers in charge and took the family on holiday. She claimed she'd put itching powder in his underpants if he didn't do as she said. And they all knew she was sufficiently batty to do just that.

'Nobody's eating maggots, Dad,' Genevieve reassured him. 'It's only Nattie being silly.'

Across the table Nattie stuck out her tongue. Genevieve returned the gesture and got up to make herself a cheese and pickle sandwich. She no longer felt guilty for deserting her sister.

When it was time to go home to Cheshire, Genevieve left her packing to the last minute, more reluctant than usual to return to Brook House Farm and the start of the autumn term. She was going to miss more than just the happy sense of freedom she always enjoyed in Angel Sands; she was going to miss Christian. They had swapped addresses with the intention of staying in touch. But she knew that wouldn't happen. They would go home, pick up the lives they'd left behind, and forget each other.

She was proved right. Every morning for three whole weeks she watched for the postman, but there was no letter for her. And although she enjoyed telling her best friend at school, Rachel, all about the good-looking boy she'd met on holiday – conscious that she was boasting, and, to her shame, omitting to say he was deaf – she couldn't bring herself to write to Christian. Not when there was the risk he might not write back. How humiliating would that be? There was also the small matter of her appalling handwriting and embarrassing spelling to consider.

No. It was better all round to put him completely out of her mind.

Chapter Ten

The following summer, Genevieve and her family arrived in Angel Sands on a chilly, wet evening, to find that it hadn't stopped raining for over a week and the roof of their rented cottage had sprung a leak. Either the previous occupants of Thrift Cottage had turned a blind eye to the problem or they hadn't used this particular room. The sloping ceiling in Genevieve's bedroom, with its pretty eaves and dormer window overlooking the cornfields, was bulging ominously and dripping onto the sodden carpet. Always at his best when confronted with a DIY challenge, their father threw himself with gusto into the project, instructing them to fetch buckets and pans. 'Quick as you can,' he commanded from his front-line position, where he could keep an eye on the ceiling that threatened to give way any second. 'Some towels to mop up the carpet wouldn't go amiss,' he called after them as they stampeded downstairs to raid the kitchen cupboards.

Mercifully the ceiling didn't give way, but that night Genevieve lay awake listening to the steady plop, plop, plop of rainwater filling the circle of pots and pans on the floor. Her parents had wanted her to sleep with Nattie and Polly, but she'd said she'd be okay where she was. She wanted to be on her own. Was even grateful for the plop, plop, plop that kept her awake. It meant she had a full night ahead of her to prepare herself for the possibility of seeing Christian tomorrow.

If he was staying in Tawelfan again, and *if* she saw

75

him, she was going to play it very differently from last summer. She was thirteen, a whole twelve months wiser than the silly girl who'd hoped he'd write. Her disappointment had been short-lived, but it still rankled that his words had been so empty. And hadn't he promised to send her some photographs that he'd taken of her?

The worst of it had been putting up with Nattie's teasing. 'What else did you expect?' she'd crowed. 'Boys always lie.' During the long journey down, in the back of the car, squeezed in with all the suitcases and boxes of food and toilet rolls, Nattie hadn't been able to resist a sly goad every now and then. 'I bet you he's found some other girl to hang around with,' she muttered. 'He won't even remember you.'

Her sister was probably right, but Genevieve was quick to remind herself that it didn't matter. Hadn't she spent the last ten months hardly giving him a thought? And hadn't she only started to think of him again because there was the chance of bumping into him?

All true. But equally true was the hope that they *would* bump into each other so she could show him how changed she was. She'd got rid of her childish ponytail and had her hair cut shorter, to look more grown-up. It had been Rachel's idea and they'd gone to the hairdresser's together. Like her best friend, she was now allowed to wear a bit of make-up. Except she couldn't really be bothered; she'd much rather help her father on the farm, or flick through her mother's cookery books, her mouth watering at the pictures. But Rachel could sit for hours in front of a mirror, happily messing about with her collection of lipsticks, eyeshadow compacts and wands of mascara. As for nail varnish, her best friend had hundreds of little bottles, all lined up along the window ledge. The colours ranged from glittery baby-pink to the deepest shade of purple, so dark it was almost black and made Rachel's hands look as though they were rotting at the ends. Occasionally Genevieve applied some varnish to her own nails, but try as she might she could never get them to grow as long as Rachel's.

'You need to eat more jelly,' her friend would advise, 'that's the way to strengthen your nails. And put Vaseline on them before you go to bed.' Rachel was an expert on most matters these days; she read all the magazines and kept some of the more explicit ones hidden from her mother.

Genevieve had been friends with Rachel Harmony since they'd both started at the local high school. Genevieve had moved up from the nearby primary school, but Rachel was new to the area and hadn't known a soul. Their teacher, Mr McKenzie, a fierce Scot with a purple birthmark on his neck, had assigned to Genevieve the task of taking Rachel under her wing. Before the end of that first week, they were best friends, although their roles had reversed. Whereas Rachel knew all the right things to wear, could sing all the latest pop songs and knew exactly which bands were in and which were out, Genevieve was not so well-informed. She had been brought up on a nostalgic diet of Judy Garland and Broadway musicals. Thanks to her mother's sentimental taste in music, she knew all the words to 'Some Enchanted Evening', 'Meet Me in St Louis' and 'Zing! Went the Strings of My Heart', but didn't have a clue about hits by Duran Duran or Spandau Ballet. Rachel was mad about Simon le Bon and Tony Hadley and had pictures of them on her bedroom walls. The only pictures Genevieve had were embarrassing pieces of artwork she'd done in primary school which her mother had framed and insisted on keeping. And although her bedroom was large, it was, as she'd come to realise, shamefully old-fashioned in comparison to Rachel's.

Beneath a threadbare rug were floorboards that creaked if you so much as looked at them, and gaps between the boards wide enough to let the draughts in. Its furniture included a bed with a rattly old brass bedstead, a chest of drawers her mother had haggled for at a second-hand shop and painted white, and a mahogany wardrobe the size of a small house, which was always used as a hiding place when they played sardines at Christmas. The wallpaper, coming away in places, was ancient and flowery and had been chosen by Gran when she and Grandad had run the farm and lived in the two-hundred-year-old farmhouse.

In contrast, Rachel lived on a recently built development of houses and her bedroom, though smaller than Genevieve's, was a vision of colour coordination and honey-gold pine. The walls, what you could see of them through the posters, were decorated with a smart, modern striped paper. The duvet was made of the same fabric as the curtains. The carpet was cream – Gran and Mum would have scoffed at the folly of this – and went right to the four corners of the room. Fitted cupboards housed Rachel's many clothes, most of them from Miss Selfridge and Top Shop, or from America, and in front of the window stood a proper dressing table with a three-way mirror and padded stool. There were shelves for her magazines, record player and growing collection of records, and the room was always perfectly tidy, not a thing out of place. It was as far removed from any room at Brook House Farm as it could be.

Rachel said her parents were boring and obsessed with keeping the house straight. Genevieve knew she wasn't exaggerating. She had once dropped an ice-lolly on the patio at a barbecue given by Mr and Mrs Harmony. When Rachel's father had seen the raspberry-coloured puddle, all hell broke loose, with him acting as though she'd dropped an atom bomb. Serena, on the other hand, had a much more relaxed attitude and expected Genevieve and her sisters to keep their own rooms tidy.

'If you want to live like pigs, it's entirely up to you,' she'd say. 'Just make sure you keep the mess inside and the door closed.'

If Genevieve had to name one thing of Rachel's that she truly envied, it would be the television in her friend's bedroom. Two years ago Serena had declared the box that stood in the corner of the sitting room was one of the great evils of the modern age, and had banished it to the loft. But the wonderful thing about Mum was that she was never afraid to do a U-turn, and on Valentine's Day last year she got their father to dig out the television set so she could watch Torvill and Dean win the gold medal at the winter Olympics in Sarajevo. With a deadpan face she justified her actions by saying it was a one-off event, a moment in sporting history that she didn't want her children to miss.

But Genevieve knew it wasn't sport or history her mother was interested in; she was an incurable romantic and wanted to see for herself the are-they-aren't-they? chemistry between the two skaters. 'Of course they're madly in love with each other,' she sniffled when the couple got up from the ice and the audience went berserk, throwing flowers and applauding wildly. 'Only love could produce something as magical as that.' She reached out to Daddy Dean and gave him a soppy look. He squeezed her hand in unspoken agreement.

The next day Serena insisted the television was returned to the loft, and Genevieve hungered for it. She couldn't even turn to Gran and Grandad to satisfy her hunger, for they hadn't got around to replacing their broken black and white set with the coat-hanger sticking out of it. In those days, Gran wasn't the addict she was later to become. So whenever she stayed at Rachel's house, she binged on what her mother would have condemned as mind-rotting trash. It could have been worse, of course. She could have been hanging about on street corners with a gang of boys, as Nattie was now itching to do. Instead, with guilty greed, she feasted on episodes of *Dynasty* and *Dallas* and *Emmerdale Farm*.

Often she watched the telly while lying on Rachel's bed, as her friend, indifferent to what was on since she was never denied it, flicked through her magazine collection.

Genevieve was sometimes glad she was dyslexic; some of the articles in Rachel's magazines were too embarrassing for words, page after page of mushy relationship stuff. And sex. But Rachel lapped it up and relished reading the articles out aloud.

'Listen to this,' she'd say, swinging round from her dressing table. 'It says here, "Think of the happiest and most incredibly satisfying moment of your life and times it by a thousand and that's how good an orgasm feels."'

Genevieve had tried to imagine sinking her teeth into a jam doughnut, tasting the dusty crust of sugar, feeling the sweet swell of soft dough roll around her mouth, jam oozing from the corner of her lips: a perfect explosion of heavenly sweetness. She then tried to imagine the experience increased by a factor of a thousand, as instructed, but could only imagine feeling sick. Would sex make her feel sick too?

The next morning, the first proper day of the holiday, she awoke to brilliant sunshine and a roof that had stopped leaking. Before breakfast was over, her father had borrowed a ladder from the neighbours and was investigating the damage.

'Nothing to it,' he announced, coming back into the kitchen to finish off his mug of cold tea, 'a couple of slates. I'll ring Mrs Jones and tell her I'll fix it myself.' Mrs Jones was the owner of Thrift Cottage and lived in Cardiff. 'Now then, let me fetch my tool kit from the car.' Their father never went anywhere without his red plastic tool box.

'You think more of that tool box than you do of me,' Mum would say. 'If the house was on fire and you had to choose between me and that wretched box, I wouldn't come out alive.'

'Nonsense, darling,' he'd argue good-humouredly. 'You're such a slip of a thing I'd sling you over my shoulder and carry the box in my other hand.'

'You see! I get *slung* over your shoulder and the box is lovingly carried.'

Their arguments were playful, never vindictive.

'Okay if I go for a walk?' ventured Genevieve.

Everyone looked at her. This was a major event in her family, catching everyone's attention at the same time. Even Polly took time out from *Charlie and the Chocolate Factory* to glance in her direction.

'What?' Genevieve asked. 'What did I say?'

Nattie sneered – she had sneering down to a fine art these days. Genevieve was sure her sister practised in front of the mirror, devoting hours to the curling of her lip and the letting out of just the right amount of condescension in her breath.

'I suppose you could run a few errands at the shop for us,' her father said. 'Some sausages for breakfast tomorrow morning would be nice.'

'Um . . . I wasn't thinking of going in that direction.'

'I bet you weren't.'

'Oh, don't be so cruel to your sister, Nattie. You too, Dean.' Her mother put down the frying pan she was washing at the sink and turned to Genevieve. 'If you want to go and catch up with that young man, then off you go. Be back for lunch at one, though. I'm doing macaroni cheese.'

'Thanks, Mum!' She escaped before she could be forced to endure another of her sister's jibes.

The day was fresh and bright, the deepening blue of the sky a welcome sight after the rain. A warm, salty wind raced across the cornfields, rippling it like the sea in the distance. She walked happily down the lane towards the village. Either side of her, quaint little cottages, trim and whitewashed, stood to attention, their doors and window frames painted cheerful colours, their small gardens pretty and well-tended. Some of them had window boxes full of tumbling flowers; vivid scarlet geraniums mixed with blue and white lobelia and orange nasturtiums. She came to a small junction where one road twisted down to the centre of the village, and the other led up the steep hill out of Angel Sands, towards Tawelfan beach. She took the latter and began the climb.

Reluctantly she tugged off her sweatshirt. It was brand new, like her trainers, and chosen especially because it hid her chest, which to her increasing horror seemed much too big.

'Wow,' Rachel had said before the end of term, when they'd been changing for PE. 'When did your breasts get so big? I wish mine would get a move on like yours.' So typical of Rachel to come right out and use the word 'breasts'. Boobs, or bosoomers as Gran called them, would have seemed less graphic. Perhaps smaller too.

But her friend was right. Overnight her breasts had suddenly decided to grow. For ages they'd been hinting at appearing, just little bumps, and then the next moment, *wham*! There they were, tender and ballooning.

'Oh, that's quite normal,' her mother had said, when Genevieve had plucked up the courage to tell her. 'Any sign of your period yet?'

'Um . . . I don't think so.'

'Well, you'll know it for sure when it does start. Meanwhile, we'd better get you sorted with your first bra.'

Genevieve draped the sweatshirt around her shoulders, using the sleeves to hide the cause of her embarrassment.

Thirty minutes later she was looking down onto Tawelfan beach and could see that only a handful of people had staked a claim to the curving stretch of sand. There was no direct access by car, which meant it was never very crowded, the main reason she loved coming here. It was also why Christian's parents, so he had told her, had bought Pendine Cottage, less than a mile away.

The path down to the beach dipped sharply and she had to watch her footing on the rocks, worn smooth and shiny by years of constant use.

Her father had nicknamed them 'the Pembrokeshire Pilgrims' when they first set out from Angel Sands to spend a day at Tawelfan – Dad carrying the deckchairs and cold box, Mum a few steps behind with the travel rug and windbreaker, and Genevieve and her sisters following, with a fishing net and rolled-up towel under one arm, and a bucket and spade dangling from the other. 'We're following in the footsteps of countless other pilgrims,' he'd say, 'pilgrims en route for St David's.'

Genevieve made for her favourite spot in the sand dunes that backed the beach, with the broad expanse of heath behind. It was sheltered and even warmer here. Removing her sweatshirt from her shoulders, she folded it into a makeshift pillow and lay back, her eyes closed against the sun. Perfect. Like wrapping herself in her favourite dressing gown and sitting in front of the fire, drinking a cup of hot chocolate with whipped cream melting on the top of it.

Listening to the sound of the sea, then the plaintive call of a distant bird – a curlew, perhaps? – she thought of the bird-spotting book Grandad had given her on her thirteenth birthday. It had belonged to him when he was a boy and now it was hers. Rachel had thought it an odd sort of present to give anyone, a tatty old book (especially for a dyslexic), but Genevieve treasured it. Grandad had written on the front page: 'To my bonnie Genevieve, may this give you as much pleasure as it has me.'

Lost in thought, she felt a shadow pass over the sun. She snapped open her eyes. At first she didn't recognise him, not with the sun directly behind him, reducing his face and body to little more than a silhouette. It was his voice, though, that clinched it.

'Hello, Genevieve, I hoped I might find you here.'

Oh, that was casual of him. He'd lied through his teeth about staying in touch, and now he was expecting her to believe that he hoped she'd be here.

She sat up. 'Really? Why's that?'

He frowned, then sat down beside her, his long legs stretched out in front of him. 'Because I've been looking forward to seeing you again.'

She noticed his voice was deeper than last year, and its pitch was better, less up and down. He looked thinner in the face, which made him seem more grown-up, and just visible through his wavy brown hair, longer and thicker than last summer, was a hearing aid tucked behind his left ear. She didn't know why exactly, but the sight of this quelled her antagonism towards him.

When she didn't say anything, he said, 'How are you, Genevieve?'

'Fine. I'm fine.'

He touched her lightly on the arm and said, 'I can't see what you're saying.'

She felt herself colour and apologised, looking him self-consciously in the eye. 'Sorry, I forgot about that.'

'The same way you forgot to write to me?'

No way was she going to let him get away with that. 'It was *you* who never wrote to *me*.'

He shook his head. 'I couldn't. I lost your address. I

waited for you to write so I could send the photographs I promised you.'

He was lying, just as Nattie said all boys did. 'I don't believe you – ' But seeing the earnest expression on his face, she faltered. Deep down she wanted to believe him. 'Did you really lose my address?'

'Yes. I threw it away by accident. And when I didn't hear from you I assumed you didn't want to stay in touch, so I had no choice but to let it go. Why didn't you write to me?'

She thought of fibbing, of saying, 'Hey! What a coincidence! I lost your address, too.' But she was hopeless at telling bare-faced lies. She told a half-truth instead. 'I decided to wait for your letter to come first. And when it didn't . . . well, I thought the same as you, that you hadn't meant to write, that it was just a polite thing to say.' She omitted to mention anything about the fear of him judging her by her inability to spell.

When he'd taken in her words, his face broke into a slow smile. 'So now we've got that straightened out, does that make us friends again?'

'I think it does,' Genevieve said shyly. She scooped up a handful of sand, let it trickle through her fingers and wondered why her stomach felt so odd.

Chapter Eleven

It was proving to be Genevieve's best holiday ever. Each morning a patchy sky would greet her when she drew back the curtains, but very soon a warm breeze would chase the clouds away and the sun would burst through. She met up with Christian almost every day and together they followed the same routine: a swim at Tawelfan beach (including a performance of the Towel Dance), followed by a walk along the cliff top until they found a suitable spot for a late picnic lunch.

Today they had climbed down onto a sheltered ledge where spongy cushions of thrift, pink and bright, grew in the cracks of the rocks. They were eating egg and cress sandwiches that Christian's mother had made for them.

'Other people's sandwiches always taste better than your own,' Genevieve said, helping herself to another.

'I know what you mean. Your mother's sandwiches are . . . ' he hesitated, as if seeking the right word, 'unique,' he said, with a smile.

'Now you're just being polite.'

Serena's sandwiches were a challenge and not for the timid. Ever since Band Aid's 'Do They Know It's Christmas?' Mum had decided there was too much waste in the world and had taken to making sandwiches using the previous night's supper leftovers. Yesterday, unbeknown to Genevieve, her mother had made them a stack of spaghetti bolognese sandwiches.

'Not bad,' Christian had said, after a tentative bite, then a bigger and more adventurous mouthful. 'Better than you'd think.' Once again he was politeness personified, something Mum loved about him.

'That boy is the most polite young man I've ever come across,' she sighed, after Christian's first visit to Thrift Cottage, when all he'd said was, 'Thank you, Mrs Baxter, but I can't stay for tea, my parents are expecting me back.' From then on, Christian could do no wrong in Serena's eyes. Especially when she learned how he'd lost his hearing.

His mother had contracted German measles when she was pregnant and he'd been born with a partial loss of hearing in one ear, which, his parents had been told, would gradually get worse. But then at the age of four he was diagnosed as having a brain tumour. It was benign, but needed to be operated on immediately; if not, he'd die. However, the operation meant he would lose the hearing in his good ear. It was fortunate, the doctors told his parents, that he'd already learned the necessary speech skills to carry him through life.

'Oh, the poor boy!' Serena had cried, when Genevieve told her the story. 'And what must his poor parents have gone through? If it had been me I would have been beside myself with worry.' It was typical Mum, to put herself firmly in another person's shoes and relive every moment of the drama.

When they'd finished lunch, they both leaned against the rock and closed their eyes. When they were silent like this, Genevieve sometimes made the mistake of thinking that Christian was listening, as she was, to the sounds around them; the waves crashing on the jagged rocks below, the cries of the gulls wheeling above, and the occasional bleat of distant sheep. Earlier in the week, while they'd been sunbathing in the sand dunes, she had patted his arm and pointed out a skylark. 'Its trill sounds just like a telephone ringing, doesn't it?' she'd said.

'I'll take your word for it,' he'd replied.

He never seemed to mind her clumsiness, but she cared deeply. It was important to her that she didn't offend him. It meant that at times she was over-careful, wanting to ask something, to understand the world he lived in, but holding back for fear he'd think her rude. One mistake she'd made was to assume that he heard nothing at all, that his world was silent. But it wasn't. He'd told her that sometimes his head literally roared with the distortion of sounds around him.

Sitting companionably in the bright sun, she touched his arm lightly and said, 'When you found me on Tawelfan beach last week, you were wearing a hearing aid. Why haven't I seen you using it since?'

He shrugged – he did a lot of that. It was another of the changes she'd noticed. Just as she'd grown taller and changed her hair, so had he. He was still thin, didn't quite fill out his clothes, and his shoulders, broad and angular, reminded Genevieve of a coat-hanger. He was quieter too, told fewer silly jokes than he had last summer. In answer to her question, he said, 'It's new. Some piece of state-of-the-art technology that's supposed to help.'

'And does it?'

Another shrug. 'A bit. Depends on the situation. But I still instinctively rely on lip-reading.'

Before she could ask what kind of situation, he added, 'I'm so used to being without a hearing aid, I feel kind of weird with one. As if I'm trying to be someone I'm not.'

'How long have you had it?'

'Just a few weeks.'

'Then maybe you need to persevere and get the hang of it.'

'You sound like my parents. Next you'll be telling me to get my hair cut.'

She surveyed his thick hair that had a hint of New

Romantics about it. She knew he never wore it too short because of the scar from his operation. 'Looks fine to me. I like it.'

Sensing that this was as personal as they'd ever got, she turned away and brushed her hand over a cushion of thrift that was as springy as his hair looked. She was suddenly shy. Almost as shy as she'd felt the first day they'd gone swimming together last week. Revealing her new shape – short of wearing a sweatshirt, there was simply no way to hide what was trying to appear over the top of her swimsuit – she had plunged into the chilly water, hoping against hope that Christian hadn't noticed anything different about her. Perhaps if she had gone to a mixed school she might have been less embarrassed, would have held her head up high and been proud of what Rachel envied so much. She never caught him looking directly at the cause of her discomfort, but who knew where his gaze roamed when she was looking the other way. Gradually she relaxed and the need for concealment became less of a priority. She was happy to lie down on the sand beside him in nothing but her swimsuit and not worry what he might be thinking.

'Boys think of sex every ninety-five seconds,' Rachel had once told her. It had occurred to Genevieve that maybe her friend thought of it more often. Rachel's encyclopaedic knowledge on the subject of sex included the dos and don'ts of flirting. 'Forget all that old-fashioned stuff about fluttering your eyelashes,' she'd told Genevieve. 'All you need to do is comment on a bloke's appearance and he'll know you're interested.'

Flirting had been the last thing on Genevieve's mind just now when she'd remarked on Christian's hair, and she hoped he wouldn't read anything into her words.

'By the way,' he said suddenly, 'I meant to say how

much I liked your hair. It suits you. What made you get it cut?'

Help! Was he flirting with her?

They had walked further than usual, so it took them longer to get home. They always parted at Tawelfan beach, he to go inland to Pendine Cottage, she to follow the coastal path to Angel Sands. On this occasion, while they were arranging to meet the following morning, he took her by surprise; he held her hand for the last few yards. Nervously, she let her hand rest in his.

A big smile accompanied her back to Thrift Cottage, but when she let herself in, the smile was instantly wiped from her face. At home, at Brook House Farm, Grandad had suffered a heart attack. He was in intensive care and they were driving home at once. Genevieve's first thought wasn't that she might not see her grandfather alive again, but that she wouldn't see Christian tomorrow. The shameful selfishness of this thought haunted her for a long time afterwards.

Genevieve had always thought of Granny Baxter as a big, strong woman. But seeing her stooped over the cooker as she attended to the ancient jam pan, she revised her opinion. Granny Baxter had shrunk.

Four weeks had passed since Grandad's funeral, the first Genevieve had attended. When their mother's parents had died the girls had been too young to attend. But they'd all been there this time round, neatly lined up in the front pew of the church where they came for Sunday School. Genevieve had been instructed to sit between her sisters; Polly on her left, Nattie on her right. Polly had sat perfectly still throughout the service, her head lowered as she searched through a Bible for something interesting to read, and Nattie, fidgeting and chewing the inside of her lower lip, played with a hanky she'd screwed into a grubby ball. Before setting off for St Augustine's – or St Rattle Bag's as Grandad had called it – their mother had given each of them one of their father's freshly laundered handkerchiefs. 'Just in case,' she'd murmured.

When they were outside in the hot August sunshine – so hot that it made the dark top Serena had forced Genevieve to wear itch against her clammy skin – the time came to lower the coffin into the ground. Clutching her father's hanky, and trying to keep herself from thinking of Grandad's dead body just feet away, Genevieve applied herself to making a list of all the 'just in case' uses for which the handkerchief might come in handy. Just in case she tripped over and cut her knee . . . just in case she needed a lift home and had to flag down a passing car . . . just in case she spilled a drink and needed to mop it up.

She kept the list going, right on until they were back at Brook House Farm and her mother asked her if she was okay. 'I'm fine,' she'd lied, knowing it was the required answer with so many guests to see to.

Four weeks on and Genevieve still had her father's handkerchief, carefully folded just as it had been the morning of the funeral. Now it was in her jeans pocket as she sat at the kitchen table, thinking how frail Granny Baxter looked as she stirred the damson jam. She felt for the 'just in case' handkerchief, just in case she might cry.

Everyone except her had cried when Grandad died. Even her father. That had shocked her, but not enough to bring on her own tears. You're nothing but a selfish cow, she'd told herself, willing the tears to appear. But they wouldn't come, despite the harsh words she scourged herself with: *How could you think of Christian when Grandad was dying in agony? What kind of a grand-daughter are you? The worst kind! That's what you are. Selfish and stupid!*

She didn't know for sure if Grandad had died in agony, but she needed to believe he had, to worsen the crime she'd committed. Now all she had to do was find a suitable punishment to fit it.

She dabbed at the crumbs and smear of butter icing on her plate and licked her finger clean. She looked at the remains of Gran's homemade Victoria sponge cake in the middle of the table, and was tempted to ask for another slice. She couldn't recall a day when there wasn't something 'fresh out' of the oven when she called on Gran – ginger biscuits, vanilla cream slices (Gran made the best puff pastry), exquisite choux buns, melt-in-the-mouth shortbread, creamy egg custard tart, and rock cakes sweet and fragrant with allspice.

Egg custard tart had been Grandad's favourite, and it had been a longstanding joke in the family that nobody had a sweet tooth like he did, or the same appetite.

'I'm famished,' he'd say, after spending a day out on the farm with Daddy Dean. 'I could eat a horse between two mattresses and still have room for a double helping of suet pud.' He was a big man, but not what you'd call fat; big-boned was how people described him. To Genevieve, when she was little, he'd been a giant of a man, and wonderfully warm-hearted. 'Come on my Bonnie girl,' he'd say to her, 'climb up here on my lap and I'll read you a story. We'll have a bun too, shall we? And maybe a mug of hot chocolate.' There was a twinkle of mischief in his eyes when he said this, as though the two of them were being naughty and breaking a rule together.

Since his death, Genevieve had expected her grandmother to stop baking completely. But, if anything, she was cooking twice as much and the pantry was filling up fast. 'It's to keep her busy,' Mum said. 'To stop her dwelling on Grandad.'

'Damn and blast!'

Granny Baxter's cursing made Genevieve start. 'What is it, Gran? Have you burnt yourself?' Genevieve went to see.

'It's nothing,' her grandmother said. 'Nothing that a bit of cold water won't put right. Stir this while I run the tap.'

Genevieve did as she was told, keeping a wary eye on the spluttering pan of damsons and the other on her grandmother as she held the inside of her forearm under the tap. 'Jam's the very devil for burns,' Gran said. 'Instead of pouring hot oil on the marauding hordes in the middle ages, they should have used boiling jam.'

Looking up from the pan, Genevieve said, 'I think this is about done now, Gran.' She had helped Granny Baxter so many times in the past, picking the fruit, cleaning it, topping and tailing it, and stirring in the sugar and lemon juice, she knew to the second when it was on the verge of setting.

They filled the jars that had been drying in the warm oven, and Genevieve was given the job of sealing them with circles of waxed paper, cellophane and rubber bands on top, while Gran wrote out the stick-on labels. When the last one had been labelled, sealed and carried through to the pantry, Genevieve said, 'It doesn't seem right that all this goes on without Grandad. He should be here.' She swallowed, not quite sure what had made her say such a thing. When her grandmother didn't respond, she looked at her unsteadily and saw something like confusion on her face. 'I'm sorry, Gran. I shouldn't have said anything.'

'Nonsense, if that's how you feel, then that's just what you should have said.'

'But does it make it worse for you? Hearing people talk about him?'

Gran put down the pan she'd been about to carry to the sink. 'Genevieve, I'd much rather hear you talk about your grandfather than hear nothing from you at all. In fact, I'd go so far as to say you've been much too quiet these last four weeks.'

Genevieve knew it had been a mistake to start the conversation. She could feel the backs of her eyes prickle. Needing something to provide a diversion, she said, 'Here, let me wash that pan for you. Then I'd better be going.'

'No,' Gran said. 'I have a much better idea. Why don't I cut you another slice of cake and make us some mugs of hot chocolate.'

The comforting reminder of her grandfather was too strong for Genevieve, and she fought hard to hold back the stinging tears. But it wasn't working. She yanked the 'just in case' handkerchief from her pocket and pressed it to her eyes. She cried and cried, for what felt like for ever, her head resting on her grandmother's shoulder. She sobbed for all those times she'd curled up on grandad's lap and had been made to feel so special. But mostly she cried because she had thought of herself and not him when she'd been told he'd had a heart attack.

If she had thought the stream of tears would bring her some relief, she was wrong. The world still felt black to her. Horribly black and empty, with nowhere for her to hide her shame.

Chapter Twelve

Gran told Genevieve that the worst of the pain would pass. She didn't believe her, but gradually Genevieve found she could think of her grandfather without being overcome by a rush of painful guilt. She had been tempted to share with Gran what was really troubling her in the kitchen that day, but had let the opportunity slip by. Ironically, as autumn gave way to winter and the days turned colder and darker, the blackness that had eclipsed her world lightened, and life didn't seem so bad.

But Grandad's absence from the family on Christmas day was hard for them to bear.

'It's like celebrating Christmas without Father Christmas,' Nattie said, in a moment of rare insight as they set off in the bitter wind to St Rattle Bag's for the traditional morning service. Later, to everyone's surprise, Polly sat at the piano and sang a song she had secretly written for Grandad. She had a beautiful voice and the words were so poignant they brought a stunned silence to the room. Gran was the first to cry, then the rest of them joined in. Even Genevieve. And because she cried so openly she knew she was over the worst.

On New Year's Eve she made a resolution to do better at school. Last term her school work had taken a downward slide. Her teachers had made allowances because of Grandad, but now she wanted to work harder and to concentrate more during lessons. In fact, she'd been told that concentration wasn't the problem, that there was even a danger of over-concentrating, which explained why she had so many headaches. She'd also been told that people who suffered from dyslexia had a thought process many times faster than those who didn't. This was because dyslexics had so much more to contend with – they were constantly trying to break the secret codes everyone else had cracked within the blink of an eye. No wonder she felt so tired most of the time!

But thank goodness she had Rachel to cheer her up. Rachel's latest craze was a quest to find the perfect everlasting lipstick. 'I've given up on flavoured lipgloss,' she announced in Boots one Saturday morning, after they'd taken the bus into Macclesfield. 'I've tried them all and they're a waste of money. Gloss looks great for five minutes, but it either turns into a gummy mess or disappears altogether. Honestly, they've put countless men on the moon; you'd think the least they could do was invent a lipstick that does what it claims, sticks to your lips. It's not asking too much, is it?' Genevieve envied her friend for having so little to worry about.

Easter was early that year and brought with it a letter from Christian.

There had been others. The first, with its Pembrokeshire postmark, had arrived the day before the funeral, and had told her how sorry he was to hear of her grandfather's death. They had left Angel Sands so hurriedly there had been no opportunity for her to explain. But word had soon gone round the village – everyone knew the Baxters who stayed at Thrift Cottage – and by lunchtime the following day, after he'd given up waiting for her on Tawelfan beach, he had knocked on the door of Thrift Cottage. A neighbour told him they'd gone, and why. Genevieve had read the letter again and again, until it gave her a headache, and concluded that he was genuine in his need to let her know he was thinking of her.

But she had thrown the letter away. She didn't want

him to think of her. And she certainly didn't want to think of him. Not when it reminded her of her selfishness.

A week after the funeral she relented and sat cross-legged on her bedroom floor, pen in hand. An hour later, the rug was covered in screwed-up balls of paper. The harder she tried, the more the words and letters slipped away from her. In the end, deciding it didn't matter what he thought of her, she scribbled a few lines and slipped the piece of paper into an envelope. She'd thanked him for his sympathy and hoped he'd enjoy being back at school when term started. There was no mention how much she'd enjoyed seeing him again, no hint that she expected another letter in return. She didn't.

A month passed and another letter did arrive. It contained some carefully wrapped photographs, two of her alone, and one of the pair of them. She thought how stupid she looked – all eyes and silly grins – and threw the letter and pictures in the bin. Then a Christmas card came, asking if she'd received his last letter with the photographs. She sent one in return, his name at the top of the card, hers at the bottom. She wanted to deny all knowledge of receiving the photos but she didn't want to lie, so she wrote a few words of thanks, adding that it was a shame she looked so awful in them.

Now, five months later, a third letter had arrived. She sat in the garden beneath her favourite cherry tree, blossom drifting down in the soft breeze, and caught the sound of her father driving the tractor across the top field. She opened the envelope, her mind made up. This time she would write a proper letter back to Christian. She understood now what she'd done; she'd used him to punish herself. She'd been a fool. A misguided fool who had deliberately hurt someone who'd gone out of his way to be nice to her.

This new-found knowledge had been slow to dawn on

her, but the truth was plain and it was time to do the right thing. It wouldn't be long before summer was upon them and she didn't want to turn up in Angel Sands with things unsaid. Christian deserved a sincere apology from her.

She opened his letter, her heart racing a little as she anticipated his words, that he was looking forward to seeing her again in Angel Sands.

But her happy anticipation skittered away. She read the letter through several times, hoping she'd misunderstood something. He hoped she and her family were well and that she would spare a thought for him next term when he had to sit his exams, after which he was going on a student exchange trip to Spain for the whole of the summer holiday. He didn't know how he was going to manage lip-reading in another language – a language he couldn't even speak – but his parents had decided it would broaden his horizons. He would send her a card from Madrid, where he'd be staying. If that was okay with her.

No! It wasn't fair. She didn't want him to go to Spain. Not when she'd just got used to thinking of him again. She suddenly remembered the way he'd held her hand, and wished she could turn back the clock. She'd give anything still to be on the beach at Tawelfan and for her grandfather to be fit and well and asking Gran to make him one of her creamy egg custard tarts.

She folded the letter, slipped it into the envelope and went inside. She needed something to eat. Something sweet and comforting.

Chapter Thirteen

Almost a year later, Rachel suggested to Genevieve that she needed to lose weight.

Genevieve had been thinking she ought to do something ever since she'd given up competitive swimming, but somehow she could never raise the enthusiasm. Her friend's exact words were, 'Don't think I'm being rude, Gen, and I'm only saying this for your own good, but I've heard some of the girls at school calling you names behind your back.'

They were in Genevieve's bedroom, Rachel lying on her front on the bed with her legs in the air, Genevieve sitting on the ledge by the open window. Her friend's words caused a coldness to grip Genevieve and her insides drained away.

'What names?' she asked, turning from the window.

'Oh, you know, the usual kind of unimaginative drivel: Fatso Baxter and wobble wobble, here comes jelly Gen.' Rachel's voice was matter of fact.

Genevieve's heart slammed. The coldness became a burning heat that seemed to swallow her up whole.

'Tell you what,' Rachel continued, 'I'd been thinking of going on a diet myself. We could do it together if you want.'

The offer was absurd. Rachel was stick thin; never in a million years would anyone call her Fatso Harmony. She had the kind of graceful body Genevieve could only dream of. The only trouble she had in buying clothes was finding a pair of jeans tight enough for her minuscule bum. But in that moment Genevieve loved her friend for her thoughtfulness. 'You'd do that for me?' she said, her voice small and croaky.

'Of course. Why wouldn't I?'

'Because you don't need to. You're . . . you're perfect as you are.' She had wanted to say 'beautiful', but thought it might sound a bit weird.

Rachel turned over and sat up, her back as straight and poised as a ballerina's. 'You must be blind, Gen. Look at me!' She lifted the blouse of her school uniform and revealed a stomach that was enviably smooth and taut. She pinched the skin – what she could get hold of – and said, 'That can go for starters.'

Genevieve wasn't convinced. Yet aware that her friend was trying to help and encourage her, she said, 'What sort of diet shall we go on?' She knew nothing about dieting, but was confident Rachel would know all there was to know.

Rachel was on her feet now, standing in front of the full-length mirror on the wardrobe door. She smoothed down her school skirt that was three inches shorter than the regulation length and showed off her slender Barbie doll legs. Genevieve thought hers were more like Cabbage Patch doll stumps. 'We'll cut out all carbohydrates,' Rachel said.

Well, that sounded easy enough. No potatoes or pasta. Or rice.

'That means no cakes or biscuits,' Rachel said with stern authority, hitching up her skirt another inch.

No cakes or biscuits. That wasn't so easy. Especially as for a special treat, Gran had invited the two of them for tea that afternoon.

They took the shortcut to Gran's bungalow, along the footpath that circled the field known as Solomon's Meadow, where the newborn lambs were put because it was so sheltered. It was late afternoon and clouds of dizzy gnats danced in the warm May air. Normally Genevieve would have enjoyed the walk; she would have ambled along spotting birds' nests in the hedgerow or hoping for the first sighting of a particular wild flower. Today, having been told by Rachel that exercise and dieting went hand in hand, she set off at a cracking pace, hardly noticing her surroundings. All she could think of was the humiliation she felt at what the girls at school were calling her behind her back. Had Rachel not been with her, she would surely have been in tears. She was lucky to have such a good friend. And knowing Rachel, she'd probably spared her the cruellest names.

It wasn't the first time she had been made fun of. When she was twelve, Katie Kirby and Lucinda Atkins, the brightest and most popular girls in the class, were always teasing her because she came bottom in almost every test. But when their sniggering turned to outright bitching in front of the whole class, Genevieve's normally stoic indifference caved in and she burst into tears that evening at home.

Genevieve had recently been officially declared dyslexic, and her mother marched into the headmistress's office the following morning and insisted that the two girls were made to apologise and had the facts – the ABC of dyslexia, as Serena had clumsily put it – explained to them.

'Dyslexia is a rare and special gift,' she told the headmistress, 'unlike ignorance. Be sure to make that clear to them. Their parents too.'

When Serena Baxter was provoked, she became frighteningly self-possessed and fiercely to the point. Nothing angered her more than bullying. She was as protective of Genevieve and her sisters as any lioness guarding her cubs. But because she allowed them more freedom than most other children, she didn't always know if they did need her protection. Rachel was in awe of this.

'Your Mum's great. She just lets you get on with your own thing. Wish mine was more like her.'

Now, marching on ahead of Rachel, Genevieve wondered if so much freedom was a good thing. Another mother might have noticed her daughter piling on the pounds and done something about it.

But that wasn't fair. It was no one's fault but her own that she'd got so fat. Besides, her mother didn't know the half of what she ate in secret. She couldn't name the day or place when she started eating too much, but she suspected it began some time after last summer.

Angel Sands hadn't felt the same without Christian. She had missed their swims together, and their long walks. But most of all she'd missed what might have been between them. More holding hands. Maybe even a kiss. She was plagued with visions of him meeting an attractive Spanish girl in Madrid. At night she had tossed and turned, picturing this imaginary girl, whom she eventually named Rosa. She was olive-skinned, dark-haired, dark-eyed and stunningly beautiful. And of course, she was as skinny as Rachel and wore one of those fantastic Flamenco dresses. She had only to stamp her feet, click her fingers and Christian would be hers for ever.

What hope for a plain girl such as Genevieve Baxter? How could she ever compete?

She never told anyone what was going through her mind, not even Rachel. And whenever Nattie teased her about pining for her long-lost boyfriend, she'd pretend not to hear.

Three weeks after driving home from Angel Sands, a postcard had arrived from Madrid – it was the only communication she'd had from Christian since the spring when he'd written to say he'd be spending the summer in Spain. She'd taken it upstairs to read in her bedroom, away from Nattie's prying eyes. She'd unwrapped a

Twix, hidden inside an old shoe box at the bottom of her wardrobe. Perched on the window ledge – and only when she'd eaten the two sticks of chocolate – she ventured to read the card. She took it slowly.

Hi Genevieve,
    As you can imagine, Madrid is very different from Angel Sands. It's much hotter, for a start. The family I'm staying with are nice, but it's a nightmare trying to understand them! I have to rely on my phrase book and gesture a lot.
    Miss you,
    Christian.

She rummaged around inside the shoe box again and pulled out a packet of Rolos, then returned to her seat to read the card again. There wasn't much to go on, but the connection, small as it was, gave her a tingly feeling, a tiny glow of happiness.

Miss you.

She put a Rolo in her mouth, sucked it for a moment, then rolled it gently round her teeth and tongue until the chocolate melted. Then came the taste of softening toffee; its smooth sweetness spreading through her mouth like the golden warmth of the sun. All too soon it was gone.

Miss you.

Had he written that because he genuinely missed her? Or was it just one of those meaningless signing-off things you said, like, 'See you soon' or, 'Lots of love'? Rachel always signed her cards with 'Luv Rachel' followed by a full stop with a heart drawn around it. It didn't mean anything.

By the time she'd finished the packet of Rolos Genevieve had convinced herself that *Miss you* meant nothing more than a polite 'Best wishes'. Even so, to be equally polite, she composed a brief letter in return so that it would be waiting for Christian when he came home. It took her more than an hour to write, not because she kept getting the letters and words in the wrong order, but because she badly wanted to say the right thing.

As the months passed, the number of letters exchanged between them increased, as did her weight. Her jeans no longer fitted, but it didn't matter; jogging suits were the thing to wear anyway. She didn't dare weigh herself, but she reckoned she'd put on a stone and a half. Perhaps more.

Granny Baxter was waiting for them. Ushering the girls inside, she pointed in the direction of the sink and told them to wash their hands. Genevieve knew this would annoy Rachel – they were both fifteen, after all – but Gran treated everyone as though they were five years old, even Mum and Dad.

'I've done your favourite, Genevieve,' the old lady said. 'Egg, sausage, beans and chips. And there's treacle tart and custard for afters. Or ice-cream if you'd rather.'

Rachel threw Genevieve a look of eye-rolling horror. Their backs were to Gran as they stood at the sink. 'There are enough calories in that lot to kill us. Tell her you're not hungry,' she hissed.

'But I *am* hungry.' Actually, she was starving and the thought of Gran's delicious homemade chips sprinkled with salt made her mouth water.

'We're on a diet, Gen. Remember?'

'What are you two whispering about over there?'

'Nothing, Gran.'

But Genevieve couldn't do as Rachel said. She couldn't hurt Gran's feelings by refusing to eat what she'd gone to so much trouble to cook. So she ate everything, even made up for what her friend left on her plate by having seconds. Later that night, when everyone had gone to bed, she thought of what Rachel had told her as they'd walked back through Solomon's Meadow, that all the famous models threw up to keep slim. She crept along to the bathroom and made herself sick. It was the most revolting thing she had ever done. But it was also strangely consoling.

Chapter Fourteen

In their last exchange of letters, Genevieve and Christian had arranged to meet on Tawelfan beach, even if it was raining.

It was. As Genevieve waited for Christian to appear – in her eagerness, she'd got there far too early – heavy rain pattered noisily against the hood of her cagoule, making her feel as though she were inside a tent. She pressed herself into the hollow of the rocks, glad that the tide was out and had provided her with a place of relative refuge. The beach was deserted and a strong wind was gusting, whipping up the sea and adding a salty taste to the rain. Doubt seized hold of her. Maybe Christian wouldn't show up. He'd have to be nuts to do so.

There had been much made of her meeting Christian again. Nattie, now thirteen going on twenty-three, had discovered horses and boys (in that order) and seldom talked about anything else. She was of the opinion that Christian definitely had the hots for Genevieve. 'Why else would he have kept writing to you?' she'd said.

'Because he likes me as a friend?'

'Because he fancies you!'

Genevieve would have given anything to have Nattie's confidence and certainty. Admitting this to herself, she knew it spoke volumes about her feelings for Christian. She was desperate for him to view her as more than a friend.

She hadn't seen Christian for two years, which, as Gran said, was a long time in which to recreate a person, to turn him into something he probably wasn't. But Gran was old and couldn't have a clue what it was like to be young, to know the joy of lying awake in bed just happy to think of being with Christian again.

But at least Gran listened and didn't make fun of Genevieve when she told her how her feelings for Christian had changed. She had confided in her grandmother while helping to pick the first crop of raspberries from the canes Grandad had planted long ago. In response, Gran had said, 'You know, your grandfather wasn't the first man I fell in love with.'

This was news to Genevieve, a revelation on the scale of Gran suddenly confessing that she used to be a stripper. 'Really?'

'Oh yes. There was Hugh before him. And John, and of course, there was Igor too.'

'Oh Gran, surely you never went out with someone called Igor?'

'I did, as a matter of fact. And we called it courting in those days.'

Genevieve did the sums. 'You must have been very young when you went out – sorry, when you were *courting* with those men. You were twenty when you married Grandad, weren't you?'

'A little bit of experience never did anyone any harm, my girl. Remember that. Too many eggs in the one basket is rarely a good idea. Some get broken. Some tip out.'

'Are you referring to Christian?'

She patted Genevieve's hand. 'Let's just say that Christian is all very well for the here and now, but there's a whole world out there for you to explore and enjoy. What's more, there are many different kinds of love. For instance, there's love that hurts and love that heals. You need to experience both to know the one from the other.'

Genevieve knew what Gran was getting at, but her grandmother was wrong. What she felt for Christian really was love. Okay, she was only fifteen – sixteen in September – but she knew, as she stood waiting for him with the rain dripping off her hood and splashing onto her face, that it was the real thing.

Her biggest fear was that he'd met someone else, but wouldn't he have told her that in one of his letters? 'Oh, by the way, I've met this really great girl. You'd love her, she's funny, intelligent and so very slim.'

Just over two months had passed since she'd first made herself sick, and though she hated herself for doing something so disgusting, the weight had dropped off. She'd lost a stone already and intended to lose another. But rather than show off her slimmer self, she kept her clothes baggy, not wanting to attract attention to what she was doing. She'd stopped swimming competitively ages ago, but now she wouldn't go near a pool – gross as she was, there was no way she could let people see her in a swimsuit. She told her mother she didn't want the chlorine from the pool wrecking her hair, and was told she was old enough to make her own decisions. Three cheers for such a liberal, easy-going mother!

But she knew Mum would go ballistic if she discovered the truth and she had to be careful that she was seen to be eating normally. It was easy to miss meals, though. There were plenty of times when she was able to get out of tea, usually just saying she was in a hurry to get to Rachel's, or that she'd already eaten at Rachel's, was enough. Occasionally, when she was feeling low, if she'd had a bad day at school, she would binge on a comforting boost of crisps and chocolate bars in her room. And of course, there was always something to eat at Gran's. But so long as she had her secret weapon, she could do what she'd previously thought was impossible: she could eat *and* make herself slimmer and more attractive. For the first time she could remember, she felt in control of her life.

Rachel had said they needed to give themselves a reason to lose weight, something that would spur them on. Rachel's goal was to become a wafer-thin model, but Genevieve's target was more modest: she wanted to get into size ten jeans. But she had another incentive. She wanted to look good for Christian. She knew in her heart she wouldn't stand a chance with him if she was anything but slim. And thanks to her friend's encouragement, and occasional bullying, she was back in size twelve jeans and feeling more confident – and hopeful.

What with the noise of the wind and rain, and being deep in thought, she didn't hear footsteps approach. Not until he was standing right next to her did she look up and see Christian.

'Hi there,' he said.

Like her, he was dressed for the awful weather, and all she could see of him was his smiling face peering through the porthole of his hood. But it was enough to tell her that he'd grown even more good-looking in the two years that had passed. She still hadn't returned his greeting when he said, 'It's great to see you Genevieve.'

Then, unbelievably, he threw his arms round her and actually hugged her. And it didn't stop there. He kissed her on each wet cheek. How grown-up he seemed! Or was that a continental souvenir from Spain, perhaps?

'Come on,' he said, 'let's walk. You don't mind the rain, do you?'

Her head spinning, she nodded. She didn't care what they did. He could ask her to paddle across the Atlantic in a cardboard box and she'd do it. He helped her clamber over the rocks, and they headed across the beach, to the other side of the bay and the steeply wooded path that would take them up towards the cliff top. When they reached the grassy headland they stopped to catch their breath. Miraculously – as if she needed any further evidence that there was a God – the rain stopped. They flung back their hoods and simultaneously took a moment to see how changed they were.

'You've grown your hair,' he said.

Immediately she put a hand to her head, self-conscious of the mess it must be with all the wind. Despite being enveloped in the unflattering cagoule, she pulled in her stomach for good measure. 'And you're – ' And what? What was Christian, other than perfect? He'd definitely grown more handsome. Had filled out too and easily looked older than seventeen. He was a man now. A man who most certainly would be looked at twice. With her mousy brown hair and nondescript features, she felt incredibly plain beside him, the kind of girl no one would look at twice. She noticed that he wore no hearing aid and realised that there had been little trace of that characteristic 'hollowness' in his voice. No one meeting him for the first time would realise he had such a severe hearing problem. He stared at her, his gaze fixed intently on her mouth as he waited for her to finish what she'd started. She'd forgotten how focused he had to be. 'And you're taller than ever,' she managed.

He laughed. 'I was warned it would happen. That if I ate my greens I'd grow.'

They walked on, the strong wind tearing the clouds apart until at last the sun broke through. They stripped down to their tee-shirts and tied the unwanted clothing around their waists. Genevieve could see how muscular Christian had become; his angular, coat-hanger shoulders were no more. Where was the skinny boy she'd met three years ago? *Bet he looks a real hunk in his swimming shorts*, she imagined Rachel whispering in her ear. Then, noticing the pair of scruffy old walking boots he was wearing, Rachel's whisper turned scornful. *What a turn-off!* It had to be Reebok or Nike trainers as far as Rachel was concerned.

Christian had caught the direction of her glance. 'I know what you're thinking,' he said, 'that I ought to give them a good clean, but what's the point? I spend most weekends tramping the hills.'

'Alone?' The question was out before she registered why she'd asked it. Was he tramping the hills with a pretty girlfriend?

'Usually with Dad, though more often on my own. He's away a lot these days. I was hoping you and I would get the chance to do some really long walks together.'

Her heart swelled. 'I'd like that,' she said.

He eyed her trainers doubtfully. 'Do you have any proper boots?'

'I'll get some.' To hell with Rachel's scorn. Her friend would never see her in them anyway.

Now there was no Grandad to help on the farm, Dad couldn't get away for as long as he'd like. But Mum, being Mum, insisted that it was no reason for her and the girls to lose out.

'We only go on one holiday a year,' she complained. 'I don't see why we should have to forgo it.'

So Dad came for just one week, leaving 'his girls' plus Gran to enjoy a further two weeks without him. It was strange having Gran on holiday with them – made it feel more like home. A home from home, in fact. After their father had set off for Cheshire that time, Mum started to talk about how nice it would be to live in Angel Sands permanently.

'It's not so daft,' Christian said when Genevieve told him of Serena's latest lunatic plan, to sell up the farm and buy a house to run as a bed and breakfast. 'You can pick up property relatively cheaply round here.'

On their way to St Govan's Chapel, they were having

lunch at a café in Stackpole Quay, a pretty little harbour which, until today, Genevieve hadn't given much thought to. Certainly she'd never considered its history or geography. But Christian made it come alive. He told her how the quay had been constructed in the eighteenth century to land cargoes of coal, which was then taken to Stackpole Court. Instead of the boats going away empty, they were then filled up with limestone. He knew all about Stackpole Court, a huge house built in 1735 but demolished in the Sixties by its then owner, the fifth Earl of Cawdor. All those years of history, gone. Poomph! He wasn't lecturing her, or showing off that he knew so much about the area.

'If I'd had a history teacher half as good as you, I might have carried on with it,' she said, stirring her glass of Coke with a straw and wondering if she dare eat the rest of her bacon bap. Her stomach was longing for it, but the slim, attractive girl inside her was telling her it was poison.

'It's a difficult subject to teach well,' he said. 'I've been lucky, I've had some brilliant teachers. Really inspiring. Are you going to leave that?'

Saved! 'I'm full. You have it.' She pushed the plate across the wooden bench table, wanting to please her constant companion, the slim, attractive girl. 'So how come you know so much about property prices round here? Thinking of becoming an estate agent?'

'No. But I am interested in houses. Or more particularly, their design. I'm going to study architecture at university next year. Or maybe do a gap year first then go to college.'

She was impressed. Doubly impressed because, against all the odds, he'd made it through mainstream education. He'd told her once how his parents had been determined he wouldn't go to a special school for the deaf, that there would be no half-measure, he was to be a part of the hearing world whether he wanted it or not.

'You've got it all worked out,' she said.

He smiled. 'You once said that I was the most organised person you knew. Remember how you made fun of my perfectly packed rucksack?'

'I never made fun of you.'

'You did.'

'Didn't!'

'*Did*!'

They were still arguing and laughing when they left the café and continued with their walk on to Govan's Chapel. As they climbed the steep steps up the hill and looked back onto the tiny harbour, Christian rested his arm on her shoulder. Just like the time he'd held her hand two years ago, it seemed the most natural thing in the world.

And that, she decided, was what she liked – *loved* – about Christian. There was no artifice to him. No pretence to be anything other than he was.

Why can't my life be as perfect as this all the time? she thought that night, lying in bed, for once not thinking guiltily about how much she'd eaten, and whether or not she should creep along to the bathroom.

The first time Gran met Christian, she made the mistake of forgetting he was deaf – or had 'impaired hearing' as he now preferred to call it. It was an easy mistake to make. He was so good at lip-reading, even Genevieve forgot sometimes. And Nattie, being Nattie, had decided that maybe he wasn't as deaf as he said and had tried several times to catch him out. But no matter how many times she tried to creep up behind him and see if he jumped when she clapped her hands, he remained completely unaware of her, or that he was being tested.

To her shame, Genevieve still hadn't told Rachel about

him being deaf; she was afraid of her friend's reaction. Rachel had very rigid ideas about what was acceptable. Only a Simon le Bon or Tony Hadley look-alike would do.

'There's nothing wrong in being choosy,' she would say, usually at some school disco or other. Every other term they were allowed to socialise with the local boys' school and Rachel was invariably one of the girls the boys most wanted to dance with. She had perfected the art of looking bored, as though a school disco was beneath her, but at the same time appearing interested enough to be an all-important part of it.

Once Gran had realised her gaffe, she made the further mistake of talking to Christian with her voice raised to the rafters. 'Genevieve tells me you want to be an architect,' she bellowed across the sitting room at Pendine Cottage, where the entire Baxter family (minus their father) had been invited for tea. Genevieve wanted to die. Trust Gran to choose today to do her impression of a dotty old lady. While Gran listened to Christian's reply, Genevieve tried subtly to attract her grandmother's attention by clearing her throat several times, in the hope that she might realise her mistake and lower her voice. But Gran wasn't looking her way; she was listening attentively to Christian's every word. Mrs May – Ella – passed Genevieve a plate and a napkin and whispered, 'Don't worry, we're quite used to it. A ham sandwich?'

Genevieve took the offered sandwich, dainty and crustless. Hardly any calories at all, she told herself happily. *Don't you believe it*, Constant Companion warned her. She cleared her throat; this was not the time or place.

Gran threw her a sharp look. 'Genevieve, whatever is the matter with you? I'm trying to talk to Christian and all I can hear is rattle, rattle. Are you ill?'

Genevieve didn't know what to say. But Nattie did.

'She's not ill, Gran, but unless you keep your voice down, we'll all end up deaf. Talk to him normally. He's not some subspecies.'

After an excruciating moment when no one seemed to know what to say, everyone laughed politely and busied themselves with sandwiches and cups of tea, but Genevieve could see from the expression on Christian's face that he hadn't managed to lip-read what Nattie had said. He turned to Genevieve and gave her a questioning look. She shook her head and mouthed, 'I'll tell you later.'

When tea was over, at Philip May's suggestion they all went out to the garden to play croquet.

'You don't know what you're taking on,' she told Christian. 'We Baxters are experts at this game.'

'Yes, but we Mays cheat to win.'

'And you think we don't?'

Gran and her mother were notorious for cheating at croquet. For that matter, they were a rule unto themselves with any game: Snap, Ludo, Scrabble, Monopoly, Rummy. You name it, they'd cheat at it. There was almost a competition between them to see who could get away with the most.

It wasn't long before the game disintegrated into a raucous shambles. Leaving Nattie and Polly to supervise the adults, Genevieve and Christian found themselves a quiet spot elsewhere in the garden. Unlike Thrift Cottage, the Mays' holiday home had an enormous garden. Christian had once told her that his mother was a fanatical gardener. There was no view of the sea, but it was beautiful, sheltered by beech and oak trees with deep borders full of pretty flowers and shrubs, all carefully chosen to withstand the extremes of a seaside climate.

They lay on a tartan blanket on the soft grass and stared up at the cloudless blue sky through a lace-work of tree branches. Genevieve couldn't remember ever feeling so happy. In the distance she could hear Gran and Serena bickering, and closing her eyes, she thought that Christian was lucky not to be able to hear the cacophony of noise her family was generating.

The warmth of the sun on her face was making her drowsy. Floating between that state of not quite awake, yet not fully asleep, she pictured herself drifting away on a magic carpet with Christian. As she was floating high above the roof tops, she felt something tickling her cheek. An annoying fly. She flicked it away, but it came back. Irritated, she opened her eyes, and saw that Christian, raised up on one elbow, was leaning over her with a blade of grass in his hand.

'Caught red-handed,' he said with a smile. Then, very gently, he stroked her cheek some more.

She didn't stop him.

Chapter Fifteen

Genevieve was frequently told by her family that she felt things too deeply. Where others could let problems and worries slide off their backs as easily as winking, she could not. Nattie, that well-known psychology expert, said she turned everything into a colossal big deal and that one day she would worry herself to death. However, once more according to Nattie, two weeks spent in the company of Christian was having a positive effect on her. 'You're not half so gloomy when you're with him.'

'It must be love,' declared Serena with embarrassing enthusiasm from the front of the car as they set off to Tenby to have a look round the shops. 'That's why you're not eating.'

Defences up, Genevieve was instantly on the alert. Squeezed in between Gran and Nattie – it was Polly's turn to sit in the front passenger seat – she leaned forward. 'What do you mean, I'm not eating?' Too late she realised she shouldn't have reacted so quickly. Or seized on the eating reference. Anyone else's first thought would have been to deny they were in love.

'Don't look so serious, darling, I was just the same at your age. The weight simply dropped off me. It's called love-sickness. You can't eat, sleep, concentrate or sit still for thinking of the object of your desire.' Serena sighed. 'I remember the day I met your father . . .'

Genevieve almost sighed with relief too. She was off the hook. For the rest of the journey, with the windows down and the wind blowing at their hair, Serena told them the story of how she and Daddy Dean had fallen in love. It was a story they knew by heart, but never tired of. They loved hearing how Serena had arrived at the barn dance late because the heel of her favourite pair of shoes had dropped off just as she'd been leaving the house, how when she'd arrived at the church hall, wearing a pair of her mother's shoes, she had caught sight of a handsome man fiddling nervously with his tie and had made a beeline for him. By the time they were in Tenby hunting for a parking space, Serena had reached the punchline of the story, the bit when she'd tripped over, and all of them, including Gran, chorused together 'and Zing! Went the strings of my heart; that was the moment I knew Dean Baxter was the man for me!'

It was one of those barmy moments that the Baxters did best. With an ache in her heart, Genevieve realised that since Grandad had died, these moments had been fewer and further between.

They were allowed to split up and go their separate ways in Tenby. Polly had run out of books to read, so Mum said she'd take her to the bookshop. Nattie wanted to go to the amusement arcade and took Gran by the arm, sure in the knowledge that their grandmother, equally addicted to slot machines, especially those ones that slid in and out, would step in with a purse full of pennies and, later, would probably treat Nattie to a stick of rock, or maybe some candyfloss.

Which left Genevieve happy to wander the narrow streets and cobbled alleyways on her own. It being August, the town was packed with holidaymakers. Genevieve liked it here. She enjoyed the hustle and bustle, the pretty shops and cafés decked out with colourful flower boxes and hanging baskets, and the nearby beaches with their sand so golden and inviting. Rachel wouldn't approve of it, though; the shops weren't big enough or fashionable enough for her. Rachel and her family went to America for their summer holiday, as well as at half-term in the autumn; she always came back with tons of new clothes.

It was funny, but it was as though there were two Genevieves: the cautious, uptight one who lived at Brook House Farm, and who was best friends with Rachel Harmony, and the other one who was relaxed and care-free at Thrift Cottage, and was best friends with Christian May. When she thought about it, the two were incompatible. While Rachel was obsessed with not just her own appearance but everyone else's, Christian didn't give a hoot about what people thought of him. He wore exactly what he wanted, and did exactly what he wanted. A bit like Nattie, really. He set no limitations for himself or those around him. But Rachel, for all her rigidity, was the best friend ever.

Buoyed up with a sense of well-being, Genevieve paused for a moment on the crowded pavement to look at the display of clothes in a shop window. Her gaze was distracted by a girl staring back at her. She was smiling, her long hair tucked behind her ears, her cheekbones forming a heart-shaped face. She was dressed in a tee-shirt that was drab and too big for her, but there was no mistaking the curvy outline of the body beneath it.

Genevieve noted all this in less than a split-second, then she was brought up short by the realisation that the girl was *her*. Despite the number of people – some with pushchairs and young children carrying beach balls and fishing nets – all trying to get past her, she continued to stare at herself, mesmerised. She knew she wasn't any-where near as slim as Rachel but, and this took her breath away, she wasn't the Incredible Hulk she'd believed herself to be. Elated by this discovery, she felt like hugging the nearest person. 'Look at me,' she wanted to cry, 'I'm not fat any more!'

To celebrate, she shoved open the shop door. Mentally

counting out her holiday money – five pounds that she'd saved, five pounds from Mum and Dad and another two pounds fifty from Gran – she scanned the racks of clothes. A top, perhaps? It wasn't the kind of place where Rachel would buy anything; there was no loud music and no surly girls wearing too much make-up and giving Genevieve the kind of stare that said the outsize shop was down the road. She started sliding a row of garments along the rail. A woman about the same age as her mother appeared at her side.

'Can I help you?'

'Um . . . I'd like to try one of these, please.' She pointed to the rail.

The woman hesitated. She looked at Genevieve, then back at the row of tee-shirts. 'I'm not sure we have any of your size left.'

Genevieve's heart sank. She should have known the reflection in the window had been a cruel illusion.

'Everything on this rail is much too large for you,' the woman carried on. 'How about these over here? I know we have your size in those tops. Do you see anything you like?'

Clutching her carrier bag and its size ten strappy top – *size ten!* – Genevieve left the shop in a giddy state of euphoria. Nothing in the whole wide world could make her feel any happier.

But she was wrong.

If Christian had thought it odd that she hadn't wanted to go swimming before now, he never said anything. He'd probably put it down to a 'girl thing', though why it had extended over two weeks may have given him cause to wonder. But today, twenty-four hours after the outing to Tenby, with her confidence at an all-time high, Genevieve suggested they went for a swim.

There weren't any full-length mirrors at Thrift

Cottage, but last night, after stripping down to her underwear and standing on the edge of the bath, holding her breath to help her balance, she had studied her body in the mirror above the basin. This was something she hadn't dared do since she had started trying to lose weight. Seeing the truth of her naked body would be more than she could bear. But she had been pleasantly surprised. Okay, she still had a way to go, but all in all she was in better shape than she'd thought possible. Perhaps she'd risk a swim with Christian after all.

A loud thump on the door, followed by Nattie demanding to know if she was going to be in there all night had her wobbling backwards and crashing into the empty bath.

'Gen! What the hell are you doing in there?'

'Nothing.'

Now, on Tawelfan beach, as she and Christian stripped down to their swimwear, the taunting voice of Constant Companion whispered in her ear. *Are you sure you want to do this? And just as it was going so well.*

She banished the voice and nervously wriggled out of her jeans. Ever the gentleman, Christian turned from her and unzipped his trousers. While his back was to her, she ripped off the rest of her clothes. Instinct made her want to reach for a towel, but she steeled herself, picturing the girl in the shop window yesterday, and the new strappy top she planned to put on after their swim.

But she wasn't prepared for the sight of Christian in his swimming shorts. He was all muscle; his legs looked firm and toned, presumably from all that walking. He looked so good she had to turn away and catch her breath. When she'd recovered, and risked a glance back at him, she saw his eyes on her. She flinched when his gaze settled on the back of her thigh. Constant Companion whispered, *I warned you!*

'That looks painful,' he said. 'How'd you get that?'

She twisted to see what he was referring to – a mound of wobbling flesh? – and saw an ugly, purplish bruise the shape and size of a pork chop. Ah, a legacy from last night's bathroom antics. 'Too embarrassing to say,' she replied. 'Ready for that swim?'

They picked their way through the sunbathers, playing children and windbreakers, and dipped their toes in the water.

'It's freezing!' she gasped.

He smiled. 'It's the Atlantic. What did you expect? Race you in!'

Suddenly she was that twelve-year-old girl again, the one who had met Christian on the beach and had defiantly risen to his challenge. And before she could think of a reason not to, she was in the water. He came in after her, dived beneath the waves when it was deep enough, then surfaced beside her, his shaggy hair plastered to his head and neck. He stood up – the water came to his chest – and pushed his hair back into place.

'The tide's coming in,' he said, 'so it'll be safe to swim round the headland. Do you fancy doing that?'

She did. It was so long since she'd swum properly she'd forgotten how free and energised it made her feel. By the time they'd swum all the way into the next bay, then returned to Tawelfan beach, they were starving.

'How about a burger?' he asked, towelling his hair dry, then draping the towel around his shoulders.

Constant Companion materialised in a flash. *Oh, that's a good one! A burger. One hundred per cent pure unadulterated poison. Still, there's always the head down the toilet routine to fall back on.*

'Maybe a sandwich,' she compromised.

But as they joined the queue at the kiosk, the temptation of a sizzling, big, fat, juicy burger was too much for her. She told herself that she had just swum nearly a mile, so she'd earned it. She could always pass on tea that evening.

They took their burgers and cans of Coke back to the dunes and found themselves a sheltered spot. It was there, quite unexpectedly, that Christian kissed her. She had imagined this moment for so long, had spent hours daydreaming of The Perfect Kiss, but nothing could have prepared her for the real thing. The softness of his mouth against hers, so light and fleeting, lasted for no more than a few seconds, but it was enough to make the world stop spinning, for a fluttering warmth to spread through her and for her senses to become aware of everything that was going on around them. Music was playing close by on a radio, Elvis Presley singing one of her mother's many favourite songs, 'The Wonder of You'. Looking into Christian's eyes – soft brown flecked with green and gold – she could only think, with painful poignancy, how appropriate the lyrics were: 'When no one else can understand me, when everything I do is wrong, you give me hope and consolation, you give me strength to carry on.'

'What are you thinking?' Christian asked her.

She pointed to the radio. 'There's a song playing and it's …' Her voice trailed away.

'And it's what?'

She lost her nerve, unable to share with him that the lyrics summed up how he made her feel.

Later, when they still hadn't moved from the dunes and he was kissing her again, she knew that there would never be anyone else for her. So full of happiness she thought she might burst, she smiled to herself. Just as her parents had 'Zing! Went the Strings of My Heart' as their song, she and Christian would have 'The Wonder of You'.

Chapter Sixteen

Genevieve didn't know why, but Rachel was in a strange mood; nothing she said or did seemed to help. She decided to keep quiet and ignore her friend's sullen silence. It was probably that time of the month. But Genevieve didn't care; she had a letter from Christian in her blazer pocket.

They were on the school bus, and with another ten minutes to go before they'd be at school, Genevieve's hands itched to pull out the letter and read it through one more time: Christian had invited her to stay with him in Shropshire for the autumn half-term. 'If the weather's nice,' he'd written, 'Dad says we might drive down to Angel Sands for a few days.' Half-term was only three weeks away and Genevieve was fidgety with excitement. She wanted to show Rachel the letter, then run up and down the packed bus telling everyone the brilliant news. She found herself smiling broadly at the thought of seeing Christian again.

'Oh, for crying out loud, Gen, give it a rest, won't you!'

'What? What have I done?'

Rachel shifted in her seat and looked out of the window at the passing shops and houses, her shoulder to Genevieve. 'You know jolly well,' she muttered.

Genevieve frowned. 'Have I done something to annoy you?'

Silence.

'Rachel?'

The shoulder turned a few degrees. 'If you must know, yes. Yes you have. You're always going on about bloody Christian this, and bloody Christian that. Ever since the summer holidays you've been a real pain. I thought I was supposed to be your best friend.'

Genevieve was stung. 'But you *are* my best friend. And always will be.'

'Yeah. That's why you're running off down to some godforsaken place in Shropshire for the whole of half-term. What about me? What am I supposed to do while you're away?'

'But I thought you were going to Florida, like you always do.'

The shoulder was back in place, the face turned even more to the glass. 'We're not going. Mum and Dad have changed their minds.'

'But you always go.'

Rachel whipped round. 'Don't you think I know that, you big fat moron!'

Appalled at the strength of her friend's attack, Genevieve stared straight ahead, concentrating on the neatly plaited hair of the girl in front. They completed the rest of the journey without another word. At school they avoided each other, and during the bus ride home at the end of the day, they sat together, but in tight-lipped silence.

Genevieve got off the bus and walked home with her sisters. They were all at the same school now, but there was an unspoken agreement between them: they were never to sit near each other. Genevieve and Nattie sat upstairs – Nattie on the back row with her rowdy friends and Genevieve in the middle with Rachel – and Polly downstairs, usually at the front, predictably lost in whatever book she was reading. Nattie and Genevieve frequently had to drag her off the bus before she missed their stop. Occasionally, if she didn't have anything to read, she would sit with her eyes closed and hum to herself, causing those around her to smile and point. Nobody ever bullied her for it, though. Not if they didn't want to face the music with Nattie, who wouldn't think twice about lashing out in her twelve-year-old sister's defence.

'So what's up with you, Gen?' asked Nattie, stopping to roll down the waistband of her skirt so Mum wouldn't know how short she wore it for school. 'You've got a face on you like a dog's bum.'

'Thanks.'

'I mean it. You look as miserable as –'

'Enough of the compliments. I've had a horrible day, so please don't make it any worse.'

'Suit yourself. Only I'd have thought you would have been deliriously happy, what with going to see Christian at half term.'

'Have you had a fight with Rachel?' This was from Polly.

'What makes you say that?' Genevieve said warily.

'I noticed you didn't sit next to her during lunch. She was with Katie Kirby and Lucinda Atkins.'

Nattie whistled. 'You must have had a bust-up if that's the case. So what did you argue about?'

'We didn't argue.'

'Liar! Why else would she set up camp with the school she-devils? Hey, interesting point; I thought it was only the real hardened bitches who were allowed to hang out with the Queens of Spite. So come on, what's been going on between you two?'

Genevieve gave in. There was no point in prevaricating with Nattie when she was in full flow. She told her sisters about Rachel's behaviour on the bus that morning, although she couldn't bring herself to repeat her friend's exact words. *You . . . big . . . fat . . . moron!*

'She's jealous,' Nattie said. 'Jealous as hell.'

More kindly, Polly said, 'Perhaps she's frightened of losing you as a friend.'

This wasn't exactly the revelation her sisters thought it was. Genevieve had worked out as much for herself. Question was, why? As far as she was concerned, nothing had changed between her and Rachel.

Gran had the answer when Genevieve called in to see her after finishing her homework and told her grandmother what had happened. 'What's annoyed that girl most is you've done something without her approval.'

'Oh, that's just silly, Gran.'

'All I'll say, Genevieve, is this. Rachel's not as clever or as confident as she makes out. I suspect that she needs you as a friend more than you need her. And because of that, she'll soon make it up with you. Now then, how about a piece of cake?'

'No, thank you.'

'A slice of treacle tart perhaps? I could pop it in the oven for a few minutes and make some custard for you. Or would you prefer some whipped cream?'

After feeling so low as a result of Rachel's hurtful outburst, nothing would have suited Genevieve more than to gorge herself on several slices of Gran's butter-rich treacle tart. But she fought hard to resist the temptation, picturing not Constant Companion tapping her foot and wagging her finger at her, but Christian's letter, now under her pillow ready to read one more time before switching off the light. In three weeks she would be seeing him, and she had no intention of arriving in Shropshire looking as big as The Wrekin.

You . . . big . . . fat . . . moron!

How could Rachel have said that? When she, of all people, knew how hard Genevieve had worked to lose weight?

After returning from Angel Sands, back in the summer, Genevieve had rushed to see her friend; the first thing she had done was to take off her jacket and show Rachel the top she'd bought in Tenby. 'Look,' she'd laughed. 'It's size ten. Can you believe it?'

Rachel looked up from her magazine. 'Really?'

'Yes! Isn't it amazing? I must have lost at least a stone.'

'Haven't you weighed yourself to check?'

'No. I can't bring myself to do it, just in case I haven't lost as much as I think I have.'

Sliding off her bed, Rachel said, 'Well, let's do it now.' She pulled some scales out from under the bed and said, 'On you get. The needle of doom never lies.'

This was what Genevieve had nicknamed the black marker that decided her fate. 'Do I have to?'

'Don't be a chicken, Gen.'

Still Genevieve held back.

'Oh all right,' Rachel said. 'I'll go first. I bet I haven't lost as much as you.'

No, thought Genevieve, but you didn't need to in the first place.

'Bang on seven stone,' said Rachel in a satisfied voice. 'Your turn.'

'Can I take off my jeans?'

'I kept mine on.'

Genevieve stepped onto the scales. 'You read it for me.'

'Eight stone and eight pounds,' Rachel announced, almost straight away.

'But I wasn't ready!'

'What do you mean, you weren't ready?'

'I was still moving. I hadn't got into position.'

'Then hurry up and get into position!'

She did, but this time she watched the needle herself, saw it wobble, then hover into place. 'Eight stone and . . . and six pounds. And that's with my jeans on.' She smiled and hopped off the scales. 'I was right, I've lost a whole stone. Isn't that great?'

'It is. Well done. Now you don't have to bother any more, do you?'

'Oh, no, this is just the start. Now I know I can do it, I want to lose another stone at least.'

Rachel went back to lying on the bed. 'Believe me, Gen, you've lost all the weight you need to. If you get any thinner you'll look stupid.' She twirled a lock of hair between her fingers. 'And if you want my honest opinion, I think you ought to put a bit back on. Your face looks too thin to me.'

Genevieve couldn't believe what she was hearing. Rachel had to be joking. She went and stood in front of the dressing table mirror. But before she could say anything, Rachel said, 'So what's your secret? How did you lose the weight? Before you went on holiday, I swear you'd never have been able to get into that top. Not in a million years. Have you started smoking like those models I told you about?'

It was then that Genevieve told Rachel all about her and Christian. 'Mum keeps going on about me losing weight because I'm in love. I know it sounds silly, but I think she might be right.'

Rachel rolled her eyes.

Now, as Genevieve waved goodbye to her grandmother and walked home through Solomon's Meadow in the dusky twilight, listening to the noisy blackbirds chirruping before settling in their nests, she thought of Rachel's reaction when she'd told her that Christian was officially her boyfriend. With hindsight she could see that Rachel had been distinctly cool about the news.

'But you're not really going out with him, are you?' she'd said. 'It's not like it's a proper relationship.'

'Yes, it is. We've kissed and everything!'

Rachel had laughed. 'That means nothing. He's probably just using you as a holiday fling. What's more, he might be lying to you. I bet there's a girlfriend at home he's not telling you about.'

'There isn't. I know there isn't. Besides, he isn't that sort of boy. He wouldn't lie to me.'

'Yeah, well, you might be right. But you didn't throw yourself at him, did you?'

'Certainly not!'

'Good. Otherwise you'll just end up feeling cheap when he dumps you.'

But Christian never made Genevieve feel cheap. Special was how she felt. Uniquely special. He'd even told her he thought she was beautiful. He said it when they'd been lying on the beach one hot, sunny day. Opening her eyes, she'd found him staring down at her.

'What are you thinking?' she'd asked.

'I'm thinking how beautiful you are,' he'd said simply. For days and weeks afterwards, she spent long, dreamy moments recalling his words.

Saying goodbye at the end of the holiday had been horrible, though. He'd come to Thrift Cottage to wave them off and while no one was looking they had sneaked a final kiss and promised to write straight away.

'I'll miss you,' she'd said, still in his arms, but pulling back so that he could see her lips.

'And I'll miss you too. Let's try and meet up some time soon.'

'I'd like that.'

'Go on, you'd better go. Your mother's trying to pretend she hasn't noticed what we're up to.'

Without fail they wrote every week. On her sixteenth birthday he sent her the most romantic present ever; a bunch of red roses. It seemed so grown-up. And because she'd plucked up the courage to tell him about the song that had been playing on the radio when he'd first kissed her, he also gave her a CD of Elvis songs, including 'The Wonder of You'. She hadn't the heart to tell him she couldn't play the CD because they didn't have a CD player at Brook House Farm – with her prized collection of Broadway musicals, Mum was refusing to believe that vinyl would soon be a thing of the past. Rachel had a CD player, but Genevieve hadn't wanted to play it in front of her friend.

Thinking about it now, perhaps she *had* treated Rachel badly. She shouldn't have talked about Christian so much, or been so ridiculously happy whenever a letter arrived. It had been insensitive of her. Hearing the cows stomping their hooves in the cowshed as she turned into the farmyard, she realised that from where Rachel was sitting, she must have become a real bore, with her Christian this and Christian that. She knew then what she had to do, and after she'd waited for Nattie to come off the phone, she called Rachel to say she was sorry, that she wanted to be friends again.

She apologised again on the bus in the morning, and any trace of coolness that had remained on the phone last night was gone. Rachel accepted her apology with good grace. She even managed to say sorry herself.

'I shouldn't have called you what I did. I don't ever want you to think that I'm jealous of you having a boyfriend, Gen,' she added. 'I'm not. You haven't slept with him, have you?'

'*No!*'

'Good. And even if he says he loves you, don't believe him. They all say that just so they can get you into bed. It's all they ever want to do. The longer you hold out, the better.'

Keen to please her friend, Genevieve nodded and changed the subject. She asked how Rachel had got on with the English essay they had to hand in that morning.

But perversely Rachel seemed eager to discuss Christian. 'What I don't get is why he never rings you. Why does he only write?'

Genevieve had never considered the possibility that Christian would be able to use a phone, but this summer he'd told her that up until last year, he had in fact been able to use a special telephone, a specially amplified one. But then he'd found that what residual hearing he had had diminished to the point that even with the extra amplification, he couldn't make out more than a blur of sounds. His parents had said they might buy him a text-phone, but as he said, what use was that unless the person he was talking to also had a textphone? And he certainly didn't want to talk with her through a third person.

But Genevieve still hadn't got around to telling Rachel about Christian's deafness – her friend could be cruel sometimes and she couldn't bear the thought of Rachel belittling Christian, or worse, making fun of him. Deciding to answer her friend's question, and to hell with what she might think or say, Genevieve said, 'I would have thought it was obvious why he doesn't ring me.'

'Obvious? In what way?'

'He's deaf. Don't you remember me telling you?' She stared out of the window and hoped she wouldn't be struck down for such a blatant lie.

'*Deaf!* You mean, deaf as a post?'

'Yes.'

Rachel poked Genevieve with her elbow, to make her look at her. 'You never told me he was deaf. I'd have remembered a thing like that.'

Genevieve met her friend's gaze, ready to defend Christian should she have to. 'Maybe I forgot to tell you. Either way, it's no big deal.'

'But *deaf,* Gen. Now that's what I call weird. I mean, how do you communicate with him? Hand signals?'

'We talk as normally as you and I are doing right now.'

'How?'

'He reads my lips.'

'Pardon?'

'I said, he reads my –'

Rachel burst out laughing. 'Got you!'

'That's not funny.'

But Rachel was still laughing to herself when they got off the bus, and for the rest of the day Genevieve was subjected to countless I-beg-your-pardon-you'd-better-speak-up jokes. By the end of it, Genevieve was ready to slap her friend's face.

Chapter Seventeen

'I'm afraid we all have to make allowances for Rachel,' Mum said through a cloud of steam as she thumped the iron down. 'She's going through a tough time. It's not easy for her.'

Over by the sink, Gran looked up from the new potatoes she was scrubbing and said, 'If Genevieve were to bend any further backwards for that girl, she'd be a contortionist!'

'I agree with Gran: Rachel's a complete pain in the backside. Just because her parents have split up, it doesn't give her the right to be such a bloody awful bitch.'

'Natalie Baxter, I've told you before about swearing!'

'Mum, I'm nearly fifteen. I'm a mass of hormonal angst; swearing is a vital outlet for my pent-up emotion.'

'Then I'll thank you to do it elsewhere. Now put your angst on hold and pass me your father's shirt to iron.'

Genevieve listened to her family discussing her friend, who was upstairs using the last of the hot water. Again.

It was five months since Rachel's mother had discovered her husband had been living a double life; turned out he'd been having an affair for years. All the times he'd said he was away chasing deals for his construction business, he'd been down in Kent seeing the other woman in his life. He'd even taken her on holiday. That was what had given him away. He'd been spotted by one of his wife's closest friends in a hotel in Paris. Mrs Harmony had kicked him out, sworn vengeance on his wallet and refused to let him see Rachel, until he hit back with the law on his side and claimed his right to see his daughter. It was horrible for Rachel, Genevieve could see that, caught between her parents and expected to take sides. She could never imagine doing that if her parents were ever to split up.

'Mum's using me to punish Dad,' Rachel told Genevieve on the bus one morning, 'and I hate her for that, almost as much as I hate him for what he's done.'

Overnight, Rachel's behaviour at school changed. She became moody, rude and surly, even to the teachers. She disregarded all the rules, dyed her lovely blonde hair a dirty shade of black and teased it about a foot high, then hardened it with gel and hairspray. She had several more holes pierced in her ears, and was constantly late with handing in her homework, if she bothered to do it at all. She also started smoking, and then began to skip school altogether. Her parents were 'invited' to discuss the matter with the headmistress, as they were only weeks away from sitting their GCSEs. 'Boring!' was Rachel's only comment. Things picked up a bit as a result of the meeting and she got through her exams – the last one for them both had been two weeks ago. Then, at the weekend, she had arrived at Brook House Farm with yet more shocking news.

Sitting on the fence behind the Dutch barn where no one would see them, she had lit up the first of many cigarettes after knocking back a large mouthful of vodka from the bottle in her bag. She told Genevieve she never wanted to see her father again.

'He's a lying cheating bastard and I hope he rots in hell for what he's done.'

'What's he done now?'

'I don't want to talk about it. Can I doss down here with you for a while?' Taking a long drag on the cigarette, she flicked the glowing stub of it into the air. It landed several yards away in the sun-dried grass.

Genevieve leapt down from the fence and stamped it out. 'You mustn't do that, Rachel, you could start a fire.'

Rachel shrugged and raised the vodka to her mouth. 'Lay off, Gen, I get enough nagging from Mum at home. If she isn't screaming at Dad on the phone, she's having a go at me. So can I stay?' She held out the bottle.

Genevieve took it but didn't drink any. In her friend's current mood she wasn't sure she wanted her around full-time. Pushing this selfish thought aside, she said, 'I'll ask Mum.'

Minutes passed as they sat in the gathering dusk. After striking a match for another cigarette, Rachel said, 'Apparently I have a sister.'

'A what?'

She snatched the vodka out of Genevieve's hands. 'You heard. My father has another child, with that woman.'

Imagining this was a recent event, Genevieve said, 'When was it born?'

'That's the good bit. Five years ago.'

'*Five years!* You're kidding?'

'Oh, yeah, like I'd go round joking about a thing like that.'

'And he's kept it a secret all this time? But that's incredible.'

'That's one way of putting it.'

Another silence fell between them.

'Her name's Christine,' Rachel said bitterly, 'and if we can believe a single word my father says, she looks just like me.' She slipped down from the fence and swayed unsteadily. 'How can he say that? How can he even compare the two of us? He always said I was special. That I was his –' Her voice trailed away and she slumped over the fence, her shoulders heaving with angry sobs.

Genevieve put her arm around her friend. She knew exactly what Rachel had been going to say, that her father had always called her his Special Little Princess.

Poor Rachel, her crown had been taken from her a long time ago and she'd never even known it.

But remaining sympathetic towards Rachel wasn't easy. She had been staying with them for five days now and so far she'd argued with Nattie at least once a day, almost coming to blows over whose turn it was to have a bath; she'd been rude to Mum about her cooking; she'd broken one of Dad's fishing rods; and, in Genevieve's eyes, had committed the cardinal sin of laughing at Gran behind her back when Gran had reprimanded her for smoking.

'Ever thought of taking a shotgun to your crazy Gran's head and putting her out of her misery?' Rachel said. 'I hope I die long before I get like her.'

'Keep smoking at that rate and your wish might be granted,' Genevieve told her sharply. Another remark like that and Rachel would get more than she bargained for.

When Genevieve heard the bath water running away, she went upstairs. It was time for some plain speaking. Rachel needed to be told she'd outstayed her welcome.

'Hi, Gen,' Rachel said, appearing on the landing just as Genevieve reached the top of the stairs. She was wearing Genevieve's brand new dressing gown and a towel fashioned into a turban on her head. 'I've just had this great idea. Why don't I come on holiday with you? I can't face Dad this summer, and Mum's turned into a right psycho. What do you say?'

There were any number of reasons why Rachel shouldn't come to Angel Sands. To name but two, she'd drive them all mad, and there really wasn't room at Thrift Cottage. But Genevieve's main concern was that she didn't want Rachel to ruin what had always been special to her. It was selfish, but Angel Sands was like a precious old toy that no one but Genevieve was allowed to play with.

There was also Christian to consider. Having Rachel around would spoil everything: she and Christian wouldn't be able to see as much of each other as they'd planned to. His last letter had been full of all the things he hoped they'd be able to do. Now that he could drive, they'd been looking forward to going further afield.

But all that was about to be wrecked and it was as much as Genevieve could do to be polite to Rachel as they sat in the very back of the family Volvo – in the dickey seat. She answered her friend's annoying questions about Angel Sands. How many pubs were there? What were the locals like? Should she – ha, ha, ha! – have brought her passport? And was it true what they said about the Welsh and sheep?

Eventually Genevieve feigned sleep and wished her parents weren't so generous. Despite Genevieve saying she didn't think it would be a good idea, Rachel went behind her back and asked her parents if she could join them on holiday. And because Mum and Dad both felt sorry for her, they'd said she was more than welcome to join them, but warned her that it would be a bit of a squash.

After the longest and hottest journey Genevieve had ever known, they'd arrived and were unpacking. There were four bedrooms – one for Gran, one for her parents, one for Nattie and Polly, and the smallest, the room that had always been Genevieve's, was home for her and her friend for two weeks.

'When your mum and dad said it would be small, I didn't think they meant dolls house small,' Rachel said rudely, still with half a case to unpack. 'The place is tiny. Where on earth shall I put all my clothes?'

'I told you not to bring so many. Here, put them in the cupboard. I'll use the shelves.'

Genevieve wasn't at all sure she'd survive the holiday. Or that her happy memories of the place would remain intact.

Driving through the centre of the village, passing the shops with their supply of seaside bric-a-brac – the colourful buckets and spades, the inflatable beach toys, the gaudy sticks of rock and racks of flip-flops – she had tried to look at it through Rachel's eyes. But what she'd seen before as quaint and relaxed, now seemed backward and old-fashioned. Where were the High Street stores that her friend would crave? The only saving grace was that the hot weather had brought out the holidaymakers and the beer garden in front of the Salvation Arms was packed, as was the beach. A deserted, rain-sodden Angel Sands would never have survived Rachel's scorn and ridicule.

Their father was keen to try out the new barbecue the owners of the cottage had supplied, and after they'd finished their unpacking, Nattie and Polly were sent down to the village to buy some chops and sausages. 'And you two,' their father said, looking at Genevieve and Rachel, 'can go over to Pendine Cottage, and see if Christian and his parents would like to join us.'

This then, was the moment of truth. And as they set off in the late afternoon sun, Rachel taking the opportunity to smoke, Genevieve knew that if Rachel said one disparaging word about Christian she would never speak to her again. In fact, she'd insist that her parents made her go home.

She had written to Christian to let him know that she would be bringing her friend with her, and warned him to ignore anything rude Rachel might say when they met. Last year, in October, when Genevieve had spent half-term with Christian, she had kept from him the falling-out that she and Rachel had had. But later, during the February half-term when she was invited to go down to Shropshire again, she told him that Rachel had been jealous of her having a boyfriend. Putting an arm round her, he'd said, 'Then she ought to find one of her own and stop worrying about yours.'

It was only then that Genevieve wondered why Rachel didn't have a boyfriend. All those magazines teaching her how to have the perfect relationship and she hadn't even come close to one.

'You never said it would be so pretty,' Rachel said, as they looked down onto Tawelfan beach, where the sea glistened in the sunlight and the golden sand looked as though it had been washed and dried specially for their benefit.

Genevieve checked her friend's face for signs of sarcasm – she was, after all, used to the glamorous beaches of Florida. To her surprise she saw that Rachel was smiling. For the first time in a long while, she looked happy. Perhaps Mum and Dad had been right to bring her with them, and a relaxing no-frills holiday away from her warring parents was just what she needed. Ashamed of her selfishness, Genevieve turned and walked on.

As it turned out, Christian and his parents couldn't come to Thrift Cottage that evening as they were going to meet some friends staying in St David's.

'So at last I meet Genevieve's mystery boyfriend,' Rachel said, when Mr and Mrs May left them alone in the garden to talk. 'Mind if I smoke?'

'I'd prefer it if you didn't,' Christian said.

Unsure how her friend would react to such directness, Genevieve watched Rachel put the packet of cigarettes back inside her bag. She was relieved when Rachel's lips curled into a smile and she said, 'I like a man who speaks his mind. Shows he knows what he wants in life.'

Sitting on the grass and looking up to where Genevieve and Rachel were sitting on the wooden bench,

Christian smiled too. Genevieve's heart gave a sudden lurch; she thought she'd never seen him look more attractive. He was dressed in an open-necked checked shirt and jeans, his feet bare and very tanned. His hair, still thick and springy, was wet from having just come out of the shower and was pushed back from his forehead giving him a sexy pop-star kind of look. Just the sight of him made her want to leap up from the wooden seat and throw herself at him.

'So what's this about me being Genevieve's mystery boyfriend?' he said. 'I don't think there's anything remotely mysterious about me.'

Rachel turned to Genevieve and laughed. 'Shall I tell him or will you?'

Frowning, Genevieve said, 'I would if I knew what you were talking about.' She glanced at Christian as if to say, please, just humour her.

'Well, the mystery to me is why Genevieve kept your disability such a big secret.'

Genevieve froze. She felt the colour drain from her face.

Christian's face altered too. Gone was the smile. 'And what disability would that be?'

Rachel switched her gaze from Christian to Genevieve. She slapped a hand over her mouth. 'Oh God, Gen! Have I said the wrong thing?' Then looking back to Christian, 'I'm so sorry. All I meant was; it was only recently that Gen told me you were deaf and I don't know why she did that. Kept it a secret, I mean. 'Cos, there's nothing wrong in being deaf, is there? Who cares about that kind of thing these days? Certainly not me.'

When neither Christian nor Genevieve spoke, Rachel puffed out her cheeks and said, 'I'm going for a walk. I need a fag.'

They watched her go. When she was out of earshot, Genevieve spoke. 'I'm sorry for what she said.'

141

He got up and joined her on the bench. 'It's okay. You did warn me.'

'But she shouldn't have said that. You're not disabled. It was an awful thing to say.'

'Clumsy maybe, but not awful.' He put his arms around her. 'Technically I am disabled. So let's leave it at that. Don't suppose you'd like to get your lips a bit nearer so I can read them better?'

Seeing that he was smiling again, she moved so that her face was just inches from his. 'Close enough?'

He shook his head. 'Closer please.'

She pressed her mouth against his. His lips parted, and with her eyes closed, her heart thumping in her chest, she opened her mouth and welcomed the soft, slow movement of his tongue against hers. The feel of his hands around her neck made her skin tingle and a dizzying warmth flooded through her. But there was something new, a burning heat deep within that made her want him to undress her and touch her all over. She knew for sure then, that if there was an opportunity during the holiday, and he asked her to, she would go all the way with him.

They were still kissing when Rachel returned. Neither of them noticed her until she was almost upon them.

'Bloody hell, you two! It's a good thing I'm here or the pair of you would be at it.'

On their way back to Angel Sands, Rachel slipped her arm through Genevieve's. She had started doing this recently and Genevieve wished she wouldn't; people often stared at them.

'Sorry about putting my huge foot in it,' Rachel said. 'Am I forgiven?'

Still high on kissing Christian, Genevieve said, 'Of course. Although it was pretty awful what you said. You must never use that word again in front of him.'

'What word?'

'The D word: disability.'

'Oh, that. He was fine about it. Especially once you got your tongue down his throat.'

Trying to hide her embarrassment, she said, 'You shouldn't have been watching.'

'What else could I do? You were in full view of me. But I'll say this. Your taste isn't bad. He's totally dee-lus-cious. He looks much older than eighteen. More like twenty-two. And that deaf thing really isn't a problem, is it? I love the way his eyes flickered over my mouth whenever I said anything. Very sexy. I could even fancy him myself.'

Genevieve's heart swelled, any earlier misgivings over her friend's blunder now gone from her mind. 'You really thought he was nice?'

'Get real! He's a drool object! A heartbreaker too, I shouldn't wonder.'

'Oh, no,' Genevieve said, 'you've got him all wrong. Christian's not like that.'

'Gen, you sweet little innocent. Haven't you realised yet that *all* men are like that?'

Thinking of Rachel's father, Genevieve didn't argue the point. Instead, she took pleasure in her friend's approval of something so important to her.

She also felt a sense of relief that Christian hadn't questioned her on why she had waited so long to tell Rachel he was deaf.

Several days after their father had left them to return home to the farm, Genevieve overheard her grandmother say, 'Serena, I wouldn't trust that little minx as far as I could throw her.'

Wondering who she and her mother were discussing – Nattie perhaps – Genevieve hovered outside the kitchen door.

'Oh, she's harmless enough. She's just a little mixed up these days. It'll pass.'

That ruled out Nattie: she'd been mixed up all her life.

'Well, don't say I didn't warn you. But if you take my advice, you'll do something about it.'

'But they're young, they have a lifetime of lessons to be learned, some harder than others.'

'I don't care how young they are, these things stay with you, and if Genevieve gets hurt, I'll never forgive myself for keeping quiet.'

Genevieve's heart pounded. Hurt? Who would deliberately hurt her? Agonising seconds passed as she waited for her mother to say something. She tried to make herself go back upstairs, where only minutes ago she had been lying in bed unable to sleep. Just turn and go, she told herself. But she didn't, and regretting the thirst that had made her come downstairs for a glass of water, she inched a little closer to the door, taking care not to breathe too loudly or step on anything that might creak and give her away. The blood pulsing in her head, she heard Gran say, 'You're making a big mistake, Serena. Mark my words, she's a viper in our midst.'

'Oh, now you're being melodramatic.'

'I'm not. She's a girl who wouldn't think twice about making a play for her best friend's boyfriend. She's wicked and cunning, and the sooner this holiday is over, the better.'

Genevieve felt sick as slowly she climbed the stairs. Staring down at the bed next to hers, where her friend lay sleeping soundly, Rachel's words came back to taunt her. *Gen, you sweet little innocent. Haven't you realised yet that* all *men are like that?*

Yes, she thought, but only because there are girls out there like you, Rachel Harmony.

*

144

Instead of confronting her friend, or confiding in her grandmother, Genevieve took the coward's way out and for the remaining days of the holiday, she watched Rachel with a constancy that bordered on paranoia.

She watched Christian too.

But while it was true that Rachel paid Christian an inordinate amount of attention, asking him endless questions and forever touching him to make sure he could see what she was saying, for his part, he was always polite and answered her questions with humour and patience.

Goodness! Genevieve had never seen her friend show so much interest in another person. But his manner towards her was no more attentive than it was towards Nattie or Polly: in other words, he was his normal friendly self. If doubt crept up on her, Genevieve reminded herself that it was her hand he held, her lips he kissed, her shoulder he put an arm round, and it was for her benefit alone that he would mouth some private joke or comment.

She could hardly believe it when they reached the end of the holiday, the luggage was stowed and Christian was still her boyfriend.

Was it wrong of her to feel victorious?

Chapter Eighteen

September was a month of enormous change that year. Genevieve and Rachel were settling into the sixth form, Christian was preparing to go to university at the end of the month, and his parents were selling Pendine Cottage to buy a place in the Dordogne to do up. It set Serena off again about them doing a similar thing, finding a house in Pembrokeshire and running it as a bed and breakfast. She spoke of little else, and very soon their father was caught up in the idea too, and began seriously to consider the offer made by a large building firm for Brook House Farm and its lucrative land.

Despite finding her A-level work even harder than she'd anticipated, Genevieve's confidence was rock steady. At last everything seemed to be going well for her. She had never raised the conversation she'd overheard between her mother and Gran, and certainly she'd never broached the subject with Rachel, which meant she would never know if Gran had been right to be worried. But with a resolve that surprised her, she put the episode firmly in the past, concluding that Rachel had probably been doing nothing more cunning than practising her flirting technique. And – *hurrah!* – it had been wasted on Christian.

The weekend before Christian was due to take up his place at Exeter, it was Genevieve's seventeenth birthday and her parents suggested he came to stay, and they'd throw a little party. Everyone knew that there was no such thing as a 'little' party when Serena was involved.

She loved arranging them, and when Genevieve and her sisters had been younger she had, once or twice, gone too far. A Halloween party she was particularly proud of had been so lavish and scary – lights suddenly switched off and homemade skeletons popped out of cupboards – terrified children had wet themselves and begged to be taken home early.

Christian arrived on the afternoon of the party. To have some time alone together, Genevieve took him for a guided tour of the farm. She showed him the milking parlour, explained how the machinery worked, and how her father would have to computerise it if he was going to make it more economical.

'That's if we stay,' she added, as she led him outside and across the yard to the old hay barn.

'You think you won't?' Christian asked, taking hold of her hand.

'Mum's become obsessed with us moving down to Pembrokeshire.'

He smiled. 'It would be nearer Exeter.'

'It would, wouldn't it?'

Looking back towards the house, where Nattie was pulling a face at them through the kitchen window and pretending to gag, he said, 'Is there somewhere we can be alone?'

From having the sun on it all day, the barn was warm and stuffy, the air heavy with the sweet smell of hay. Climbing the ladder up to the loft, where Genevieve and her sisters had often played as children, they sat on the dusty floor. 'This would make a fantastic house,' Christian said, taking off his sweatshirt and glancing round at the space. 'I'd love to do that kind of work when I'm qualified as an architect. Converting old buildings into houses would be such a great thing to do.'

But for once Genevieve wasn't interested in what Christian had to say. Since the moment he'd arrived she'd wanted to kiss him and suddenly feeling light-headed and breathless, she pushed him onto his back. She kissed him slowly on the lips, wanting so much for him to know what he meant to her. He returned her kiss, his mouth deliciously soft and tender. And feeling strangely weak, yet fantastically strong at the same time, she slipped a hand under his tee-shirt, wanting to touch the smooth hardness of his stomach. His hands, too, began to work at her clothes and when she sat up and took off her top, he stared at her, his eyes shining, his breath huskily audible in the stillness. She had never felt more sure of a thing, but when she put her hands behind her back to undo her bra, he suddenly looked nervous.

'Gen, don't. Please don't.'

'It's okay. I want to.'

He put out his hands to stop her. 'I want to as well. But . . . but not here. Not now.'

Her heart slammed in her chest. 'Don't you love me?'

'It's not that. It's . . . ' His voice broke off.

'You don't fancy me? Is that it?' She could feel everything fall away from her, everything she had believed about him, about the strength of his feelings.

He smiled and put his arms around her neck. 'Oh, I fancy you all right. But I don't want to take any chances. You know, doing it without protection. I don't have any condoms.'

Condoms! Of course. How stupid she'd been. Relief flowed through her. She tilted her head back so that he could see her face. 'Another time, perhaps?'

He stroked her cheek. 'You better believe it.'

Rachel was the last guest to arrive, and she was fabulously over-dressed in a slinky white dress that showed off her perfect figure and, if Genevieve's suspicions were right, the lack of a pair of knickers. On her head was a pink baseball cap with the words 'Spoiled

Rotten' written in sparkly fake diamonds.

'A present from my father,' she said, catching Genevieve's glance. 'The dress too. It's his way of saying sorry and I'm quite prepared to take advantage of him.' She handed over an expensively wrapped package. 'For you. Happy seventeenth birthday, Gen.'

'Thanks, Rachel. It looks gorgeous before I've even unwrapped it.'

'Think nothing of it; it's more guilt money extracted from my father. The well is deep and given the chance, I'm going to run it dry.' She took in the other guests. 'There are a lot of people here. Who are they all?'

'Mostly our farming friends.'

'Ah, yes, you told me once that farming blood is thicker than anyone else's and you all stick together like treacle. So where's Christian?'

'He's helping Dad with the barbecue.'

Serena breezed through just then, carrying a large bowl of salad, the smell of spring onions and peppers filling the air. She looked at Rachel. 'Hello dear, I do hope you'll be warm enough. That dress is gossamer-thin.'

Rachel laughed. 'Oh, I expect I'll find some way to keep warm. Gen could always lend me something if I get desperate.'

'She might even lend you some knickers if you're nice. Now, if you'll excuse me, I must get this salad on the table. Have fun!'

When they were getting ready to cut the cake – the Baxters liked nothing better than a good drum-rolling, cake-cutting moment – Genevieve went to look for Christian.

'Have you seen Christian?' she asked Nattie. 'Mum wants to take some photographs of us all together.'

Her sister, who'd been drinking cider for most of the

evening, shrugged. 'No, but I'm seeing two of you if it's any help?'

When Genevieve couldn't find Rachel either, a chilling fear crept into her heart.

'I saw Rachel talking to Christian earlier,' Polly said. 'Do you want me to help you find them?'

'No. It's okay. You tell Mum and Dad to hold back the cake for a few minutes more. I won't be long.'

I'm being irrational, she told herself, but despite her firm words, the chill took a stronger hold on her. Determined to find them both, to know the worst, she checked the house.

No sign of them there.

She tried the hay barn and, almost inevitably, that was where she found them. She didn't need to climb the ladder up to the loft, where only hours ago she and Christian had lain – where she'd been rejected – to know what they were doing. It was obvious. Rachel was gasping loudly and Christian was breathing hard, the floorboards creaking rhythmically.

Genevieve wanted to run, to run right out of the barn, but mesmerised by the trickles of dust falling through the gaps in the wooden floor above her head, she moved slowly towards the ladder. She had to see for herself. Had to know she hadn't imagined it. Her hands trembling, she reached for the ladder and began the nightmare climb upwards. But before she'd stepped onto the second rung, the growing pain inside her exploded and she let out a cry of sickening anguish and dropped to the ground.

Only Rachel could have heard the cry, but probably her expression would have alerted Christian and made him realise something was wrong. The rhythmic creaking stopped. Knowing what was about to happen – that Rachel and Christian would peer down at her – Genevieve picked herself up and fled.

She stumbled outside and ran, blinded by tears, across

the yard to the house. She didn't stop running until she was upstairs and had thrown herself onto her bed. How could he? How could he betray her like that, and with Rachel of all people?

She was sobbing so hard into her pillow, she only realised Gran was in the room when she felt the mattress dip. She opened her eyes, plunged her head into her grandmother's lap and sobbed even harder.

'Oh, Gran,' she gulped, 'I . . . I saw them . . . they were together . . . in the barn . . . and they were . . . he was . . . I hate them both!'

'It's all right, sweetheart,' her grandmother soothed. 'You cry. You cry for as long as you need.' She rocked her gently. The moment was so reminiscent of that day in Gran's kitchen when finally Genevieve had cried for her grandfather, that the tears flowed as though they would never stop. The ache, already burying itself deep inside her heart, was so profound, she knew it would never leave her.

PART III

Chapter Nineteen

'I bet your father wanted to beat the little sod to a pulp! I hope he did.'

Genevieve smiled at Adam. 'You should know Dad better than that. Nattie, on the other hand, didn't waste any time in giving him a piece of her mind. Just as he was getting into his car to drive home, she slapped his face so hard, she knocked him clean off his feet.'

'That's my girl!' Adam laughed heartily, jiggling Lily-Rose on his lap. She was back in the kitchen again, quietly helping herself from the packet of raisins on the table. 'So what happened next?'

'Heavens! Haven't you heard enough? Surely you must be bored to death with all this memory lane stuff?'

'Sorry, am I being insensitive?'

'No. Not at all. But I guess the straight answer is, I recovered from a broken heart and grew up.'

'And the complicated answer?'

'Ah, well. I made myself ill, dropped out of school and drifted aimlessly until I finally got my act together.'

He looked thoughtful. 'How ill, Gen?'

'Oh, you know; the full works. Depression. Anxiety. And starving myself in the belief that Christian had betrayed me because I was a big, fat, unlovable moron. All I could think of was making myself slowly disappear, taking all my problems with me. It became a way of life. Towards the end I was living off peas and toothpaste; the only things I'd allow myself to eat.'

Adam reached across the table and laid his hand on

top of hers. He didn't say anything, just shook his head. Lily-Rose, thinking it was a game, added her small hand to the pile. Giggling, she got back to the packet of raisins, eating them steadily, one by one.

'Why have you never mentioned any of this before?' Adam asked quietly. 'Or for that matter, why haven't your parents or sisters ever spoken of it?'

'It's called shame. Plus that well-known Baxter trait, an inability to talk about anything really important. Let's face it, it's why Mum's currently swanning around some winery in New Zealand and Dad refuses to get his head out of the sand.'

'But there's nothing to be ashamed about.'

Genevieve shook her head. 'Look at it from Mum and Dad's point of view. In their eyes they allowed me to slip through the net. What with Nattie's wildness to control and Polly's musical gifts to nurture, I was the easy-going daughter they didn't need to worry about. Okay, there was my dyslexia, but all in all, I was the one they didn't need to lose any sleep over.'

'But they can't still feel guilty, surely?'

'I think they do. The first thing I remember Mum saying when I was taken into hospital, was, "Where did we go wrong?" You see, with nothing tangible to blame, they blamed themselves. They thought they should have been better parents. Then when I recovered, we all started to push my illness under the carpet, and before long it became known as *That Time When She Wasn't Well*. A tidy euphemism for something we wanted to put behind us.'

Adam frowned. 'I'd never have guessed you'd gone through so much.'

'That's because we Baxters are adept at covering our tracks and keeping schtum.'

'So what happened to Rachel? After you'd torn her limb from limb.'

'She stayed on at school, though I never spoke to her again after that night. Other than to tell her what I thought of her the next day.'

'Strikes me that was something you should have done a long time before. Your Gran was right about her.'

'Hindsight's a wonderful thing, but you know, I think Gran was also right about Rachel not being as clever or confident as she made out. I just couldn't see it at the time.'

Adam scoffed. 'Don't start making excuses for her, Gen. She knew exactly what she was doing. She deliberately manipulated you, filled your head with a lot of dangerous nonsense to plump up her own ego. Do you know what she went on to do?'

'The last I heard – this was years ago – was that she went to live with her father.'

'And Christian. Did he ever say he was sorry?'

'I didn't give him much of a chance to apologise. He wrote to me, but I returned all his letters unopened. After his parents sold Pendine Cottage, he never showed up in Angel Sands again.'

'And now the dirty love-rat is about to appear on the scene again. How do you feel about that?'

She got to her feet to make some fresh tea. 'For a start, I don't view him as a dirty love-rat. Don't forget, we were little more than children. Teenage love isn't designed to last. My mistake was to take it too seriously. But then, that's the prerogative of the young. And as my mother said, there were important lessons to be learned.'

'A very pretty speech, Gen. How about you answer my question?'

With her back to him, staring out of the window, the rain still coming down, Genevieve tried, as she had so many times, to think what her answer really was. How she felt about the memory acquiring its final chapter.

'I'm curious,' she said at last, turning to face Adam.

'Curious to see if I still think he's as perfect as I once thought he was.'

Adam left Lily-Rose to her raisins, and came over to Genevieve, his expression serious. 'I'd have thought he settled that matter in the barn that night.'

She smiled. 'Are you protecting me? Worried I might still be carrying a torch for him?'

'And aren't you?'

'I told you, I'm intrigued. Nothing more.'

From outside came the sound of Henry kicking up an almighty row again. Adam switched his gaze from her to the garden.

'The sooner you find that donkey a pal, the better. Now then, I'd better get going. You won't forget to give Gareth and Gwenda a call about the wedding buffet, will you?'

Chapter Twenty

Genevieve was aware some people would say that as a teenager she'd been a pathetic wimp. That she'd let Rachel walk all over her, had allowed her to have her way over the slightest thing. And worse, she had willingly let Rachel manipulate her like a puppet. No two ways about it, she had only herself to blame for being so feeble.

Well, there was never any point in preaching to the converted – Genevieve knew better than anyone that she should have been more assertive. But ultimately it had been the axis of her friendship with Rachel that had been at fault. Their relationship had been based on too much mutual neediness. As she'd told Adam, hindsight was a wonderful thing, but at that young age she had been ill-equipped to deal with the complex circumstances in which she'd found herself.

She didn't need to be a psychiatrist to know that her low self-esteem in those days, a direct result of being dyslexic, had made her subconsciously pick out a dominant friend to hide behind, and Rachel, with her desperate need to feel superior, had carefully nurtured Genevieve to play the necessary supporting role. So in that respect, neither of them was to blame.

But what Rachel had done with Christian was another matter altogether. Genevieve would always view that as a malicious and calculating act. Rachel had known exactly what she was doing that night and had deliberately gone all-out to destroy what was most precious to Genevieve.

Genevieve could only surmise that it stemmed from Rachel's parents splitting up. Just as Genevieve had been set on a particular course when her grandfather died, so too had Rachel when she realised she was no longer her Daddy's Little Girl, his Special Princess.

Cause and effect.

But that was then.

Now, today, with the wedding buffet to oversee, she had enough to think about without wasting any more time dwelling on the past. She could change none of it, and perhaps, if she was honest, she didn't want to change it. The experience had taught her two invaluable lessons: to take responsibility for herself, and never to allow anyone to manipulate or bully her. Though perhaps a more important lesson would have been to learn the trick of being more open about her feelings. That was a concept she and her family had yet to get the hang of.

Making her final round of checks, she looked in on the marquee in the garden, seeing if the florist had arranged the flowers on the tables as she'd asked. Yes. They were all there, beautifully displayed; baskets of yellow roses and creamy white irises.

Going back outside into the blazing June sunshine, such a contrast to the rain of last week, she pondered why Adam was going to such lengths to organise her. He seemed determined to make her start up her own catering business, having engineered what she was doing today – providing a buffet for eighty-five wedding guests who would be arriving in less than an hour. Since last week, when he'd asked her to rescue Gareth and Gwenda's daughter's wedding party, he'd been on at her almost daily to consider his offer to back her. In the end, just to silence him, she'd told him about George and Cecily Randolph and the money George had left her in his will. It wasn't an enormous sum, but it was enough to help set herself up in business, should she so wish. It had been almost the last conversation she and George had had when he was dying in hospital.

'You've been so good to me,' he'd said, his voice so low she had to bend down next to him to hear, 'and I'm sure Cecily would have wanted you to have the money. It's such a small amount, so please don't refuse it.'

'So you see,' she'd told Adam, 'you don't have to take pity on me.'

'I wasn't doing anything of the kind.'

'Good. Now please don't mention the money to anyone. I don't want people knowing about it. They'll only ask questions that I shan't want to answer.'

'Mr Discreet, that's me. But one more thing. If you have the wherewithal, why don't you get stuck in to something?'

'Because if I'm going to do it, I'll do it when I'm good and ready. I won't be bullied by anyone, not even you, Adam.'

He'd looked hurt at that. 'I've never bullied anyone in my life, Gen. I'm the least manipulative person in the world.'

'You're a dear friend,' she said, giving him a hug.

Inside the house, the sound of laughter was coming from the kitchen. Nattie, who was helping to serve along with Donna, had decided to dress for the part and was wearing a French maid's outfit. Gran, resplendent in one of her best party frocks, said, 'I think she looks great. How I wish I had those legs.'

But Daddy Dean was wearing his disapproving father's hat. 'You don't think you ought to change into something a little less indecent, Nattie? You do realise the vicar's been invited, don't you?'

Nattie grinned wickedly and hitched up her skirt to reveal stocking tops and suspenders. 'Hey, great idea, we could make it a Tarts and Vicars party.'

Genevieve wondered what Adam would make of his beloved parading herself so provocatively.

At their father's insistence, the welcome party was changed. Instead of Nattie and him standing at the entrance to the marquee to offer arriving guests glasses of champagne, as originally planned, Donna was assigned the task in her place. He judged it prudent to wait until the guests had downed a mellowing drink or two before Nattie was let loose on them.

The bride and groom, plus parents, were the first to arrive. The four of them looked with relief at the marquee and pretty garden with its dramatic backdrop of sparkling blue sea; they were clearly impressed. But having thought they'd be reduced to raiding the local supermarket for its limited selection of mass-produced canapés, and putting on a DIY do at home, Genevieve guessed that anything would have been a welcome sight. Polly was playing her part too. She was providing background music. Last night Adam had helped Dad move the piano from the guest sitting room to the conservatory, so that music would flow out into the garden. Now, as the guests began to arrive, Polly struck up with the first of her popular music pieces, 'Love Changes Everything'. On the cliché scale, it was joint first with 'Lady in Red', but as with most clichés, it was entirely appropriate. Catching her eye from across the lawn, Gareth and Gwenda gave Genevieve the thumbs-up.

So far so good.

Back in the kitchen, there was no sign of Gran or Lily-Rose. But with a foot on a chair, cursing loudly, Nattie was adjusting one of her suspenders.

'Bloody thing, it won't stay put. Ah, that's got it.' She lowered her black stilettoed foot to the floor and straightened up. 'How the hell do women manage in these things?'

'I haven't a clue. Are you sure you're going to cope in those shoes? They look lethal.'

'They are, but they'll do wonders for Dad's precious lawn. I'll aerate the grass as I go. Any sign of the vicar yet? I'm dying to see his face. Adam's too.'

With so much to do, Genevieve let Nattie's remark go. 'If you could put your Ann Summers outfit to one side for a moment, you could help me get these trays in the oven.'

After setting the timer and leaving Nattie in charge to remove the canapés when they were cooked – please God, let her perform that simple task! – she went outside to make sure everyone had a drink. Donna and Dad had done their job, and the guests, glasses in hand, were circulating well. Some of them were openly admiring the garden. This would please her father; he'd worked hard all week bringing it up to scratch. The lavender-blue spikes of the neatly formed bushes of hebe contrasted prettily with the silvery-grey leaves of the senecio with its profusion of yellow, daisy-like flowers. Sheltered by the escallonia hedge were beds of hardy fuschias, santolina, sea holly and cat mint. Pots of begonias and geraniums lined the terrace, and against the south-facing wall of the house, Dad's treasured palms were bathed in golden sunlight.

Genevieve felt a satisfying glow of pride that she had pulled it off. She hadn't seriously considered she would fail, but it was gratifying to see just how well, with help from her family and Donna, she had arranged everything.

Echoing her thoughts, a voice said, 'You've done a fantastic job, Gen. Just like I said you would.'

It was Adam, dressed immaculately in a lightweight suit, its effect sadly marred by a tie depicting a pink flamingo.

'Thanks,' she said. 'But I didn't do it alone.'

He shook his head. 'Just take the credit and have done with it, will you?'

She laughed. 'Okay, if you say so.' More seriously, she said, 'Have you seen Nattie yet?'

'No. Why do you ask?'

'Oh, no reason.' Changing the subject, she said, 'By the way, I had a word with that man you recommended over in Saundersfoot.'

'And?'

She pointed towards the far end of the orchard. 'See, or rather, listen. It's worked. Henry's been as good as gold, not a peep out of him. He hasn't left Morwenna's side since Nattie and Dad fetched her first thing this morning.'

'Morwenna?'

'Nattie's choice. It's Welsh for maiden. But she's cute, isn't she, with that light sandy face and chocolate body?'

'I can't honestly say that donkeys do it for me, Gen, but – *Sweet Moses on a bicycle made for two!* What the hell does she think she's doing?'

Adam's gaze, no longer directed towards the orchard, had swung round to the middle of the lawn and was fixed on the object of his desire. Carrying a large tray of canapés, Nattie had finally made her appearance.

He wasn't the only one to stare. 'Why?' he said simply. 'Why does she do it?'

'Because she loves to stand out. It's why you're mad about her, Adam. Remember the first time you set eyes on her; she was on a table doing her Madonna "Like a Virgin" impersonation. Now if you'll excuse me, you're here as a guest, but I'm not. I still have a hundred and one things to do.' She hurried away, leaving him to try to comprehend the impossible – what in the world made Nattie Baxter tick?

Before heading back to the kitchen, Genevieve popped into the conservatory to see how Polly was getting on.

She had moved on to playing Elton John's 'Your Song'. But she had company. Lily-Rose was sitting on the floor under the piano, stirring a bowl of melting ice-cream.

'I thought Gran was supposed to be looking after Lily,' Genevieve said.

Her fingers still moving expertly over the keys, Polly replied, 'I think she may have got the wrong end of the stick.' She inclined her head towards the marquee.

There was Gran, a glass of champagne in one hand and a canapé in the other. She looked every inch the wedding guest, and not the handy baby-sitter she had offered to be.

'It's okay,' Polly said, 'I can manage. Lily's not a distraction.' But she spoke too soon. Suddenly aware of the piano pedals her aunt was working, Lily-Rose leaned forward to take a closer look. She grinned and tapped one of Polly's bare feet with her spoon; a blob of ice-cream landed on Polly's big toe. Professional to the end, Polly played on.

Genevieve bent down and held out her arms to her niece. 'Okay little missey. Out you come.'

Lily-Rose frowned and backed away. With a quickness of hand a magician would have been proud of, she dolloped another blob of ice-cream onto Polly's other foot. Before she got it into her head to tip the bowl over both her aunt's feet, Genevieve grabbed her around the waist and slid her out on her bottom. Still brandishing the spoon, the little girl used it to try and stop Genevieve spoiling her game, bopping her on the forehead with it and then the nose. Snatching it out of her hand, Genevieve slipped the spoon into her pocket. 'You're becoming more like your mother every day. Now behave or I'll be forced to put you in a lobster pot and throw you out to sea.'

Her words had no impact at all on Lily-Rose and, wriggling out of Genevieve's hands, she suddenly pointed through the open conservatory door and let out a cry of delight. '*Adam*!'

The man in question heard her squeal and turned round. She ran helter-skelter towards him and head-butted his kneecaps.

'Hello Rosey-Posey,' he laughed, 'how's my best little girl?'

'We've got a new donkey. Do you want to come and see her? Her name's Morwenna.'

'In a moment maybe.'

'I know it's a cheek, Adam,' said Genevieve, when she'd caught up with her niece, 'but I don't suppose you'd like to keep an eye on her, would you? Gran's decided she'd rather be guzzling champagne than helping out.'

'No problem.' He bent down to Lily-Rose and lifted her onto his shoulders. 'Let's go and see if we can find something to eat, shall we?'

'But what about Morwenna?'

'Food first. Then Morwenna.'

Wide-eyed with delight, Lily-Rose beamed and grabbed hold of his ears. 'Giddy up, giddy up!'

'Thanks, Adam,' Genevieve said. 'What would we do without you?' She touched his arm lightly and leaned in to kiss him. But the sight of two men appearing round the side of the house caught her eye, and she froze.

She had a pretty good idea who the taller and darker of the two was, but the other . . . the other, without doubt, was Christian.

Chapter Twenty-one

Genevieve would never have thought it possible to take in so much in so short a time. As though a spell had been cast, everything around her became a muffled blur while, across the lawn, Christian was picked out in sharp focus.

He'd changed, of course. As much as anyone would in the thirteen years since she'd last seen him. He'd filled out more and his hair – cut shorter than she'd ever seen it – looked as though, finally, it had been tamed. His eyes were hidden behind sunglasses, but she could tell from his stance, hands pushed into the pockets of his loose-fitting trousers, head slowly turning, that he was scanning the garden, searching for someone.

Question was, who?

His gaze fell on her. His body stiffened and his hand reached for his sunglasses. It was obvious he was as stunned as she was. He turned to his companion, said something, then started to walk towards her. The spell grew stronger and the moment became heart-stoppingly surreal. Behind her, in the conservatory, Polly was playing 'Fly Me to the Moon' – something Genevieve would have paid good money to do right there and then. Everyone else, oblivious, continued to chat and laugh; they had no idea she had become a convert to the school of thought that time really could stand still.

Then the spell was broken. Next to her, Adam said, 'Gen, what's wrong? You look like you've seen a ghost.'

She moved closer to him, as if seeking his protection. 'I have,' she whispered. 'It's Christian.'

167

'*What*? Where?'

For a second it was tempting to raise an accusing hand and shout, 'There! That's the bastard who broke my heart!' Instead she murmured, 'He's heading this way. Don't leave me, whatever you do.'

'Anything you say.' Adam lowered Lily-Rose from his shoulders and, holding her hand, set her on the grass. 'We'll get something to eat in a minute, sweetheart.'

It felt as though an eternity passed before Christian was standing in front of her.

'Genevieve.'

That was it. That was all he said.

'Hello Christian.' She forced herself to look him dead in the eye. 'I was wondering when you'd show up.'

He looked puzzled. 'You were? I don't understand.' His voice still had that characteristic flat, hollow timbre to it. The absence of any real inflection.

Over the years she had imagined bumping into Christian, showing him she harboured no ill feelings, that she was a superior being who had always had better things to do with her emotions than waste them on bitterness. She had pictured them catching up on old times, perhaps even becoming friends again. But now, as she stood face to face with the past, she felt a weight of hostility towards him, wanted very much to let him know just how badly he had hurt her.

A childish response? Yes. Proud of it? She didn't care. She even took a twisted, cruel delight in knowing that he appeared more uncomfortable than she did.

'I live here, Christian,' she said, in answer to his question. 'At the moment we all do, Mum, Dad, Gran, Nattie, Polly and me.'

'Really? Where?'

'Here.' She glanced around the garden, up at the house. 'This is our home.'

'Paradise House?' If it were possible he seemed more awkward than ever.

'We run it as a bed and breakfast . . . just as Mum always wanted. Remember her dream?'

'I didn't know. Really I didn't.'

'Why would you?' Her voice was sharp. 'Why are you here, Christian? I don't mean, in the area, everyone knows about Ralph's barn being sold and some architect doing it up – we soon realised it was you. But why are you here at Paradise House?'

He turned away, stared at some distant point out to sea, shifted his feet, then looked back at her. 'You're not going to believe this, but we came here hoping there might be a couple of rooms available. We've just discovered the hotel we'd booked into has been closed down. We were pointed in this direction and told that Paradise House was the best place to stay these days.' He paused. 'But given the circumstances –' He paused again. Shifted his feet once more. 'Honestly, Genevieve, I didn't know you were living here. I swear I had no idea. I'm sorry. I'll tell Jonjo we'll try somewhere else.'

Then, as though only just noticing them, he glanced at Adam and Lily-Rose. His gaze rested on the little girl and something almost like a smile passed across his face; it took away some of the awkwardness from his expression. Genevieve was almost struck with pity for him – but not quite.

'She looks just like Nattie,' he said.

Realising his mistake, Genevieve said, 'That's because she's Nattie's daughter.'

He raised his glance back to her. 'What's her name?'

'Lily-Rose.'

'Look,' he said, more to Adam than to Genevieve, 'I'm sorry for barging in. You're obviously in the middle of a party. I'd better go.' He turned to leave, but hesitated, and just stood there staring at her. 'It's . . . it's good to see you again, Genevieve. You're looking well.' His eyes flickering briefly over Adam and Lily-Rose, he turned and went.

She watched him walk away, back to find his companion, presumably their neighbour-to-be, Jonjo Fitzwilliam. She felt a hand on her shoulder.

'You okay, Gen?'

Still watching Christian's retreating figure, she nodded. 'I'm fine, Adam. Thanks.'

It soon became clear that Christian had lost his friend amongst the wedding guests. Soon he was approaching Genevieve once more.

'Sorry about this,' he said, 'but I can't find Jonjo. It's so typical of him. He has the attention span of a goldfish.'

'Do you always speak so highly of your friends?'

Adam's comment went unnoticed by Christian – he'd been looking at Genevieve for a response. Sensing that her friend's hostility towards Christian was more palpable than her own, she said, 'I'll help you find him.'

'Thanks,' he said. 'Then I promise we'll get out of your way.'

They didn't have far to go before they found Jonjo. He was in the conservatory with Polly. They looked like a pair of Jane Austen characters: he was leaning attentively over the piano, watching her, and Polly, probably assuming he was one of the guests, concentrated on playing 'Strangers in the Night'. But Genevieve recognised all too well the spellbound expression on Jonjo's face. She had seen it countless times before; men slain by Polly's bewitching charms. Even Christian stood for a moment to stare at Polly. The last time he'd seen her she'd been a child.

As if the moment couldn't get any more unreal, a strident voice burst into the conservatory.

'Is it only Donna and me feeding this lot? I'll tell you

this for free, if one more bloke asks me to bend down for his napkin, I'll poke a cocktail stick up his bum. *Bloody hell!* What're you doing here?'

Not even Polly could maintain her professionalism in the face of so many distractions. She caught sight of Christian and abruptly stopped playing.

In the silence that followed, Jonjo said, 'Christian, you never told me what my neighbours would be like in Angel Sands. Not a word did you say about musical angels or even fallen angels.' He eyed Nattie's outfit.

Genevieve saw that Nattie was dangerously armed with a plate of used cocktail sticks. 'Seeing as you're here, Christian, perhaps you and your friend would like a drink?' she said.

'Are you completely off your head, Gen?' demanded Nattie. 'How can you even *think* of allowing him to stay?'

They were in the kitchen, grabbing more food to take outside to the guests.

'It's called acting civilly. Something you should try.'

'I'd rather take up growing bamboo shoots through my toes than be polite to that pig of a man. What he did to you was beyond – '

'Oh, shut up, will you! Now pass me that chilli and garlic dip for the prawns. Okay, that's it. Out we go. Go on. Get a move on! People are waiting.'

Jonjo had eagerly accepted the offer of a drink, blind to Christian's discomfort. As Genevieve passed round a tray of canapés, she observed the two men sitting on the stone steps outside the conservatory. She had the feeling that neither was much interested in listening to the other. Jonjo, who she would bet a king's ransom didn't know the history between his friend and the Baxters, was being pulled like a magnet to stare at Polly, who was churning out another schmaltzy love song. Christian was picking absently at the moss on the steps, his glass of wine untouched. Perhaps she hadn't done the right thing suggesting they stay for a drink. He looked like he'd rather be anywhere but here.

Served him right.

Having attended to the guests, and with only a few canapés left on her tray, she went over to Christian and his friend. 'Any takers for asparagus tips wrapped in smoked salmon, and Thai prawns with chilli and garlic?'

Christian was instantly on his feet. 'Genevieve?'

'Yes?'

'I don't think this is a good idea.'

'Oh. Well, why don't you try one first?'

He brought his eyebrows together then looked at the tray. 'No, I didn't mean that. I meant me being here.'

Jonjo was now on his feet too, brushing away any dust that might have been clinging to the back of his linen trousers. He'd taken off his jacket, hooked it over the handle of the conservatory door, and Genevieve could see just how finely toned his body was. His black tee-shirt clung to his broad chest and shoulders, the perfect advertisement for the health and fitness centres he ran. She suspected, though, that he might be as vain as he was attractive. He seemed an unlikely choice of friend for Christian. Or for the Christian she used to know.

'But we can't go yet, Christian,' Jonjo said. 'I haven't had a chance to talk to the future Mrs Fitzwilliam. May I?' He helped himself to a couple of canapés.

Christian rolled his eyes. 'Just zip up your brain, will you?'

'I will, the day you channel that sarcasm into something called humour.'

'Take no notice of him, Genevieve. He's only allowed out at weekends.'

For the first time since the two men had appeared, she smiled.

'But seriously,' he said, 'I don't think your family want me here. Nattie's made that very clear.'

'My sister doesn't speak for all the Baxters.'

He glanced about him. 'I don't see any others queuing up to chat. Your father and grandmother keep giving me blood-curdling looks.'

'I'm talking to you, aren't I?'

'Only out of politeness.'

'True.'

'Mm . . . these are great. Any more going? Now tell me, Genevieve, when does your enchanting sister get time off? How can I propose to her if she's chained to the ivories until the end of time?'

'I told you, Jonjo, give it a rest. This is one family you really don't want to mess with.'

'What the hell have you done to upset the natives?'

Seeing that Christian didn't know how to answer or silence his friend, Genevieve said, 'It's okay, you can stay if you like. I'll have a word with Dad to go easy on the dirty looks.'

'There's no need. Come on, Jonjo, we're going. Before you make a complete arse of yourself.'

Jonjo reached for his jacket and threw Polly one last dazzling smile through the open door. 'I hate to pull the plug on a fine idea, Christian, but where exactly are we going? As far as I'm aware, we still don't have a place to rest our weary heads tonight.' He turned the full force of his magnetic smile on Genevieve. 'I don't suppose your sister would take pity on me and make room for a little one, would she?'

'You could try the Salvation Arms,' Genevieve said, trying not to laugh. 'Although the rooms are a bit on the small side, I believe.'

He pulled a face. 'Is that as bad as it sounds? A flea-ridden doss house for the down-and-outs?'

'It's the local pub, you idiot,' snapped Christian. 'And

if you want to set off on the right foot with your new neighbours, I suggest you put some thought into showing them some respect.' He turned to Genevieve. 'Thanks for the recommendation. We'll try there next.'

'Good luck. And . . . '

'Yes?'

'If you're really stuck, you could sleep in the marquee tonight, after the guests have all gone home.'

He smiled, a little stiffly. 'You never know, we might just have to take you up on that offer. A night closely confined with Godzilla here holds few attractions for me.'

Chapter Twenty-two

The following morning, Genevieve was up early. She didn't have a wedding reception to prepare for, but she still had ten breakfasts to cook. It was also Sunday, which was often a complete changeover day – every room vacated and re-occupied within a matter of hours. As a consequence, it was often the busiest day of the week. Today was such a day. The last of the clearing up from yesterday remained to be done: the marquee would be taken down by the firm who supplied it, the chairs and tables collected, along with the hired crockery, cutlery and glasses. Once all that was out of the way, she would feel that Paradise House was back to normal and she was in control again.

Routine had become important to her when she realised she had to stop viewing food as a weapon, something with which to punish herself. Structure and order replaced the chaos of what had gone before, and very soon they had become an integral part of her life. Her bedroom went from a ramshackle mess to the tidiest area in the house. She took to keeping a wipe-board by the side of her bed so that if a thought or worry came to her as she was drifting off to sleep, she could switch the light on and jot down the concern before her brain turned it into a major anxiety. She'd been told by the psychotherapist during her stay in hospital, and afterwards, that she should be aware that there was a danger of swapping one addictive habit for another. So she policed her thoughts and actions, watching for anything that had the potential to get out of hand and become a compulsion or obsession.

She still kept the wipe-board by the side of her bed and used it most nights, not as she used to, to offload, but to help her marshal her thoughts for the following day. Her Things To Do list. Ironically, her behaviour scored her a double whammy, because the need to keep her life carefully ordered, to be in control, was a trait often displayed by both dyslexics and anorexics. In short, control was 'her thing'. Remove it, and panic would rise inside her like a soufflé.

Another irony, perhaps one that her family would never understand, was why, since she'd made a full recovery, she now spent her days surrounded by food. She'd read an article once that said this wasn't uncommon, that it helped some sufferers to regain a natural sense of control by cooking for others, proving they were in control, not just to themselves, but to those around them.

'You're not trying to punish yourself some more, are you?' Gran had asked, afterwards confessing that it was Daddy Dean who had put her up to the question. Poor Dad, the world in which he'd found himself was too alien for him to comprehend. Both he and Mum had attended sessions with a therapist to help them understand that it wasn't just a simple matter of their daughter gaining weight, that the weight gain was only the beginning.

Dad had made the mistake one day of saying how well he thought Genevieve looked. 'You've put on a few pounds, haven't you? Well done!'

Just those few words undid weeks of uphill struggle. Panic and self-loathing kicked in – weight gain equalled ugliness – and she was almost back to square one. From then on Dad crept around her, terrified of saying the wrong thing. He and Mum were told that she needed to feel safe to eat, but it was a concept beyond his understanding.

'How can she not feel safe?' Genevieve overheard him saying to her mother. 'We're her family. We love her, for God's sake! How much safer can we make it for her? Tell me and I'll do it. Whatever it is, I'll do it.'

But he'd got the wrong end of the stick. It wasn't her surroundings, or the love of her family that were in question; it was her fear of food itself that needed changing.

With her usual breakfast of tea and a slice of toast and marmalade, Genevieve wandered out to the garden. It was going to be another beautiful day, like yesterday. She settled herself on the wooden bench that overlooked the bay and sipped her tea. She was exhausted. Mentally as well as physically. Not surprisingly, sleep had eluded her for most of the night. Turbulent dreams of Christian staying at Paradise House had merged with nightmares of the robbery. In the most violent of the dreams, she'd viciously beaten one of the robbers with a poker, but after she removed his mask, she'd found it was Christian.

What had shocked her most about Christian's reappearance yesterday was not her reaction to him, but her family's. They were protecting her, she knew, but even so, it annoyed her that they thought she was so fragile she couldn't cope with meeting Christian again. All things considered, she thought she'd handled the situation pretty well. Better than Christian had. He seemed much more uptight than she did. But then, as Adam had pointed out as he was helping to clear up after the revelry, Christian had unwittingly found himself slap bang in the middle of the lion's den.

'I suppose it's to his credit that he did feel so uncomfortable being here,' Adam had said. 'He did at least have the savvy to make a hasty exit.'

'Hardly surprising, given that everyone was giving him such a hard time.'

'I barely said a word to him.'

'Exactly!'

'Oh, for heaven's sake,' Nattie had interrupted, 'what did you expect us to do? Kill the fatted calf and put out the bunting?' She had exchanged her French maid's outfit for her pyjamas – vest top and shorts – and was sitting on the worktop, pouring herself a large glass of milk. She was quite happy to watch Adam and Genevieve stack the dishwasher. Just the three of them were in the kitchen. Lily-Rose had gone to bed hours ago, Polly was in the shower, and their father was walking Gran home. All of them had had their say on the matter, but it was, as always, Nattie who was the most vociferous. Genevieve suspected this was because Nattie had grown fond of Christian all those years ago, and had felt almost as betrayed as Genevieve had. She was firmly of the opinion that anyone who messed with a member of the Baxter family had her to answer to.

Such fierce protectiveness should have been a comfort, but it wasn't. They were making too much of it, and Genevieve hoped they'd get it out of their systems. Especially if Christian was going to be around over the coming months, or however long it took to turn Ralph's barn into a holiday home for his friend.

And what a character that Jonjo was! All that absurd talk of Polly being the future Mrs Fitzwilliam. How many times a week did he say that? Genevieve wondered, as she chewed her toast and watched a speck of a figure in the distance walking the cliff top. She remembered Christian's words: *'I told you, Jonjo, give it a rest. This is one family you really don't want to mess with.'* The terse reprimand certainly implied he'd heard the routine, or something similar, more than once before.

It had been odd, hearing Christian speak like that, so curt and out of sorts. It was only when they were leaving that he'd sounded more like his old self, or the person she knew from thirteen years ago, the easy-going boy with a warm sense of humour.

Soft footsteps behind her made her turn. 'Mind if I join you?' her father asked, a mug in his hand.

She made room for him on the bench. 'You're up early.'

'Not as early as you. Things on your mind?'

'A few.' She knew exactly what was on *his* mind. Knew also that he wouldn't come right out and say it. 'It went well yesterday,' she hedged. 'Thanks for your help. I couldn't have done it without you all.'

He slurped his tea. 'Every commander in chief needs his foot soldiers.'

'I'd hardly describe myself as a commander in chief.'

'Then you should. Adam says you should do more of this specialised catering lark.'

'Adam says a lot of things.'

'Most of which make a good deal of sense.'

Watching the distant figure on the cliff – he or she was getting closer – Genevieve thought of Adam's parting question last night. 'So has your curiosity been satisfied?' he'd asked. 'Does he seem as perfect as you once thought he was?'

'I'll let you know when I'm in a position to think straight. For now it's as much as I can do to wish you goodnight.'

As though picking up on her thoughts, her father said, 'Was it very much of a shock seeing him again?' She noticed he couldn't bring himself to say Christian's name.

'At first, yes. But then I began to feel almost sorry for him. He seemed so awkward, and everyone was making him feel unwelcome.'

'Your mother would have given him what-for, had she been here. I was tempted myself.'

Genevieve smiled. 'Liar. You're the biggest pacifist going, Dad.'

179

'And perhaps that isn't something I should be proud of. But I'll tell you what I am proud of, Gen, and that's you.'

She shrugged off the compliment with a shake of her head. 'Now you're being silly.'

He placed his mug on the arm-rest. 'It's true. I'm more proud of you than I can say. You know how I dry up when it comes to putting things into words.'

'But words aren't always necessary, Dad,' she said. She thought of all the occasions at school prize givings, when he'd give each of his daughters a single red rose, whether they'd gone up on the stage to collect a prize or not. Polly was forever out of her chair collecting another accolade; a merit certificate here, a highly commended certificate there, or as she did for three years running, the overall Year Achiever cup. But no matter how badly Nattie and Genevieve trailed behind her, their father was always on hand to give them his own special award and gesture of congratulations. It had meant a lot to Genevieve.

'I disagree,' he said. 'Words stay with a person. If they didn't, why would there be all that poetry?'

'So is there something special you want to say to me?' Genevieve asked, almost dreading what he might say.

He cleared his throat. 'Yes. Your Gran told me about the robbery.'

For the first time in the conversation, she turned and faced him. 'But *I* told you about it.'

'No, Genevieve. You told me what you wanted to tell me. That's not the same. Why did you tell your grandmother the robbery had been so brutal, but not me?'

She sighed, glad she hadn't told Gran everything. 'Because I didn't want to worry you. You had enough to think about with Mum going.'

'I don't understand. I'm your father. I'm supposed to worry about you.'

'Perhaps I feel I've given you sufficient worry over the years.'

She could see he wasn't buying it, but he let it go. 'You're all right, though, aren't you? I mean . . .'

She switched on the reassuring smile she knew he needed to see. 'Dad, I'm fine. Really. I get the occasional bad dream, but that will go with time.' She said nothing of the flashbacks she'd experienced in the days and weeks after the break-in. Of the fear of being alone. And of the sleeping pills she'd taken to try and ward off the nightmares. She kept all this to herself, determined to put it behind her. As indeed it was. Apart from last night's glitch, she had started to sleep better, and the fear of being alone had passed. What point would there be in telling her father any of this? He'd only feel guilty that he hadn't been able to do more to help.

Turning the spotlight onto him, she said, 'You didn't seem so nervous around Donna yesterday. If I'm not mistaken, I think I caught you chatting with her, and not just when you were on welcoming duty handing out drinks.'

A ghost of a smile passed across his face and he picked up his mug of tea. 'That's because I think I'm off the hook.'

'Really? How's that?'

'Donna's switched horses, you could say. I pointed her in Tubby's direction. I mentioned several times during the day that he'd been on his own for too long and that, though he'd never admit it, what he needed was someone to take care of him.'

'You sneaky old matchmaker, Dad! So is that why Tubby turned up towards the end of the party?'

'Yes. I invited him for a drink, then got them together. Next thing, just as I hoped he would, he's offering to walk Donna home. I think they'll make an excellent couple.'

'I'm impressed.'

She truly was. In his own quiet way, her father had resolved matters better than she and her sisters could have done. The combination of Donna and Tubby seemed so perfect, Genevieve wondered why they hadn't thought of it before. And hadn't Polly said they ought to find Donna a boyfriend?

Noticing the time, Genevieve said, 'I'd better go inside and make a start on breakfast.'

Her father got to his feet with her. 'I'll help you.'

'There's no need. I can manage.'

'But I'd like to.'

'You never helped Mum.'

His face dropped. 'Maybe I should have.'

Trying to undo the harm she'd done, Genevieve said, 'Oh, you know what Mum was like, she had some daft notion that the kitchen was no place for a man.'

'*Is*, Gen. What Mum *is* like. Please don't put her in the past tense.'

Genevieve could have kicked herself. That was twice now, in as many breaths, that she'd said the wrong thing. What was the matter with her?

He led the way back up to the house and she followed behind. But not before she noticed that the person who had been walking the coastal path was staring across the bay towards Paradise House. Despite the distance, she knew who it was – Christian.

Perhaps he'd had things on his mind and hadn't been able to sleep, either.

Gran appeared after lunch, just as the men finished loading the dismantled marquee onto their van. She swooped on Genevieve and offered to help peg out the third load of that day's washing.

'That's okay, Gran. Why don't you sit down and enjoy the sun. There should be some newspapers somewhere, unless the guests have taken them.' She hid behind a large duvet cover, anxious not to be left alone with her grand-mother who, ominously, was wearing her Gestapo Gran face. Genevieve had wondered how long it would be before she showed up. Although, of course, she could go on the attack and ask Gran why she'd broken her promise and gone tittle-tattling to Dad.

Ignoring her, Gran stooped to pick out a pillow case from the laundry basket. She pegged it alongside the duvet cover that was flapping in the breeze. 'I saw him this morning,' she said.

'Saw who?'

Her lips compressed, Gran looked at her for a long, uncomfortable moment. 'Don't be obtuse with me, Genevieve Baxter. You know jolly well who I'm talking about. Now stop fiddling with that washing and come and talk to me.'

'I'd love to, Gran, only I have a lot to get done today.' With a loud flap she shook out a small hand-towel and pegged it to the line. Feeling Gran's eyes burning into her back, she reached for what was left in the basket, a double sheet, and concentrated on finding its corners. But Gran could be as patient as she was determined, and she kept quiet until Genevieve knew she couldn't put her off any longer. 'Okay,' she said, picking up the basket and bag of pegs, 'I give in. What do you want to talk to me about?'

'You.'

No surprise there, then.

Rather than go inside the house, where Nattie was in the kitchen mixing up a cocktail of henna to redo her roots and Polly was teaching Lily-Rose to play the piano, Genevieve tried to gain the upper hand by suggesting they sit on the terrace, away from prying ears and any acerbic opinions Nattie might feel inclined to offer.

'In the absence of your mother,' Gran began, 'I'm taking it upon myself to look out for you.'

'Gran, I'm thirty years old! I don't need looking out for.'

'Age doesn't come into it. Do you think I've ever stopped worrying about your father? I just don't think I would ever forgive myself if I stood back and allowed you to make yourself ill again.'

'Oh, Gran –'

Rattling on like a runaway train, her grandmother didn't give Genevieve the chance to finish what she was saying. 'No, don't interrupt me. I've come here to say my piece, and I'm not leaving until I have. You mean the world to me, Gen, and there's nothing I wouldn't do to ensure your happiness. I added to your problems all those years ago, so it's my duty now to make amends in any way I can.' She paused to draw breath.

Genevieve seized her opportunity. 'Gran, I've told you before, you didn't have anything to do with my problems then; it was me. It was my way of coping.'

'But what if it starts again?'

'You really think that because Christian's here in Angel Sands I'm going to revert to being a confused teenager?'

'It's possible, isn't it?'

Poor Gran. So caring, so concerned. And so wrong. But Genevieve could understand her anxiety, for it had been Gran who had found Genevieve unconscious on the bathroom floor, Gran who'd called for an ambulance, convinced that her eldest granddaughter was dying. At the hospital the old lady and her parents were told that despite months of punishing her body by starving it, Genevieve was far from death's door. Even then her grandmother had difficulty believing that she'd live.

'Gran, I'm touched, but really, there's no need for you to worry. I'm fine.'

'But seeing him again might stir up all those old

memories . . . remind you of things you thought you'd put behind you.'

Genevieve took hold of her grandmother's hands and squeezed them gently, forcing her to look her in the eye. 'I'm stronger than you think, really. I know you see Christian as a trigger, but he isn't. I'm not that precariously balanced, Gran. Honestly. A relapse is about as likely as me becoming Poet Laureate. Or Nattie winning the Nobel Peace Prize.'

Withdrawing her hands, Gran said, 'Good. So you won't be cross when I tell you I've arranged for you to meet Christian properly.'

'*What*!'

'You heard. That's what he and I were discussing.'

'When?'

'Do try and keep up, Genevieve. I told you I saw him early this morning. In the newsagent's, as a matter of fact. He said he'd just been for a long walk, reacquainting himself with the area.'

So it *had* been him she'd seen. 'So why the change of heart, Gran? Yesterday you were giving him death-threat looks.'

'He said there were things he wanted to say to you. He mentioned the word apologise.'

'He said that of his own accord? You didn't push him up against the shop window and force it out of him?'

Gran looked aggrieved. 'There were witnesses present if you don't believe me. Tubby heard every word.'

'Oh, great, just what I need. Everyone for miles around knowing my business.' She had a sudden mental picture of Gran shouting at Christian like she used to, thinking it would help him to hear. 'But I still don't understand why you've changed your stance. For years you wouldn't even call him by his name.'

'It's called disclosure, Genevieve. They were talking about it on *Kilroy* the other day.'

Genevieve frowned. Then smiled. 'I think you mean closure.'

Gran shrugged. 'Any which way, I told him to come here at four o'clock.'

'Out of the question. I have far too much to do. There are guests arriving around that time.'

'That won't be a problem. Your father and Nattie can deal with them.'

'But I said I'd make them tea.'

'And how difficult is that? Come on, Gen, you're making excuses, and that's not like you.'

Christian arrived exactly on time, just as he always had. In those days he blamed it on his school, saying the teachers were sticklers for punctuality and would beat it into the pupils. Today, though, she could see it was nervousness that had him ringing the door bell on precisely the stroke of four.

A walk seemed appropriate.

They set off in silence, the way he'd just come, to the centre of the village, and up the hill towards . . . where else, but Tawelfan beach?

When they'd emerged from the steep path through the woods and were looking back down onto Angel Sands, she touched his arm to attract his attention. 'So what was it you wanted to talk to me about?'

'Do you mind if we sit down? We'll be able to talk better that way.'

'Here? Or at Tawelfan?'

'Here will do. If that's okay with you?'

She nodded.

They wandered away from the main path and found a patch of soft, dry grass to sit on. For a moment they both kept their gaze on Angel Sands and Paradise House. This was where he was standing this morning, she thought. Had he been watching her?

'When did you and your family move here?' he asked, removing his sunglasses and slipping them into his shirt pocket.

Noticing the scar on his head for the first time, she acknowledged that there had to be a degree of small talk, and gave him a brief potted history.

'And the wedding party yesterday, is that a regular thing?'

'No. That was a one-off, Adam's idea. He's a terrible bully sometimes. But his heart's in the right place. He's the son my father never had and gets away with more than he should.'

'From the little I saw of him yesterday, he looks like he fits in well.'

'So how about you? You obviously became the architect you always wanted to be. Where are you living these days?'

'I've moved around a bit, but now I live in a little place you've probably never heard of. Stony Stratford, it's in –'

'Northamptonshire.'

He bowed his head. 'I stand corrected.'

'It's okay. A long time ago I had a boyfriend who was a compulsive obsessive when it came to Formula One. He took me to Silverstone once. And do you live in an amazing house you've designed yourself?'

'No. I'm still waiting to find the time. Clients keep getting in the way of any dreams I might have.'

'Clients like Jonjo?'

'He keeps me pretty busy with the fitness centres, and now there's this barn to do as a personal project for him. So yes, he's currently the most time-consuming client, for sure. But he's also a good friend. And as we all know, friends take the most enormous liberties. They rob us blind.'

He lowered his gaze as they both took in his blunder.

'Well, that's as good a way as any to broach the subject,' he said.

Genevieve suddenly wished he wouldn't say any more. It had been quite pleasant just sitting here, catching up with each other. Like two old friends. She was more than happy to settle for a filling-in-the-blanks session.

But his solemn face told her she would have to endure what he'd come here to do.

Chapter Twenty-three

'Genevieve, I know it's been a long time, but did you ever . . . did Nattie ever tell you about the letter she sent me?'

'Nattie? When?'

He swallowed and stared intently at the grass between his legs. 'When you were unwell.' His eyes slid back to her face.

'You knew I was ill? But how?' Then very slowly the penny dropped. Nattie had written to him behind her back. Annoyed, the colour rose in her face. 'What exactly did my sister tell you?'

'That it was my fault for making you so ill you very nearly died.'

'And you believed her?'

'What was I supposed to think? She said you were rushed into hospital, that you were there for several weeks, that you'd lost so much weight it was touch and —'

She stopped him from going on by raising a hand. 'Okay, okay,' she said, 'I get the drift. And before you ask, yes, I did end up in hospital with a tube down my throat, and yes, I was a fully fledged anorexic who had to be taught again how to eat properly as well as trust people when they said a mouthful of mashed potato wouldn't kill me.'

She watched him piece together her words, then saw him wince. 'I had no idea,' he said, 'I didn't . . . Oh, Genevieve, I'm sorry. I'm sorry I did that to you.'

'You didn't.' Her voice was firm. '*I* did it. Everything that happened to me was a direct result of my own decisions and actions. What I did was like taking drugs. It made me feel strong and invincible, whereas the reality was I was making myself weaker and weaker. I did that to myself, not you. Or anyone else for that matter.'

'But if –'

'No. No ifs and buts. Do you blame your mother for you being deaf? No, of course you don't. So I don't blame anyone for my anorexic days. And just for the record, I had my bulimic moments as well.' She paused, realising that she had raised her voice, was practically lecturing him. 'Look, it all started well before my seventeenth birthday,' she continued, and less heatedly, 'not long after my grandfather died. So you see, you have no cause to blame yourself. My problems were exactly that: mine.'

Again she could see him piecing together what she'd said. When he'd caught up, he didn't look like he believed her. 'I'm still sorry about . . . about that night in your father's barn.'

Her tone softened. 'It's okay, you can say her name. Rachel.'

But he didn't register what she'd said. 'To this day, I don't know what the hell I thought I was doing.'

Genevieve raised an eyebrow. 'Don't insult me, Christian. From where I was standing, you gave the impression of knowing exactly what you were doing.'

'No, what I meant was, it shouldn't have been her. It should have been you.'

For the first time in the conversation, Genevieve floundered, unable to find the right response. A wave of nostalgic longing for Christian swept over her. She thought of all those times as a naïve girl when she'd lain in bed and dreamt of furthering their kisses and tentative touches. There had been days when she'd literally ached with desire for him, had itched and burned to feel his hands and mouth explore her body, the whole of it. Some days it had been all she could think of.

Ordinarily, when confronted with an unpleasant conversation, Genevieve could turn away and give a muttered response, but with Christian she couldn't do that. There was no hiding from him. To talk to him, she had to look him full in the face. She did so now. 'Did you stay in touch with Rachel, afterwards?'

'No!' The vehemence rang out in his voice.

'Why not?'

'Why do you think?'

'The last thing she ever said to me was that you'd invited her to stay with you at university.'

'Another of her lies.'

'She'd lied before?'

He picked at the grass between his legs. 'At the time I didn't realise it was a lie, but the night of your party, she told me you'd been seeing someone else, that you had been stringing me along for over a year.'

Genevieve was horrified. Rachel had told her Christian had made all the running, that he hadn't been able to take his eyes – or hands – off her all evening. Instinctively Genevieve knew who to believe now. But she couldn't let him off the hook entirely. 'So you thought you'd get your own back and shag my best friend? Is that it? Asking for my side of the story was out of the question, I suppose.'

'I was angry and wanted to hurt you.'

'Trust me, it worked.'

They fell silent, the cry of a gull filling the space between them as they both stared out at the sea. In the dazzling sunshine, the horizon was an indistinguishable blur of sky and water. As indistinguishable as the truth. Or what they'd both thought had been the truth.

She touched him lightly on the arm. He turned. 'Why did you believe her, Christian? Why did you think I'd be capable of doing that to you?'

He fiddled with his watch, running his finger back and forth under the steel strap as if it was irritating his skin. At length, he said, 'Put it down to too much to drink and . . . and colossal insecurity.'

'You! Insecure? Never.'

He tilted his head and frowned. 'You always thought I was so confident, didn't you? But think about it. I was an outcast, a swotty deaf kid totally lacking in any street cred.' He smiled ruefully. 'I'd be called a nerdy geek today. An anorak. You were the nearest thing I had to a best friend in those days, the one person I felt totally at ease with. You accepted me without question. And you never made allowances for me. From the moment you pushed me into the water, the day we met, I knew we were on the level.'

Picturing the scene, and the grin on his face when he yelled at her to speak up, she said, 'I didn't ever see it that way. Compared to me, you had confidence coming out of your –' She hesitated at the inappropriateness of what she was about to say.

'Ears?' he finished for her. 'Don't go all coy and PC on me, Genevieve. Anything but that.'

She smiled and relaxed a little. 'I was just trying to say that I used to wish I had your confidence. Nothing ever got you down. It sounds over the top, but I was in awe of you. Do you remember that day when we were in the sand dunes and –' But once more she held her tongue, on the verge of going a reminiscence too far.

'Go on.'

'No. I was going to say something silly. Something I'd regret.'

'You were thinking of that day on the beach when we first kissed, weren't you?'

She nodded.

'And later you told me about the song that was playing on the radio at the time – "The Wonder of You".'

She cringed. 'Please don't make me squirm.'

'"When no one else can understand me, when everything I do is wrong, you give me hope and consolation, you give me strength to carry on."'

She looked at him. 'You remember the words?'

'Course I do. They came to mean as much to me as they did to you. Why do you think I gave you that CD?'

There didn't seem anything Genevieve could add. 'It's getting late; I ought to be making tracks. There are guests arriving soon.'

She was almost up on her feet, when he put out a hand. 'Please, can we stay a little longer? I feel we still have so much to say.'

But she'd had enough. More than enough. 'No harm in keeping it for another day,' she said lightly.

As they retraced their steps, he said, 'Genevieve, you haven't asked why I didn't try to get in touch with you again after Nattie wrote to me.'

'I imagine it would have something to do with the nature of her message. Nattie, as you probably recall, can be very assertive when she wants to be.'

'It wasn't that I was being a coward,' he said, once again putting out a hand to stop her.

They were standing on the beach at Angel Sands, surrounded by holidaymakers making the most of the late-afternoon sun. The tide was out and several four-wheel-drive vehicles were parked in the shallow water; jet skis and power boats were being winched onto trailers. Distracted by a shout from one of the men rudely yelling at a woman, presumably his wife, to help with the boat, Genevieve glanced away from Christian. It was the only thing about Angel Sands that she, and everyone else in the village, didn't like. The PBP – Power Boat People – were brash and always noisier than anyone else. They strutted about the beach with their flash cars and smelly boats as if they owned it. She felt Christian's hand move from her arm, and looked back at him.

'Sorry,' she said, 'I was just thinking how much better the beach would be without all the noise.'

'Ah, the upside of being deaf.'

Seeing that he was smiling, Genevieve smiled too. 'I've never thought of you as being a coward,' she said, 'if that's what you're worried about.'

It was a while before he answered, as though he'd had trouble understanding her. 'I wrote back to Nattie,' he said finally, 'asking her to pass on a message to you, but she returned the letter, just as you'd done with all the others. She said I was never to get in touch with you, that any contact might make you ill again. I felt so responsible for what had happened, but had no way of helping you. So I did what Nattie told me to do. I kept away in the hope you'd get better, telling myself it was the right thing, the only thing I could do. I've never felt so guilty in all my life.'

Genevieve didn't know whether to be furious with Nattie for meddling or touched that she'd been so concerned. 'Well, all's well that ends well, I guess. Come on, I really need to get home.'

When they were standing outside the Salvation Arms, Christian said, 'Genevieve, while I'm down here with Jonjo, can I see you again?'

'Okay. If that's what you want.'

She could tell from his face that it wasn't quite the reaction he'd hoped for. What did he expect? High-five enthusiasm?

'Would you like to come and see Jonjo's barn tomorrow?' he said. 'If the weather's nice, and you have the time, we could walk and take a picnic. I'd appreciate your comments on some of the ideas I have.'

She hesitated, trying to remember what she had to do tomorrow, convinced that there was something. She visualised her wipe-board by the side of her bed and remembered what it was. 'I'm sorry, but it'll have to be another time. I've promised Lily-Rose I'll do something special with her tomorrow.'

'Oh.' He looked disappointed. But then his face brightened. 'Why don't you bring her? If you think she'd enjoy it.'

After saying goodbye, Genevieve returned to Paradise House alone. She had set out cursing her grandmother for interfering; now she was returning home to exchange some stern words with Nattie. It was nothing new, but that girl had definitely overstepped the mark.

When she walked round to the side of the house, all thoughts of Gran and Nattie's meddling were forgotten. Sitting in the garden with Polly, his arm creeping along the back of the wooden bench they were sharing, was Jonjo. A dangerous mixture of adoration and sparkling mischief lit up his handsome face. But there was no denying what a striking couple they made. Polly's delicate fairness seemed all the more ethereal next to Jonjo's dark good looks. As to whether they were any kind of a match, it was too soon to tell. She wasn't being cruel, but the little she had seen of Jonjo made her suspect that they were poles apart.

'I didn't think you'd be back until after six,' she said to Polly.

'Oh, hello, Genevieve. My last lesson in Milford Haven was cancelled so I came home early.'

'And just as well she did,' said Jonjo, 'or I'd have had a wasted journey.'

In contrast to the charming shade of pink that Polly had turned on seeing Genevieve, there was no awkwardness to Jonjo, no jumping to attention and removal of his arm, just the relaxed air of a man behaving as though he was an old and trusted friend of the family.

'How was your walk with Christian?' he asked. 'I hope you left him buried in the sand up to his neck. He's been such an edgy devil since yesterday afternoon. No chance of you shedding some light on what's giving him the hump?'

Genevieve got the feeling that Jonjo seldom expected an answer to any of his questions. She was about to ask if he or Polly would like a drink, when he pre-empted her.

'I've been trying to persuade your lovely sister to see my new home tomorrow. Do you think you could help me twist her arm? I know, why don't you come too?'

She explained about Christian's invitation. And that Lily-Rose was also included in the outing.

He turned to Polly, like a small boy who'd just been told he could stay up late. 'There! It's as good as settled. Now you'll have to come.'

'I thought you were never going to put the poor man out of his misery,' Genevieve said, when they'd waved Jonjo goodbye and were checking on Henry and Morwenna.

'I wasn't teasing him, if that's what you think.'

'I didn't say you were. But you do realise he's going to keep chasing you until he gets what he wants?'

'Well, that rather depends on what he wants and if I have it. How was your walk with Christian?'

'Um . . . interesting.'

If Nattie had been there she would have pounced on Genevieve. 'Interesting?' She would have barked. 'What's that supposed to mean?' But Polly was no interrogator. It wasn't that she didn't care, she just believed in letting people do things their own way.

They strolled back through the orchard and up to the house where Polly was bound for the guest sitting room to put in an hour's piano practice. Some of their regular guests would hang around at this time of day in the hope that Polly would play for them. Today, though, the sitting room was empty and Genevieve left her sister to it.

'Interesting' really was the best description she could come up with to describe the hour she'd spent with Christian. Because there were no overlaps in their lives – no mutual friends who would pass on snippets of gossip – it hadn't occurred to her that he might have found out how ill she'd been. Not even Rachel could have told him, because she'd moved away long before Genevieve had been rushed into hospital.

But trust Nattie to take things into her own hands.

The opportunity to plan what she was going to say to her sister was put on hold when she pushed open the kitchen door and saw the mess. Nattie had agreed to provide afternoon tea for the arriving guests, and as though to prove she'd been true to her word, the crockery had been left to find its own way into the dishwasher. A pair of large bluebottles were feasting on the remains of a ginger cake Genevieve had made that morning. 'Whatever isn't eaten,' she'd told her sister, 'be sure to put away in the cake tin. Don't leave it out, otherwise the flies will think they've died and gone to heaven.'

She was so furious with Nattie she felt like throwing the ginger cake, plate and all, hard against the wall. And she might well have done, had it not meant more for her to tidy up.

Chapter Twenty-four

For Genevieve, picnics were synonymous with sandy beaches and temperamental summers, and as she added salt and white pepper to the egg mayonnaise rolls (never black – it turned the filling a dirty grey colour), she thought how Christian and her eating disorder would always be inextricably bound: she would never be able to think of one without the other. But she had meant what she'd said yesterday; Christian hadn't caused her problems. Low self-esteem had been the culprit. He'd merely been caught up in the chaos of her adolescence. Getting herself straight had been slow and painful, but once she'd made the break from her old self, had killed off Constant Companion, she'd begun to enjoy life in a way she never had before. She discovered the incredible freedom of letting up, of not giving herself a hard time.

Tearing off pieces of cling film, she began wrapping the rolls and putting them in the hamper, with a storage box of potato salad, a tub of cherry tomatoes, and the salmon and broccoli quiche she'd made last night. Next she added a foil-wrapped tray of chocolate brownies, a selection of Lily-Rose's favourite cartons of juice, and lastly some crisps, plates and glasses, and knives and forks. Christian had said he'd see to wine and anything else he thought they'd need to drink. Which was just as well; she could barely lift the hamper off the table as it was.

From upstairs she could hear the sound of Donna vacuuming. The guests had conveniently departed several hours ago, leaving Donna and Genevieve free to blitz the bedrooms and bathrooms. With the picnic now ready, and Jonjo and Christian arriving in less than ten minutes, Genevieve went to look for Polly and Lily-Rose. The last time she had seen Lily, the little girl was having a bad hair day – literally. Her blonde curls had blossomed like a ball of candyfloss overnight, and she was screaming at her mother to sort it out before she and Daddy Dean met up with Tubby to go to a furniture auction in Pembroke.

Genevieve found her youngest sister and niece – hair now tamed – on the top landing. Dressed in a bright orange ra-ra skirt, purple T-shirt, red sandals and yellow sunglasses, Lily-Rose was squeezing a cuddly toy into her small rucksack: it bulged as though she had packed for a fortnight's holiday.

'I suggested that just the one teddy would suffice,' Polly said, helping to get the zip done up, 'but she couldn't choose which one to take. So she's bringing them all.'

Swinging the bag over her shoulder – it was in the shape of a butterfly, and two large wings now appeared to grow out of her back – Lily-Rose adjusted her sunglasses and stuck out her chest with a wide, beaming smile. 'Ready now,' she said.

They were halfway down the stairs when the doorbell sounded. Genevieve's heart gave a little jolt, just as it always had when Christian called for her.

Jonjo had overruled any plans for them to walk to Ralph's barn, as it would always be known to everyone in Angel Sands.

'I don't mind carrying Lily-Rose if she gets tired,' he said, 'but a weakling like Christian won't last two seconds with that hamper. What have you got in it, Genevieve? A microwave?'

Again he seemed not to expect an answer. He threw

open the boot of his Land Rover Discovery and stowed the hamper inside. 'Now then,' he instructed them, 'Polly in the front with me, and the rest of you, sort yourselves out in the back.'

Seeing a new side to Jonjo, Genevieve exchanged a look with Christian. 'What's brought on the bossy sergeant major act?' she mouthed.

'He gets like this now and then. Just pretend he doesn't exist.'

'I've told you before, Christian, not everyone's deaf, so keep the insults to yourself. Right then, let's be on our way.'

Ignoring his friend, Christian said, 'He's excited about showing off his new house. He's always like this with a new project. Here, do you want some help?'

'It's okay,' Genevieve said as she struggled with the buckle of Lily-Rose's seat belt. She had refused to remove her rucksack and her wings were getting squashed. 'There, that's got it.'

Ralph's barn was situated half a mile inland from Tawelfan beach, a stone's throw from Pendine Cottage. As they drove down the bumpy track, Genevieve asked Christian if he'd ever been back to see the house.

'No. Never.'

'What about when you came here with Jonjo to view the barn?'

'He came alone. I saw the place for the first time the day before yesterday.'

'What's that you're saying in the cheap seats?'

When Christian didn't answer – presumably he didn't realise his friend had spoken – Genevieve said, 'I was just asking Christian why he didn't view the barn with you when you were buying it.'

'A good question, Genevieve. It was as much as I could do to get him to take on the job. You should have seen his face when I showed him the details and where it was on the map. He even tried to talk me out of it, said why didn't I look for something in Cornwall or Devon. But I told him this was exactly where I wanted my rustic bolt hole, if you'll pardon the expression. I came here once as a young boy and always knew I'd come back.'

Christian hadn't caught any of this conversation; he was staring out of the window. Genevieve was left to ponder why he'd been so reluctant to revisit the past.

When they arrived, a pair of crows, startled by the sound of doors slamming, clattered their wings and launched themselves off the roof. The derelict barn didn't look like much, but Genevieve knew that with careful design, and a great deal of money, it could be turned into an amazing house. Especially given the views from the rear. And although she had never seen anything Christian had designed, she felt instinctively that he would do an excellent job. Nattie would be disappointed not to have a crusading save-the-environment fight on her hands.

Jonjo led the way. It was fortunate that the weather had been as dry for as long as it had, as otherwise the ground would have been a skidpan of mud. Where there wasn't bare earth, they had to negotiate rampant nettles and brambles.

'There,' said Jonjo, when he'd moved an old milk churn and swung open one half of the wide double doors. 'What do you think?'

His question was clearly aimed at Polly. Genevieve went and stood in the middle of the gloomy barn. Beams of sunlight filtered through the holes in the roof and the mixture of damp, dust and mouldy hay made her nose twitch. In amongst the cobwebs and shadows there was a graveyard of rusting old farm implements, rubber tyres and ripped tarpaulins. It was far from inspiring.

Christian came and stood next to her. His face was caught in a beam of sunlight and she noticed the flecks of green and gold in his brown eyes. She'd forgotten that his eyes were such a mixture of colour. She waited for him to speak. When he didn't, she said, 'I remember you saying this was just the kind of work you'd like to do; converting barns into houses.'

He stared at her hard. 'I remember it too. I said it the afternoon of your birthday.'

Recalling the scene in her father's hay barn, she turned away, embarrassed. She was glad when Jonjo suggested they explore outside.

The view from the rear was as perfect as she'd known it would be. All that separated them from the sea was a sloping, narrow stretch of heath and the sand dunes that backed the unspoilt beach. It was beautiful. She turned to Christian and saw from his expression that he thought the same.

'I'm going to design it with the living area of the house upstairs,' he said, looking back at the barn. 'Each of the bedrooms will have a door leading out onto the garden. The main bedroom will catch the rising sun and the sitting room will have a fantastic view of the setting sun.'

'It sounds good.'

'Thanks. It'll mostly be open plan. I want to take full advantage of the natural light as well as bring the landscape inside. I don't like houses that shut people out. That's the trouble with a lot of buildings; the doors and walls limit the space available.'

'Do you wish you were designing it for yourself?' she asked, when they were returning to the car to fetch the picnic. Jonjo and Polly were walking on ahead, while Lily-Rose, who'd been unusually quiet since leaving home, was holding Genevieve's hand and sliding occasional sideways glances in Christian's direction.

He came to a stop and looked the way they'd come. 'Yes. It's pretty much what I'd like for myself.'

'And will that affect your judgement when working on it?'

'It might do. But my job is to remain objective, to take

into account the client's taste more than my own.'

'And does this particular client have good taste?'

He laughed, which made her realise how solemn he'd been till now. 'Believe it or not, Jonjo does. Look how taken he is with Polly.'

The flippancy of his remark made her say, 'You have told him that he'll have Nattie and me to answer to if he does anything . . . anything silly.'

The laughter vanished from his face. But he didn't answer her.

They carried on walking and glancing at her sister, who seemed quite at ease in Jonjo's larger-than-life company. Genevieve touched Christian's arm lightly to make him turn. 'I get the feeling that Jonjo doesn't know our history? Am I right?'

'Yes.'

'Why's that?'

He pushed his hands into his trouser pockets and frowned. 'Because it's none of his business.'

It wasn't a very satisfactory answer, but she didn't pursue it, not with Lily-Rose pulling at her hand so they could catch up with the others.

They had their picnic in the dunes, in a quiet, sheltered spot where a gentle breeze rustled the marram grass. Any wariness Lily-Rose had shown previously towards Jonjo and Christian was now gone. She sat cross-legged between them, slyly adding more crisps to her plate when she thought no one was watching. Even Christian seemed to be relaxing now and was telling Polly how he and Jonjo had got to know each other.

'It was love at first sight,' he joked, 'our eyes met across a crowded gym –'

'Hey,' interrupted Jonjo, 'not any old gym, I'll have you know. It was the first one I set up, my pride and joy. This arrogant bastard told me it was a mess, that he knew a man who could have made a far better job of it.'

'Watch your language,' said Christian, eyeing Lily-Rose. 'What you have to know about this guy is that anyone who disagrees with him, or knows more about a subject than he does, is automatically classed as a bigoted know it all.'

Jonjo grinned. 'Can I help being such a good judge of character?'

'Is that why you commissioned me to design your second gym?'

'Call it a moment of weakness.'

'And the subsequent six fitness centres?'

Genevieve smiled at Polly and, while Lily-Rose wasn't looking, removed half the crisps from her plate. 'So is this something you specialise in,' she said, turning to Christian, 'designing commercial properties?'

'It wasn't my original intention, but the work's plentiful and varied.'

'What he means is that it's lucrative, stinging hard-working blokes like me.'

'And do you run your own practice?' asked Polly.

'No, more's the pity. I keep thinking about it, but the time never seems quite right to take the plunge. For now I'm tied into a medium-sized set up, with the prospect of one day becoming a partner.'

Jonjo tutted. 'I keep telling him to get on and go it alone, like I did, but he's too cautious for his own good. Now Polly, how about another glass of bubbly and then we go for a walk?'

'I want to go for a walk,' piped up Lily-Rose. She tossed aside her plate and leapt to her feet.

'Not so fast, sweetheart,' said Genevieve. 'Have something more to eat. All you've had so far is a few crisps.'

She shook her head and rested her hands on her hips, a classic Nattie pose.

'It's okay, Gen,' said Polly, 'I'm sure Jonjo won't mind the extra company.'

Smart move, thought Genevieve, as she watched her sister, dressed in one of her particularly pretty jumble sale dresses, take her eager little chaperone by the hand. If Jonjo was at all disappointed to be denied a romantic stroll along the beach, he didn't show it. Instead, he took hold of Lily-Rose's other hand and said, 'Christian, make sure you behave yourself while we're gone.'

'You must be very proud of her,' Christian said, when they were alone.

Thinking he was referring to Polly's out-manoeuvring of Jonjo, she said, 'I am. Polly may be the quietest and least worldlywise Baxter, but she's no push over.'

He frowned. 'I didn't mean Polly. I meant your daughter. She's really cute. How old is she?'

It was Genevieve's turn to frown. 'Oh, no! No, you've got it wrong, I'm not her mother. Nattie is.'

'Nattie? But you . . . at the party . . . you and Adam, and Lily-Rose.'

Seeing his confusion, she tried to recall the exact moment in the garden at Paradise House when he'd commented on Lily. All she could think was that he must have misread her lips. Of course, that was it! He'd been looking at Lily and had missed her explaining that Nattie was her mother. Before she could say anything, he said, 'But you and Adam . . . you are married, right?'

She laughed. 'Absolutely not.' She told him about Adam being hopelessly in love with her sister. 'He's mad, of course. As I keep reminding him.'

'But you seemed,' he paused, as if conjuring up the right words, 'such a couple. I was convinced you were married.'

'As cheesy as it sounds, we're just good friends. Nattie gives him a hard time and I'm the sympathetic shoulder he's come to rely upon.'

'And you're not . . . remotely interested in him?'

'What is this? Are you trying to fix me up?'

He laughed now, and at last seemed relaxed. 'I wouldn't dream of it. How about some more of Jonjo's champagne while he isn't looking?'

She held out her wine glass. 'This is very decadent, isn't it, drinking champagne on the beach? Quite a step up from swigging back cans of coke like we used to.'

'You can always depend on Jonjo for the grand gesture. I had a bottle of wine ready to bring but he wouldn't listen. He said, "I'm not drinking that rubbish to toast my new home."'

'Well, here's to many more of his grand gestures.'

He chinked his wine glass against hers, 'And . . . to old friends.'

His words hung in the air as they both stared out to sea and sipped their drinks.

Christian said, 'Jonjo and I are leaving tomorrow evening.'

'Oh.'

'But we'll be back.'

'That sounds worryingly like a threat.'

He tilted his head and looked puzzled. 'It wasn't meant to be.'

Realising he'd missed the joke, she said, 'Any idea when you'll return?'

'I'm not sure. But soon.'

Another silence followed. And then, 'Genevieve, you won't hold the past against me, will you? I'd hate to be forever defined by a mistake I once made.'

Unable to answer him, she turned away.

Chapter Twenty-five

Some guests were more troublesome and ungrateful than others, and Genevieve was checking in one such couple now, who, so far, had complained about almost everything. According to them, the roads were too narrow and winding; the weather was too hot; the beach was too small and pebbly; and lastly, and for future reference for other unwary guests, Angel Sands needed to be better signposted. Thank God they were only stopping the two nights; any longer and she might run out of patience. From experience she knew they were the type to hunt out all that was wrong with their room – the window that rattled; the toilet that didn't flush properly; the plumbing that gurgled; the floorboards that creaked, and of course, the lumpy bed that kept them awake all night.

Bracing herself for the first of the criticisms about their accommodation, she led the way upstairs, offering to carry the woman's luggage, but leaving the man to carry his own; he looked quite strong enough to manage the small case and suit-carrier. She unlocked the bedroom door and stepped back to let them in. All the rooms at Paradise House were large and airy and had been named by Serena, her inspiration coming from songs made famous by Judy Garland; the most obvious being the Rainbow suite. Most guests, when entering the April Showers suite, commented on its size. It was the largest bedroom in the house and the most impressive, with a four-poster bed and chintzy décor straight out of *House and Garden*. The next comment, invariably, would be to admire the south-facing view over the garden and the sea beyond.

But not Mr and Mrs Grumpy. They gave the room a cursory glance, pushed open the door to the en suite bathroom and asked where the bathrobes were kept.

Bathrobes! Where did they think they were staying, the Ritz?

'I'm sorry, but we don't supply them.' She watched the couple mentally chalk up a point against her and added, 'If I could just draw your attention to the sign on the back of the door, you'll see what to do in case of a fire. Oh, and there's no smoking in any of the rooms. When you've settled in, perhaps you'd like a cup of tea. Or coffee? Maybe a scone or some shortbread?'

'We'll have tea and scones,' Mr Grumpy said, without consulting his stony-faced wife.

'Excellent. I'll see you downstairs in the sitting room. Better still, shall I look for you in the garden? There are plenty of tables in the shade,' she said, remembering the complaint about the heat.

In the kitchen Genevieve loaded up a tray, making doubly sure the crockery was squeaky clean and not chipped. People like the Grumpys didn't intimidate her; she viewed them as a challenge, to be humoured. All the same, she would make sure Nattie didn't get anywhere near them, or they really would find something to complain about. Even after all these years of their home being a guest house, Nattie still had a tendency to treat visitors as unwelcome intruders.

Hearing footsteps on the stairs, then voices in the hall, she poured boiling water into the china teapot – one that she knew never dripped – and added it to the tray, giving the tea things one last glance to make sure there was nothing she had forgotten.

She found Mr and Mrs Grumpy in the shade, as she'd recommended. She set down the tray on the wooden table and left them to it. Tubby would be here later and she wanted to go through her shopping list before he arrived. Sometimes she wrote down things that even she couldn't make sense of. Grpefroot, apel, letise, avodaco were typical misspellings, but once, when in a hurry, she'd written witbadge and couldn't for the life of her work out what it was. Days later, when she wanted to make some coleslaw, she realised it was white cabbage. Loyalty was important in a close-knit community, so as her mother had, Genevieve always got their fruit and veg from Tubby. Basic everyday staples like bread, tea and eggs came from the mini market in the village, and bacon, sausages and black pudding from the Lloyd Morris brothers with whom they had a regular order placed. Every fortnight, armed with a computer-generated list, her father would head off to the supermarket in Pembroke to stock up on the bulkier items, such as breakfast cereals, fruit juice, toilet rolls, cleaning products and washing powder.

After checking her list for Tubby, she gave some thought to what she was going to say in answer to Christian's letter.

It was a week and a half since the day of the picnic. This morning, after their father had intercepted the postman, he had handed her a letter with a Northampton postmark. He'd made no comment, just sorted through the rest of the mail and left her alone. It was so reminiscent of years gone by that she had taken the letter outside to the garden to read. But unlike those childhood handwritten letters, this one had been done on a computer, and the typeface was bold and clear, as though he'd remembered her dyslexia and was trying to help. What he didn't know was that these days, she wore specially tinted glasses to help her read more easily. Nattie called them her rose-tinted spectacles. Rarely did she wear them in front of people who didn't know her well because, vainly, she thought they gave her a strange unflattering look, like a pink-eyed rabbit.

The gist of Christian's letter was that once he'd recovered from the shock and unease of their meeting, he had really enjoyed catching up with her. Would she, he wondered, like to go for a proper walk the next time he was down?

In contrast to the one brief communication she'd had from Christian, Polly had been the subject of numerous calls from Jonjo. Often Polly wasn't around when he phoned and Genevieve ended up chatting with him instead.

'By the way,' he said during one conversation, 'Christian's told me everything. And what a piece of work he turns out to be! Hardly the saint I had him down as. But it's not too late to exact revenge. I'd willingly do it myself on your behalf. What do you think? A hate campaign? Letters of abuse and unspeakable things shoved through his letterbox? Personally, I'm all in favour of publicly naming and shaming.'

'Or we could be very dull and just let sleeping dogs lie.'

'Spoilsport!'

The biggest and most ostentatious bouquet of flowers that had ever been delivered to Paradise House arrived at the weekend. It was for Polly, and the accompanying card said:

There was a sweet maiden called Polly,
As tasty as a strawberry ice lolly,
Call me a poet but wouldn't you know it,
I'd sooner lick her lips, by golly.

'The man's a fool,' declared Nattie when she read out the limerick to see who the flowers were from. Polly was absorbed in playing a piece of Mozart. 'And an inept one at that. Those last two lines are cringingly awful.'

And not the rest? thought Genevieve with amusement.

Polly stopped mid-chord and gave the flowers a measured glance. She then returned her attention to the pages of music in front of her and began playing again. But not before Genevieve saw a small smile illuminate her face.

Since then there had been numerous phone calls and a further bunch of flowers. The man was certainly persistent, and if Genevieve was honest, not as dangerous as she'd first thought. More importantly, Polly appeared quite capable of taking him in her stride.

Hearing the sound of Tubby's van coming to a stop at the front of the house, Genevieve roused herself and went outside.

As a result of her father's intervention, romance was very much in the air. Tubby was positively glowing with it, bursting to share his happiness. It didn't come as a surprise, though. Donna had not been shy in sharing her own new-found happiness with Genevieve during their coffee breaks. It was funny, but Donna and Tubby were so wrapped up in each other, it was impossible to imagine there was ever a time when Daddy Dean had been under threat.

'Donna cooked me supper last night,' Tubby announced, before Genevieve had even had a chance to inspect his tomatoes. 'And not just some trifling little snack. It was the full works. Prawn cocktail, braised steak with mushrooms and mash, and bread and butter pudding to finish. A feast fit for a king!'

'Well,' said Genevieve with a smile. 'Who'd have thought it? Old Tubby Evans falling in love.'

He blushed and reached for a paper bag, then shook it open. 'I tell you what, *cariad*, a man could get used to it.'

Helping herself to some tomatoes – firm but on the verge of softening – and passing them to him, she said, 'So how come you've been on your lonesome for so long, Tubby?'

There had always been faint mutterings about Tubby in Angel Sands. Some said that he'd never got over the death of his first wife in his mid-twenties, the one true love of his life. And some said that his second wife divorcing him ten years ago had put him off women altogether. What were those gossipers saying now? Genevieve wondered.

'Let's just say I've been biding my time,' Tubby said. 'Waiting for the right woman. A woman with a bit of spirit.'

'Well, I think it's great. You deserve some fun.'

An hour later, after Mr and Mrs Grumpy decided they might risk the late afternoon sun and go for a walk, her father appeared in the kitchen where Genevieve was taking advantage of the peace and quiet to get on with some bookkeeping. Fortunately it was a task that came relatively easily to her – for some reason she'd never truly understood, her brain could handle basic arithmetic; it was something to do with order, sequence and time – and she'd readily taken on the job in her mother's absence, knowing her father hated anything that didn't involve a spirit level or some Black & Decker accessory.

'All alone, Genevieve?' he asked, despite the obviously empty kitchen.

'Looks like it,' she said. 'Nattie and Lily-Rose are still down at Gran's and Polly's not due back until after seven.'

'Oh.'

She took in his shuffling awkwardness as he moved round the table where she was totting up a column of figures. Watching him fill the kettle then plug it in, she sensed there was something he wanted to say, that finding her alone had perhaps been fortuitous.

'Coffee?' he asked.

'Tea please. And there's some bara brith in the

cupboard, if you're interested. And some of Tubby's special butter in the larder.'

Watching him as he rounded up mugs, plates and slices of Welsh tea bread, she wondered what was on his mind, and hoped he wasn't still worrying about her. At last he sat down in the chair opposite her. 'Have you got a minute, love?'

She took off her glasses. 'Of course I have. What's up? Nattie hasn't gone and rescued another donkey, has she?' Her tone was deliberately light, but she could see from her father's expression that they were heading into the choppy waters of A Serious Chat.

'No, it's nothing to do with Nattie. It's your mother.' He pulled out a letter from his back pocket and placed it on the table between them. 'It came this morning.'

'You never said anything.'

'You had other things on your mind.' A tiny stab of guilt pricked at her conscience. If she hadn't taken herself off to the garden to read Christian's letter, her father might have . . . She let the thought go.

They hadn't heard from Serena since their father's birthday and, with each day that passed, it seemed to Genevieve that the gap their mother's absence had initially created at Paradise House was slowly closing. She hated the thought that they would all eventually get so used to Serena not being around, that one day they'd get on with their lives as though she'd never existed. She hadn't said anything to anyone, but Genevieve was beginning to feel angry towards their mother. How could she do this to them, to Dad in particular? She felt the anger rise in her now as she looked at the letter on the table. Or was it fear she felt? Had Mum finally made her decision? Had she written to say that she was never coming home?

'What does Mum say?' she asked.

'You can read it if you like.'

She put on her glasses again.

My dearest Dean,

I know it's unforgivable of me to have left it so long before writing again, but goodness, I just don't know where the time goes. As you know, it's winter here and Pete and I have been spending time away from the winery and staying in Wellington, visiting old friends of his who used to be neighbours. It was fun staying in The Big City. Wellington is such a sophisticated place – so many art galleries, coffee houses and trendy bars. Don't laugh, but I've developed quite a taste for vodka martinis! There's this bar Pete took me to, where they mixed, or rather, shook them to perfection. You must try them yourself, but I doubt if anyone down at The Arms has a clue how to make a cocktail.

I miss you and the girls and often think of you. Give my love to your mother (although I doubt she'll want it) and a special hug and a kiss to little Lily-Rose (if she hasn't already forgotten who I am).

All my love,

Serena.

PS. I expect you've become quite used to me not being there. Sometimes it feels as though Paradise House was where someone else – not the real me – used to live.

Giving herself time to think, Genevieve pretended she was reading the letter again. She wanted to think carefully about what her mother had written. On the face of it, it looked like Serena was rubbing their noses in it, telling them what a thoroughly enjoyable time she was having, living this new and exciting life of cruising bars and knocking back cocktails. But maybe there was a more important message hidden behind her words.

Was it possible that Serena was trying to make Dad jealous? Until now the name and sex of the friend in New Zealand had never been divulged. Previous letters had referred obliquely to 'we' or 'us', but now, without a word of explanation, Serena had deliberately slipped in a bombshell guaranteed to make their father sit up and take notice. If Genevieve was right, and she had a gut feeling she was – her mother wouldn't be so cruel as to flaunt a real lover so openly – it meant that Serena wanted to provoke her husband into doing something. Question was, what? And if Genevieve's guesswork was correct, it meant she would have to play her part. It was down to her to reinforce the message that if her father didn't act promptly he would lose Serena. But how to do it without hurting him more than he already was?

She removed her glasses, refolded the letter and pushed it across the table. She met her father's gaze, which was as searching as she knew it would be.

'Who's this Pete character?' he asked. 'Where's he sprung from all of a sudden?'

'He's the old school friend you were supposed to think was a woman,' she answered truthfully.

His eyes widened. 'You knew? You knew all along?'

She tried not to flinch at the pained disbelief in his voice.

'I'm sorry,' she murmured. 'But we thought it would hurt you too much to know the truth.'

'*We?* Your sisters knew as well?'

She nodded. 'We kept it from you because we never thought there'd be anything in it.'

He bent over the table and raked his hands through his hair. 'I've lost her,' he groaned. 'I lost her months ago, and never realised it. What an idiot I've been.'

Genevieve wasn't her grandmother's granddaughter for nothing. 'Dad,' she said, summoning up her most authoritative voice, 'look at me. And listen hard. You haven't lost Mum. But you will if you don't do something to get her back. You can't go on pretending this isn't happening, or kid yourself that she'll come back when she's ready. Whoever this old friend is, you have to prove to Mum that he's nothing compared to you. You know, and I know, there's only one man for Mum and his name isn't Pete. It's time for action. Right?'

He blinked back tears and managed a nod. 'Right,' he repeated, but with a lot less conviction than Genevieve would have liked.

In bed that night, Genevieve began to doubt what she'd been so sure of earlier. What if she was wrong about her mother's letter, and Pete genuinely meant more to Serena than she'd thought? What then?

Chapter Twenty-six

She wasn't entirely sure she was doing the right thing, but Genevieve decided to talk to Gran. Other than Serena, Gran was the only person who could make their father do something he didn't want to.

After lunch, while Dad was mending a faulty shower head – thank goodness there were so many DIY jobs to keep him occupied – Genevieve set off for Gran's. Yesterday's heat had been cooled overnight by a strong, chilly wind and the air was fresh and tangy. Predictably, Mr and Mrs Grumpy had complained at breakfast that they'd been woken in the early hours by a rattling window. Save for a few hearty souls, the beach was almost deserted. A brief spell of cooler weather – better still, wet weather – was good news for Huw and Jane up at the Smithy and also for Ruth and William at Angel Crafts; their takings were always boosted by inclement weather. Passing the first of Angel Sands' teashops, she saw that it was packed. Next door was Debonhair. Scissors and comb poised, Debs smiled at Genevieve through the window. Genevieve gave her a small wave and continued on her way as briskly as the wind that tugged at her hair. She was still annoyed that Debs had been openly gossiping about her.

Two doors up from Debonhair was Angel Crafts. She waved to Ruth, then stopped at the Post Office. She slipped a cream-coloured envelope into the box and stupidly looked over her shoulder to see if anyone was watching her. She half-expected to see Debs craning her neck round the salon door, making a note of her movements. Two thirty-five: Genevieve Baxter posts a letter, recipient as yet unknown. Possible recipient: childhood sweetheart, Christian May.

Had the letter been addressed to anyone else, Genevieve wouldn't have felt so paranoid, but as it was, she felt the whole of Angel Sands would be putting two and two together. But there again, they had plenty to go on, what with Gran broadcasting to the nation the day she bumped into Christian in the newsagent, and the two subsequent occasions Genevieve had been seen with him – their walk and then the picnic. One thing you could be sure of in Angel Sands: nothing was private. Under the guise of taking an interest in one's neighbours, gossip was a fact of life. And let's face it; she couldn't be holier than thou about it. She and her sisters liked nothing better than a tasty titbit coming their way. Just so long as it wasn't about them, of course.

Gran opened the door to Genevieve, and immediately turned her back on her.

'Put the kettle on, dear, I'm watching *Murder, She Wrote*.' Nothing new in that, Genevieve thought with a smile. But what was new was the state of Gran's kitchen. It was several weeks since Genevieve had been inside Angel Cottage, and she wondered what was going on. Was her grandmother having a spring clean? As far as Genevieve could see, Gran must have emptied every cupboard and drawer and stacked the tins and packets of food, crockery, pans and cutlery wherever she could find space on the small table and work surfaces. Opening one of the cupboards where the tea caddy was normally kept, and then another, Genevieve found that she was right. The cupboards were empty.

She unearthed the kettle, filled it, then hunted through the toppling mess on the table for some tea bags. Once she'd located them, she joined her grandmother in the sitting room. 'What's going on in the kitchen, Gran?'

'Ssh!'

Genevieve looked at the television screen and saw that Jessica Fletcher was in the final throes of showing the confused cop how the crime was committed. When the credits rolled, Gran said, 'I've seen it before but I was hoping someone else would have done it this time.'

Genevieve was used to her grandmother's unfathomable logic. 'Are you having a major spring clean, Gran?' she said.

Her grandmother looked at her as though she were mad. 'Now why would I be doing that in the middle of June?' She rose from her chair. 'I thought you were making some tea.'

'I am. The kettle's on.'

'Good. I'm parched. Now come with me; I need your help.'

Thinking Gran wanted a hand with putting everything away, Genevieve followed her back into the kitchen. The kettle was boiling, producing its customary rumbling noise, but the sound was amplified by the emptiness of the cupboard beneath it.

Gran suddenly grabbed hold of her arm, making her jump. 'There! Did you hear it?'

'What?'

'There it is again!'

But all Genevieve could hear was the kettle clicking off. Puzzled, she made the tea and watched Gran. It struck her that her grandmother had a tendency to appear 'odder' when she was within her own four walls. Or was it because when she was at Paradise House, her eccentric behaviour blended in with that of the rest of the family?

'Are you sure you can't hear it, Gen?' On her knees now, the old lady was peering into the cupboard beneath the sink.

Genevieve got down on the floor with her. 'What does it sound like?'

Gran backed out from the cupboard. 'What a silly girl you are sometimes. Since when has a mouse sounded like anything other than a mouse?'

Ah. Now things were beginning to make sense.

'Have you got any traps?' Genevieve asked. 'I could set them for you, if you want.'

Gran shook her head vehemently. 'I don't approve of setting traps. It's too sneaky.'

This, coming from a farmer's wife, was bordering on the ridiculous.

'So how are you hoping to get rid of them? Shake them by the paw and ask them to set up home elsewhere?'

A withering glance told her to be quiet and pour the tea. She wondered when the mouse problem had started. Dad hadn't said anything when he'd come back after visiting Gran the day before yesterday.

'How long's this been going on, Gran?' she asked, at the same time inspecting the sugar bowl for mouse droppings.

'Since last night. I couldn't sleep and came down to warm some milk, and I heard the little blighters. But they're cunning so-and-sos, they wait till I'm not looking, then start to squeak and patter about the place.'

Genevieve was just passing Gran her mug when the old woman whipped round and nearly knocked it out of Genevieve's hand. 'Look, it's coming from there!' Once more on her hands and knees, Gran peered round the back of the cooker. She let out a curse. 'I'm just not fast enough!'

'Are you sure you've got mice, Gran? I didn't hear anything.'

Gran stood up with a creak of joints. 'I hope you're

not insinuating that I'm becoming vague and dotty, young lady.'

Genevieve laughed. 'You've been vague and dotty all your life. Now drink your tea and let me talk to you. I need your advice.'

Back in the sitting room, the television switched off in order to have Gran's full attention, Genevieve filled her in on Serena's letter.

Gran was furious. 'The little madam. I'll give her cocktails! Who does she think she is?'

'What Mum's drinking or who she thinks she is, isn't the point,' Genevieve said firmly. 'It's what she's trying to make Dad do that we have to focus on. I'm convinced she wants him to nail his colours to the mast.'

Gran narrowed her eyes and pursed her lips. 'I know who I'd like to nail to the mast.'

'Stop it, Gran. You know you're not supposed to bad-mouth Mum.'

Her grandmother sat back in her chair and sniffed. 'You may not have noticed, Gen, but we're in my house, which means my rules apply; so I'll say exactly what I want.'

Exasperated, Genevieve said, 'But only if it's relevant. Now what do you think is the best way to tackle Dad? We have to make him realise he's the one to change things. He keeps saying Serena has to make her choice. That he can't *make* her come home. But I don't think that's what Mum wants. If she's the woman I think she is, she wants some old-fashioned Judy Garland drama. A husband to sweep her off her feet. A husband worth coming home to.'

Gran stirred her tea, her back ramrod straight with obstinate reproach. 'If it's drama she's after, I know just the thing. It's been on my mind for a while that they're both behaving like a couple of idiotic children. What they need is their bottoms spanking. That would bring them to their senses and give them some drama they wouldn't forget in a hurry.'

Genevieve gave up. Gran wasn't in the best of moods to offer constructive advice. She walked home, disappointed, taking care to keep her gaze on the pavement as she passed Debonhair, just in case Debs was ready to pounce on her.

A shout from the other side of the road, outside Roy and David's butcher shop, made her look up.

'Gen, it's me!' With a bulging carrier bag in each hand, Adam waited for a car to pass, then crossed the road. 'I was calling and calling to you, but you must have been in another world.'

She smiled. 'I was. A very strange place; my head.'

'Ooh, scary. How about you recover from the ordeal by having dinner with me tonight? My treat.' He indicated the bags of shopping. 'Roast lamb's on the menu.'

Nattie was full of scorn when Genevieve said where she would be eating that evening. 'Bloody hell!' she crowed. 'You're letting him cook for you? I'd sooner lick out the loo.'

'Thank you, Nats, for sharing that. Let's hope Dad and Polly don't think the same when they sit down to eat what you've cooked for them this evening.'

'You're expecting *me* to toil away in the kitchen? I don't think so.'

'Honestly! How that daughter of yours has survived, I'll never know. There's a lasagne in the fridge. I'm sure even you can manage to put that in the oven. Throwing a salad together can't be beyond your capabilities either. I'm going for a bath now.'

'He's using you,' Nattie called after her. 'He's trying to get to me through you. Any fool can see that.'

Something in Genevieve snapped. She whirled round and came back to where her sister was feeding carrots to

Henry and Morwenna. 'Don't you dare say that about Adam! He's the last person to use anyone. And you know what? If I didn't know better, I'd say you were jealous. You don't want Adam for yourself, but you can't bear the thought of him being my friend.'

She marched away in a state of high dudgeon, arms swinging, teeth gritted. Sometimes Nattie just went too far! If she wasn't careful she was going to feel the full force of her anger. It was years since she and Nattie had had an all-out fight, but the way things were shaping up, Genevieve knew she was inches away from losing control where her sister was concerned.

Adam was on the phone when she rang his doorbell. He ushered her in, pointed at the open bottle of wine in the kitchen and disappeared to finish his call.

Whereas Paradise House was Edwardian and possessed a comfortable faded charm, Cliff View was all-singing, all-dancing, brand spanking new. Adam had employed the services of an interior designer from Cardiff, much to the derision of the regulars down at The Arms, and had spent a fortune on kitting out the eighteen-month-old house with up-to-the-minute furniture and soft furnishings; black leather sofas, subdued oatmeal carpets, glass and marble units, remote controlled lighting, several wall-mounted plasma screens, and every electronic gadget a boy could wish for. The kitchen was a high-gloss black and chrome affair with gleaming granite surfaces. There was a huge built-in American fridge the size of a small terraced house, and a range of appliances that you had to play hide and seek to find. If it wasn't for the delicious smell of roast lamb coming from the oven, the kitchen might easily have been nothing more than a film set, it was so pristine and immaculate. To her knowledge, Adam rarely entertained; he always claimed he preferred to eat out. Certainly this was the first time she'd been invited to sample anything created by his own hand.

French doors led out onto a neat patio edged with hardy oriental grasses and pots of spiky palms, tall and erect. The wind had dropped and Genevieve went outside to enjoy the view, very different from the view she was used to seeing from across the bay. She wondered if Adam ever had to pinch himself: he'd come a long way from his roots as a car mechanic in Wolverhampton.

Adam was in casual mode – a striped rugby shirt tucked into belted jeans. Watching him carve the lamb, Genevieve itched to pull out the shirt and loosen him up. No two ways about it, he needed taking in hand.

'Just goes to show that you can have all the money in the world and still have lousy taste,' Nattie had said of him. The annoying thing was, there was an element of truth in that.

'I know what you're thinking,' Adam said, adding another slice of meat to one of the plates.

'You do?'

'Yes, that I'm making a mess of this carving. You being the expert and all.'

She didn't disagree with him, and after they'd taken their plates through to the smaller of the sitting rooms, the one Adam usually used, he set up the DVD for them to watch on the enormous screen on the wall.

'You're sure you don't mind a tray supper?' he said.

'Not at all. This is fine. Much more relaxing.'

The film was the much-hyped sequel to *The Matrix*, which Adam assured her was a classic. If she'd seen it she might have stood a chance of understanding the impenetrable plot of the one they were now watching. It seemed to be nothing but head-spinning effects and incomprehensible dialogue.

'Is it me, or are they muttering?' she asked.

Adam smiled and picked up the remote control. 'You're not enjoying this, are you?'

'It must be too deep for me.'

He laughed and zapped the film. 'I'm sorry, you should have said something.' He refilled their glasses of wine. 'Now tell me what you've been up to. It seems ages since I last saw you.'

'It is. It was the day of the wedding reception.'

'You have been paid, haven't you?'

'Oh, yes, the money's been banked.'

'Good. So what's next? Have you another job lined up yet?'

'If your ulterior motive for inviting me here was to bully me again, think on.'

He chewed what was in his mouth and looked thoughtful. 'Actually,' he said, 'I do have an ulterior motive.'

'Aha, we're getting to it now.'

'It's a bit awkward, but I want to talk to you about something.'

'I don't ever recall a conversation between us being awkward.'

'Well, this is different.' He took a sip of his wine. 'It's about your sister.'

'Oh, in that case, awkward doesn't come close. I hope you're not expecting me to be nice about her. She's far from being my favourite person just now.'

'Don't worry, I'm not expecting anything from you, other than a friendly ear. The thing is, I've come to an important decision. I can't go on as I am. I have to get her out of my head, or she'll drive me nuts. Do you understand what I'm saying?'

Genevieve put her finished plate on the glass-topped table in front of them. 'You're asking *me*? The girl who nearly starved herself to death over a boy? The girl who for years afterwards measured any boyfriend by that one example and found them all wanting?'

It was difficult to know who was more surprised by what she'd said and, for a moment, neither of them seemed to know what to say next. Adam looked away and Genevieve took a moment to reflect on what she'd always taken for granted: she had been wary of committing herself to any boyfriends in the past because she'd found it difficult to trust them. But now she realised it went further than that. It was not a comforting thought.

'Sorry,' Adam muttered, 'that was clumsy of me. It was a stupid question.'

'Forget it,' she said lightly, reminding herself that it was Adam's problems they were discussing, not hers. 'So what's brought all this on? About you and Nattie.'

He sighed. 'Months and months of frustration. And I don't mean sexually,' he added with a smile. 'I've reached a crossroads, you could say. I want to settle down, to share my life with someone special. It doesn't seem much to ask, does it, but I don't seem to be making much headway in that department?'

'Adam, you're only thirty-three, there's plenty of time yet for you to meet the right girl.'

He smiled again. 'You know me. Always in a hurry. I hate to let the grass grow under my feet. Everything done yesterday.'

'Well, now that you've decided to untangle yourself from Nattie, the opportunity to meet the right person will probably arise of its own accord.'

He reached for the bottle of wine and topped up their glasses. 'Now you're just being kind. You may not have noticed but I'm butt-ugly, and odds on the only reason a girl's ever going to be interested in me is because I've got a buck or two.' He swirled his wine round and stared into the glass. 'Maybe that's why I hung on, hoping for Nattie to give me a break. I knew the money wasn't an issue for her. I'd probably have stood more of a chance if I'd been dirt poor. She'd have treated me as a rescue case then.' He sighed and stretched out his legs. 'Maybe I just have to face it, I don't have an abundance of shag-appeal.'

Genevieve leaned forward in her seat. It was time for some straight talking. 'First thing,' she said, 'you're not butt-ugly, and second, there's nothing wrong with your shag-appeal, although it could benefit from some –' Her voice broke off. Could she tell him? Could she really suggest that if he spruced up his wardrobe he might attract the right sort of girl?

'Go on,' he said, 'finish what you were going to say.'

She cleared her throat. 'I don't mean this unkindly, Adam, but I think you might do better if you . . . if you took a closer look at what you wear. Your clothes are a little . . .' The baffled expression on his face stopped her from continuing. She wished she'd never started.

'A little what?' He prompted.

She took a large gulp of wine and steeled herself. 'Confusing,' she said. 'Your clothes give out the wrong sort of messages.'

He stared at her, dumbfounded. 'What's wrong with them?' He glanced down at his jeans. 'These weren't cheap you know, they're Armani. Not market stall tat.'

'I didn't think for one moment that they were. But have you ever thought maybe you try too hard?'

He pushed his plate away and seemed to contemplate what she'd said. She hoped she hadn't gone too far.

'Okay,' he said slowly, 'if that's what you really think, why don't we go upstairs and you can explain where I'm going wrong.'

She laughed. 'If that's one of your chat-up lines, you might like to work on it.'

He laughed too and pulled her to her feet. 'I was referring to my clothes, not my mind-blowing skills in bed. Though, who knows, maybe that's my real problem.'

They stood in his bedroom, which was directly above

the main sitting room and looked over the sea. After drawing the curtains, blocking out the moon that shone brilliantly in the night sky, Adam switched on the lights and flung open the doors on the bank of wardrobes.

She whistled. 'Look at all those suits! And so many shirts! I've never seen so many.'

He smiled, proudly. 'And a different tie for each one of them.' He pulled open a drawer and revealed rows and rows of neatly laid out ties.

This was when she knew she had to be cruel to be kind. She held up a particularly awful specimen – Goofy blowing smoke from the barrel of a gun – and said, 'Now there's no gentle way to break this to you, Adam, but believe me when I say that novelty ties are a huge turn-off.'

'But I thought they were supposed to show the warm, funny side of a man's nature. Isn't that the guaranteed ticket to a girl's heart?'

'It can be if you go about it the right way.'

'But women are always saying they want a man with a sense of humour. GSOH, it's there in the ads. Not that I read them. Well, not much.'

She smiled at his embarrassment. 'We all read them, Adam, there's no shame in it. But back to the ties.' She picked out another one, a toothy mouse nibbling on a wedge of cheese. 'This shouts from the rooftops that you haven't grown up yet, that you're as sexy and sophisticated as Donald Duck. Which anyone who knows you properly, knows isn't true. But to a potential date, well, let's just say, it's going to have her running in the opposite direction.'

He took the ties from her and threw them on the bed. 'Anything else? Any more tricks I need to learn?'

'Yes. Let your personality show you're warm and funny, not your clothes.' She caught sight of his gold bracelet on the bedside table. 'And you need to lose some of the flash, be more understated.'

'You mean dull?'

'No. Understated equals classy. Trust me.'

He smiled. 'I do. Completely.' To her surprise, he came over and hugged her. 'You know what? You're the perfect friend.'

When he'd released her, she said, 'And talking of friends, haven't any of them ever told you what I just have?'

'No way! Blokes don't discuss clothes. Cars, sport and gadgets, that's what we talk about. Oh, and money.'

'Well, that would be the problem, then.' Seeing as he'd taken his medicine so painlessly, she went for one last piece of advice. 'Right, this is going to hurt you a lot more than me, but raise your arms to your sides.'

Puzzled, he did as she said, and she untucked his rugby shirt. 'There, that's better. Don't you agree?' She turned him round to look at his reflection in the full-length mirror.

With a doubtful frown, he said, 'It looks untidy sticking out like that.'

'It looks *better*,' she replied. 'Now get used to it.'

'I feel like I've been through the wringer several times over,' he said later, when they were downstairs in the kitchen and he was playing with an expensive coffee machine. 'I had no idea you could be so tough.'

'A mistake other people keep making,' she said.

'Anyone in particular?'

'Not really. It's just that ever since Christian showed up, I get the feeling I'm being watched, in case I have a bad reaction to him.'

He passed her a large cup of frothy cappuccino. 'I did hear you'd been to see Ralph's barn with him.'

'Yes, but did you also hear that Jonjo, Polly and Lily-Rose were with us?'

'No. That minor detail was conveniently omitted.'

She rolled her eyes. 'Great! Why spoil a good story by including the facts?'

'So how did it feel, seeing him again?'

She dipped her finger into the creamy froth of her coffee, then licked it. 'In the end it was fine. I've agreed to see him again when he makes a return trip to look at the barn.'

'And are you doing that to prove to everyone, including yourself, that he doesn't mean anything to you any more?'

'Certainly not. I've agreed to see him because he's good company, just as he always was.' Changing the subject, she raised her cup and took a sip. 'Mm . . . this is delicious. Ten out of ten for the perfect cup of coffee.'

He put down his own drink, moved in close, and with his thumb, gently stroked her top lip. 'I like you better without the moustache.'

She lowered her gaze. But when he didn't step back, she suddenly found it difficult to look up at him again. Something weird had just happened and she wasn't sure she understood it. What she was sure of, though, was the overwhelming need to feel Adam touch her again. Just acknowledging this extraordinary thought seemed to open the floodgates and a tremor of pure lust ran through her. Fearing the wobbling cup in its saucer would give her away, she put it down on the counter with a clumsy bang.

A body starved of touch for too long does the craziest of things, she told herself. Trying to keep calm – *remember this is Adam, your old pal and friend* – she forced herself to look up. When she did, she found he was staring at her in a way she'd never seen before. The blueness of his eyes had darkened and they were fixed intently on her own. She cleared her throat and said, 'It's getting late, I ought to be –'

But she got no further. As though the very air between

them had imploded and sucked them in, they were suddenly in each other's arms. His mouth was deliciously warm, and when he pushed her against the counter top and pressed his body against hers a thrill of excitement shot through her. Old friend or not, it didn't matter. She wanted him and he wanted her.

Chapter Twenty-seven

The next morning, breakfast was a shambles. Toast was burned, eggs were dropped, orders were mixed, and tempers lost. And it was all Genevieve's fault. She couldn't even blame Nattie, who, in contrast to her as she blundered from one mistake to another, was waiting on the tables in the dining room with polished professionalism.

'What the hell's the matter with you?' Nattie demanded, bursting through the kitchen door with a tray of rejected food. 'Table four ordered poached eggs, not scrambled!'

Daddy Dean was hot on Nattie's heels, a plate in his hands. 'You've forgotten the beans,' he said, more reasonably.

When at last the guests had left the dining room, her father asked if she was okay.

'I'm fine,' she lied.

'The hell you are!' said Nattie. 'I've never seen you so disorganised.' She ripped off her apron and threw it on the table. 'Right then, that's me done for the day. Do you think Polly would mind looking after Lily-Rose a bit longer? Only there's something I need –'

'Oh, why bother asking?' Genevieve rounded on her. 'Do what you always do, just leave us to take care of your daughter!'

'Oo-er. Listen to who got out of bed the wrong side this morning.'

Her sister's blithe tone incensed her. 'Save the sarky

attitude for someone who gives a toss. I've had enough of it. You're nothing but a selfish cow. I knew it would be a mistake, you moving back here. That you'd make more work for everyone else, me especially.'

Eyes blazing, Nattie opened her mouth to speak, but their father stepped in between them. 'Steady on, you two.'

The telephone prevented the row from developing further. Glad of the diversion, Genevieve pushed past her sister and snatched up the receiver.

It was Adam.

Her face and body burned with shame.

All Genevieve could think to do was go for a walk. The longer the better. A thick sea-mist had rolled in during the night, and it had yet to clear. The muted gloom of the morning had a calming effect on her, and gradually she slowed her pace sufficiently to notice that the grass was glistening with droplets of water and the path was slippery.

No one else was about on the cliff top. Standing in the spot where she and Christian had sat not so long ago, she paused to catch her breath – she'd taken the steep climb so fast, she'd given herself a stitch.

Oh, but what had she done? What had possessed her to act in such a way? And now Adam wanted to see her, to talk it through. How could she face him when she couldn't even face herself in the mirror? She had told him she'd ring back when she had a free moment. Now all she had to do was contrive to be busy for the rest of time.

Poor Adam.

Wrapping her arms around herself, she recalled how they'd scrambled upstairs to his bedroom, ripped off the last of their clothes and fallen onto the bed, crushing the ties and shirts she'd earlier discarded from his wardrobe. Desperate to get on with it, Adam had reached for his bedside drawer. 'Better play safe,' he'd said. But the moment she heard him rip open the small packet, the reality of what they were doing crashed in on her. She pulled away from him, sat up straight.

'Gen?' he'd said.

But she couldn't speak. She lowered her head and reached for one of his rejected and much prized Hawaiian shirts. He sat up too, put his arm around her.

'Gen?' he repeated. 'What is it?'

Still she said nothing.

He must have realised then what the problem was. He slid off the bed, and disappeared to the bathroom, leaving her to get dressed. No easy task, given that her clothes were scattered to the four corners of his house. She threw on what she could find – her knickers were nowhere to be seen – and silently vanished into the night before Adam could follow her downstairs.

She had behaved badly, she knew. Atrociously. And to a dear friend. A better person would have stuck around to apologise, but she'd proved that she could be as cruel and uncaring as Nattie. Perhaps that was why she'd blasted off at her sister in the kitchen just now: she'd seen herself looking back at her, and it was not a pretty sight.

The dampness was seeping through her clothes. Shivering with cold, she started walking again. She had a vision of herself walking for the rest of eternity so she didn't have to face Adam again.

For as long as she could remember, she'd hated confrontation. She knew it was cowardly, but avoidance always seemed a better option. Sometimes, though, not having the courage to speak her mind served only to make a bad situation worse. Ending things with boyfriends had always been tricky for her. With the last one, Mike, she'd hoped he'd realise for himself that their six-month relationship had run its course. But annoyingly, he'd seemed quite happy with the status quo; the occasional disagreements over staying in or going out (he always wanted to stay in and watch the football), and the lack of things they had in common. Rather than offend him by saying she'd had enough (if she was really honest she'd have told him she found him boring), she had fallen back on the old standby of dropping hints of settling down, of making their relationship more permanent. It worked. He was gone within days, panicked by the mere thought of commitment. But more importantly, she'd allowed him to leave with his pride and dignity intact. She would never deliberately take that away from another person, not when she knew how humiliating it could be.

The thought brought her back to Adam. Rejected now by two of the Baxter girls, he must be feeling horribly humiliated. However, unlike Nattie, she would make amends. Just as soon as she felt able to look him in the eye, she would apologise. Would their friendship ever be the same again? For a crazy moment she wondered if it might have been better to have gone through with what they'd started, because at least then she wouldn't have hurt Adam's feelings.

And what of her own? Didn't her feelings count as much as his? Before she had a chance to answer her own question, another formed itself. What would have happened had it been Christian in that bed with her last night?

Shocked at such a thought, she quickened her pace. She certainly wasn't going to dignify the question by answering it. But she couldn't help herself, and started to wonder what it would be like now, as a grown woman, to go to bed with Christian. To experience what she'd been cheated of when Rachel had got there first.

No! She would not go down that route.

The mist was clearing at last and a faint orb of whiteness had appeared in the overcast sky. The cries from a flock of gulls added a mournful note to the eerie gloom. Ahead of her, with a clear view of the headland and Tawelfan beach beyond, she could see a figure in a bulky waxed jacket coming towards her. He had to be someone local because, unless you were an idiot, you only walked the cliff path in this kind of weather if you knew it like the back of your hand. As the figure drew nearer, after a double-take she realised she was wrong. It was Christian.

What was he doing here? He waved to her. Something made her want to run to him, like in one of those old films her mother loved so much, but she forced herself to walk slowly. Casually.

When he was close enough to read her lips, she said, 'You're the last person I expected to see out here.'

'And there was me thinking I was the only one mad enough to be out walking.'

'The mist's taking ages to clear. There isn't enough wind to blow it away. Did you get my letter?' She was glad he couldn't hear the nervous awkwardness in her voice.

He shook his head. 'What letter?'

Then she remembered. 'Of course, I only posted it yesterday. When did you arrive?'

'Eight o'clock this morning, having got up at the crack of dawn. I had a free day and thought I'd do a lightning visit. I needed to take some more photographs of the barn.'

'But I thought you'd taken loads when you were down last.'

'I did, but stupidly I lost the roll of film.' He produced a smart little camera from his jacket pocket. 'I'm using a digital one this time. Not taking any chances.'

'So what brings you out on the cliff path?'

He returned the camera to his pocket. 'I couldn't help myself. I also thought, if I was brave enough, I'd walk as far as Angel Sands, knock on your door and invite you for a cream tea.'

'And do you think you might have been brave enough?'

'That would have depended on who opened the door. If it was Nattie I would have high-tailed it out of there.'

'After the words she and I have exchanged in the last twenty-four hours, she would have been just ready for you.'

'Oh? You two been fighting?'

'It's nothing. Just me flying off the handle.'

'Want to talk about it over that cream tea?'

She was tempted, but the thought of going back to Angel Sands, where all and sundry would observe them, made her say, 'You know what, I'd prefer to walk on to Tawelfan and grab a hot dog at the kiosk.'

After feeling so wretched, it was a relief to sit with Christian and enjoy his steady company. A breeze had sprung up, the mist had gone, and patches of delicate blue had broken through the clouds. They'd taken off their jackets and were using them to sit on as they tucked into two enormous hot dogs – onions, mustard and tomato sauce oozing from both ends.

'We'll need to go for a swim to wash this lot off,' Genevieve said, when she'd finished eating.

'Freezing cold swims are all right when you're too young to know any better, but you won't catch me doing it these days.' He picked up one of the polystyrene cups of tea they'd bought at the kiosk, removed the lid and handed it to her. 'This feels good,' he said. 'It's great seeing you again.'

'Likewise.'

There was no need to say it, but it was just like old times. They drank their tea companionably, watching the amusing antics of a family nearby as they set up a windbreaker, the father issuing instructions to his wife while the children, three of them, fought over the contents of a large cool bag.

'I'm surprised Jonjo isn't with you,' she said, turning her head.

'He doesn't know I've come. I wanted to look at the barn alone, to get the feel of it unhindered. By the way, is he still pestering Polly?'

'Almost continually.'

'Does she mind?'

'No. She's the most tolerant person in the world. She makes up for Nattie and me.'

He smiled. 'You mentioned earlier about words being exchanged between you and Nattie. What was that about?'

'If you don't mind, I'd rather not say.'

'Fair enough.'

An argument had broken out amongst the nearby family about whose sandwiches were whose. Following her gaze, Christian said, 'Having made the mistake of marrying you off to Adam with a child into the bargain, would I be making another mistake to assume you aren't, or haven't been married to anyone else?'

She faced him. 'I haven't even come close to it. Oh, there have been one or two men I thought had potential, but when push came to shove, they got a hearty shove.' She explained the technique she'd employed over the years to end things 'nicely'.

'How very considerate of you.'

'I like to think so.'

'Although, of course, there's always the risk that one day your bluff might be called.'

She scooped up a handful of sand and let it trickle slowly through her fingers. 'Now that would be a disaster. But not the end of the world. I'd then have Plan B to resort to.'

'Which is?'

'I'd force him to spend a week in the bosom of my family. That would have him backtracking at the speed of sound.'

Laughing, he said, 'I've been meaning to ask you, I haven't seen your mother. How is she?'

'For a woman going through a mid-life crisis, she's having a ball.' Genevieve told him about Serena needing time out, and about the most recent letter from New Zealand.

'How's your father coping?'

'Up and down. He's basically paralysed by fear and denial. Part of him wants to believe she'll come home when she's ready and the other part is terrified he's lost her already to this old friend, Pete.'

'What do your sisters say?'

'They don't know about the letter. Dad hasn't shown it to them and as yet I haven't had an opportunity to discuss it with either of them. Polly's busy helping with some music festival in St David's and Nattie, well, Nattie will just hit the rant and rave button. I don't know why, but out of all of us, she's the most furious with Mum.'

Seconds passed before he replied. As it had years ago, it still amazed her how good Christian was at lip-reading: rarely did he misread what was said.

'And if your father doesn't do anything,' he said at last, 'what do you think your mother will do?'

'I wish I knew. Anyway, enough of my family, tell me about yours. How are your parents? Did they ever buy that house in France?'

'They did, but Mum sold it when Dad died three years ago from cancer. Mum's health has gone downhill ever since. She's had one thing after another.'

Recalling he'd always been close to his parents, Genevieve said, 'I'm sorry about your Dad. How often do you get to see your mother?'

'Not as often as I should. I've been trying to convince her to move somewhere smaller that needs less work, especially in the garden, but she won't hear of it. You remember how she loved nothing better than to spend entire back-breaking days in the garden?'

She nodded. 'I do. Will you give her my best wishes, when you see her next?'

'I will.' He checked his watch and said, 'I ought to be going.'

'Really?'

'Yes.'

She walked to Ralph's barn with him, where his car, a Volvo estate, was parked. He threw in his jacket and exchanged his walking boots for a pair of dusty Timber-lands.

'Hop in and I'll give you a lift home.'

She had a sudden mental picture of Debs and the coven of gossipers peering out of the salon window as they drove past. 'There's no need,' she said.

'I know there's no need, but I'd like to.'

She held her ground. 'The walk back will do me good.'

He tilted his head. 'What are you scared of, Genevieve?'

Perturbed at his sharpness, she laughed a little too shrilly. 'You forget,' she said, 'I'm a Baxter and we're scared of nothing.'

'Then get in the car and stop worrying about what other people will think.'

She squared her shoulders. 'I don't know what you're talking about.'

He held the door open. 'Yes you do. Now get in.'

She said nothing until they'd dropped down the hill into Angel Sands, whereupon sod's law prevailed. A queue of traffic had built up behind a car towing a caravan, which had acquired a flat tyre and was partially blocking the road. People were out of their cars lending a hand. If she'd wanted an audience, she'd got the biggest one going. Debs, Stan and Gwen, Ruth and the Lloyd-Morris brothers were all standing in their shop doorways observing the commotion.

Slumping into her seat, Genevieve glanced sideways at Christian and saw he was smiling. She slapped him on the arm. 'How did you know?' she asked.

'That you didn't want to be seen with me? Oh, just a hunch. That and the length of time, a whole nanosecond, it took you to reject my invitation for a cream tea on your doorstep.'

'You must think me very silly.'

'Not at all. I'm just sorry you feel like that. As though any of it matters.'

'You're right. I shouldn't worry, but some old habits are harder to shake off than others.'

With his elbow resting on the sill of the open window, he twisted round further and gave her a penetrating stare. It was so intense, she felt herself back away from it. Then, to her horror, the question she had asked herself earlier – what if it had been Christian in the bed last night and not Adam? – surfaced again. She tried to wrench her gaze from his, but couldn't. She waited for him to say something, anything, but he didn't. He just kept on staring at her. Then, hearing a car horn blare from behind them, she said, 'It looks like we can squeeze past now.'

He nodded, put the car into gear and drove on, carefully mounting the kerb to bypass the caravan. It was then that Debs, along with everyone else, saw Genevieve. They all smiled and waved. Debs even had the nerve to bend down to gawp in through the car window to get a better look at Christian.

'Don't ignore your friends, Genevieve,' he said. 'Wave back or I'll stop the car and kiss you, just to give them something worthwhile to talk about.'

'You wouldn't dare!'

'Care to risk it?'

For the rest of the short journey up to Paradise House, neither of them said anything. He switched off the engine and turned to face her. For a moment she thought he was going to carry out his threat and kiss her. When he leaned towards her, raised a hand and pushed her hair away from her cheek, she said, 'Do you think that would be a good idea?'

His hand stayed where it was, pressing gently into the hollow of her neck, until slowly he lowered it. 'You're right,' he said. 'It would be a mistake, and not just because of our history.'

'What other reason could there be?'

'A very good one. Her name's Caroline.'

Chapter Twenty-eight

'Seeing someone?' repeated Nattie. 'Now who the hell would be crazy enough to go out with that lying, cheating excuse of a man?'

As ever, Nattie's views on the subject of Christian were implacable. Once she had decided a person's character was flawed, there was no changing her opinion. Genevieve suspected that if Christian were to bring about world peace, then discover a cure for cancer, Nattie would still find a way to condemn him.

Busying herself with pulling on the tangle of towels jammed inside the washing machine, she wished that the house had been empty when Christian had dropped her off. Externally she had been all politeness, appearing hardly to have noticed that Very-Nearly-A-Kiss moment when they'd said goodbye, but internally she was experiencing a tumultuous wave of confusion. Why on earth had he even hinted at wanting to kiss her if he was involved with someone? It was difficult not to think in terms of leopards and spots.

Nattie had been in the kitchen with Lily-Rose when she'd come in from waving Christian off. Perhaps because she needed to confide in someone – even her hostile sister, who was still bristling from Genevieve's earlier loss of temper – she had stupidly blurted out what he had just shared with her.

'And if he has a girlfriend,' Nattie continued now, in the utility room, 'why has he been down here sniffing round you?'

Genevieve dropped the heavy bundle of untangled towels into the basket in front of the machine and stood up to take it outside. But Nattie was barring her way, standing in the doorway, a shoulder resting on the frame, one ankle crossed over the other. Behind her, Lily-Rose was sitting at the kitchen table waggling a paintbrush in a jam-jar of cloudy water.

'You have such a way with words, don't you?' Genevieve said, her voice low so that her niece couldn't hear their conversation. 'All we've been doing is catching up with one another. Nothing more.'

'He hurt you once before, Gen, I'd hate to see it happen again.'

'You make him out to be some kind of serial heart-breaker.'

'What can I say? His actions speak for themselves. But I notice you haven't answered my question. If he has a girlfriend, why would he want to be so pally with you?'

Genevieve shifted the laundry basket to rest it on her hip. 'Oh, don't be ridiculous. The days of having only same-sex friendships are long gone. Just look at Adam and me. Honestly, sometimes I think you live in a totally different world from the rest of us. Now, I have things to do, like putting these towels on the line. Unless you'd like to do it.'

She was almost through the door, wishing the reference to Adam hadn't proved her sister's point exactly, when Nattie said, 'By the way, Adam called for you. Twice in fact. I told him to lay off, that the last thing you needed was a nuisance caller.'

Outside in the garden, Genevieve considered what was going on. In less than twenty-four hours she had very nearly gone to bed with a man for whom she'd never harboured a single amorous thought, and then, unbeliev-ably, she had come close to being kissed by a man she had once hoped never to set eyes on again.

But the immediate problem she had to sort out was Adam. Hiding from him indefinitely wasn't the answer. In a place as small as Angel Sands, she would soon run out of hiding places. She had no choice but to speak to him and plead a moment of insanity. But would that upset him further? *Sorry, Adam, but I only stripped off all my clothes with such eagerness because of a wild mental aberration. It goes without saying that in a sane and level-headed mood I wouldn't dream of doing such a thing.*

Oh, yes, that would really make him feel better.

Eleven o'clock the next morning, following breakfast, Genevieve was tidying the dining room with Donna's help. One of the guests had spilled a bowl of muesli on the floor. Scooping up the soggy mess, Genevieve was listening to Donna's latest news bulletin on her romance with Tubby.

'I came here looking for a new life,' Donna said, gathering the pots of homemade jam and marmalade and adding them to her tray, 'but I never thought I'd fall in love. Not at my age. Well, you don't expect it, do you?'

'You're not old, Donna.'

Donna gave one of her husky laughs, the sexy, full-throated one that only weeks ago had had Dad running for cover. 'I'm hardly in my first flush, though, am I? Although at fifty-four, I reckon I cook better than a lot of women.' She wiggled her tightly wrapped hips and struck a pose like a woman destined never to grow old gracefully.

Getting up from the floor, Genevieve said, 'So it's love, then, is it? You and Tubby?'

'Either that or we're both in lust!' She let rip with another husky laugh.

Whatever misgivings Genevieve might have had about Donna working at Paradise House had long since been replaced with a real fondness. Her life hadn't always been happy. 'Let me tell you, living with a vicious drunk was no picnic,' she'd told Genevieve one day. But she was always cheerful and positive.

Later, while they were sorting out the cleaning things for upstairs, Donna took Genevieve by surprise.

'I know it's none of my business,' she said, 'but do you think it would help your Dad if Tubby and I had a word with him?'

'What about?'

Hoisting the vacuum hose over her shoulder as though it were an enormous handbag, Donna said, 'About your mother, of course.'

Genevieve was taken aback. This was a conversation she'd never touched on with Donna. 'Oh, I don't know if that would be a good idea. Dad's very private, he doesn't –'

'He's also very lonely and miserable,' Donna cut in. 'Anyone can see that. And they're two things, in my opinion, which should never be allowed to fester in a man. It can turn them into things they weren't ever meant to be – drunks, like my ex, or prowling womanisers.'

Smiling uneasily, Genevieve said, 'I think that's a bit simplistic. I can't quite see Dad turning into either of those things.'

'Oh, well, like I say, it was just a thought. Knowing how well your father and Tubby get on, I thought it might help.'

'Was it Tubby's idea?'

'Lord help us, no! He's as dim-witted as the next man when it comes to discussing his feelings. Still, we wouldn't have them any other way, would we, love?'

They were halfway through making the beds and cleaning the bathrooms when Genevieve heard the doorbell. She went to answer it. Once again it was the florist,

Rhys Williams, who had twice now delivered flowers for Polly. He greeted Genevieve warmly, while handing over a bouquet of beautiful pale pink roses.

'Seems like I'm always here. Whoever the admirers are, keep them coming; I'll be able to retire early at this rate.'

Genevieve took the flowers through to the guest sitting room and put them on the piano. They had to be for Polly. But she couldn't resist a peek at the label.

Dear Genevieve, sorry for what I very nearly did. Please forgive an old friend . . . if you can.

Well, that did it! Now she had to apologise to Adam. If he could be so sweet and thoughtful and ask for her forgiveness, it was only right to summon every miserable scrap of her courage and face him.

That evening, when she could see the lights on in Adam's house across the bay and knew he was at home, Genevieve told her father she was slipping out for a few minutes.

'I shan't be long,' she said, leaving him to watch the television in peace. The guests were all out, Lily-Rose was in bed, Nattie was having a bath and Polly was at a concert in Milford Haven where one of her pupils was playing.

She took with her a gift of her own making; a lemon meringue pie, which she knew was one of Adam's favourite desserts. He looked as awkward as she felt when he opened the door to her. She thrust the foil package towards him.

'It should be humble pie, but I thought you'd prefer lemon meringue laced with a double helping of whipped apologies.'

He closed the door after her. 'Come on through to

the kitchen and I'll make us some coffee.'

'Not if it's going to lead us into temptation again,' she said with a nervous laugh.

'Tea, then? Would that be safer?'

'Actually, a large glass of wine would be better.'

It was warm enough to sit outside. The sky had grown darker, insects hovered in the air and the sea surged below in the bay.

'I'm glad you felt able to see me, Gen. I'd hate for anything to come between us.'

'I know; I feel exactly the same.'

He shook his head. 'I bet you don't. I bet you feel used. As though I tried to take advantage of you the other night.' He looked away into the gathering darkness. 'You probably hate me.'

Appalled, she said, 'No, Adam. That's not true at all. I never once thought you were using me. In fact, I think it was me who started it.'

He turned his head. 'You don't have to spare my feelings, Gen. But you must believe me when I say it wasn't Nattie I imagined I was in bed with.'

Of all the thoughts that had careered through her head, this one hadn't featured. She'd been so wrapped up in her own guilt and embarrassment, she hadn't once thought what might have been going through Adam's mind.

When she didn't respond, he said, 'Look, Gen, I'll be straight with you. I've been guilty of it before, with other girls. I'd take them to bed and make love to them, all the while thinking of Nattie. I'm not proud of that, but it wasn't the same with you. I swear.' He took a large gulp of wine. 'It . . . it's difficult to explain, but it sort of felt right with you. It made me realise how good it must be to have sex with someone you really care about. You know, to experience the whole package. Something I haven't done before.' He suddenly banged his fist down on the arm of his chair. 'Shit! What the hell do I sound like?'

She reached over to him and touched his arm lightly. 'Oh, Adam. I'm sorry. Sorry that it turned out the way it did.'

'And you know what? I wish I could say I don't know what came over me, but I can't. I knew exactly what I was doing.'

'The same goes for me. But for the sake of our friendship, we have to put it behind us.'

He looked up. 'I can, if you can.'

'Good,' she said resolutely. 'So no more embarrassment?'

'And no more hiding from me?'

'It's a deal.' Relieved they'd dealt with the problem so easily, she said, 'By the way, you're looking good this evening. Have you been shopping?'

'I took your advice. I had to go to Swansea this afternoon, so I scooped up a load of new shirts and trousers. You don't think this blue shirt looks a bit boring, do you?'

'No. It looks great. Casual but stylish. The colour matches your eyes.'

He drained his glass and looked glum. 'And for what? Or rather, for whose benefit?'

'Hey, that doesn't sound like the Adam I know and love.'

'Yeah well, it's been a strange couple of days, one way or another. Anyway, no more feeling sorry for myself.' A welcome smile appeared on his face. 'I reckon I might never be allowed the opportunity again, so I'm going to say it now, Gen. You've got a great body, you know. *Very* sexy. I had no idea you had such good legs, either. I can't recall an occasion when I've had so much as a peep at anything higher than your ankles. Perhaps that's why I found the whole thing such a turn-on.'

She blushed and sat back in her chair, arms folded.

'Don't scowl at me, Gen. It's true. You have a fantastic figure. I don't think you have any idea just how attractive you are.'

'That's enough. You can stop right there!'

'No! You had your say with me, about my tacky shirts and ties, now you can have a taste of your own medicine. Polly may be the brightest and prettiest Baxter girl and Nattie the most spirited, but you're the best of the bunch. And you know why? It's because you're not only kind and generous, but you connect with people. You're also damned sexy into the bargain. I can quite understand why your old boyfriend couldn't keep his eyes off you when he was down here. And why he's been back so soon.'

Genevieve snapped forward. 'He's done no such thing!'

'You sure about that? So how come I saw the pair of you on the cliff path yesterday morning, after I'd tried speaking to you on the phone?'

'Adam Kellar, have you nothing better to do than spy on your neighbours? Why weren't you hard at work earning an honest crust?'

He grinned. 'I was. I was working from home.'

'Mm . . . clearly not hard enough, or you wouldn't have had time to watch my movements. And what about all that mist? You couldn't possibly have seen us.'

'Binoculars are a wonderful invention. You should try them.' Then leaning forward to top up her wine, he said, 'So how's it going between the two of you? The old magic still there?'

'I think I preferred it when you were miserable and contrite,' she muttered. 'At least you didn't poke and pry.'

'Answer the question, Miss Huffy-Pants. Which reminds me, you left a pair here the other night. They're washed and ready for you to take home. Unless you want me to keep them as a souvenir?'

She blushed again. 'You realise, don't you, that you're being quite intolerable?'

'Another few glasses of this Merlot and I might show just how intolerable I can be. Now tell me, has he made a move on you? You know, just for old time's sake?'

Genevieve pictured the scene in Christian's car. Was that what it had been? A split-second when he had idly wondered what it would be like to turn back the clock and rekindle a time when their days together had been so innocently intimate and uncomplicated? She decided to be honest with Adam.

'I think it did occur to him to try to kiss me, just to see what it would be like, but fortunately he thought better of it.' She explained about the girlfriend back home.

'And how did you feel when he said that? Were you disappointed? Relieved? Hurt? Or maybe plain old angry?'

'A bit of all those things,' she said, after taking a long sip of wine. 'And your point?'

'Well, if you'd been indifferent, you'd be immune from his charms. As it is, you risk –'

'Yeah, I know, being hurt again. In her own inimitable fashion, Nattie's already gone to great lengths to warn me of that peril. But what you're forgetting is that I'm a big girl now and with there being a girlfriend on the scene, he's out of bounds.'

'And if the girlfriend becomes history? Does that bring him within range?'

'As I said, I'm a big girl. I can handle the likes of an old flame curious to take a trip down memory lane. Something I'm not in the least bit interested in pursuing myself.' It was time to change the subject. 'Now then,' she said, 'before I skedaddle out of here and forget why I came, I must thank you for the lovely flowers. There was no need to send them. If anyone needed to ask for forgiveness, it was me. I shouldn't have snuck away like that, but I didn't know what to say.'

He gave her a blank look. 'Sorry, I'm not with you. What flowers?'

'You know, the roses. They came this morning.'

The blank expression was replaced with a slow smile. 'Remind me what the card said.'

Annoyed that he was playing games with her, she said, 'The wording went something like, "Dear Genevieve, sorry for what I very nearly did. Please forgive an old friend . . . if you can."'

Adam looked at her steadily. 'Like I said, the guy couldn't keep his eyes off you.'

Chapter Twenty-nine

Even at the best of times, Granny Baxter wasn't the most reliable of people. Her memory, so she claimed, was in perfect working order; it was others who confused her by deliberately playing tricks, like hiding her glasses. Exchanges such as, 'But Gran, you're wearing them!' 'Well, who put them there? Was it you?' were frequent. As was wondering why Genevieve or some other member of the family had arrived in the car to take her shopping in Pembroke or Haverfordwest. 'But Gran, it was your idea!' 'What nonsense. But seeing as you're here, you can take me anyway. I could do with a change of scene.'

Over the years, Genevieve and her sisters had witnessed many a scene when their grandmother had turned a perfectly logical situation completely on its head. Today, though, she seemed intent on turning Angel Cottage on its head and giving it a good shake. Convinced that the mice plaguing her kitchen had now taken up residence in the dusty confines of the understairs cupboard, she was issuing orders to Genevieve and her father.

'Careful where you stand, you might step on one!' And, 'Try not to make too much noise; we need to take them by surprise.'

The Mice Thing, as it had become known, was close to being an obsession with Gran. Every conversation anyone had with her was punctuated with some new complaint. The mice were either keeping her awake at night with their squeaky cacophony in the chimney breast, or they were shredding her nerves with their prolonged silences. Either way, their presence was driving Gran mad. Yet it was difficult to use the word 'presence' because, as yet, no one had had an actual sighting. Other than Gran, no one had even heard so much as a squeak.

But now, because Gran was so insistent that the mice had moved from the kitchen to the understairs cupboard, the small hallway of her cottage was strewn with what looked like museum pieces – two ancient vacuum cleaners, boxes of chipped crockery and jam jars, bundles of faded newspapers, cracked old shoes without laces, and one solitary, fur-lined ankle boot.

'What's the point in keeping this, Gran?' asked Genevieve. She held up the boot for her grandmother to see.

The old lady took it from her and turned it over as though trying to place it. 'Well, I'll be darned,' she said at length. 'I was wondering where it had got to. Clever you for finding it. Here, give me a hand.' Leaning against Genevieve, she kicked off her slipper, pushed her stockinged foot into the boot and was just about to pull up the zip when she let out an ear-splitting yelp. 'There's something in it!'

She put all her weight against Genevieve, making her stagger, and tried to shake off the boot. Meanwhile, still digging around in the cupboard for more lost family heirlooms, Daddy Dean emerged to see what all the fuss was about and promptly banged his head on the low door frame.

'Bugger!' he yelled above the noise of Gran's shouts, while rubbing the top of his head. 'What the hell's going on?'

But Gran was beyond answering questions.

'She thinks there's something in it,' Genevieve shouted. 'Get it off before she has a heart attack!'

It was some minutes before Gran was in a calm

enough state to drink the tea Genevieve had made. The three of them were in the sitting room, squashed on the sofa, Gran between Genevieve and her father.

'It was a mouse, I tell you,' Gran muttered, more to herself than them. 'It was there, right at the end of the boot. I felt it wriggle under my big toe.' She shuddered and spilled some of the tea from the mug in her hands.

Daddy Dean took the mug from her and put it on the coffee table. 'Mum, it wasn't a mouse,' he said very firmly. 'It was a small ball of wool. Look.' For the third time he showed her the flattened remnant.

But seeing wasn't believing, and Gran turned her weepy eyes on him. 'I know what I felt. It was a *mouse*.'

He put his arm around her. 'It only felt like a mouse because that's what's on your mind at the moment.'

Her expression turned stern. 'Don't treat me like a child. I'm not a simpleton. Don't think you can bully or patronise me.'

'I wouldn't ever think of patronising you,' he soothed. 'Now drink up your tea.'

She took it from him with a look of such fierce petulance, Genevieve was reminded of Nattie. She held back a smile. But deep down, Genevieve was concerned. The Mouse Thing was getting to Gran and she wondered if she ought to suggest to her father that they get Gran checked out by a doctor. Senile dementia or Alzheimer's were not words she wanted to start bandying around, but if Gran was beginning to imagine things, then perhaps it was their responsibility to find out why. Right now Genevieve would give anything to see a family of mice trotting across the sitting room carpet.

She was just wondering which one of them would be brave enough to broach the subject, when her grandmother said, 'And while we're on the subject of bullying, I hope you're going to do exactly what Genevieve thinks you should.'

Uncertain which way the conversation was about to go, Genevieve looked anxiously at her father. 'And what would that be?' he said.

'Doing something about you and Serena, of course.'

It should have been a relief to see Gran revert so quickly to her normal self, but Genevieve flinched on her father's behalf. This was a conversation her father was going to have to face. But watching him remove his arm from his mother's shoulder, she could see him withdrawing already.

'And if you leave it much later, Daddy Dean, you'll go to rack and ruin and no woman in her right senses would be interested in you. No, don't look like that. I'm only speaking the truth. Which reminds me, you're beginning to bear an uncanny resemblance to that silly man on the television.'

'And which silly man would that be?' Dad's voice was tight.

'Oh, you know. The one who waves his arms about a lot.' Gran screwed up her eyes to assist her concentration. 'No, don't rush me, I'm thinking. Oh, dear, whatever is his name? My brain's turned to quince jelly. It sounds like dog. Something dog. Dog. Dog. Ken Dodd! That's who you remind me of.'

Genevieve stifled a laugh but her father looked offended.

'You do!' Gran persisted. 'When was the last time you had your hair cut? Look at it; it's sticking up all over your head. You need to make an appointment with Debs and get yourself tidied up, my boy. Or what will Serena think when you fly to Australia to sweep her off her feet?'

'Serena's in New Zealand, Mum. And I don't know where you've got this notion that I'm setting foot on any kind of an aeroplane.' He got to his feet and looked at his reflection in the mirror above the fireplace. 'I don't look anything like Ken Dodd.'

Gran made a small grunting sound. 'If you don't go and see her, it might well turn out to be the biggest mistake of your life. It's time you brought that wife of yours home where she belongs. It's not just you who misses her.'

Taking her cue, Genevieve said, 'Gran's right, Dad. You can't go on as you are. I really think you should go and see Mum. If you don't, she might start to think you don't want her back.'

In a gesture of despair, he raked his hands wildly through his hair. 'But how can I compete with this old friend who's giving her such a new and exciting time? What have I got to offer?'

'There!' cried Gran, 'now you really do look like Ken Dodd.'

Her father refused to speak another word on the subject for the rest of the day, and it was with a weary heart that Genevieve sat alone in the small office that night. She ignored the pile of paperwork that needed filing, and instead switched on the computer to check her emails.

It was three weeks since she had written to thank Christian for the roses. But even as she penned the note, she half-expected to receive a reply from him that said, 'What roses? *I* didn't send any.' But he'd replied a week later asking if she had a computer and was online. 'Emails are so much more convenient,' he'd written. He'd given her his email address and she'd replied with the message: 'Bet you thought we Baxters were too primitive for such hi-tech equipment, didn't you?' She pointed out that for years now she'd preferred to use a PC when writing letters. 'Spellchecker is the mother of all godsends for me.' He, in turn, pointed out that emailing and texting were easily the most useful forms of communication available to him.

Since then, there had been no more than a couple of

brief exchanges, mostly news bulletins about Ralph's barn. Then silence. Perhaps, in view of Caroline, he'd felt it was inappropriate to correspond too often. This had a strange effect on Genevieve: it made her feel guilty, as though somehow she had become the Other Woman in his life.

Of course, nothing could have been further from the truth, despite what Adam wanted to believe. And even if Christian was tempted to turn back the clock, she wasn't. While she had forgiven him for what had happened, she had no intention of getting romantically involved with him. Not because she didn't find him attractive – she most certainly did – but because for once in her life, her head was ruling her heart. And her head was very clear on one crucial point of survival: she would never, ever, *ever*, allow anyone, herself included, to hurt her again.

The flashing white envelope on her screen showed that she had just one email waiting for her: it was from Christian. She clicked on OPEN and realised straight away why she hadn't heard from him. His mother was in hospital. Cancer. She'd had surgery to remove a lymph node from under her arm, but, from what Christian said, it seemed it had come too late. The cancer had spread.

Genevieve responded immediately, offering what few words of encouragement she could in the circumstances.

Having recently had many nights of relatively peaceful, nightmare-free sleep, she went to bed only to be kept awake by the day's events tumbling through her head: Gran's hysterical turn, her father refusing to see sense, and now Christian's mother, who was probably dying. Listening to the wind blowing in from the sea, she lay staring up at the ceiling. She was troubled by how helpless she felt. It was so frustrating that she couldn't do more to put her grandmother's mind at rest over the Mice Thing, and that she couldn't galvanise Dad into doing more to bring Mum home. She decided, though, to let this last worry go. Her father had resolved the Donna issue without anyone's help, so maybe he would do the same with Serena. Perhaps all that was needed on her part was patience. Something she seemed to be in short supply of these days.

Chapter Thirty

By the middle of July, no one needed a weather forecaster to tell them they were experiencing a heatwave. It had started last week, and Angel Sands was tripping over itself with visitors. The usual complaints were heard, that it was too hot and the gardens could do with a drop of rain, but all in all, anyone running a business off the sunburnt backs of holidaymakers was rubbing his or her hands and praying on bended knee that the weather would hold for the rest of the season.

In the garden at Paradise House, Genevieve stood for a moment in the breathless heat to look down onto the beach. It was packed. The tide was in, leaving only a small amount of sand and pebbly surface to sit on, but every square inch was occupied. Rarely had she seen it so busy. 'Who needs to go abroad when the weather's like this?' all their guests were saying.

She had now started cooking evening meals for those who wanted them and, after a two-week trial period, it was proving to be a success.

Predictably, Nattie was muttering that it was more work for the rest of them. 'I'm not spending all my evenings dishing out food,' she said, 'and then tidying up afterwards. Not when I've been on the go all day with Lily-Rose.'

This was too much for Genevieve. 'And I suppose I haven't been on the go all day!'

'Yeah, but that's your choice. You've decided to make all this extra work. Why should I be lumbered with it?'

'Because it's a family business. We're all in this together.'

'I notice you don't go on at Polly like you do with me.'

'And for a very good reason. She's not an idle beggar like you. She's out teaching most days, but during the school holidays she always does her bit. Honestly, Nattie, it's time you grew up.'

'And became a boring adult like you? Not bloody likely!'

As ever, Adam had come up trumps and recommended the niece of a friend of a friend who was spending the summer in the village and would appreciate the unexpected pocket money. Her name was Kelly Winward, a seventeen-year-old student from Bolton, and she was far more helpful than Nattie would ever be.

Now that things were back to normal with Adam, he had been on at Genevieve again about putting her supposed skills to better use. 'I hate to see good talent go to waste,' he said, when she asked him why he was so concerned about her.

'But if I take on too much, I won't be able to run Paradise House. Now that I'm doing evening meals, I have even less time for anything else.'

'And is that what you want to do for the rest of your life?' he'd asked.

Christian had asked her much the same question during one of their email exchanges. Her answer had been vague. Sometimes she thought she would like nothing better than to stay in Angel Sands for ever, continuing to do exactly what she was doing. But as someone had once told her – probably Gran in one of her wise old lady moments – everyone should have their own dream, and Paradise House had been her parents' dream or, more specifically, her mother's. For the time being, she was happy to be the caretaker of someone else's dream, but sometime soon she would have to chase her own. She did have something in mind, but until the right opportunity arose, she didn't want to tell anyone about it. For now it was a tentative plan with a small p. But given time, it would become her Plan with a capital P.

Meanwhile, she had plenty to do. Thanks to Adam and the wedding party, she now had two party bookings, one for August and another for September. Donna and Kelly would waitress for her, but come the autumn when Kelly was back in Bolton, Genevieve would have to think again.

News from Christian about his mother went from bad to worse. The emails he sent were sporadic; some were just a couple of lines, while others were over a page long. Genevieve sensed he needed someone to talk to. She hoped Caroline, whom he never mentioned, was a good listener. The latest email said, 'Mum's having all the treatment, but I know her heart's not in it. Mentally she's given up the fight and it makes me so angry. Not cross with her, but impotent and furious that I can't do anything to stop the pain or the inevitable.'

Genevieve wished she was better with words and could say something incisive and helpful. But the best she could do was reassure him he was doing all he could by being with his mother as much as possible.

Walking back up the garden to the house, Genevieve thought how wrong Adam was. Other than that Very-Nearly-A-Kiss moment, Christian hadn't given her any cause to worry that he might want more than just friendship. It was a relief, one thing less for her to worry about.

The house was empty so, switching on the answerphone, she walked down the hill to call on Gran, to see if there was any shopping she needed doing. The air was drenched in the smell of suntan oil and the area of parched grass in front of the Salvation Arms was carnival-like, awash with reddening bodies swigging back beer and soft drinks. The shops were also busy, and across the road, outside the mini-market, Stan looked like he was wrestling with a killer whale – he was actually restocking his display of inflatable beach toys. Waving to him, Genevieve carried on up to Angel Cottage.

Since the Mouse-In-The-Boot incident, their father had insisted on getting a pest man in. Reluctantly Gran had agreed and even when her house was declared a pest-free zone, she wasn't convinced. 'Modern mice are more cunning than they used to be,' she said.

The very next day she claimed to have been woken in the night by squeaking, but the funny thing was, she was no longer irritated by the noise. It was as though the enemy had become her ally. Heroes, even. They had beaten the pest man and won her respect.

To Genevieve's astonishment, her father had broached the subject of Gran seeing a doctor. Her reaction, unsurprisingly, was to hit the roof and tell anyone who would listen that there was nothing wrong with her. She told Stan and Gwen in the mini-market, she told Ruth and William in church, and, of course, she told Tubby – because, as everyone knew, if you wanted important news relayed, Tubby was your man.

'It's so embarrassing,' Nattie complained. 'She's making out that we're trying to have her put away.'

'But no one would believe it,' said Polly. 'Everyone knows that's the last thing we'd do.'

'Don't you be so sure,' their father muttered from behind his newspaper. 'The way I feel, I might just lock her up myself.' He was still smarting from the Ken Dodd comparison.

Genevieve knocked on Gran's front door.

She knocked again. And again. And still Gran didn't appear. Genevieve moved to the window where she cupped her hands around her eyes and peered in. The television wasn't on, and there was no sign of Gran. Perhaps she was in the kitchen at the back of the house.

Nothing for it, Genevieve thought, and took the unprecedented step of using the key she'd been entrusted with.

'Gran?' she called out anxiously, shutting the door behind her. 'It's me, Genevieve.'

The house was refreshingly cool and still after the heat outside. It was also unnaturally quiet. She poked her head round the sitting room door, then went through to the kitchen. Still no sign of Gran. She investigated further, calling out all the while – better not give Gran a heart attack by creeping up on her.

When she stood on the small landing, she thought she heard something. 'Gran?' She strained to hear the noise again.

Yes. There it was. It was coming from the bathroom. A faint moaning noise. She pushed open the door.

Her first thought was that subconsciously this was what she'd always dreaded . . . finding Gran dead.

Chapter Thirty-one

The doctor saw himself out, leaving them to hover around the bed like actors in a second-rate television drama.

'If you're trying to annoy me,' Gran grumbled, 'you're doing a good job of it. You look like a bunch of greedy mourners who've been called to the bed once too often. Any minute now you'll start squabbling over who's going to inherit the most from my vast fortune.'

'Good, I'm glad we're annoying you,' said Nattie, 'because you scared the hell out of us! If you're planning another dizzy do, let me know so I can make arrangements to be some place else.'

'That's enough, Natalie,' her father murmured. Pale-faced and anxious, he dropped into the chair nearest Gran's bed. He rubbed his hands over his face. 'You're sure you're okay?' he said. 'You're not pretending, are you? I know what you're capable of.'

The old lady drew her eyebrows together. 'Please, I wish you'd all stop fussing. I'm as fit as a fiddle.'

'No you're not! What's more, you're under doctor's orders to stay in bed for the next two days.'

Gran raised her head off the pillow. 'I clearly heard Doctor Shepherd say that all I needed to do was take things slowly. He didn't mention anything about staying in bed gathering bedsores. Now is there any chance of a cup of tea, or am I denied that basic human right too?'

Genevieve and Polly volunteered for the job. In the kitchen, while they put together a tray of tea things,

Genevieve said, 'She's at her most imperious when she's hiding from the truth, isn't she?'

'You're right. Beneath it all, she must be as shocked as the rest of us. But how are *you* feeling? It must have been awful finding her like that.'

'I'm fine,' Genevieve said, conscious that she was lying in the same glib way her grandmother just had. When she'd found Gran slumped in a heap on the bathroom floor – her hand still clutching a J-cloth and a puddle of pine fresh cleaner on the carpet – her brain had registered the obvious, that Gran was moving and therefore alive, but her heart had been several paces behind, causing panic to thump in her chest. She'd turned the old lady over, seen the gash where she must have cracked the side of her head on the basin as she fell, and was about to rush downstairs to phone for an ambulance, when Gran had opened her eyes.

'Gran! Can you hear me? Are you okay? Is it your heart?'

Her grandmother had winced and raised a hand to her head. 'Why are you shouting, Genevieve?' Then, looking about her, 'What are we doing here? Why are we on the bathroom floor?'

The calmness to her voice told Genevieve an ambulance wasn't necessary, but a doctor was. After she'd helped her grandmother to her feet and got her to sit on the edge of the bed – lying *in* bed was out of the question: 'Don't be absurd, Genevieve, you're making such a drama of it!' – she phoned the local surgery. Then, remembering she'd put the answerphone on, she called her father on his mobile. All the while, Gran kept grumbling at the fuss.

'I've only bumped my head. Anyone would think I'd severed a major artery the way you're carrying on.'

'And maybe that's your next party trick,' Genevieve

had answered back. 'That really would frighten me to death.'

'Oh, well, if it's death you're fretting about, save yourself the worry. There's nothing you or I can do to stop it happening.'

'Oh, be quiet, Gran. At least have the decency to act like you've had a narrow escape.'

Dad arrived within minutes, followed hotly by Polly and Nattie with Lily-Rose. Finally Dr Shepherd joined the throng and, after a few minutes alone with Gran, he pronounced his patient shaken but in reasonably good health.

'From what she says, it seems she had a blackout,' he told them. 'Her blood pressure's a little higher than I'd like, but I don't see any point in causing alarm by whisking her into hospital for exhaustive tests that will probably tell us no more than we already know. I suggest we leave things be and see how she gets on over the coming days. Don't hesitate to ring the surgery if you have any concerns.'

Part of Genevieve had wanted to disagree with the doctor and demand that the exhaustive tests he dismissed so lightly were carried out. But now, pouring boiling water into Gran's old brown Betty teapot, she saw the sense in what Dr Shepherd had said. Gran's blood pressure would soar if she was forced to lie in a strange hospital bed and subjected to endless prods and pokes. It would be better to keep an eye on her at home.

Polly went ahead of her to open the bedroom door, while Genevieve carried the tea upstairs and considered the best way to take care of Gran over the next few days. The simplest thing would be for her to move in with them at Paradise House, except there wasn't really room. The Rainbow Suite would be free at the weekend, but until then, unless Genevieve moved in with Polly and gave Gran her bedroom, she didn't see how to do it.

As she set the tray on Gran's bedside table her father said, 'Despite a difference of opinion, your grandmother will be having a guest to stay. Me.' Ignoring Gran's scowl, he added, 'It seems the easiest way, so long as you can handle things on your own, Genevieve?'

Relieved that a solution had been found so quickly, she said, 'I'll manage perfectly.'

As usual she had imagined that it would be she who had to sort things out. It struck her then that she was beginning to behave as though she didn't trust anyone else to get things done. When had that started? When had she begun to be so controlling of others? Was it because she thought she had her own life so tightly controlled that she imagined she could do the same with other people? Maybe Nattie had been right to criticise her for lumbering her with extra work because she wanted to cook something more challenging than bacon and eggs. Could it be that, deep down, she was as bossy and selfish as Nattie?

During breakfast the following morning, Genevieve had to give Nattie her due; without their father around, she was definitely trying to be more helpful. Nothing had been said, but a truce seemed to be in place. Prepared to bite her tongue if there was any lapse on her sister's part, Genevieve was relieved that Nattie hadn't once taken umbrage at being asked to do anything, and that she had even greeted the guests with something that resembled a welcoming smile as she took their orders. Her first negative comment of the day came now as she stood by the open back door trying to escape the sweltering heat of the kitchen.

'It beats me how that lot can still tuck away a fry-up in this weather. You'd think they'd want nothing more than a chilled glass of orange juice and half a grapefruit.' Then turning to Lily-Rose, who was sitting at the table and eating paper-thin slices of apple, she said, 'Pumpkin-Pie, how about a little paddle down at the beach when your Auntie Genvy's finished with me?'

Poking her finger through one of the slices of apple, Lily-Rose looked at Genevieve. 'Will you come as well?'

'I'd love to,' Genevieve said, spooning hot oil over the eggs in the spitting pan, 'but while Daddy Dean is keeping an eye on Gran, I need to go to the supermarket to do a big shop.'

'Mummy could help you.'

Genevieve laughed. 'An important rule, Lily-Rose: never push your luck. Especially not with a sister.'

The little girl looked thoughtful and proceeded to poke at another slice of apple. 'Mummy?'

'Yes.'

'When am I going to have a sister?'

Expecting Nattie to mutter something like, 'When hell freezes over,' Genevieve was surprised to hear her say, 'When I find one as gorgeous as you sleeping with the fairies at the end of the garden.'

Smiling, Genevieve slipped the cooked eggs onto the warmed plates of bacon, black pudding, sausage and tomatoes, and handed them to her sister to take through to the dining room.

When Nattie had gone, Lily-Rose said, 'How often does Mummy look at the end of the garden?'

Before Genevieve could think of a suitable reply, the phone rang. She switched off the radio and lifted the receiver.

'Genevieve, is that you?'

She hadn't spoken to him in a while, but she recognised Jonjo's voice at once. 'Hello, Jonjo. If you're hoping to speak to Polly, she's not here. She left for work over an hour ago.'

'I know; I've just spoken to her on her mobile. She said I needed to speak to you. The thing is; you're my last hope. I know it's last-minute stuff, but is there any chance of a couple of rooms being available this coming weekend? Christian and I are planning to meet with the builders and it's the only time we can both make it, assuming of course that Christian's mother doesn't get any worse. We've tried the pub in the village and they're fully booked. Like just about everything else. So, any room at the inn?'

Genevieve checked the diary to make sure no one else had taken a booking without letting her know. 'If you don't mind sharing, we've just had a cancellation, but I'm afraid it's –'

'That's brilliant! But tell me it's not a double bed. The thought of sleeping with Mr May doesn't appeal.'

'No it isn't. You're quite safe, it's a twin-bedded room, so people won't gossip too much.'

'Better and better. Now, depending on the traffic, we aim to be with you around lunchtime, is that okay?'

'Yes. One of us should be here to meet you. Probably me.'

'Oh, and before I forget, Christian says "Hi".'

'How's he doing, Jonjo? He was always so close to his parents.'

'He's coping pretty well, but I think the change at the weekend will do him good. Splitting up from his girlfriend probably hasn't helped either.'

This was news to Genevieve. 'When did that happen? He never mentioned anything in his emails.'

There was a silence and for a second Genevieve thought they'd been cut off. 'Are you still there, Jonjo?'

'Er . . . yes. Look, forget I said anything. If Christian hasn't mentioned it to you, it's certainly not my place to talk about it behind his back. I'd better go, my other phone's ringing. See you on Saturday. Thanks so much, Genevieve. Don't forget to give your cruets an extra polish for me, will you?'

Putting the receiver down, Genevieve was left with Adam's words echoing in her ears: *And if the girlfriend becomes history? Does that bring him within range?*

It might do, her treacherous heart whispered.

But her head had other ideas. No! She told herself firmly. Not again. She would not allow it to happen. She would not fall in love with Christian all over again.

That afternoon, she took a quiche and some ready-made salad she'd bought at the supermarket down to Gran's so that her father wouldn't have to worry about cooking an evening meal.

'How's she behaving?' Genevieve asked when he let her in at Angel Cottage.

'Like a badly behaved child. I'm nearly out of patience. I've threatened her with another visit from Dr Shepherd if she doesn't do as she's told and stay in bed.'

'Poor you. I don't envy you one little bit. She's not overdoing it with the Baxter Bell, is she?' The Baxter Bell was a small, brass hand-bell that came out from the bathroom cabinet whenever anyone was ill in bed.

'I'm surprised she hasn't broken it, but it's no more than you'd expect from her. Any news from up the hill? Anything I should know about?'

She told him about Lily-Rose wanting a sister, which she knew would amuse him, and then the conversation she'd had with Jonjo, about him and Christian booking in.

'And you're happy with that, for . . . for Christian to stay under the same roof?'

She was touched her father still had difficulty saying Christian's name. 'Christian and I have moved on. Life's too short to harbour grudges, Dad.'

'I know, Gen, but the moment he steps out of line, he'll have me to answer to.'

She smiled and, mimicking her grandmother, said,

'Goodness, Daddy Dean, you're becoming so brutish these days, I hardly know you!'

'Good! Because I've been doing some thinking and have reached an important decision. As soon as I think your Gran can be trusted to be on her own again, I'm going to New Zealand to see your mother.'

'You are? Really?'

'Yes, I'm going to do what I should have done weeks ago. I'm going to try and make her come home.'

Genevieve hugged him fiercely. 'So what's brought on this change of heart?'

'It was your grandmother's fall. It shook me up, made me realise we have no way of knowing what's around the corner, and maybe not everything should be left to resolve itself. Plus, your grandmother has just made a bargain with me; she promised to behave if I stopped being a coward and went and faced Serena.'

'Oh, Dad, you mustn't be too hard on yourself. We're all cowards sometimes.'

'I've buried my head deeper than most. I've let things go on and get worse because I couldn't bear the thought of losing your mother altogether. But it's a risk I have to take. I see that now. Some people say we only have one chance to get things right. Well, I disagree. I think if we're lucky, we get two. Either way, if we let those chances slip through our hands we have only ourselves to blame.'

This was nothing short of radical stuff coming from her father. She never dreamed she'd hear him talk so openly. Her hunch that he might resolve matters himself had been right, after all.

Above their heads, as if to add a musical flourish to his words, came a noise followed by the tinkling of the Baxter Bell.

'Let me go to her,' Genevieve said. 'You've earned a break.'

Genevieve had an ulterior motive; she was keen to

thank her grandmother for shaking up Dad. But when she stood in the doorway of Gran's bedroom, she saw that the old lady, head slumped to one side on the pillows, was asleep – the sound had been the bell falling out of her hand and landing on the floor. Genevieve crept into the room and was just placing the bell on the bedside table when her grandmother stirred.

'Sorry, Gran, I didn't mean to disturb you.'

Gran straightened her neck and looked at Genevieve through sleepy eyes. 'It's a bit late to be sorry, Serena. But I suppose it's better late than never. I hope you've apologised to Daddy Dean and the girls. You've caused them no end of heartache.'

'Gran, it's me, Genevieve.'

'Genevieve? Oh, I've no idea where she is. She's always so busy these days. But now you're home, she won't have to work so hard.' The old lady suddenly yawned and, closing her eyes, she leaned back against the pillows. 'Would you mind closing the door after you, Serena? I think I'll snatch a quick forty winks. I can't think why I'm so tired.'

Genevieve knew it was common for old people to muddle up members of their family, even imagining they were talking to a relative who'd died years ago, but Gran confusing her with Serena upset Genevieve more than she could say. But when she joined her father down in the kitchen and saw the look on his face – the upbeat look of a man who had, at last, decided to act – she knew she couldn't tell him of the conversation she'd just had with Gran. He would put off going to see Serena.

Later, as she walked home in the bright sunshine, threading her way through the crowds of trippers, she consoled herself with the thought that Gran was just tired. It was perfectly understandable that she could be confused, especially as Genevieve did bear quite a strong resemblance to her mother.

Chapter Thirty-two

The next morning, in a hurry to get all the chores done, Genevieve found herself thwarted at every turn. The telephone kept ringing and Donna was in one of her turbo-charged chatty moods. And it didn't matter which direction the conversation went – the weather, the ever-lowering interest rates, the mess in one of the bathrooms – she managed somehow to bring Tubby into it. On any other morning, Genevieve would have been amused by Donna's tales of what she and Tubby had got up to, but today she was tired and all she wanted to do was get down to Angel Cottage and put her mind at rest.

She'd lain awake in bed for hours last night worrying about her grandmother. Listening to the sounds of the seashore through the open window, then knowing she would never get to sleep, she'd crept downstairs to make herself a drink. She'd sat in the conservatory, watching the moonlight dancing across the water, wishing she didn't feel so anxious about Gran. For years they'd joked about her not being the full shilling, but Genevieve couldn't bear the thought that her beloved grandmother might really be losing her marbles. And what a silly expression that was, to describe an elderly person's heartbreaking decline into a world where they could no longer be reached.

She had eventually gone back to bed and snatched an hour's sleep before her alarm clock went off.

'So what do you think, Genevieve? Is it a good idea that will go down well in the village? If we make a reasonable fist of it, Tubby reckons it might become an annual event. A tradition.'

Realising she hadn't been paying attention to Donna, Genevieve looked up from the pillow she was knocking into shape. 'I'm sorry, Donna, what were you saying?'

'You okay? You seem sort of distracted. Still worried about your Gran?'

'A bit,' she said non-committally. 'But tell me what you were saying. What does Tubby think might become an annual event?'

'We've had this idea of putting on a charity talent contest at The Arms. You know the kind of thing, *Stars In Your Eyes*, people dressing up and belting out tunes we all know and love. There'd be an entrance fee and an extra charge if you want to take part, and any money we raise, after giving out some prizes, will go to a local charity. What do you think? Will people go for it?'

'Oh, I should think there are any number of people in Angel Sands who'd go for it like a shot. Look how they all enjoy karaoke nights.'

'So what about you? Will you take part?'

'Me? Good Lord, no! I can't hold a note to save my life.'

Donna laughed. 'That's the point. People would pay good money to hear you try.'

'No way! Absolutely not.'

'Is that your final word?'

'Yes. But I'll help in any other way you want. I'm better at the backstage stuff.'

Unlike Donna, she thought, when she walked down into the village an hour later. 'Who do you think I should have a crack at?' Donna had asked Genevieve. 'Bonnie Tyler or Tina Turner? Or there again, I can do a mean Shirley Bassey popping her cork and all.'

But Genevieve couldn't conceive of anything worse than performing in front of an audience. No matter how friendly or mellowed by alcohol they were.

She was doing her usual eyes-fixed-on-the-pavement routine as she passed Debonhair when a loud tap-tap-tap on the glass forced her to glance up. Brandishing her scissors and comb, Debs was standing over a petrified-looking man sitting in the chair nearest the window. It was a moment before Genevieve recognised her father. She went inside. The tiled floor around him was covered with a mat of thick grey hair.

He said, 'I only asked for a trim and look what she's done!'

'Get on with you!' Debs laughed. 'I'm giving him a makeover, just what he needs.' She swivelled his chair to face the mirror and began snipping at the nape of his neck, which was bone-white compared to the rest of his neck and face.

'Not too much off the back,' her father said, raising his head to speak, but Debs pushed it down again. From the depths of his chest, he mumbled, 'I thought I'd be in and out, Gen. I told your grandmother I'd just be a few –'

'You'll be out when I've finished with you,' Debs interrupted sternly. 'Just remember, I'm the one with the scissors in my hand.' Then to Genevieve, she said, 'Has Donna told you about the talent contest she and Tubby want to put on? I've offered to do everyone's hair, and if they want wigs, I can get hold of them, no problem. I'm trying to get your father to do a turn, but he won't have it. How about you, Gen? Are you going to loosen your stays and show us the real you?'

'Oh, I think you all know the real me,' Genevieve said.

Debs winked. 'A bit of letting go never hurt anyone.' Her voice was silky smooth. 'By the way, how's that young man of yours? I hear he's coming here again at the weekend. Staying at your place, too. That'll be cosy for you, won't it?'

Daddy Dean jerked his head up. 'Please,' he begged, 'I only came in for a trim. And that was nearly an hour ago.'

When finally Genevieve could get away – it really was breathtaking how much Debs knew about everyone – she left her father with the promise that she would send out a search party if he wasn't back by dusk.

A large herring gull was standing guard on Gran's gate. It eyed Genevieve suspiciously with its enormous beady eyes, and made no attempt to move until she clapped her hands loudly. It squawked, flapped its wings and flew off.

She let herself in. The sound of the television told her that Gran wasn't where she ought to be.

'I thought you were supposed to be in bed,' she chastised her grandmother, at the same time glad to see that there was plenty of colour back in her face. 'I've just spoken to Dad, and he said you'd promised to be good while he was having his hair done.'

'Your father, baloney! That man is getting above himself and if he doesn't watch his step – oh, be quiet a minute, it's *Bargain Hunt* and the auction's about to start. Come and sit down with me, Genevieve. Then I'll make us a nice cup of tea.'

Genevieve. Not Serena! So it had only been a one-off memory lapse. All the anxiety of last night instantly faded, and Genevieve sat on the sofa with her grandmother. She put her arm around the old lady and kissed her.

'What's that for?'

'For being your usual self.'

'And who else would I be?'

'Ssh! We're missing the programme. Yuck! What's that when it's home?'

'The Victorians used it for syringing out their ears and the Red Team stupidly paid twenty-five pounds for it.

Your father could do with cleaning out his ears. I've told him till I'm blue in the face that I don't need him here, that right now he's got more important things to be doing, like bringing Serena home. There! I knew it wouldn't make any money. I'm always right.'

In that moment, Genevieve had never been keener to believe her grandmother.

Chapter Thirty-three

The strain of cooking an evening meal and then getting up early to cook breakfast was taking its toll on Genevieve. It was a misconception that running a B & B was an easy option. The hours were long, practically twenty-four, and the pace relentless: to maintain the word-of-mouth recommendations and repeat bookings, which were essential, you couldn't afford a momentary drop in standards. And of course, during peak season, there was no chance of a lie-in, something Genevieve felt she badly needed right now. But given the choice, she'd rather be working long hours in Angel Sands than any-where else.

She was making the most of a short lull, relaxing on the steps outside the guest sitting room, watching Nattie read to Lily-Rose on the lawn. Polly was playing the piano. It was a beautifully restful and harmonious piece she'd heard her sister play before. She had no idea what it was, or who the composer was, but it matched per-fectly both the weather – there was a gentle breeze rippling the sea and cooling the intense heat – and Genevieve's mood. Despite being so tired, she felt calm: Gran was back to normal, bossing them all about with renewed vigour, and Dad, sporting his dramatic new haircut, was making arrangements to go and see Mum.

And on top of that, she was looking forward to seeing Christian and Jonjo. They wouldn't be arriving for another two hours, but she had everything ready. If they hadn't eaten on the way, there was plenty in the fridge.

Stretching her legs in front of her and lifting her long skirt above her knees, she thought of what Adam had said about her having great legs. Silly man! Okay, they weren't the worst legs in the world, but they were hardly a match for Kylie's or Nicole Kidman's. As a girl she had badly wanted to be a ballerina, and at their mother's instigation all three sisters had attended Miss Marian White's School of Dancing, but only Polly had stayed the course. Nattie had said she'd rather shoot herself than prance about like a prissy idiot (this was after her one and only lesson) and, by the age of eleven, Genevieve had grown too tall. Standing head and shoulders above all the other girls made her feel cloddish and clumsy. That was when she'd taken up swimming. Even today, if she heard the opening bars of *Swan Lake*, she instinctively closed her eyes and pictured herself as a sylph-like ballerina en pointe: she was always dressed in pale blue chiffon and was as light on her feet as Polly.

For years she had envied Polly her long, graceful legs and delicate features, and Nattie her straight up-and-down, tomboy shape. Now, eventually, she had come to terms with the way she looked. She took after her mother, with what Serena called a golden-age Hollywood hour-glass figure. 'Where would Rita Hayworth, Jane Russell, Marilyn Monroe, or Betty Grable have been without their sashaying hips and luscious cleavages?' she had often told Genevieve.

Adam had also described her as attractive and sexy. She liked being called sexy, even if there was no one to share her sexiness with. Anyone eavesdropping on that rather odd conversation might have leapt to the conclusion that there was a danger of Adam transferring his affections from one sister to another. But Genevieve knew Adam was much too sensible to make that mistake. Strangely though, she knew that from now on things would be different between them, now he wasn't trying to win over Nattie. It was going to take some getting used to not being the sympathetic shoulder. She wondered, though, if he could really do it – give up on Nattie. There again, he was one of the most decisive men she knew. So perhaps he could.

Behind her in the sitting room, Polly had started playing something else, something brisk and robust. She closed her eyes and wondered whether it might be fun to organise a picnic tomorrow, like the last time Jonjo and Christian had come down. It would depend on how busy they were, and if they would be around long enough after their meeting with the builder.

Before long, the piano music and Nattie's voice as she read to Lily-Rose, became as distant and muffled as the cries of happy children playing on the beach below, and she slept. She dreamed she was floating on her back in the sea, the waves lapping around her, caressing her lightly, but best of all, her mother was there too, at her side. It was a lovely dream and when the sound of an approaching car shooed it away, she opened her eyes reluctantly. Assuming the car belonged to a guest – they all had a key to let themselves in – she stayed where she was. Then she heard footsteps and a familiar voice.

'Hel-*lo!* Anyone at home?'

Jonjo and Christian? Already? She checked her watch. It was almost twelve. She stood up and straightened her skirt in time to see them coming round the corner of the house.

'You're very early. Was there less traffic than you expected?'

'We decided to set off earlier than planned,' said Jonjo, 'in case the roads ground to a halt or the tarmac melted in the midday sun.' He cocked his ear and smiled. 'Is that the light of my life serenading my arrival?' Without giving Genevieve a chance to respond, he walked the length of the terrace and stepped inside the house to the guest sitting room: the music stopped abruptly.

'If I start apologising for him now,' Christian said with a weary shrug, 'I could spend the entire weekend doing it. Can you just accept that he's a lunatic and humour him?'

'Come off it, Christian, he fits in perfectly with us Baxters. Anyway, officially you're both guests so I have to humour the pair of you.' Then taking in how tired he looked, she said, 'How are you?'

'Completely knackered. Any chance you can find me a quiet spot in the garden where I can sleep for the next twenty-four hours?'

'You're in luck. Dad's rigged up a hammock in the orchard.'

'Lead me to it!'

While Polly showed Christian and Jonjo their room, Genevieve prepared lunch, a choice of mini baguettes filled with smoked mackerel pâté and fresh crab. As she buttered the baguettes, she reflected on Christian's appearance. He hadn't been exaggerating when he'd said he was knackered. Fatigue was etched around his eyes; he looked burdened. She doubted whether he'd slept or eaten properly since his mother had gone into hospital. More than once she'd had to repeat something she'd said, and there was a difference in his voice – some of the sounds seemed to get caught in the back of his throat. She remembered how, as a teenager, whenever he'd been tired, it had been more of an effort for him to keep the timbre of his voice evenly pitched and to keep up with the conversation. The strain of his mother's illness was clearly affecting him deeply.

'I thought we'd eat in the garden,' Genevieve said, when Polly came into the kitchen. She looked flushed, Genevieve noticed. 'How are our guests settling in?'

'Jonjo loved the view.'

'I bet he did! Right, I think I've got everything ready for lunch. Will you give me a hand taking it outside? Oh. By the way, where's Nattie and Lily-Rose?'

'They've gone down to see Gran.'

'And Dad?'

'Helping Tubby to creosote his garden fence.'

Genevieve wrinkled her nose. 'What a revolting job for a day like today. Okay, you take the plates and cutlery and I'll manage the tray.'

They ate their lunch in the private area of garden in the shade. Jonjo did most of the talking. He raved about Christian's designs for his new home and boasted that it would be the best house in the area. Occasionally Christian would roll his eyes and exchange a smile with Genevieve, but his input to the conversation was minimal. When they'd finished eating, he offered to help Genevieve clear away.

'There's no need, there's hardly anything to do,' she said.

'But if I don't move, I'll nod off. Besides, I'm under orders from the Boss to make myself scarce.' He nodded in Jonjo's direction.

Leaving Polly and Jonjo alone, they went inside the house. They worked in silence at first, then she asked him again about his mother. She'd asked him in the garden, but he'd avoided going into any detail.

'She's had a run of good days,' he said, 'which is why I agreed to come down. But it won't last, the doctor says. The prognosis is weeks rather than months. What I can't handle is the suddenness of it. One minute the doctor is saying she's anaemic and the next she's in hospital having lumps cut out of her.'

'Oh, Christian, I'm so sorry. I don't know how I'd cope if I were in your shoes.' She told him about Gran and how worried she'd been over her fall. 'I know it's nothing compared to what you're going through.'

He disagreed. 'You're probably as close to her as you are to your parents. She's always been there for you. You know, I always envied you your family.'

'And I always envied you your quiet, self-contained little unit of three.'

He turned and looked out of the window. She heard him say, 'And then there was one.'

At six o'clock Christian and Jonjo returned from Ralph's barn after a lengthy, but according to Christian successful, meeting with the builder, a man from Haverfordwest who had been chosen because he'd worked on barn conversions before. But with six evening meals to prepare, there was no time for Genevieve to sit and chat, or to admire the intricate model Christian had made of the house-to-be. Christian said he and Jonjo wouldn't add to her workload and would eat out. 'We'll try the Salvation Arms,' he said.

'I don't mind cooking for you.'

'But it doesn't feel right, you waiting on us hand and foot.'

'But it's my job. It's what you're paying me to do.'

In the end, a compromise was reached. Jonjo asked Polly to go out with him for the evening and Christian said he'd eat whatever Genevieve wanted to cook, on the condition he ate in the kitchen with her.

'Not a good idea,' she said, 'Nattie will be around. Tell you what; we'll eat after everyone else, in the garden. Agreed?'

Smiling, he said, 'I don't remember you driving such a hard bargain.'

She cooked him sea bass with polenta and a salad with a sweet balsamic dressing. At midnight, they were still sitting in the garden. The night air was heavy and soft, a faint breeze skimmed her bare arms, and the incoming tide, slowly creeping up the moon-washed shore, rattled the loose pebbles in the sand. The calming sound was lost on Christian, but Genevieve could tell from his face, through the flickering candlelight on the table, that he was more relaxed than when he'd arrived. The tense lines had gone from his brow, and his voice was more evenly pitched. She wondered if now was the right time to ask him about Caroline. Perhaps not. It was none of her business, after all.

'This is so good,' he said simply, gazing out at the moon trailing its silvery reflection across the flat sea. He turned to look at her, his eyes dark and intense.

'It's one of the reasons I came back,' she replied.

'What were the others?'

'You don't want to know.'

'A boyfriend?'

She laughed. 'You're obsessed! Always trying to dig around in my patchy romantic past.'

'I think obsessed is stretching it a bit. Interested is nearer the mark.'

'Well, it didn't have anything to do with a failed relationship.' She could have told him about the robbery, about George and Cecily, but decided against it. She didn't want to think of anything that would spoil the moment.

By the time Christian and Jonjo made it down to the dining room for breakfast the next morning – Jonjo boasting that he'd already been for a jog – the rest of the guests had either left for the day or were in the garden reading the papers before deciding what to do.

'Where's Polly?' enquired Jonjo, when Genevieve asked them what they'd like to eat.

'At church with Gran and Lily-Rose. She plays the organ when the local man is off sick or on holiday.'

His disappointment showing, he said, 'What time will she be back?'

Genevieve checked her watch. 'In about an hour.'

His face brightened. 'So time for me to grab a slimline poached egg on a slice of wholemeal toast and a glass of orange juice before I surprise her and God? Is the church far?'

'Ten minutes' walk.' She told him where St Non's was, then turned to Christian. 'A healthy breakfast for you too?'

'No chance. Give me the works. Whatever you've got, please. I slept like a log and now I could eat a hog!'

'In that case, I'll do you a Paradise Special. Tea or coffee?'

'Tea, please. And if it's no trouble, see to Jonjo's breakfast before mine. I don't want him hanging about making derogatory comments about my fat intake.'

Jonjo was off as soon as he'd finished his breakfast, and Genevieve sat with Christian while he ate the Paradise Special – eggs, bacon, sausage, black pudding, fried bread, tomatoes, mushrooms and waffles to finish.

'I feel very rude eating in front of you,' Christian said. 'Why don't you have something to keep me company? Even though I was famished, I'll never get through all this.'

'If it makes you feel better, I'll pinch one of your waffles.'

'Is that all? How about a sausage? Or some bacon?'

'No. You need building up.'

'I do?'

'Yes. You've lost weight, haven't you? Remember, I know all about weight loss. I know a shrinking body when I see one.'

'It's not been deliberate, I just haven't had time. I've

been working all day, then spending every evening with Mum.'

'But you mustn't make yourself ill. That isn't what your mother would want. Have you been in touch with her since you arrived?'

'Yes, by text.'

Genevieve was impressed. 'She's quite a techno-whizz, then? I can't imagine either of my parents getting their heads round text messages. Come to think of it, I'm not that hot myself. I don't even own a mobile. I'd probably lose it or forget how to work the wretched thing.'

He smiled. 'Mum's always been at the forefront of anything new. But there again, texting has been a part of our lives for years. We've arranged for the hospital to call me if ... if there's an emergency.'

'So how is she?'

'She says she's okay. But we both know that's a lie. She tells me what she thinks I want to hear.'

'That might well be true. But you have to bear in mind that people who are ill need rules to play by.'

He stirred his tea. 'You're right. But I'm lousy at pretence. It doesn't come naturally to me.'

'You should be more like us Baxters. We've mastered the art of denial.'

'Is that what you did when you were . . . ' He stopped stirring his tea and looked awkward.

'It's okay, Christian, you can refer to my starve, binge or bust days without embarrassing me.' Then, changing the subject, she said, 'Presumably we're still on for the picnic?'

'Absolutely.'

The guest list for the picnic kept growing.

When Polly arrived back from St Non's with Lily-Rose and Jonjo, she said they had invited Gran to join them.

Or more particularly, Jonjo had invited their grand-mother.

'You're sure it won't be too much for her?' asked Genevieve.

'She seemed her sprightly old self in church,' Polly said, 'so I don't see why not. Anyway, Jonjo can always take her home if she gets tired, since it was his bright idea. She seems very taken with him.'

'And why wouldn't she be?' interrupted Jonjo. He put his arm round Polly's waist. 'All in all, I think I made quite an impression on the old ladies at St Non's. My only disappointment was that Polly hardly batted an eyelid when I slipped into the front pew while everyone was praying and blew her a kiss. And there was me thinking she'd fall off her stool straight into my arms. I had plans to carry her up to the altar and ask the vicar to marry us there and then.'

Something in Polly's smile told Genevieve that had Jonjo carried her up to the altar, she wouldn't have protested. She thought back to that night when they'd all been in Polly's room and her sister had been standing at the window dressed in a pair of their father's old pyjamas, but had still managed to look like the proverb-ial princess waiting for her prince. So was Jonjo her prince? Certainly he was charming, but was he a stayer? Or would he, once he'd had his wicked way – to extend the fairy tale analogy – be off, leaving Polly with a broken heart? Only time would tell.

Meanwhile, Nattie, back early from seeing a friend, announced that she and Lily-Rose would be joining the picnic. She said she'd enjoy the chance to grill Jonjo and Christian on what they would be doing to Ralph's barn. Then, of course, it would have been heartless to leave Daddy Dean at home on his own, so he too was added to their number.

Eventually they set off, picking up Gran on the way,

and drove in two cars to Tawelfan beach, chosen above Angel Sands by Gran, who insisted that Jonjo show her where he'd be living, even though she was perfectly well acquainted with Ralph's barn. Polly's comment that Gran was quite taken with him was a massive under-statement; she was utterly enamoured.

'Such a delightful young man,' she whispered in Genevieve's ear, after they'd bounced along the rutted, sun-dried track towards the barn and were unloading the boot of Jonjo's Discovery. 'So handsome. If Polly has any sense she'll hang on to this one. They'd have the most beautiful children.'

Apart from Gran, they all carried something – light-weight chairs, the hamper, the cool bag of drinks, towels, two parasols, a fishing net, a bucket and spade and an inflatable dolphin, which Lily-Rose carried like an enor-mous baby in her arms. As they made the trek through the sand dunes to the beach, Genevieve was reminded of long-ago picnics with their father leading the way. On this occasion he was at the rear of the group, walking slowly with Gran, a supporting hand discreetly resting under her elbow. Genevieve had yet to hear her father exchange more than two gruff words with Christian.

As they'd expected, the beach was busy. They found themselves a suitable plot and began setting up camp. Quick as a flash, Lily-Rose stripped down to her fluores-cent pink bikini bottoms and said she was going for a paddle.

'Oh, not yet,' yawned Nattie. 'Can't you wait ten minutes?'

'That's okay,' Genevieve said, 'I'll take her. Where's the suncream?'

Her sister tossed her the bottle. 'Thanks, Gen. I owe you.'

'Anyone else fancy a paddle?' asked Genevieve,

rubbing factor thirty-five into Lily-Rose's smooth skin. 'Gran?'

'No thanks, love, I've just got settled.' She was already installed in her deckchair. 'Oh,' she said, as though suddenly remembering something vitally important. 'You did pack a thermos of tea, didn't you?'

'Of course I did, Gran.'

'And my favourite almond shortbread?'

'Need you ask? Lily-Rose, we won't be going anywhere unless you stop fidgeting and let me finish putting this cream on you. There now, that's you done.'

Slipping off his deck shoes and pulling his tee-shirt over his head, Christian said, 'Mind if I come along as well?'

Lily-Rose grabbed hold of his hand. 'Do you want Genvy to rub some suncream on your shoulders?'

He didn't catch what the little girl said. He turned to Genevieve for help, and she felt herself unaccountably blush at the thought of touching his bare skin. 'Lily was just asking if you were ready to go.'

'Ooh, you little liar!' smirked Nattie from behind Christian's back. Genevieve glared at her.

Christian left his mobile with Jonjo, and they set off for the distant water's edge – the tide was out. Lily-Rose scampered on ahead, a castle-shaped plastic bucket swinging like a handbag from her wrist. Genevieve was again reminded of the past, of herself and Christian, hand in hand, walking this very same stretch of beach. She wondered if he was thinking the same. They soon caught up with Lily-Rose and, holding her wrap-around skirt above her knees, Genevieve ventured into the first rush of shallow water.

Christian, beside her, glanced back up the beach. 'They all rely on you heavily, don't they?'

Genevieve shrugged. 'Do they? I've never thought of it quite that way.'

'They'd find it hard to manage without you.'

'They did before I came back.'

'But that was when your mother was here.'

'Look! *Look!*'

Both Genevieve and Christian bent down to see what Lily-Rose was pointing at: it was a starfish, about the size of Lily's hand. 'Can I have it? Can I put it in my bucket to take home?'

It was obviously dead. 'I don't see why not,' Genevieve said.

The little girl picked it up and carefully put it into her bucket. 'I'm going to show Mummy my lucky starfish,' she said proudly. She ran off excitedly, hopping skilfully around the pebbles and other people on the beach. They watched her until she was safely with the family.

'Shall we walk to the rocks?' Christian said.

They walked along the shore. As they approached the rocks, a group of teenage girls, who had been using them to sunbathe on, swam off. Dangling their legs over the side of the sun-warmed rocks, Genevieve touched his arm lightly. He turned to face her.

'This is where I pushed you into the water, isn't it, the day we met?'

'It's also where I thought you were the nicest and prettiest girl I'd ever met.'

'Your memory must be playing tricks on you. I was never a pretty child.'

He shook his head. 'I'm not going to argue with you, Genevieve, so be quiet and accept the compliment.'

His words, said so forcibly, amused her. She swirled the water round with her feet, enjoying the sensation of her toes being gently pushed apart.

'Genevieve?'

She turned back to him. 'Yes?'

'Do you remember me saying at breakfast that I like to be honest and play it straight?'

'I do. But if this is a complaint about the standard of your accommodation, or that you're suffering from indigestion, forget it; you're not getting a discount on your bill.'

He smiled, but somehow still managed to look serious. 'No, it has nothing to do with that. It's something I want you to know. Several weeks ago I stupidly tried to kiss you; at the time you wisely pointed out that it wasn't a good idea. As we both know, you were right, and for two reasons: one, our complicated past, and two, because I was in a relationship.' He paused, just long enough for her to see how hard this was for him. And for her to feel guilty that she already knew what he was about to say. 'The thing is,' he continued, 'I'm not in a relationship any more. Caroline and I . . . well, I've ended things with her. I just wanted you to know that.'

Genevieve didn't bother to feign surprise. Instead, she said, 'And the reason?'

'Do you really need to ask that?'

'I think I do.'

He took a deep breath. 'It wouldn't have been fair to go on seeing her, not when – ' He broke off and swallowed. 'Genevieve, you must have realised that ever since our paths crossed again, I haven't been able to get you out of my head.' He turned away. 'I promised myself I wouldn't say anything, but I guess I'm being selfish. I want you to know how I feel. More than that, I want to know how you feel, too.'

She touched his leg to make him look at her. 'Perhaps it's nothing more than curiosity you're feeling? A desire to relive the past.'

He blinked. 'All I know is that I can't think of you and not wonder what it might have been like between us. It's always there.'

'Some might call it unfinished business.'

'No. It's more than that. There's something between

us. Something that will always link us.'

She was surprised by his vehemence. Surprised too by her calm reaction.

'So where does that leave us?' he said. He looked and sounded wretched.

'Precariously placed, I'd say.'

He frowned and stared hard at her lips. 'What placed?'

'Precariously,' she repeated, trying to speak more distinctly, even though she knew it annoyed him and didn't really help. 'We either do nothing and go on wondering for the rest of our lives what might have been, or we throw caution to the wind and you try kissing me.' So much for her head ruling her heart!

His solemn face softened instantly. 'I think I favour the second choice.'

'Me too.'

He had just raised his hand to her neck, and tilted his head to lean into her, when he hesitated and drew back. Following his gaze, over her shoulder, she turned to see Jonjo hurrying towards them, waving Christian's mobile. The look on Jonjo's face made her reach out for Christian's hand.

'I'm sorry, Christian,' he said, 'but it's your mother. The hospital's just been in touch. We need to get going.'

PART IV

Chapter Thirty-four

Christian's mother died three days later. She spent the last thirty-six hours of her life in a coma with Christian at her side. Saddened by his loss, Genevieve was touched when Jonjo phoned to say that Christian wanted her to be at the funeral. Polly too, to keep her company.

Now, as Genevieve turned off the A44 and joined the B4361 heading towards Ludlow, happy memories of staying with Christian all those years ago, came flooding back. Along with some fond memories of his mother. Ella May had been a kind, straightforward woman with a sense of humour, not averse to teasing her husband or her son. Genevieve had always been struck by how supportive she was of Christian, without overprotecting him. A lot of mothers might have wrapped him in cotton wool. Not Ella; she had always encouraged him to go one step further than he thought he was capable of.

Ella had been a considerate host as well, and had always made Genevieve feel part of the family, whether it was at Pendine Cottage or here in Shropshire. During one of Genevieve's visits to Pendine Cottage, in a light-hearted moment after they'd been playing cards, Ella had told Genevieve that she would have liked more children, especially a daughter. Certainly, in Christian's current situation, a brother or sister would help to share the load with him. Though Polly was impractical, and Nattie a pain on occasion, Genevieve knew that in a crisis they would be there for each other. From what Jonjo had told her, Christian had no close family members to turn to.

'There are plenty of ageing rellies he hardly knows,' Jonjo had said on the phone, 'but no one who really matters to him.'

Following the directions Christian had emailed, Genevieve turned into a winding country lane lined either side with verdant hawthorn and wilting cow parsley. It was instantly familiar. She recalled a time when Christian had chased her down it. The rain had recently stopped and, wearing a pair of his too-large Wellington boots, she'd tripped and pitched, almost headfirst, into a squelchy ditch. He'd been so concerned that he didn't realise, until he was pulling her out, that she was laughing and not crying. Catching him unawares, to get her own back, she'd pushed him into the muddy ditch. They'd returned home wet and filthy. After they'd washed and changed, Mrs May had laid out an old-fashioned tea of hot buttered crumpets in front of the fire.

The house was just as Genevieve remembered it: a pretty, half-timbered, thatched cottage (originally it had been two) with an off-centre porch swamped in honeysuckle. Sunshine bounced off the polished, leaded windows, and Genevieve felt heartened that the house hadn't been allowed to slide into decline. She parked the car next to Christian's Volvo and nudged Polly.

'We're here, Polly. Wakey, wakey.' Having been up since five, Genevieve would have liked the opportunity to doze as well. Determined in some small way to help Christian, she had offered to take care of feeding the funeral guests and had put together a modest buffet. It was in the boot and she hoped it had survived the journey.

Leaving Polly to stir herself, Genevieve got out of the car and went round to the boot, but before she'd got it open, she heard footsteps. Christian was coming towards her, dressed in a dark suit with a white shirt, open at the neck. She had never seen him in a suit before and at once thought how dazzlingly handsome he looked. Her heart fluttered and she felt a tightening in her chest. But his face, pale and sombre, showed her the inappropriateness of her reaction. Without a word passing between them, they embraced. Held within his firm grasp, she could feel the tension in his body.

The funeral was to be held in a small local church that would take them no more than ten minutes to reach. The procession of cars moved sedately along the narrow country lanes. Following behind in Jonjo's Discovery, Genevieve sat in the back and stared out at the flowering hedgerows; she left Polly and Jonjo to their murmured conversation in front. Christian had wanted her to sit in the lead car with him, but there hadn't been room: a surprising number of distant relatives had turned up. They had appeared en masse for a pre-service glass of sherry. Confirming what Jonjo had told Genevieve, Christian admitted they were practically unknown to him.

By the time Jonjo had found somewhere to park, they were the last to arrive. They slipped in at the back of the crowded church – friends and neighbours had shown up in force – but within seconds Christian appeared and said he'd saved them a seat at the front with him.

'Please,' he said, taking hold of Genevieve's hand, 'I don't want to be alone.'

The service was much the same as any other funeral she had been to: hymns were sung, prayers were spoken, emotions were strained. But then the vicar, looking straight at Christian, asked him to step forward to say a few words about his mother. Letting go of Genevieve's hand, which he'd been holding during most of the service, he walked towards the lectern. From the pocket of his jacket, he pulled out a piece of paper and unfolded it slowly, the microphone in front of him picking up the noise, amplifying it to a crackling roar. Oblivious, he stared at his audience and visibly composed himself.

'All mothers have an extraordinary capacity to love and to encourage,' he began, 'and mine was no exception. She taught me to love and respect others as I would want to be loved and respected. It's a tall order sometimes, and I know I've fallen short more times than I care to admit, but my mother never did. She –' His voice cracked and he briefly closed his eyes. Genevieve's throat clenched and she willed him to carry on. 'She was unfailingly constant,' he continued, his tone less clear, 'a constant beacon of love and hope. Someone we could all aspire to be. I shall miss her more than I can say.' He bowed his head, folded the piece of paper and stepped away.

Around her Genevieve could hear people, including Polly and Jonjo, clearing their throats and blowing their noses. She blinked hard and kept her gaze on the flower arrangements either side of the coffin. She felt, rather than saw, Christian take his seat beside her. She turned to face him and mouthed the words, 'Well done. That was beautiful.'

He nodded and squeezed her hand. 'Thank you.'

He thanked her again when they were back at the house and the last of the guests were leaving. Jonjo and Polly were at the door, waving them off.

'You've been such a help,' Christian said as she moved round the sitting room with a tray, gathering plates and glasses.

'It's nothing,' she said. 'Canapés aren't difficult to make, just a bit fiddly and time-consuming.'

He took the tray from her. 'But you must have been up so early to make them.'

'I was. But I shall sleep well tonight.'

'You are staying, aren't you?'

'If the offer's still on. Yes.'

Jonjo and Polly came back into the room. Jonjo said, 'I blame you, Genevieve. If the food hadn't been so good, we would have been shot of that lot hours ago.'

Christian smiled – the first time he had that day – and said, 'I don't know about the rest of you, but I've had enough. I vote we leave the rest of the tidying up till later. Let's go and sit in the garden with a bottle of wine.'

It was only ten o'clock when Genevieve started to yawn. 'It's no good,' she apologised, stifling yet another yawn, 'I have to go to bed.'

Everyone else agreed that they were tired too, that it had been a long day. After locking up and turning out the lights, they went upstairs. Just as Genevieve remembered, there was a long, L-shaped landing with five bedrooms and two bathrooms leading off. Christian opened the door of the first room and told Polly that it was hers. Next door was Jonjo's room, and going further along the landing, missing out his parents' room, he said, 'I thought you'd like to sleep in the room you stayed in before. If you need anything, I'm in the room the other side of the bathroom.'

It felt slightly comical as they all stood on the landing and said goodnight to each other. Typically it was Jonjo who summed up the moment. 'Anyone for a bedroom farce?' he asked, with a mischievous grin. He kissed Polly on the cheek, and after watching them disappear to their respective rooms, Christian said, 'Well, then, I'll say goodnight. Remember, anything you need, I'm –'

'I know; you're just the other side of the bathroom.'

She had only been in bed a short while when she heard footsteps, followed by the sound of a door creaking open, then shutting. Jonjo and Polly, no doubt. She smiled sleepily to herself. The bedroom farce had begun.

*

She didn't know how long she'd been asleep, but she awoke with a start. Footsteps. She could hear footsteps. Someone was in the house. A burglar! Her mouth went dry and fear bubbled up inside her. She tried hard to keep calm. To think logically. To put the night of the robbery out of her mind. It's probably Christian, she told herself. Or maybe Jonjo and Polly. But what if it wasn't?

Her heart began to beat faster. She pushed back the duvet. She couldn't just lie here. She had to check. She hadn't acted fast enough once before, but not this time. She crept onto the landing and stood for a moment to make out where the noise was coming from and to orientate herself.

She took the stairs slowly, grasping the balustrade and holding her breath. For a second she wondered what the hell she was doing. If it was a burglar, what was she going to do?

Go back upstairs, her head told her. Knock on Christian's door. Get help.

But he wouldn't hear, would he?

Knock on Jonjo's door, then.

No. He was in with Polly.

Not knowing quite how she'd got there, she found herself at the bottom of the stairs. Where was the noise now? But she couldn't hear anything other than her pulse banging like an enormous drum inside her head. This is madness, she thought. I shouldn't be doing this. Yet still her body betrayed her and she reached for a heavy vase on the hall table as her feet carried her forward.

To the sitting room.

Burglars always made for the sitting room first. For the hi-fi. The video. Antique knick-knacks. Stuff they could easily sell on with no questions asked. She pushed open the door and stepped in. The french doors were open, the curtains billowing. She was right! A gust of cool air rushed at her and she knew what she had to do.

She had to fetch help. She couldn't do this alone.

She turned to retrace her steps, but the sight of a shadowy figure coming into the room rooted her to the spot. The vase slipped from her hands and she screamed.

But no sound came out of her mouth. *Oh God, it couldn't happen again!* The blood drained from her, her legs buckled and she fell to the ground.

She came to with a painful jolt of panicky fear and let out a small cry.

Arms held her and a voice said, 'Genevieve, it's okay. It's me, Christian.'

Confused and light-headed, she tried to focus. Christian's face became clear. As did the reason she'd come downstairs. *The burglar!* Where was he? Agitated, she looked around, took in that she was lying on the sofa, that there was a lamp on, and that Christian was kneeling in front of her. Beside him, on the carpet, was a broken vase, and behind him, the french doors were open and the curtains still moving. Her agitation grew and she sat up with a jerk.

'Have you called the police? Did he get away?'

'No, Gen. There's no need. It was me you saw. I'm so sorry I frightened you. I couldn't sleep and –'

'No. I would have recognised you. Of course I would. It wasn't you. It was . . . '

He took her hands in his and rubbed them gently. 'It was dark, Gen. There were no lights on. You couldn't see properly.'

She forced herself to listen to him, to believe what he was saying. Looking at the broken bits of china, she slowly realised that the only intruder had been the one inside her head. She covered her face with her hands. 'Oh, God. I'm so sorry. I feel so –' Stupidly she began to tremble. When he took her in his arms she started to cry.

'It's okay,' he murmured. 'It's my fault, I shouldn't

have scared you.' He held her close, and she cried all the more.

She had had to tell the policemen all about that dreadful night with George and Cecily, but she'd told no one else exactly what had gone on. She'd told Gran the most, but each time she had been tempted to unburden herself fully, the thought of reliving the robbery was too much and she was almost physically sick.

But now she knew that the time had come to tell someone. She didn't want to be haunted by the memories any longer. Wrapped in Christian's arms, she felt safe enough to relive the trauma.

When the two masked men had demanded the code for the safe and George had refused, the robbery had turned into something altogether more terrifying. One of the men had seized hold of Cecily and beaten her savagely, kicking and punching her frail body, his boots smashing into her in a terrifying frenzy of mindless violence. It was only the other man pulling him off that made him stop. The terror and pain in Cecily's eyes, as the two men then argued and yelled at each other, was too much to bear, and both Genevieve and George had tried to shuffle over to her so they could comfort her. But the men, seeing what they were doing, stepped in and the more violent of the two struck out and viciously kicked George. He then turned on Genevieve, catching the side of her head with such a ferocious blow she was knocked back against the wall, to feel a further thud of pain. The sickening look of pure sadistic pleasure on his face had frightened her most and it haunted her still. He ripped the tape from George's mouth, just long enough for him to give them the code for the safe. After they'd taken the jewellery and what-ever else they wanted, they left.

As soon as Genevieve was sure they were alone, she

wriggled to slide her wrists, which were tied behind her back, under her body and brought them up to her mouth to remove the tape, using her teeth she slowly released her hands. She then shuffled across the room to George and Cecily and uncovered their mouths. Almost as though opening her mouth and breathing in a gulp of oxygen was too much for her, the old lady grimaced and cried out.

By the time the ambulance arrived, Cecily was already dead: her heart – weakened by an earlier heart attack – had failed. Poor George never recovered from the shock. He died a month later in hospital following a massive stroke. Although desperate to go home to her family, Genevieve had stayed on in the house on her own and visited George every day; she'd held his hand, helped him to eat, and read to him, albeit very badly. He and his wife had no children. They'd both been nearly ninety and most of their friends had already died, so Genevieve was his only regular visitor, other than his solicitor and accountant.

At last she fell quiet.

Christian said nothing, just held her hand and stroked her hair.

The relief at having finally unburdened herself was so great that Genevieve began to cry silent tears.

Christian continued to hold her close. 'It's okay, Genevieve, you're safe now.'

It was light when Genevieve awoke. She turned over and saw that Christian had been true to his word. There he was, asleep in the chair in the corner of her bedroom, a blanket sliding off his legs. She had been so shaken that he had refused to leave her alone. He'd been so very kind and loving. He'd sat with her for more than an hour, passing her tissue after tissue, holding her, reassuring her, then making her a drink and bringing her upstairs to bed. It was a miracle they hadn't disturbed the others.

Feeling groggy from all the crying, she remembered how brave people thought she'd been during and after the robbery; how well she'd coped. But she hadn't coped in the right way. Just as she'd bottled up her feelings about her grandfather when he'd died, she'd tried to suppress the horror of that night. During the robbery, when they'd had their mouths taped, they'd been unable to cry out or scream. She realised now that was why she hadn't been able to scream last night in the sitting room. Her brain had played some kind of sick trick on her. Yet reliving her terror had released something inside her. Christian had suggested that maybe now, after shedding so many tears, she would let the memories go.

'You need to be able to remember what happened without reliving it,' he'd said. 'Once you can do that, you'll know you're over it.'

She looked across the room to Christian and hoped he was right. He was still sleeping soundly. The blanket had slipped off his legs now but she resisted the urge to get out of bed and cover him again. Instead she studied his face, the face she'd memorised as a teenager, the face she'd idolised and looked up to, the face she'd thought she'd always love. Was it possible to love him again? Was that what he wanted? More to the point, was it what *she* wanted?

She sighed and thought how unfair it was that while she was asleep she undoubtedly looked awful – mouth open, hair to hell – but Christian managed to look even more attractive than usual. Younger, too. The temptation to wake him with a kiss was so strong she had to remind herself why she was here. They had buried his mother yesterday; it wasn't the moment.

There had been no opportunity since that day on the beach, when they'd so very nearly kissed, to talk about what they'd discussed or what the consequences might be if they really did resurrect their old relationship. In the circumstances she sensed that, for now, all Christian needed was a friend.

Chapter Thirty-five

Genevieve had thought for a long time that the most momentous events in her life had all taken place during the summer months.

She thought this now as she and Polly were driving home to Paradise House. Polly hadn't said anything but, judging from the radiant look of her, Genevieve didn't have to be a genius to work out that her sister had spent the night with Jonjo and had loved every moment of it. There had been no sign of the two of them at breakfast. After Genevieve and Christian had given up waiting for them, Christian had suggested they make the most of the early morning sun.

'What will you do with the house?' Genevieve had asked when they were settled in the garden.

'The sensible thing would be to sell it, but I can't think of doing that yet. It's too soon.'

'Of course. I didn't mean to sound insensitive.'

'You couldn't be insensitive if you tried, Genevieve.'

Frowning, she said, 'You really mustn't make the mistake of thinking too well of me.'

A plump woodpigeon landed heavily on a branch of the chestnut tree at the end of the garden, and they both watched it for a while as it tried to steady itself on the flimsy, wobbling branch.

Christian said, 'I know you might not want to talk about what happened last night, Genevieve, but if you do –'

'It's okay,' she interrupted, 'I think I'm all talked out on that particular subject.'

He smiled ruefully. 'Are you sure? Or are you telling me to back off?'

'A bit of both. I think I need time to recover from how stupid I've been.'

'You haven't been stupid. Far from it. You've been incredibly brave.'

'It doesn't feel that way.'

'That's because you're always so hard on yourself.'

'There you go again, thinking too well of me.'

He shook his head, but he was smiling. 'I give up. You just won't take a compliment, will you?'

'Not without a reasonable fight,' she laughed.

Up in the chestnut tree, the woodpigeon flapped its wings and flew off clumsily.

Christian stood abruptly. 'Come with me,' he said. 'There's something I want to show you.'

He led her to the bottom of the garden, to the summer house, the roof of which was almost entirely hidden beneath a fairy-tale drift of pastel-pink climbing roses. Swollen flowers tumbled gloriously, their fragrance sweet on the morning air; bees hummed drunkenly from flower to flower. When Christian opened the door of the summer house, a further fusion of smells greeted them – sun-warmed cedar wood, mildewed canvas seats, musty old garden tools. Genevieve couldn't spot anything especially worth looking at in amongst the clutter – badminton racquets, a trug and an assortment of plastic seed trays and clay flowerpots – but when he closed the door and came towards her, she realised exactly why he'd brought her here.

At long, long last, his face inches from hers, his hands placed either side of her face, he kissed her. It was thirteen years since they'd kissed, but his mouth was so recognisable against hers that the intervening years fell away. Everything about the soft warmth of his lips, the gentle pressure of his fingers on her skin, the feel of his body pressing into hers, was the same. How could a body remember that? How was it possible? But it was, and she kissed him back with a desire that made him strengthen his hold on her.

'You have no idea how much I've been longing to do that,' he said, when he released her. 'And how many times I very nearly did but always lost my nerve, or someone or something got in the way.'

'Is that why we're hiding in here?'

He smiled. 'Yes. To be sure of not being interrupted.'

'I think Polly and Jonjo have got other things on their minds.'

'In that case, I'd say we owe it to ourselves to make the most of their preoccupation with each other.'

They kissed and kissed, and would have gone on doing so if the summer house hadn't been so hot and airless, and if Genevieve hadn't promised her father she'd get back to Paradise House that afternoon.

The first person Genevieve and Polly saw as they drove into Angel Sands was Adam. He was driving out of the village. There was no other traffic about, and Genevieve flashed her lights. They pulled alongside each other.

'Hi there, you two. How was the funeral?'

'How did you know we'd been to one?' asked Genevieve.

He tapped his nose. 'Usual sources. Either of you fancy a drink in The Arms this evening? It's quiz night.'

Polly nodded her agreement, and Genevieve, having spoken to her father before setting off, and knowing there were no bookings for dinner that evening, said, 'You're on. What time?'

'The quiz starts at eight, so I'll call for you at twenty to. See you.' With a loud pip-pip of his horn, he drove off.

*

All was quiet at home. The guests were out, as was Lily-Rose, who was down at Gran's.

'I told you we could manage without you,' her father said, as he helped them in with their overnight bags and the cool boxes Genevieve had used to transport the food.

'We haven't had one single emergency,' joined in Nattie, when they went through to the kitchen.

'I never said you wouldn't be able to cope,' Genevieve said.

'Yeah, but the way you carry on, you'd think you'd need to be a brain surgeon to keep this place going.'

'Not a bit of it. I always knew if you pulled your finger out you could do it.'

Nattie laughed. 'Hey, you're on top form, girl. Funerals must bring out the best in you. So how was it?'

Polly answered for her. 'You should have been there, Nattie. Christian spoke so movingly of his mother during the service. He had us all in tears.'

'Even your crazy fella, Jonjo Fitz?'

Polly blushed. 'He's really quite serious when you get him alone.'

Nattie narrowed her eyes. 'You've slept with him, haven't you?'

Polly's colour deepened.

Nattie was triumphant. '*Yes!* I can always tell. Was he any good? With a fit body like his, I bet he was stupendous. Wow, Polly, I'm almost envious.'

It was all too much for Dad. 'For heaven's sake, girls! I'm your father, I don't need to hear about your sex lives. In fact, I'd prefer to believe you didn't *have* sex lives! If anyone wants me, I'll be down at your grandmother's, fetching Lily.' With that, he marched out of the kitchen.

Nattie closed the door and leant against it so there was no escape. 'So come on, Polly, divvy up the details on your sweet little duet.'

'Nattie! Leave the poor girl alone.'

'Be quiet, Gen, we'll get to you in a minute. And don't look so horrified. You didn't honestly expect me to believe you'd stay the night with Christian and not take advantage of him while he was in a vulnerable state, did you? Okay, Poll, while Gen's finding something to hit me with, fire away. Let's have it.'

Polly sighed and sat down. She looked as happy as they'd ever seen her. 'He's asked me to go to Hong Kong with him.'

'*Hong Kong?* Whatever for?'

'Never mind travel plans, what was the nookie like?'

'Natalie Baxter, will you, just once in your life, shut up!' Genevieve turned to Polly. 'So why Hong Kong?'

'It's a business trip. He's branching out. He wants to sell his own brand of leisure and sportswear and he's meeting with some potential suppliers. He wants me to go with him.'

'When?'

'Friday. It's the end of term for all my schools, so I'll be free. But I haven't said I'll go. Not yet.'

This latest piece of news which, typically, Polly had kept to herself throughout the journey home from Ludlow, so dominated the conversation for the rest of the afternoon and evening that Genevieve and Polly forgot all about the quiz night Adam had invited them to. It was only seeing his face at the back door that reminded them.

To their surprise, Nattie said, 'I'm not doing anything tonight. I could come with you. Dad? Do you mind babysitting Lily-Rose for me?'

Adam looked awkward. 'Actually, I was going to invite your father to join us.'

Nattie looked as though she'd just been slapped. She turned to their father.

'That's alright, Nattie,' he said. 'You go and enjoy

yourself. Another time, Adam. Thanks for the offer.'

They walked down the hill to the village, Nattie and Polly in front, Adam and Genevieve behind. It was a beautiful summer's evening, and the air was drowsy with a still warmth. Plenty of people were still on the beach. The Power Boat People were winching their boats and jet skis out of the water, making their usual unsociable din and getting in the way of a large group of people playing a makeshift game of French cricket.

Genevieve told Adam about Polly going to Hong Kong with Jonjo.

'I thought there was an extra twinkle in her eye when I saw you in the car this afternoon,' he said. 'If it's love, it suits her. So what about you and lover-boy? How's it going?'

'Oh, you know, so, so.'

'Still kidding yourselves you're just good friends?'

When she didn't answer him, he said, 'So things have moved on, have they?'

She gave him what she was hoped was an enigmatic smile and changed the subject. 'By the way, nice handling of Nats earlier. The look on her face was a treat. She looked well and truly wrong-footed.'

He slowed his step. 'Are you accusing me of something, Gen?'

'No. But you have to admit, the result was very satisfying. She's so used to taking people for granted.'

There was a good turnout for the quiz. Participants were grouped into teams of five and the atmosphere was fiercely competitive. The teams all had names and, as team captain, Adam had called theirs Adam's Angels, much to Nattie's disgust. She was further annoyed when she asked the adjudicator for some upfront points, claiming they were at a disadvantage, only being four – Adam, Genevieve, Polly and herself – but the landlord overruled her and said if anything, they had an advantage. 'You've got Polly,' he said, 'and she has more brains than the rest of everyone else put together.'

Polly soon proved her worth and was probably the only one in the entire pub who knew the answer to question five: according to John's Gospel in the New Testament, what was the name of the servant who had his ear cut off by Simon Peter? Mutterings of 'unfair' and 'fetch the bloody parson' were heard. Taking the pencil from Adam, Polly wrote down the answer – 'Malchus'.

'You sure about that?' asked Nattie.

'Don't be stupid,' said Adam. 'Polly's never wrong.'

The next question gave Genevieve the chance to shine.

'What is the middle name of J.B. Fletcher, the crime-writing sleuth from *Murder, She Wrote?*'

She grabbed the pencil and wrote the answer: 'Beetris.'

'How the hell do you know that?' asked Nattie, crossing it out and spelling it correctly – Beatrice.

'From watching too much telly with Gran.'

'Ssh, you two, we're on a roll.'

'Ssh yourself, Adam Kellar!'

He gave her sister such a stern look, Genevieve witnessed a miracle right before her eyes: Nattie looked offended.

It may have been the effect of too much wine and the excitement of Adam's Angels winning the quiz, along with a whole twenty-five pounds and a bottle of Cava, but Genevieve wasn't in the mood to go straight home afterwards. 'I fancy sitting on the beach for a while,' she said. 'Any takers?'

Nattie pointed out that it was pitch black and Polly said she wanted an early night.

'More like you want to rush back and indulge in some hot phone sex with Jonjo Fitz,' Nattie teased.

'That just leaves you and me, Adam. How about it?'

After waving the others off, they went and sat on the pebbles.

'How about we open our prize?' Genevieve said.

He pulled a face. 'You're on your own, there, kid. My Cava drinking days are a thing of the past. But if it's something special you want to celebrate, I'm willing to make an exception.'

She laughed. 'You're fishing again, aren't you?'

'Well?'

'Okay, he kissed me.'

Adam didn't miss a beat. 'I should think he did. An attractive girl like you. And did you kiss him back? Oh, Gen, you did, didn't you?' He tutted. 'What a tart you've become! I do hope you're not going to shock me with any further revelations. You know what a chaste, innocent boy I am.'

'No, I was very well-behaved,' she said primly. 'Mouth to mouth contact only.'

Laughing, he put his arm round her. 'Keeping him keen, eh?'

'It wasn't like that.'

'So what was it like?'

She sighed and rested her head on his shoulder and stared up at the velvety night sky. 'It was beautiful. Just like I remembered it.'

His voice low, Adam said, 'You will be careful, won't you, Gen? This guy obviously has quite an effect on you.'

But she didn't answer him. It was too late to think about being careful. Her heart had well and truly won the battle over her head.

Chapter Thirty-six

In the days that followed, Genevieve was filled with longing to be with Christian. In the same way that as a teenager she'd devoted hours to daydreaming of him, she was constantly distracted by thoughts of the two of them in the summer house. How pleased she was that he'd seized the moment! Occasionally, though, slivers of doubt found their way into her thoughts. Were they doing the right thing? Would getting involved again turn out to be a terrible mistake?

Despite Nattie's best efforts to extract the story from her – had she or had she not been stupid enough to sleep with Christian? – Genevieve had told no one, other than Adam, how she felt about Christian. Perhaps it was because she didn't dare put her emotions into words. It might be asking for trouble, tempting fate, and the past, to crush what was still so fragile.

She kept all this to herself, as she did the happy realisation that since the night of Ella May's funeral, when she'd been so terrified, she had begun to put the robbery behind her. She would never forget the savage cruelty she'd witnessed and experienced but, as she wrote in one of her emails to Christian, she was sure it had less of a hold on her now.

She knew from Christian's emails that there was no chance of seeing him for the foreseeable future; he was snowed under with work as well as sorting through his mother's things.

'I wish you were here to help me deal with her

personal stuff,' he wrote. 'The clothes I can handle, but I simply don't know what to do with the letters and keepsakes. There are boxes of letters she and Dad wrote to each other before they were married. What on earth do I do with them?'

His question made Genevieve think of all the letters she and Christian had exchanged as teenagers, especially the ones of his she had burned after a particularly gruesome bingeing session, when her anger and self-hate was at its zenith.

He had asked if there was any way she could get away from Paradise House so they could spend some time together, but frustratingly it was impossible. It was peak season and everything was happening at once. The big news was that Dad was leaving this morning for New Zealand. Polly was travelling to Heathrow with him – unsurprisingly, she had agreed to go to Hong Kong with Jonjo – and their flights were only an hour apart.

Nattie, not to be left out, had received an invitation to a school reunion and was going away for a couple of days. As usual she was expecting Genevieve to step into the breach and not only hold the fort single-handedly, but take care of Lily-Rose as well. When Genevieve had hinted that looking after Lily-Rose on this occasion might be the straw that broke the camel's back, Nattie wheedled, 'Oh, please, Gen, I can hardly take Lily-Rose with me, can I? Please say you'll have her? Pretty please with cherries on top? And don't forget, now that Gran's back to normal, she could always help you.'

Genevieve had given in to her sister, on the condition that when Nattie returned, she'd cover for Genevieve so she could have the day off.

Now, since time was getting on and there was a full house for breakfast, she drained her mug of tea, brushed the toast crumbs off her plate for the birds, and told herself not to worry. She'd cope. But as she walked up to the house, she couldn't shake off the feeling that she was being taken advantage of. Reminded of what Christian had said on the beach – *they all rely on you so heavily* – she wondered if this was how her mother had felt. If so, was that why she had upped sticks and run?

Till now, because Serena had left without any warning or apparent contrition, Genevieve's sympathy had lain mostly with her father, but now she wasn't so sure. What if their mother had grown tired of always being the glue that held things together? For that was what she'd been; Genevieve could see that clearly now. Cut through her mother's irrepressible romantic notions, the lapses of memory and cock-eyed way of looking at life, and what did you have? You had Serena always there for them.

After kissing Polly goodbye and hugging her father, Genevieve watched him climb into his Land Rover; he looked like a man on a mission, jaw set firm, shoulders squared. After weeks of dithering, he was at last embarking on what had to be the most important journey he would ever make. Though at times Genevieve had considered him a coward for not acting sooner, in her heart she knew he wasn't. He was just human, as emotionally frail as the next person. She hoped his nerve would hold out. But thank goodness he had Polly with him for the journey to the airport. Nattie, standing beside Genevieve, was even now giving him last-minute instructions guaranteed to make matters worse. Comments such as, 'Tell her to stop being so selfish,' and 'Drag her back by the hair if you have to,' were not only a case of pots and kettles, but highly unhelpful.

Not long after they'd left, Nattie took Lily-Rose down to the beach and Tubby stopped by with a delivery of fruit and veg and an update on the Talent Contest. To his delight, tickets were flying out the door for participants and audience alike; it was going to be a night to remember. Genevieve would have liked to talk more with him about her own contribution to the event, but she didn't have time. She had plans, and in particular a Plan with a capital P.

An hour later she was in Tenby. It took a while to find somewhere to park. After locking the car, she set off on foot for the centre of the walled town. The day was hot – the heat-wave was showing no sign of cooling. She wove a purposeful path through the hordes of dawdling, sun-tanned holidaymakers, and on past the imposing church of St Mary's with its elegant spire. She was tempted to go inside and get down on bended knee to do a bit of negotiating – a sinner's soul in return for a generous act of benevolence – but pressed on ahead until she was standing outside the bank.

Loans, so Adam had told her when they'd been sitting on the beach following the quiz, were two a penny. She was about to discover if that was true.

She pushed against the door and went inside. The air conditioning was cool and made her realise how hot and clammy she was, a combination of weather, nerves and the fact that she was wearing a jacket. She had deliberately made an appointment at this particular branch, not the one in Pembroke that the rest of her family used, because she wanted to keep her affairs private. She didn't want anyone in her family knowing what she was up to, not until she was sure of it herself.

She was shown through to a small office where Mrs Hughes, the Loans Manager, would see her. Unlike the outer office, Mrs Hughes' office didn't have the benefit of air conditioning; the stuffy heat hit her at once. A crisp-haired woman in a lightweight suit rose from the other side of the desk.

'Sorry about the stifling temperature,' she said, 'but there's nothing we can do. We've been waiting for the engineer to show up, but apparently he's inundated. Please, sit down. Now then, what can I do to help you, Miss Baxter?'

The woman seemed friendly enough. Genevieve opened her folder and leaned forward in her seat. She spent the next ten minutes setting out her plans in as businesslike a manner as she could manage, remembering all that Adam had told her.

As she let the bank door close slowly behind her, she stood on the pavement and awarded herself a small pat on the back. It wasn't exactly in the bag, but things looked promising. Her next stop was just off St Julian's Street, where she had arranged to see a solicitor, Mr Saunders. She emerged not long after and stood once more on the pavement in the bright sunshine. She was just thinking she ought to give herself some kind of treat to mark the occasion when she saw a familiar smiling face across the busy street. She waited for a break in the traffic and crossed the road.

'Adam Kellar, are you stalking me?'

'I prefer to see myself as your guardian angel. So come on, future Businesswoman of the Year, shall I take you for a celebratory drink and you tell me how it went?'

'Oh, I think we can do better than that. Let's have an ice-cream down on the beach.'

He looked doubtfully at his suit. 'No chance. Not even for you.'

'Okay then, we'll find a nice clean bench for you to sit on.'

Genevieve led the way. They pushed through the crowds along St Julian's Street, with its pretty hanging flower baskets, past the Hope and Anchor pub and the stately houses of Lexden Terrace. They got stuck behind a family with a pushchair and a panting dog. When they reached the harbour, they bought two 99s with all the trimmings. In the gardens that overlooked the Prince Albert Memorial and St Catherine's Island they spotted one free seat and quickly claimed it. Genevieve held Adam's ice-cream while he took off his jacket and laid it carefully on the back of the bench. She noticed with approval the muted tie that he was now loosening and the absence of his faithful gold bracelet. He was buffing up a treat these days.

'Why, in the name of all that's wonderful are you wearing a suit on a day like this, Adam?'

'The same reason you're dressed to impress in your cute little power number.' He indicated the skirt and jacket, an outfit that only saw the light of day for special occasions – she'd worn it for Christian's mother's funeral. 'Only difference is, my business was conducted over lunch.'

'So what are you up to now? Another caravan park?'

'No.' There was something oddly evasive in his tone.

'What, then?'

His expression serious, he said, 'Look, this is strictly between you and me. I don't want anyone knowing yet, but I'm thinking of selling up.'

Genevieve was shocked. 'You're kidding! But why? And what will you do? You're much too young to retire.'

He licked his ice-cream. 'Who said anything about retiring? No, the truth is, I'm getting itchy palms, which is always a sign I need a new challenge.'

'What do you have in mind?'

'Mm . . . too soon to say. Anyway, tell me how you got on. But first off, how about your dad and Polly? Did they get away on time?'

'They did. Dad promised he'd give me a call from the airport before his flight at seven.'

'And what time's Polly's flight?'

'Ten to six. Jonjo said he'd meet her at the check-in desk at four.'

'Well, fingers crossed all goes to plan. Now, tell me about *your* plans.'

It was good having Adam to confide in, especially as he'd been in on it right from the start, since that night on the beach when she'd first broached the subject.

She recounted her visit to the bank and then her brief meeting with Mr Saunders. 'Nothing's definite, but I've set the wheels in motion. It's a matter of wait and see now.'

'A done deal, I'd say. No question. And as I've said before, if you want any help, just give me a shout.'

When Genevieve was driving home, trying to keep up with Adam's Porsche, it hit her how very upset she'd be if Adam's plans for his future didn't include Angel Sands. If he moved somewhere new to satisfy those itchy palms of his, she would lose her closest friend.

Back at Paradise House, after hurriedly changing out of her dressed-to-impress jacket and skirt so that Nattie didn't catch her in it and start asking questions, Genevieve pushed the excitement of her visit to Tenby from her mind: there were new arrivals to check in, and dinner for two couples to prepare.

She was hulling some strawberries for a Pavlova when the phone rang. It was her father. She could tell straight away from his voice that something was wrong.

'What is it, Dad?' she asked.

'Nothing, Gen. Nothing's wrong.'

'There is. I can tell.' She glanced at the clock above the dresser. 'Has Jonjo turned up to meet Polly?'

'Yes, he was here before us. I've already waved them off.'

'So everything's okay? Dad? You're sure of that?'

The silence told her she was right to worry. More patiently she said, 'What is it, Dad?'

'Oh, Gen, I'm getting cold feet. I am doing the right

thing, aren't I? What if I arrive and find there's more going on between your mother and this Pete character than we'd thought?'

Genevieve decided to be firm. 'Either way, Dad, you have to know. But my guess is there really isn't anything going on between them. Mum wouldn't do that to you.' And to boost her father's confidence, she added, 'Mum will get such a kick when you knock on the door and she sees it's you. She'll –'

'I still think I should have spoken to her,' he cut in. 'Surprises are all very well, but if she's not there, if she's gone off somewhere else, what then?'

'Let's worry about that if we have to. For now, just concentrate on boarding that plane and staying positive.'

'You don't think I ought to phone ahead and speak to –'

'Don't you dare! We've been through this before. Mum wants drama and romance from you, not a bloody appointment. Now stop being so feeble!'

'Genevieve, I'm doing my best –'

'No you're not!' she snapped, suddenly filled with fury. 'If you'd done that Mum would never have gone off in the first place.'

Genevieve heard a sharp intake of breath down the line. Mortified at what she'd said, she apologised. 'I'm sorry, Dad, I shouldn't have said that.'

'No, Gen, you're absolutely right.' He spoke firmly. 'I'd better go now. I'll speak to you soon, hopefully with good news.' He rang off.

Genevieve put the phone down. How could she have said such a thing to her father? And where had that anger come from?

But she knew exactly what had made her do it. Picturing herself in Mrs Hughes' office discussing her Plans, she acknowledged the true source of her frustration and anger. If her father couldn't persuade Serena to come home, Genevieve would feel beholden to stay with him at Paradise House. Her own tentative plans would come to nothing.

Chapter Thirty-seven

The next morning, as soon as Genevieve had cooked the last plate of bacon and eggs and Nattie had served it, her sister was upstairs throwing a bag together for her school reunion in Cheshire. She was leaving just as soon as she'd fetched Gran to help look after Lily-Rose.

As she scrubbed the grill pan at the sink, feeling distinctly like Cinderella, the phone rang.

'Get that will you?' Genevieve called out to anyone who might hear. Then remembering Polly and her father were somewhere on the other side of the world, she peeled off her rubber gloves and grumbled her way across the kitchen.

It was Donna, to say she was sorry but she wouldn't be making it into work that morning. 'I've been up all night with the trots,' she elaborated. 'I must have lost half a stone. If this carries on my clothes will be hanging off me.'

Genevieve made all the requisite noises of sympathy and went back to the grill pan, muttering under her breath some more. Now she'd have all the rooms to clean on her own, as well as everything else. A cursory knock at the back door announced the arrival of Gran, who, as well-meaning as she was in offering to help out while Dad, Nattie and Polly were away, would very likely add to Genevieve's workload. You're being unfair, she told herself, as Gran came in and at once complained about the heat.

'Mark my words,' she said, flopping into the nearest

chair, 'we're in for an almighty storm. Probably tonight. I can feel it in my bones.' Fanning herself with one hand and wiping her forehead with the other, she added, 'I'm not exaggerating, but there's not a breath of air out there.'

'Gran, Nattie was going to fetch you in the car. You shouldn't be rushing around in this weather, it's much too hot.'

'I'm not completely daft, Genevieve. I got a lift from . . . oh, you know, what's-his-name?' She stopped fanning herself and stared into the middle distance. 'Oh, never mind. It'll come to me later. Now then, what can I do to help. Where's Lily-Rose?'

'She's upstairs with Nattie, helping her to pack. And talking of packing, where are your overnight things? You are staying the night, aren't you? If you can manage the stairs, I thought you could have Nattie's room.'

Gran gave her a withering look. 'Of course I can manage the stairs. Really, Genevieve, I'm growing tired of being treated like an old dear. Ever since I bumped my head you've done nothing but –'

'So where's your bag?' Genevieve interjected.

Cut off mid-flow, Gran looked vaguely about her. Her expression suddenly brightened. 'Adam! That's who it was who gave me a lift. I must have left my bag in his porch.'

'And what were you doing in Adam's porch?'

Her grandmother shot her another withering glance. 'I told you, Gen. He gave me a lift here in that fancy car of his.'

Genevieve smiled. 'Adam's car is a *Porsche*, Gran. Not a porch.'

Gran pursed her lips. 'Well, whatever it is, you can take that silly smirk off your face, young lady.'

Making a noisy entrance, Nattie came into the kitchen with Lily-Rose on her back and a large holdall in her hand. 'Hello, Gran. I thought I was supposed to be fetching you.'

'Adam gave me a lift. As I've just been telling your foolish sister.' She looked reproachfully at Genevieve.

Nattie dropped her holdall with a thump, then leaning to one side, carefully manoeuvred her daughter to the floor. 'You'd better be careful, Gran. That man is determined to have one of us Baxter girls.'

Gran chortled. 'Did you hear that, Lily-Rose? I'm going to be Adam's new girlfriend. Wouldn't that be the funniest thing?'

Wrinkling her nose, the little girl came towards her grandmother. Burying her elbows in the old lady's lap, she stared up into her face. 'Mummy says I have to look after the donkeys while she's away. Do you want to help me feed them?'

Gran cupped Lily's face in her hands. 'I will, just as soon as Mummy's gone. We need to give her a proper wave goodbye, don't we?'

Nattie left shortly afterwards, annoyingly taking Genevieve's car because, at the last minute, she discovered her own had a flat battery. Just as well she wasn't thinking of going anywhere, Genevieve thought as she helped Lily-Rose find some carrots for the donkeys.

Genevieve made a beeline for the rooms of those guests who had already left the house. By the time she'd cleaned, vacuumed, emptied the wastepaper bins and made the beds, the other rooms were empty. The last one to clean was the April Showers suite – the room Christian and Jonjo had stayed in. For the second night running there had been no message from Christian last night, and she was halfway to convincing herself he was regretting what they had done and, having satisfied his curiosity, he had gone back to Caroline.

In the bathroom her Cinderella mood intensified as she

scrubbed the enamel bath and wished that *she* was swanning off to some school reunion and not Nattie. Bloody hell, she must be fed up! The very thought of making polite chit-chat with her old classmates made her stomach churn. Here she was, thirty years old, yet the taunting memory of being laughed at for spelling like a five-year-old would always be there. Condemned as a slow learner. Nicknamed 'retard'. She scrubbed harder at the tide mark on the bath. Two years ago she had received an invitation to attend a reunion, written by a girl who had been particularly vicious when it came to name-calling, and she had thrown the letter straight in the bin, almost afraid that touching it would transport her back to that humiliating period in her life.

The telephone was ringing. Struggling down the stairs with the vacuum cleaner under one arm and a bucket of cleaning fluids and cloths under the other, thinking it might be her father, she dropped what she was carrying and raced to the kitchen

'Hi, Gen. It's me, Polly.'

Genevieve leaned against the wall. 'Oh, hello, Poll, everything okay? How's Hong Kong?'

'It's amazing. Very beautiful, even if it is raining. And raining like you've never seen. And, Gen, it's *so* busy. I've never seen so many people squeezed into one small space.'

'You've been out and about already?'

'Hardly at all. We only arrived this afternoon; it's evening for us now. Jonjo and I are going to have dinner and then we're going to bed early. To sleep, that is. We're both exhausted.'

Genevieve could feel hard-done-by Cinders holding back an envious sniffle. Why couldn't she be somewhere exotic, being wined and dined and taken to bed by a gorgeous man, with sleep the furthest thing from his mind?

'Gen? Are you still there? Can you hear me?'

'Sorry, Polly, I…I was just listening for Lily-Rose. Nattie left earlier.'

'You sound tired. Are you managing all right without us there?'

'Oh, I'm fine. Just a little pushed. Donna's gone down with a stomach bug so I've been tearing round the place on my own. Look, this must be costing a fortune. Give my love to Jonjo. Tell him to take good care of you.'

'He does that already, Gen. I can't believe how lovely he is sometimes. Where do you think he sprang from?'

Genevieve laughed. 'Who cares? Just enjoy yourselves.'

'Have you heard from Christian?' The question brought an instant change of tempo to the conversation.

'Um . . . not for a couple of days.'

'I expect he's busy.'

'That'll be it. Anyway, love you.'

'Love you too, Gen. Give Lily a kiss from me. Bye.'

Going back out to the hall to retrieve the vacuum cleaner and bucket of cleaning stuff, Genevieve was suddenly overcome by a desperate weariness, and for no good reason she could think of, a great weight of sadness filled her. She plonked herself on the bottom step of the stairs and sighed. It must be the weather, she thought. It's melting my brain.

As predicted by Gran, the weather broke that night. Lightning lit up the sky with a brilliant luminosity that woke Genevieve with a start. For a second she thought someone had switched on the light in her bedroom. But when the loudest clap of thunder she'd ever heard cracked overhead and rattled the windows, she got out of bed to draw back the curtains and shut the window. Rain was splattering heavily against the glass. She wasn't the least bit afraid of storms, but worried that Lily-Rose might be, she went and checked on her. She was fast asleep, a small foot and an arm hanging over the side of the bed. Genevieve then looked in on Gran, who was also sleeping soundly, outdoing the thunder with the volume of her snoring. On the way back to her room, she heard the murmur of voices from some of the guests downstairs. She sat up in bed so she could watch the diamond-bright lightning ravage the sky. She had often done this as a young child, baffling her mother and father that she could enjoy something so violent.

Eventually she fell asleep. Her last thought was to wonder why her father hadn't phoned. Surely he must have arrived in New Zealand by now.

Chapter Thirty-eight

Genevieve stood yawning at the back door, taking in the storm-damaged garden. The lawns and flower beds were untidy with a confetti of crushed petals; fuchsias were toppled, lavateria branches had been snapped off by the weight of drenched foliage, and flower heads on the hydrangea bushes looked weary and sodden. It was a far cry from the glorious sight of yesterday, when it had been bathed in hot late-July sunshine. Initially, the rain must have bounced off the parched, rock-hard lawns, but the continuous downpour had eventually reduced them to a soggy mess that would take days to dry out. And only then, if the rain kept away. It was raining now, just a light drizzle, but it was enough to put a dampener on the day, to bring out the waterproofs and umbrellas. At least the air was fresh and clear.

As she suspected it would, breakfast took longer to get through that morning. Guests were in no hurry to embrace the day – these weren't the hardy year-round variety who walked the coastal path no matter what the weather. They trickled slowly down to the dining room, having treated themselves to a lie-in and a prolonged soak in the bath or shower. They took an age over their breakfasts and eventually left the dining room clutching a selection of tourist leaflets. Should they visit Picton Castle, then drive up to St David's, or stay closer to home and see the Bosherton Lily Ponds?

Genevieve would have chosen to go up to St David's, a place she'd always loved, never more so than when she'd gone there as a teenager with Christian. He'd borrowed his father's car and after a walk around the city – the smallest in Britain – they'd wandered down to the cathedral and the Bishop's Palace. The day had been warm and sunny, and they'd eaten a picnic on the grassy slope, surrounded by other holidaymakers. Except they'd felt entirely alone, as they always did when they were together. But that was teenage love for you; the intensity of it precluded anything, or anyone, else. It was years before Genevieve understood that relationships should never isolate you from others. Her relationship with Rachel had done that, too. It was easy to see now that Rachel's actions had been based on jealousy. If she couldn't have Genevieve to herself, then she'd make sure her only friend would have no one. At the time, though, Genevieve had been so wrapped up in her own insecurity and need for approval that she hadn't seen Rachel's destructive influence for what it was.

After an apologetic call from Donna to say she still wasn't well enough to work, Genevieve made a start on cleaning the guest rooms. Gran had offered to help, but Genevieve suggested she read to Lily-Rose instead. 'If you can keep her entertained for as long as you can, I'd be really grateful,' Genevieve told her grandmother.

'But what about Henry and Morwenna?' Lily-Rose asked. 'I haven't fed them. Mummy said I had to.'

'Just as soon as the rain stops you can go and see them,' Genevieve said firmly. 'I'll be upstairs if you need me, Gran.'

She attacked her morning's work with determined energy despite feeling so tired, and was soon back downstairs filling the washing machine with towels and tablecloths. The sky, much to her surprise, was showing signs of brightening. With a bit of luck she'd get the washing on the line. If not, there was always the tumble dryer. With no sign of Gran or Lily-Rose in the kitchen, she made herself a cup of tea and sat down. Five minutes, she told herself, and then she'd tackle the ironing. After that, she'd have a shower. A long, revitalising shower to wash away her lethargy. She couldn't remember the last time she'd felt so bone-tired. She was edgy too, worried that Dad still hadn't been in touch. And then there was Christian. Still no word from him. The longer his silence went on, the more she began to worry she would never be able to trust him.

She yawned, and to taunt herself some more, she pictured herself in the summer house with Christian, in particular that moment when she knew he was going to kiss her. Within seconds, she had lowered her head to the kitchen table and dozed off. She dreamt she really was in the summer house with Christian. That he was standing behind her, kissing the nape of her neck, his hands massaging the tension from her shoulders. The next thing she knew, she was being jolted awake by the jangling ring of the telephone. *Why did that phone never stop ringing!*

Except it wasn't the phone. It was someone at the front door. She shook herself out of her disappointment, feeling cheated that there was no Christian planting warm kisses on her skin, and went to see who it was. She hoped it wasn't anyone she knew. Dressed in a grubby T-shirt, her tattiest jeans with holes in the knees and her hair tied back with a rubber band, she looked and felt a mess.

She pulled open the door.

Christian!

For what felt like for ever, she held onto the door and stared at him. Was she still dreaming? Without speaking, he stepped over the threshold, kissed her politely on the cheek and then a lot less politely on the mouth. She breathed in the fresh, clean smell of him and felt her body go limp with longing. Still kissing her, holding her tight, his hands pressing into her shoulders, he somehow shut the door with his foot. She wanted to ask what he was

333

doing here, but she couldn't. She daren't stop kissing him for fear she would wake up and he'd be gone as magically as he'd appeared. He manoeuvred her up against the wall and, tilting his head back, said, 'Please tell me there's no one else in the house?'

'I don't know. There might be some guests around.'

He kissed her again, his hands warm and firm around her neck. Frightened that any second someone – a guest, or Gran, or Lily-Rose – might appear in the hall, she pulled away. 'I've heard of doorstepping, but I don't suppose you'd like to go somewhere more private, would you?'

She could tell from his expression he hadn't understood her, so she took him by the hand and led him upstairs. Once they were in her bedroom, with the door shut and their bodies pressed against each other, all her earlier tiredness and doubts flew from her mind. 'Why didn't you let me know you were coming?'

'I wanted to surprise you.'

'Well, you certainly achieved that. But what made you do it?'

He tipped her chin up. 'I got a text message from Jonjo and Polly. They said you were a bit down. I would have come sooner, but I couldn't get away before now.'

Genevieve was touched. He had done that for her? She opened her mouth to speak, to say how glad she was to see him, when, very gently, he put a finger to her lips. 'Do you think we could leave the talking till later?'

She couldn't have agreed more. When his hands circled her waist, then slid under her T-shirt and brushed against her breasts, she steered him towards the bed, at the same time unbuttoning his shirt. He slipped her top over her head and trailed his mouth along her shoulder, then down her arm. He was just about to do the same to her other shoulder when she froze. She cocked her ear towards the door. 'What was that?'

Her gave her a half-smile. 'I didn't hear a thing.'

'There! There it is again. Oh, God, it's probably Gran and Lily-Rose.'

He groaned and held her close. 'I suppose it's pointless trying to pretend we're not here?'

'We could try.'

Smiling, he said, 'No, the thought of your grandmother bursting in on us is hardly the erotic scenario I imagined when I drove down here this morning.'

She feigned indignation. 'You knew all along you were going to get me into bed!'

He kissed her lightly on the neck. 'Are you saying it hasn't been on your mind?'

He looked so sexy, his shirt hanging open and his chest just waiting to be kissed all over, she longed to push him onto the bed and show him exactly how much it had been on her mind. 'I'll leave you to figure that one out for yourself,' she said.

'Perhaps you'd better give me a clue; you know how slow I am.'

She pulled his head down to hers and kissed him passionately. 'Does that help?'

'Oh, yes. It makes me want you all the more. Go on, I'm a desperate man. Lock the door; I promise you, this won't take long.' He started to undo her jeans.

Though it was the hardest thing to do, she pulled away from him. 'As tempting as you make it sound, I think we'd better make ourselves decent.'

She was straightening her hair while watching Christian do up the buttons of his shirt, when she heard the thumpty-thump-thump of small feet approaching. The bedroom door flew open and Lily-Rose burst in. Breathless and crying, tears streaming down her cheeks, she threw herself at Genevieve.

'Genvy, Henry and Morwenna have gone!'

*

Gran greeted Christian as though him showing up out of the blue at Paradise House was an everyday occurrence. Immediately they got down to the business of finding the missing donkeys.

'First off, we ought to speak to your neighbours,' Christian said, 'to see if they've seen them.'

He was perhaps the only one thinking logically. Genevieve was trying to calm a bawling Lily-Rose, who was taking her mother's instruction to take care of Henry and Morwenna too much to heart, and Gran was shuffling about the kitchen looking for the teapot. Plainly she deemed the situation a hot-sweet-tea emergency.

'They must have been frightened by the storm,' Genevieve said, when at last Lily-Rose was calm enough to sit on her lap, producing an occasional full-body shudder and an accompanying sniff.

'But weren't they tethered?' Christian asked.

'No. The orchard had its own natural boundaries, and they've never strayed before.'

'They could have gone anywhere,' Gran said. 'Along the clifftop path in the dark and taken a tumble down into the –'

'Very unlikely,' Genevieve interrupted. She didn't want Lily-Rose dwelling on such a disturbing thought. 'They've probably just wandered down to the beach and are giving rides to all the children in return for ice-cream.' She bounced her knees as though she were giving Lily-Rose a donkey ride. Anything to distract her from what Gran had just suggested.

Leaving Lily-Rose with Gran, Genevieve and Christian set off on foot to knock on doors. They went all round the village, but no one had seen or heard so much as an ee-aw. Gran's vision of Henry and Morwenna wandering the cliff path began to seem horribly likely.

They stood in front of the Salvation Arms, figuring out

what to do next. The sun had broken through the thick bank of clouds, but a stiff wind rippled the bunting outside the pub, making the day seem cold and bleak. Down on the beach, a handful of youngsters were playing in the rock pools while the parents, wrapped in fleeces, looked on indulgently.

'Should we go further afield?' Christian asked. 'We could drive along the coast.'

'But Nattie's got my car, and hers isn't working.'

'You're forgetting mine. Let's go back up to the house.'

Genevieve fell in step with him. 'I bet you're wishing you'd never come down here. This is the last thing you expected to be doing – a wild donkey chase.'

He put his arm round her shoulder. 'I wouldn't have missed it for the world. At least I can say I got as far as your bedroom on this visit. Who knows, next time I might actually get you into bed.'

She leaned into him happily.

The house was unnaturally quiet when they let themselves in the back door.

'That's odd,' Genevieve said, after she'd called to Gran and Lily-Rose and got no answer. 'I wonder where they've gone.'

'To your gran's, perhaps?'

'Mm . . . maybe.' She was suddenly annoyed. 'Why does my family do this to me? I spend all my time keeping an eye on them. If it's not them I'm worrying about, it's their personal crusades. These are Nattie's donkeys, she should be here to find them. Sometimes I wish I'd never come home.'

He looked at her hard, then took her in his arm. 'I'm glad you did, or we might never have met again.'

She rested her head against his chest, and could feel the thud of his heart. For a few seconds she allowed herself to be soothed by it. But then, tilting her head back to look up at him, she said, 'Do you really mean that?'

He looked offended. 'Genevieve, you have to stop doubting me.'

They spent the next hour trawling the coast road, stopping every now and then to ask if anyone had seen a pair of roaming donkeys. When it started to rain, they drove home. The house was still empty, save for two guests who were reading in the conservatory. Genevieve had just served them tea when the phone rang.

'Hi there, Genevieve.' Tubby's jolly voice boomed down the line. 'Have you lost anything recently? Like a couple of absconding donkeys?'

'Tubby! Do you know where they are?'

He chuckled. 'Yes, and I'm keeping them as hostage until I receive five thousand pounds in used bank notes in the post. Oh, and you can throw in a Ferrari as well.'

'I'll throw in Nattie too, if you're not careful. Where did you find them?'

'I was down at that new pottery and tea room near Stackpole, dropping off some strawberries, when I saw the pair of them grazing in a field. I knew it was them; they had on those ridiculous scarves Nattie makes them wear.'

'But that's miles away.'

'Not really. Anyway, I tethered them up, so they're safe for now. I can get hold of a horsebox and trailer if you like.'

'Thanks, Tubby, but we'll leave them there until Nattie gets back. She can damn well deal with it herself!'

Genevieve rang off and told Christian the good news.

'So, panic over? We can call off the air-sea rescue team?'

She laughed. 'For the time being, yes. But who knows with this family?' She glanced at her watch. 'I've just realised, you haven't had anything to eat since you arrived. You must be starving. What would you like?'

'Some of those scones would be good.' He indicated

the open tin on the table, the pot of homemade jam and dish of whipped cream.

'Tell you what, help yourself while I give Gran a ring and see how she's getting on with Lily-Rose. I don't want her wearing herself out.'

But there was no answer from her grandmother's telephone.

'Maybe she's nipped to the shops with Lily-Rose,' Christian suggested.

She shrugged. 'I know it seems silly, but something's not right. And why didn't she leave a note saying where she was going?'

'Does she always let you know what she's up to?'

'No. But –'

He put down his half-eaten scone. 'Okay, then. Let's go.'

'Let's go where?'

'To your gran's, of course.'

'But she's not there, is she? If she was, she'd have answered the phone.' He started leading her towards the back door. 'Christian, what are you doing?'

'I know you well enough to understand that if we don't check on your grandmother, you'll just sit here worrying. Go on. Out you go.'

It was raining again, so they drove the short distance and parked directly in front of Angel Cottage. Genevieve knocked on the door, then knocked again. As she'd done before, she peered in at the window, her hands cupped around her eyes. Gran was on the sofa, her face turned towards the television. But she wasn't watching it; with her eyes closed and her head leaning to one side, she was fast asleep. Genevieve tapped on the window, but got no response. She was just berating herself for forgetting her key when Christian joined her. 'Is there a way in at the back?' he asked.

They went round the side of the house to the back

garden and found the kitchen door open. Genevieve went on ahead to the sitting room.

'Gran,' she said softly, not wanting to make her start. The memory of finding her grandmother on the bathroom floor was still fresh in her mind and her heart was beginning to pound. 'Gran, wake up!'

Her grandmother stirred. By the time she was fully awake and asking if Genevieve would put the kettle on, Christian had joined them.

'Genevieve,' he said, taking her aside, 'I've searched the house and garden, but there's no sign of Lily-Rose. She's not here.'

The enormity of his words hit her like a blow. Cold panic took hold of her. Lily-Rose. Where was she?

Chapter Thirty-nine

'You're sure she's not here?' The question was futile, but Genevieve had to ask it.

'I double-checked,' Christian said. 'Where do you think she could have gone?'

'I've no idea. She's never wandered off before. She's so young. Four-year-olds don't have regular haunts of their own. Oh, God, Christian, suppose someone's taken her?'

'Let's get out there and start looking.'

Hauling herself to her feet, Gran said, 'What are you two muttering about?'

Genevieve broke the news to her grandmother as gently as she could, not wanting her overly alarmed. But Gran *was* alarmed. She clutched hold of Genevieve.

'It's all my fault,' she cried frantically. 'Lily kept wanting to look for Henry and Morwenna, and to distract her I brought her down here. I said if she was a good girl and played quietly so I could have a short nap, I'd take her to buy some sweets afterwards.'

'Then that's where she must be,' Genevieve said decisively, trying to allay her grandmother's distress – the old lady was now pacing the floor fretfully. 'You stay here, Gran. Christian and I will go round the shops.'

It didn't sound like something Lily-Rose would do. Nattie might not be the best mother in the world but she had brought her daughter up to know that she must go nowhere without an adult.

But their enquiries, as they once again dashed from shop to shop in the pouring rain, got them nowhere. No one had seen the little girl. Everyone promised to keep a lookout and told Genevieve not to worry, that Lily-Rose would show up any minute. In the mini-market, Stan and Gwen said they'd ask anyone who came into the shop if they'd seen a small girl on her own, and Ruth and William in Angel Crafts said if there was anything they could do, Genevieve only had to ask. In the salon, Debs asked how long Lily-Rose had been missing.

When exactly *had* Lily-Rose wandered off? They didn't know how long Gran had been asleep.

'Don't mess about, Genevieve,' Debs said. She was the first person not to pull her punches. 'Call the police. Do it now. Use my phone.'

'Perhaps I should just go and check Paradise House. She might have gone back there.'

'Okay, but meanwhile I'll ring a few people and alert them.'

Alone, Genevieve ran all the way up the hill. Christian had offered to return to Angel Cottage to check on Gran. After frantically searching every room at Paradise House, she drew yet another blank. Drenched to the skin, she stood in the kitchen and phoned the police. She gave the duty officer all the details she could, desperately trying to remember what Lily-Rose had been wearing. Then she made a second call; the one she was dreading. She had to tell Nattie her daughter was missing. But there was no answer from Nattie's mobile. She must have switched it off.

Grabbing a coat, she dashed back down the hill to Gran's, scanning the now-deserted beach for any sign of a child, praying like mad that when she reached Angel Cottage, Christian would tell her that Lily-Rose, all smiles and laughter, had just shown up. Passing the salon, Debs came out to her. Donna was with her. They both looked anxious.

'Any sign of Lily?' Debs asked.

Genevieve shook her head. 'No. But I've called the police. They're on their way.'

Christian opened the door to her, but his concerned expression, together with Gran still pacing the floor, flustered and muttering to herself, told her that Lily-Rose hadn't appeared. Shrugging off her wet coat, Genevieve told Christian she'd phoned the police. 'They said they'd send someone as soon as they could.'

'Good. I'll get my coat from the car.' He stopped for a moment and took her by the shoulders. 'Genevieve, we'll find her. I know we will.'

While he went to fetch his coat, Genevieve led Gran into the sitting room. Her concern for her grandmother was almost as strong as it was for her niece: the old lady was breathless and trembling. She sat with her on the sofa.

'Gran, you mustn't upset yourself.'

'How can you say that when it's no one's fault but my own that Lily's missing? I shouldn't have fallen asleep. I'll never know a moment's peace if something's happened to that poor little girl. Oh, and whatever will Nattie say?' Distraught, her eyes brimmed with tears. She looked very frail and old.

Trying not to let her apprehension show, Genevieve said, 'Gran, I need you to be rock steady. I can't get hold of Nattie, but I'm going to leave you her mobile number so you can keep trying it. You must tell her what's happened.' From her jeans pocket, she pulled out a piece of paper with the number clearly written on it; she handed it to her grandmother. 'Can you do that for me?'

With shaking hands, Gran took the piece of paper.

Joining Christian back out in the hall, where he was rummaging through a small rucksack, Genevieve pulled on her jacket. A knock at the door made her jump.

'What is it?' asked Christian.

'The door,' she said. 'It'll be the police.'

But it wasn't. A crowd of people stood outside: Tubby and Donna, Debs, Stan, Huw and Jane from the pottery, William and Ruth, the Lloyd-Morris brothers, Adam, and some of the regulars from the Salvation Arms. They were all dressed in boots and waterproofs.

'We're here to help,' Adam said, his face grim. 'Where do you want us to start looking?'

Their kindness was almost too much. Genevieve swallowed hard and took a deep, optimistic breath. With so much help, she told herself, they were bound to find Lily-Rose.

It was decided that one of them should go up to Paradise House in case Lily-Rose appeared there – Donna, still not quite recovered from her gyppy tummy, volunteered to do that – and then they split into pairs with a mobile between them. Christian produced an OS map from his rucksack and the immediate area was divided and distributed accordingly. Anything over a four-mile distance was ruled out, as there was no way a child of four could have walked so far. No one voiced the thought that if she had been taken by someone in a car, she could be forty miles away by now. The other unspoken fear Genevieve had was that Lily-Rose might have fallen into the sea. She told everyone how upset Lily-Rose had been when Henry and Morwenna had gone missing and how Gran might have put the idea in her head that they could have strayed along the coastal path in the dark during the storm and plummeted to their deaths in the sea.

'It's possible,' she said, forcing herself to voice the unthinkable, 'that Lily went to look for them and got too close to the edge.'

An uneasy murmur went round the group. They exchanged mobile phone numbers and dispersed. Genevieve checked on her grandmother one last time, explaining to her that the police would probably want a photograph of Lily-Rose. She left her to choose one from the selection on the mantelpiece. It might have been kinder to Gran if Genevieve had waited for the police herself, but she couldn't bear the waiting. She had to be out there doing something. Lily-Rose had been left in her care, and *she* had to find her. How could she ever face Nattie again if she didn't?

There was an odd number of people, so Genevieve and Christian teamed up with Adam. The three of them set off to Paradise House, skirted the headland and followed the coastal path in an easterly direction. The rain was coming down harder, making the ground slippery, and the wind, which had grown wild, whipped at the hoods on their jackets. The thought of Lily-Rose out in this weather, wet, cold and alone, sent a chill through Genevieve and she quickened her step. She soon realised the folly of this when Christian pulled at her arm.

'Slow down, Genevieve, or we might miss her.'

'He's right,' Adam said, 'we have to take it slowly.'

They continued in silence, stopping occasionally to peer down the side of the cliff. The sound of the wind roaring in her ears and the sea battering the rocks was beginning to have a mesmerising effect on Genevieve and, disorientated, she felt herself drawn ever closer to the edge of the rocks. She felt a sudden yank from behind as Christian pulled her back.

She wanted to thank him, but couldn't. Desperation was kicking in. She was beginning to fear the worst. But how could a small child disappear off the face of the earth? With a much older child, all sorts of credible scenarios presented themselves – a hitched lift into Tenby or Pembroke, a visit to friends, even a lovers' tryst. But a four-year-old? None of these things were possible.

They had walked as far as Hell's Gate. After pausing to look at Christian's map, the wind almost ripping it out of his hands, the three of them stood looking out at the rough, churning sea. The horizon was lost in the murky rain. The weather was getting worse.

'We'll never find her,' Genevieve murmured dismally. 'Or if we do, it'll be too late.' Only Adam heard her.

'We'll find her, Gen. No question.'

Christian refolded the map, stuffed it back into his rucksack and walked away from them, towards the edge of the path. Genevieve watched him anxiously. Above him, a pair of jackdaws circled, once, twice, and then flew off. Hell's Gate had always been out of bounds to Genevieve and her sisters as children; even now, seldom did they come this far. She wanted to call out to Christian to tell him to be careful, that the rocks below were treacherous, but she knew it was useless; he wouldn't hear her. She waited for Christian to stop moving, but he didn't. He carried on, getting perilously near the edge. He bent down, put a hand on a rock to take his weight and suddenly was gone. Genevieve rushed after him, Adam following behind. They came to what was very nearly a sheer drop, where Adam put a protective hand out to stop her from slipping. Below them, they could see Christian carefully picking his way over the jagged rocks towards a narrow ledge, where gulls were sheltering from the wind and spray. He stooped to pick something up. He turned, looked back to where they were standing and waved a small, bright yellow Wellington boot. Genevieve gasped and grabbed hold of Adam.

'It's Lily's,' she cried. At once she and Adam were scrambling down the rock-face. But the first signs of hope were tinged with fear. If Lily-Rose had been down here, had lost one of her boots, she must almost certainly have met with an accident. How could she have survived if she'd fallen?

Standing on the ledge together, they scanned the area beneath them, staring down into what was effectively a deep bowl cut into the rocks. The tide was coming in, and as the waves slapped and swirled, the wind roared with an animal-like baleful cry. Adam motioned for them to stay where they were, and pushed forward to a shallow cutting in the rock-face. He had to wade into the menacing water. And for what? Could they really be sure Lily-Rose was here? But it was a hope, perhaps their only hope.

Genevieve chewed on her lower lip as she watched Adam. Then, to her horror, she realised there was a lethal undercurrent where the water rushed into the bowl and couldn't get out. The next moment, Adam was sucked under. Genevieve screamed. Pulling off his bulky jacket and his shoes, Christian threw himself into the water. She watched in an agony of suspense for him to bob to the surface again. He did, but then dived back down again. When he surfaced, he was holding Adam. He dragged him over the side of the bowl and the two of them clung onto the rocks, Adam, coughing and spluttering. Genevieve could see he had knocked his head; blood was flowing from his temple. She shouted to them to be careful. After they'd caught their breath, they swam across the bowl to the shallow cutting that, when the tide was out, would have seemed to an inquisitive child like an interesting cave to play in. But with the tide coming in, it was a death-trap.

Holding the yellow boot Christian had found, she watched Adam hunker down and disappear inside the dark hole. She willed their search to be over, that somehow, miraculously, Lily-Rose was safe inside the cave. She stared hard at the opening, and suddenly she saw Adam emerge, and . . . and he had Lily-Rose in his arms. Wet through and shivering, she was clinging to Adam as he carried her to safety. But to get to the ledge where Genevieve was standing, Adam and Christian had to make it back across the bowl. Genevieve suddenly wished it was Christian who was carrying Lily-Rose; he was clearly the stronger swimmer. Then, as if reading her mind, Christian exchanged a word with Adam and took the little girl from him.

Very slowly, they lowered themselves into the dangerous vortex of water. As a huge, swelling wave reared up and almost covered them, Lily-Rose screamed and thrashed her arms and legs about. Christian had to work hard to keep his footing. More agonising minutes passed, until finally he and Adam made it to the ledge. Genevieve reached down, scooped up Lily-Rose and, wrapping the petrified little girl in her coat, gave thanks that the day hadn't ended in tragedy.

Chapter Forty

Once they'd climbed back up to the path and were heading for home, Adam took Christian's mobile – his own had been in his jacket pocket and was now useless – and phoned Donna at Paradise House with the good news. He also asked her to phone the doctor's surgery so that Lily-Rose could be thoroughly checked over.

'Ask whoever's on duty to meet us at the house,' Adam said, 'it'll be better for Lily that way. One less ordeal.'

Dr Shepherd was waiting for them when they crashed, exhausted but triumphant, through the kitchen door.

To Genevieve's enormous relief, while Donna poured them all shots of brandy and fussed for them to get out of their wet clothes – her father's wardrobe was raided for Adam and Christian – Dr Shepherd gave Lily-Rose a clean bill of health.

'She's had an amazingly lucky escape,' he said. 'Best to get her into a nice warm bath and then bed. She'll be as right as rain come the morning.' Switching his attention from Lily-Rose to Adam and the cut to his head, he said, 'Looks like a few stitches wouldn't go amiss there. Sit down and I'll see to it now.'

When he'd finished with Adam, and Genevieve was seeing the doctor out, she thanked him for coming so promptly and joked that, hopefully, it would be a while before they saw him again.

Back in the kitchen, dressed in her pyjamas and wrapped in a blanket, Lily-Rose was sitting on Adam's lap, telling him and Christian what had happened. While

Gran was sleeping she'd decided, as Genevieve had suspected, to go and look for Henry and Morwenna.

'Mummy told me I had to make sure they were all right,' she said, 'and I promised her I would.' She explained how she had quietly opened Gran's back door, slipped through the gate at the end of the garden and gone down on to the cliff path. 'It was very windy. I could see the seagulls and I went to sit with them. But they were horrible and pecked at my boots. There was a funny noise, like Henry and Morwenna calling to me.'

The rest was easy to imagine. She'd mistaken the strange-sounding wind for braying and had gone to explore. She'd found the cave and discovered somewhere to play for a while. But then the tide had started to come in, cutting her off. Another half-hour and the cave would probably have been completely under water, and she'd have drowned.

'She's her mother's child through and through,' Adam muttered. 'Intrepid to the point of stupidity.'

'Will Mummy be cross with me?' Lily-Rose asked anxiously.

It was then that Genevieve remembered Gran was supposed to be getting hold of Nattie.

'Donna,' she said, 'when you called the search off, did you ring Gran?'

'Oh, Gen, I'm sorry, I forgot all about that, what with the excitement. Shall I ring her now?'

'No, that's okay, I'll go down and see her.'

Adam shifted Lily-Rose off his lap and stood up. 'I'll walk down with you. I need to go home and change.' He glanced at Christian, also wearing Daddy Dean's cast-offs. 'I could lend you something if you like? Not that any of it will fit you properly.'

'Thanks,' Christian said.

Lily-Rose was happy enough to be left with Donna, so the three of them walked down the hill. Outside the

Salvation Arms, Adam suggested Christian went with him up to his house to shower and change.

'Shall I meet you at your Gran's?' Christian suggested.

'If you like. I'll probably be there a while. I ought to ring round everyone and thank them for joining in with the search. I'll leave the door on the latch for you.'

It was becoming a habit, Genevieve thought, as once again she was knocking on Gran's door and getting no answer. After another rap, Genevieve gave up and let herself in with her key, which she'd remembered this time.

'Gran, it's me,' she called out. She closed the door and went through to the sitting room, bursting to share the good news with her grandmother, wanting to be the one to put her mind at rest. 'Get the kettle on, Gran, we found Lily-Rose and a celebratory cuppa's just what we need.'

Genevieve stood very still in the echoing silence. In an instant she knew that her grandmother couldn't hear. Her head leaning back against the sofa cushion, lips dried and slightly parted, she was completely motionless. There was no fall and rise to her chest. No little throaty grunt Gran often made when she was napping. Very slowly, almost reverently, Genevieve bent down and knelt beside the old lady. 'Oh, Gran,' she murmured. 'You never even said goodbye.' Tears filled her eyes and, letting them stream down her cheeks, she held her grandmother's cool, still hand. Never had that knotty, age-spotted hand been more precious to her.

The day had ended in tragedy, after all. But the real tragedy was that Gran's last moments before she died would have been so tormented. She would have left this world not knowing that Lily-Rose was safe. It broke Genevieve's heart that her grandmother had died thinking she'd let them down.

She didn't know how long she'd been kneeling on the

floor sobbing, but she was suddenly conscious that Christian was beside her. She felt the steady pressure of his hand on her shoulder and, turning her tear-stained face to his, she said, 'How will we all manage without her? She was always there for us.'

He lifted her to her feet, took her through to the kitchen and cradled her, stroking her back. Eventually, she was able to think straight. There were things she had to do. Dr Shepherd would have to be sent for. Yet again. Then there was her family to notify – her parents in New Zealand and Polly in Hong Kong. And, of course, Nattie. Had Gran managed to ring her? She almost turned to go to the sitting room to ask Gran if she had, when . . . when she remembered.

The pain slapped at her. Never again would she be able to talk to her beloved grandmother. She reached for another tissue and blew her nose.

'This is when I feel so bloody useless,' Christian said.

Not understanding, she said, 'How do you mean?' Then realising she had her mouth partially covered with the tissue, she repeated what she'd said.

'I can't ring anyone for you. Do you want me to fetch Adam?'

Her first instinct was to say no, that she could manage. But the thought of Adam, decisive and always reassuring, made her say yes. 'But before you do that,' she said, 'could you send a text to Jonjo? I think I'd prefer it if Jonjo was the one to tell Polly about Gran. At least then she'll be told face to face by someone who cares about her.'

After everything had been done, including the formality of Gran's death certificate, they returned to Paradise House. Dr Shepherd had told Genevieve that the probable cause of Gran's death was that her heart had simply given out. He wouldn't commit himself to say that it was in any way a direct result of her distress at Lily-Rose's disappearance, but it haunted Genevieve to think that her grandmother had died blaming herself for what had happened. There was also the poignant similarity between Gran and Cecily: both women had died because their hearts had been put under unbearable pressure.

Donna had put a comfortable armchair from the sitting room into the kitchen for Lily-Rose, and the little girl was fast asleep in it, the head of a pink, long-eared rabbit sticking out from the blanket. Keeping her voice low, Genevieve thanked Donna for all her help and told her there was nothing else to be done just now. 'Go home, Donna,' she said, 'you've been wonderful, but I'm sure you'd rather be spending the evening with Tubby.'

'A nice thought, but unfortunately I'm working behind the bar tonight.' She gave Genevieve a hug. 'I'm really sorry about your Gran, Gen. I didn't know her for long, but it was long enough to appreciate what a great woman she was. I'll see myself out.'

Thinking guiltily that she felt better for there being one less person around, and that she wouldn't mind being alone, Genevieve looked at Christian and wondered if this was how he'd felt immediately after his mother had died. Fond as she was both him and Adam, and deeply grateful for everything they'd done, she wished they'd go. It was a selfish, unworthy thought, because if it weren't for them Lily-Rose would be dead.

Dead.

Her thoughts immediately returned to Gran. But the sound of hurried footsteps, followed by the back door flying open, put a stop to them. It was Nattie, her face as white as chalk. She took one look at her daughter, safely curled up in the armchair, and burst into tears. She cried so hard that Lily-Rose stirred, and when she saw her mother, she too started to cry.

Genevieve signalled to Christian and Adam to give her sister some privacy, and led them to the conservatory.

'What else can we do to help?' Adam asked, his hand resting on her arm.

Genevieve shook her head. 'Adam, you've done so much already.' She turned to Christian. 'And you too, Christian. Besides, don't you think you two life-saving heroes have done enough for one day?'

They shrugged off her praise. Adam, perhaps sensing her mood and that it was time to leave, said, 'You know where I am, Gen, just give me a ring if you need anything. Promise?'

She kissed him gratefully.

After he'd gone, Christian said, 'Do you want me to go as well?'

'Don't be offended, but yes. I think Nattie and I need some time alone.' She saw the disappointment in his face and felt a prickle of misgiving. It had been a long day for him and now he had a lengthy journey ahead of him. He couldn't have picked a worse day to surprise her.

'Are you sure you'll be all right?' he said.

'We'll be fine.'

But they weren't fine. Not really. Nattie was as devastated about Gran as she was. 'I know it's ridiculous,' her sister said late that night, 'but a part of me always believed Gran would live for ever.'

They were in Genevieve's room, sitting on her bed, and all they wanted to do was talk about Gran. To remember her.

'I want to be just like her when I'm old,' Nattie said. 'She was the perfect role model. Dotty as hell, a one-off.'

'She was that all right. And some.'

Nattie was silent for a while, then said, 'Gen, do you believe there's such a thing as an afterlife?'

Genevieve thought back to when their grandfather had died. 'I used to like picturing Grandad running a heavenly farm. I'd see him ploughing fields in a shiny red tractor, providing endless churns of creamy milk for the thirsty angels. A combination of Enid Blyton and the Bible.'

'Was there any ginger beer?'

It was the first light-hearted comment either of them had made. When they were little, Gran had kept them amused for hours reading Blyton adventure stories, and the memory had them both reaching for the tissue box. A collection of used ones lay on the floor around the waste-paper bin.

'I wish Mum and Dad were here,' Nattie said. 'When did Dad say his flight would arrive?'

'He wasn't really making a lot of sense when I spoke to him the second time, but I checked online, and it looks like he should get to Heathrow at breakfast time the day after tomorrow.'

'And you're sure Mum isn't coming back with him? I mean, she wouldn't deliberately miss the funeral, would she? I swear I'll never speak to her again if she does.'

'He said they couldn't get another ticket. The flight was full. He got the last remaining seat. He was lucky to get that.'

Staring into the middle distance, Nattie said, 'He wasn't the only one who was lucky today.' Then, hugging herself, she looked back at Genevieve. 'I was in such a state earlier I didn't thank Adam and Christian for what they did. You too.'

'I'm sure they understood. Anyway, you can go and thank Adam tomorrow.' She thought how brave Adam had been. He could easily have drowned if it hadn't been for Christian. 'Nattie,' she said, 'just for once, try to be nice to him. He'd never say it himself, he's far too modest, but he risked his life trying to rescue Lily.'

Nattie reached for another tissue, her eyes filling with tears. 'Don't you think I realise that?' she said gruffly.

'Here I am practically suicidal with guilt and you're lecturing me on being nice to a man who saved Lily's life. Get real, Gen!'

Chapter Forty-one

Old habits die hard, and in times of crisis, Genevieve still turned to food. She had been up earlier than usual, and instead of making herself some toast and taking it to eat outside, she'd thrown open the fridge and cupboards to see what was available. It was to be a sweet fest, she decided. A satisfying, irresistible mammoth indulgence: Welshcakes rich with allspice plus the ultimate in gooey comfort food, American pancakes, fluffy and as light as air but glossy with maple syrup. She weighed the flour for the Welshcakes then added butter and rubbed it gently between her fingers. It had been Gran who had taught her the secret of good baking. 'Keep your arms relaxed and your fingers full of kindness,' she'd say. 'Imagine you're handling a newborn baby. The more love you put into the food, the better it will taste.'

But thinking of Gran made Genevieve feel choked and breathless. The sorrow of not saying goodbye seemed too painful to bear. More than anything she wanted to keep her grandmother's memory vivid and alive. But it was too late. Already she was slipping away from Genevieve, and for a panicky moment she couldn't picture the old lady. She fought to overcome the fear and at last Gran's face popped into her head. A happy, smiling Gran.

Two hours later the guests, along with Lily-Rose, were enjoying the fruits of Genevieve's labours; she'd made sure there would be one waffle left for herself when breakfast was over. Her early morning baking session had left her feeling soothed and less tearful.

Sitting at the table, a dribble of maple syrup running down her chin, Lily-Rose was her normal happy self. Genevieve added crispy ribbons of streaky bacon to a plate of pancakes for one of the guests and listened to the little girl pestering her mother as to when Henry and Morwenna would be coming home. Nattie, pale and distracted, clearly wasn't interested in rushing to fetch the donkeys. As though suffering from delayed shock at so very nearly losing her daughter, she kept touching her. And to compound the shock, there was Gran's death to come to terms with. Lily-Rose still knew nothing about it. There hadn't seemed an appropriate moment yesterday to tell her about Gran. Last night, Nattie had said that she would be the one to break the news.

'But I don't want her to know too soon,' she'd said. 'There's a danger that she might connect the two events, and think that her wandering off in some way caused Gran's death.'

Genevieve could see the logic in this, but thought the sooner her sister got it over and done with, the better. As it was, Lily-Rose had already asked twice if they could go and see Gran after they'd brought Henry and Morwenna home. She looked at her niece, standing on a chair washing her hands at the sink. Tilting her head from side to side, she was humming to herself just like a young Polly.

How Genevieve wished Polly was here with them. Earlier, in the middle of making the pancake batter, the telephone had rung. It had been Polly calling to say that Jonjo had got her on a flight home and she was at the airport waiting to board the plane.

'Is Jonjo coming back with you?' Genevieve had asked.

'He wanted to,' Polly said, 'but I wouldn't let him. He came here because of work; he really ought to stay. How are you all coping?'

'Pretty well.'

'Oh, Gen, I still can't believe Gran's dead. I wish we didn't have to have a funeral. They're so morbid. It makes it too final.'

It was a typical Polly remark; sufficiently off-key to resonate with a note of perfectly pitched clarity. Why should there be this need to tie up the loose ends, to put a loved one in a closed box, literally, and then carry on without them? Some would argue it was the only way to accept that a life was over, but Genevieve wasn't so sure she wanted to accept that Gran would no longer be around. As Gran herself might say, 'It'll take more than death to get rid of me!'

They were in the garden having a picnic lunch on the lawn, despite the grass still being damp. The sun was shining again and it felt good to be outside, to feel the uplifting warmth on their faces. Lily-Rose had wanted the picnic. 'A proper picnic,' she'd said, 'with a blanket and a basket.' Neither Genevieve nor Nattie felt inclined to refuse her. And it was now that Nattie chose to tell her daughter about her great grandmother.

In response to her mother's explanation why they couldn't go and see Gran, and breaking off from trying to fit a Hula Hoop onto each of her fingers, Lily-Rose looked solemnly at Nattie. She didn't say anything.

'But you mustn't be sad about it,' Nattie said hurriedly, 'Gran wouldn't have wanted that. She'd want us all to be happy. For us to sit here, just as we are, having a lovely picnic in the sunshine and thinking about her.'

Lily-Rose's hands drooped; a Hula Hoop slipped off one of her fingers. Until she spoke, it was difficult to know what else either Genevieve or Nattie could say to reassure her. But from the blank look on her face, it was evident she had no idea how to react. A timely cry from a gull sitting high up on the chimney pot filled the silence and provided the distraction they needed.

'Do you remember how Gran was always putting bread out for the birds,' Genevieve said to Lily-Rose, 'but she'd chase the big gulls away?'

Lily-Rose nodded. 'She shook her broom at them.'

Nattie smiled. 'When I was little, she shook her broom at me sometimes.'

'Because you were naughty?'

'Oh, Lily, I was the naughtiest girl in the whole world.'

Lily-Rose turned to Genevieve. 'Was she?'

'Well, not all the time. There were occasions when she behaved herself. But not often.'

Removing the remaining Hula Hoops from her fingers, scattering them on the blanket, Lily-Rose stood up. She put her arms around her mother's neck and kissed her smack on the lips. Nattie hugged her tight and pressed a noisy kiss on Lily-Rose's cheek; it made her squeal and wriggle. As though the conversation about Gran had never taken place, she said, 'When can Henry and Morwenna come home?'

Genevieve was about to suggest they take up Tubby's offer of help, when she heard a noise coming from the front of the house. 'Look who's here, Lily,' she said.

Lily-Rose's face lit up. 'Henry! Morwenna!' Before anyone could tell her to slow down, she was off, dashing across the lawn to where Adam and Tubby were leading the donkeys out of a ramshackle horse box.

'They look pleased as punch to be home,' Adam said, when the animals had been led to the orchard and were grazing contentedly on familiar grass. 'And before you accuse us of interfering, Nattie, we thought you and Gen had enough on your plates without worrying about these two.'

Genevieve went inside to fetch two ice-cold beers. When she rejoined them in the garden, they, with Nattie, were watching Lily-Rose feed handfuls of grass to the donkeys.

'If she carries on spoiling them like that,' Tubby said, 'they'll forget how to graze altogether. They'll be tapping on the window waiting to be invited inside.'

They went and sat at the table on the terrace, the mood suddenly politely awkward between them. Nobody was looking anyone in the eye. That was the trouble with death, thought Genevieve; it made people act out of character, made them too deferential. Not so long ago Nattie would have been sitting here being rude and antagonistic, saying anything to wind up Adam and taking Tubby to task over whatever took her fancy.

Tubby left when he'd finished his beer, but at Nattie's invitation, Adam remained where he was. Genevieve took it as her cue to leave them alone. She joined Lily-Rose in the orchard, and suggested they walk down to the shops. 'Let's buy some sweets to cheer us up, shall we?'

Down in the village, Lily-Rose was greeted with a five-star VIP welcome. She lapped up the attention, particularly in the mini-market when Stan gave her a big bag of sweets for free. She offered one to Debs when they called in at the salon so that Genevieve could thank Debs again for putting the search party together yesterday.

'It was the least we could do,' Debs said. 'We're all just so pleased the day ended so well.' Realising her blunder, she lowered her voice so that Lily-Rose couldn't hear. 'It was a dreadful shame about your Gran. We'll miss her. You know, she had the most wonderful hair. Strong and springy, more like a fifty-year-old's.'

Regretting every bad thought she'd ever harboured about Debs, Genevieve said goodbye. They'd only gone a few yards when they saw Adam coming towards them. Lily-Rose slipped her hand out of Genevieve's and ran to him.

He picked her up and swung her round. 'And what have you got there, little Rosy-Posy?'

'Flying Saucers. They're my favourite. Would you like one?'

'No thanks. You keep them for yourself.'

Curious to know how Nattie's attempt to be nice to Adam had gone, Genevieve probed unashamedly. 'Nattie say anything pleasant to you?'

He put Lily-Rose back on the ground. 'As a matter of fact, she did. And you know what? I reckon it was the hardest thing she's ever had to do.'

'You didn't deliberately make it harder for her, did you?'

He looked hurt. 'Gen! What do you take me for?'

'I'm sorry. That was out of order.'

'Forget it. Now look, if there's anything you need a hand with, you will say, won't you? Your grandmother was a popular woman, and people will want to help if they can. You only have to say the word.'

She nodded. 'I know, but until Dad comes home tomorrow morning we're in limbo.'

'And if you want anyone to talk to, you know . . . about your Gran, my shoulder's at your disposal.' Smiling, he added, 'I've used yours often enough, it seems only right you should have the use of mine.'

His words were so sincere, she didn't trust herself to thank him. 'Come on, Lily,' she mumbled, 'we ought to be getting home. Your mother will be wondering where you've got to.'

Back at Paradise House, Nattie was sitting on the terrace where Genevieve had left her earlier. Her head was in her arms on the table and it was obvious she was crying.

Lily-Rose put a hand on her mother's arm. 'Mummy, why are you crying? Would you like a sweet?'

Nattie raised her head and sniffed loudly. She tried to speak, but couldn't. She put her arms around Lily-Rose and held her tightly, as if she'd never let her go.

*

'Sorry about all that in the garden.' Nattie was helping Genevieve get dinner ready that evening. All but two guests had opted to eat in and, on reflection, a busy evening was just what they needed. Kelly had come in to help, and they were carrying on as normal, while Lily-Rose watched a Disney video on the television in the corner of the kitchen. Genevieve was arranging plates of vegetable tempura with aubergine pickle.

'Don't be stupid, Nats, there's no need to apologise for crying.'

Kelly appeared in the kitchen. 'Table two's order,' she said, handing the slip of paper to Nattie. 'Shall I take those through?' she asked Genevieve.

When they were alone again, Nattie said, 'It was Adam's fault, of course.'

Genevieve, her head in the oven as she checked on a main course of braised lamb shank in a Madeira sauce, stopped what she was doing. She looked at her sister sharply. 'How did you reach that conclusion?'

Nattie fiddled with the stubby remains of a root of ginger. 'If you must know, he –' she glanced over to Lily-Rose, and lowered her voice, 'he told me he would have done anything to save Lily-Rose. That she really matters to him.'

'And you have a problem with that?'

'It made me realise what a – ' again she glanced over to Lily-Rose – 'what a bitch I've been to him. He really cares, doesn't he? All this time I thought he'd been using her to get round me.'

Genevieve closed the oven. 'You idiot. I've been telling you for ages what a genuine guy he is.'

'You know he's selling up, don't you?'

'He did mention it.'

'You never said.'

'He told me not to tell anyone. Besides, since when

have you been interested in what he does?'

'I'm interested now. He says he's moving out of the area. He told me there's nothing to keep him here.'

Saddened by her sister's last remark, Genevieve felt they'd let Adam down in some way.

'And what am I going to tell Lily?' Nattie continued. 'She adores Adam. She's lost her great grandmother, and to all intents and purposes her grandmother, and now Adam is deserting her. I've a good mind to make him tell Lily himself.'

'Oh, for goodness sake, Nats, stop being so selfish and always thinking of number one. Ask yourself the obvious question: why does Adam think there's nothing to keep him here?'

The opportunity for Nattie to respond was snatched from her by Kelly coming back into the kitchen with a stack of empty plates. When they were able to talk freely again, instead of picking up where they'd left off, Nattie changed tack.

'I didn't tell you about the school reunion, did I?'

Genevieve was half-tempted to say she couldn't give a damn about the school reunion. 'Was it worth the effort of going all that way?'

'Yes and no. The food was lousy, what Gran would call a pork pie and pickled onion event.'

'Isn't it the people you're supposed to be more interested in?'

'I'm coming to them. And one in particular. Remember Lucinda Atkins from your year?'

'How could I forget her? She was one of the Queens of Spite.'

'And do you remember her sister, Vivienne, in my year? Well, it doesn't matter if you do or not, but guess who she bumped into six months ago in Edinburgh?'

'Go on, I can see you're itching to tell me.'

'None other than Rachel Harmony! Except now she's

Rachel White, married with three children and living in Scotland. Her husband's an accountant, twelve years older than her, and they've just celebrated their sixth wedding anniversary. Who'd have thought it? I'd have put money on her ending up as some designer clothes addict living in London and milking dry her third husband.'

For the first time in years, Genevieve smiled as she thought of her old friend. 'Good for Rachel,' was all she said.

It was almost midnight when Polly arrived home. She was exhausted, having hardly slept during the long flight and then driven herself from Heathrow in a hire car that Jonjo had arranged. Seeing how shattered she was, Genevieve made her get ready for bed straight away and took her up a mug of tea. She and Nattie sat with her for a while, Nattie plaiting Polly's hair like she used to when they were little. They wanted to ask what Hong Kong had been like, but in the circumstances, it didn't seem right. As they were about to say goodnight and close the door, Polly yawned and said, 'Oh, I nearly forgot, Jonjo's asked me to marry him.'

They came back into the room, almost tripping over each other.

'But you hardly know each other,' said Nattie.

'What was your answer?' asked Genevieve, amused at Nattie for sounding so sensible for once, and at Polly for dropping the news so casually into the conversation.

'I said I'd think about it.'

'But you hardly know him,' repeated Nattie, clearly too stunned to think of anything else to say.

'That's what makes the prospect of marrying him so exciting. Who wants to marry someone they know completely? Where's the fun in that?' Yawning hugely, Polly pulled the covers up and closed her eyes. 'Goodnight.'

Shutting the door behind them, Genevieve thought how wonderfully simple and straightforward Polly made life seem. It was good having her home again.

The morning brought a sky of brilliant blue and a sea that was as still and shiny as glass. After breakfast had been served and tidied away, Genevieve took a short break before helping Donna – now fully recovered – clean the bedrooms. All their guests were staying on, so it was a comparatively easy day with no change-overs. Taking the post with her, she went outside to her bench. There was the usual rubbish amongst the mail, which she put aside to go straight in the bin, plus a handful of With Deepest Sympathy cards from neighbours and friends. It struck Genevieve that Gran would have loved all the attention. The thought made her smile, and her smile widened when she opened the next envelope. It was from Christian; a brief note to say that he was thinking of her and hoped she and her sisters were managing. His last comment was to say how much he wished he could be with her.

'Me too,' she sighed.

She opened the rest of the mail, including a formal-looking envelope from the bank in Tenby. She held her breath as she ripped it open. Slowly she read the letter twice to be sure of its content, to be convinced that she'd understood it properly. She then put the letter back inside the envelope and wondered if she really dare go ahead. From nowhere she heard Gran's voice, so clear she could have been sitting on the bench with her.

'You can do it, Gen. You know you can.'

She stood up to go back inside and help Donna. As she was crossing the lawn, she heard a car. She checked her watch. Could it be Dad? Still clutching the pile of mail, she went round to the front of the house and found her father stepping down from the driver's side of his Land

Rover and rubbing his lower back. Happy relief swept through her and she quickened her step to greet him.

She was almost upon him when she realised he wasn't alone. Pushing open the door on the passenger's side was Serena Baxter.

Chapter Forty-two

'But we thought you couldn't get a seat on the flight with Dad?'

'So did we. But they put me on standby at the airport. At the very last minute there was a cancellation.'

'Why didn't you tell us you were coming?' This was from Nattie and there was a distinct accusatory tone to her words.

'Oh, darling, there wasn't time. It's been such a mad, crazy rush. We just wanted to get back as soon as possible, to be with you all.'

'Does this mean you're home for good?' Again the question was from Nattie and it was suitably loaded. She had always been the least forgiving of them and her face was uncomfortably hostile. Genevieve hoped her mother was too jetlagged to take it to heart.

'Goodness,' said Serena, with a spirited show of blithe cheeriness. 'All these questions and I haven't had so much as a chance to draw breath. I'd love a cup of tea. You can't imagine how desperate I am for a decent cup of Typhoo. Where's Polly?'

They were standing in the kitchen, Daddy Dean, Serena, Nattie, Lily-Rose and Genevieve. 'She's still in bed,' Genevieve said, conscious that it was glaringly obvious to everyone that Serena had deliberately not answered Nattie.

'Actually, I'm right here. Hello Daddy. Hello Mum! What a brilliant surprise! I thought I could hear your voices.' Rubbing the sleep from her eyes and still dressed in her nightclothes, Polly stepped into the room. Her sunny presence instantly took the edge off the hostile atmosphere Nattie had generated. She kissed their father first, who had Lily-Rose in his arms, plus a fluffy Kiwi bird, then their mother. 'You look different, Mum. Have you lost weight?'

Serena smiled. 'A little. I've taken up yoga. But I'll tell you about it later. I've so much to share with you. Now then, shall I make us a drink? The kitchen looks very tidy. Better than it used to. That must be your doing, Genevieve.'

'That's okay, Mum. Why don't I put the kettle on while you and Dad freshen up?'

When she was alone with her sisters – Lily-Rose had gone upstairs with her grandparents – Genevieve filled the kettle. 'Nattie, I think you should drop the belligerent act. It's really not the time or the place.'

Nattie picked at a nail and scowled. 'I would have thought it's exactly the time and place. How can she just waltz in here as though it's the most normal thing in the world for a wife and mother to bugger off and then come back like nothing has happened? It'll take more than a toy kiwi bird to get round me. And did you catch the way she didn't say if she was home for good?'

'Yes, I did. But for now, and for Dad's sake, let's just play it her way. Perhaps we'll have to wait until after the funeral before she'll open up to us.'

But Genevieve was wrong. After lunch, while their father, who had scarcely uttered a word since arriving home, got on the phone and started organising the funeral, Serena asked Genevieve and her sisters to go for a walk with her. She said she wanted to talk to them. Genevieve had a sudden fear that Serena was preparing them for the inevitable: divorce. Nattie armed herself with Lily-Rose, counting on their mother's better nature not to say anything unpleasant with her granddaughter around.

They didn't walk far, just down to the beach, where they picked their way through the stretched-out bodies and playing children till they found themselves a place to sit on the pebbles. After kicking off her sandals, Lily-Rose took her fishing net and went to play in a nearby rock pool. Anyone looking at their long faces as they watched her would have thought how conspicuously they stood out from the crowd. Even Polly seemed muted and anxious.

Serena had changed out of her travelling clothes and was now wearing an outfit Genevieve didn't recognise. It was a simple, sleeveless, olive-coloured shift dress that suited her new shape. Her hair was cropped short, and where before it had been shot through with dowdy grey, it was now highlighted with a flattering mixture of copper and nut-brown. She'd had her ears pierced, something she'd always claimed she was too squeamish to have done, and wore a pair of star-shaped earrings with a matching necklace and bracelet. On her feet she wore a pair of smooth leather thong sandals. All in all, she looked great and glowed with a healthy radiance that couldn't be caused by sun alone. And anyway, she had just left New Zealand in the grip of winter. It was hard to admit, but Genevieve could see that the change had done her mother good. But what if it wasn't just the change of scene that was responsible for the new Serena? What if this old friend Pete was the cause?

'I've missed this so much,' Serena said, her arms embracing the shore and looking up to Paradise House.

Genevieve shot Nattie a warning glance, knowing it was probably on her tongue to say, 'Then why did you leave it so long before coming home?'

'I felt exactly the same when I came back,' Genevieve said, taking on the familiar role of mediator. 'I kept thinking I had to make the most of it in case it disappeared.'

'Oh, please,' cut in Nattie, not for a second put off by Genevieve's warning look, 'let's cut the deep and meaningful crap and get to the point. Mum, are you, or are you not, home for good?'

Serena placed a hand on Nattie's arm. 'Still the same old Natalie, then? Looking for a clear-cut answer to every question?' For a moment their mother looked and sounded as quietly composed as Polly.

But Nattie was having none of it. 'There you go again,' she said angrily, 'avoiding the question. Is that what you've been learning to do while we've been consoling Dad? I don't think you have any idea how much you hurt him. What's more, I don't think you even care.'

'Oh, but Nattie, I do. I care deeply. And not just about your father. About you, too. All of you. But did any of you stop and think about me? About why I went?'

Nattie picked up a stone and brought it down hard on another. 'As far as I can see, you went because, selfishly, you wanted to indulge yourself in a stupid mid-life crisis.'

Serena smiled. 'And is there anything wrong with that?'

'Yes, there is! You're a middle-aged woman with . . . with responsibilities. You're not supposed to go off when the whim takes you.'

Quietly, Serena said, 'Maybe I'm wrong, Nattie, but I think the reason you're so angry with me is that you're jealous. What would you give, right now, to be able to go off on your own? To go this very minute without a backward glance for any responsibilities you have? No, don't look so indignant. I know you love Lily-Rose, but I bet there's a part of you that would love to be able to do what I've done.'

Nattie gave their mother a ferocious stare. 'That's not true! And how can you say that after what nearly happened to Lily? God Mum, how can you be so bloody insensitive?' She got to her feet and marched off, her shoes grinding the stones underfoot as she went over to the rock pools to be with her daughter.

Serena sighed. 'I knew this would happen. It's one of the reasons I dreaded coming home.' She turned to Genevieve and Polly. 'Anything you two want to accuse me of? If so, best we get it all over and done with. Who wants to go first?'

Polly shook her head and Genevieve said, 'Nattie will be okay, Mum. Don't worry. You know what she's like. She doesn't accept change unless she's at the epicentre of it.'

Her mother smiled faintly, then suddenly looked tired. 'I did miss you all, you know. I badly wanted to see you again, but as the weeks and then the months passed by I began to worry if you'd want me home.'

'But our letters! We told you how much we wanted you here.'

'Yes, but why did you? For my sake? Your father's? Or your own?'

Genevieve couldn't meet Serena's eyes. 'A mixture of all three,' she said truthfully.

'What about you, Polly?'

'I just wanted you to be happy, Mum. And if that meant you had to stay away, then sooner or later we would have come to terms with it. Are you going to divorce Dad?'

'Perhaps that's a question you should be asking your father. After all, I've given him every reason to want to divorce me.'

'Oh, Mum,' said Genevieve, 'how could you even think that? He's mad about you. Why do you think he flew to New Zealand to see you? Haven't you had a chance to talk things through yet?'

'Not really. Your Gran's death has put *us* on hold for the time being. It's very important we make the right decision when we're both thinking straight. Your father

372

has to want me home for all the right reasons.'

'What about Pete?' Genevieve asked. The question came out more snappily than she'd intended. 'Where does he fit in?'

'He doesn't.'

'Come off it, Mum. You've been living with him all these months. Of course he fits in.'

'I've been *staying* with Pete, not living with him, Genevieve. There's a big difference. There's also the small matter of him being gay.'

'*Gay?*' Genevieve had to repeat the word, to make sure she'd heard right. 'But why didn't you say? Why did you leave us to suspect the worst?'

'Because . . . because I needed to. I needed to shake your father up. To see how badly he wanted me. And not just as cook, cleaner and general dogsbody at Paradise House.'

It was as Genevieve had suspected. Her mother had grown tired of always being there for everyone. She couldn't blame her for that. Being taken for granted, as she'd come to know, was soul-destroying.

'And do you know what makes it worse?' Serena said. 'It's knowing that it was all my own fault. I encouraged your father to sell the farm and live out my dream; the idyllic dream of running a cosy B and B by the sea. But in the end it turned into something I didn't want any more. Can you imagine how guilty that made me feel?'

'Mum, there's nothing wrong in waking up on Christmas morning and being disappointed by the present you'd always wanted. But have you asked Dad if it's what he still wants?'

'Oh, Polly, you know what your father's like. He always wants to please other people. He's just so infuriatingly considerate.'

'But you still love him, Mum, don't you?'

Serena turned back to Genevieve. 'As you grow older,

Gen, you come to realise that it's not just love that keeps a marriage alive.'

'What, then?' But before her mother got the words out, Genevieve knew exactly what she was going to say.

'The unexpected. The thrill of not knowing what's going to happen next. Being stuck in a rut is what kills most marriages. I suppose what I'd come to realise was that without a zing in my heart, I felt dead.'

'You need to talk to Dad,' Genevieve said.

Serena nodded. 'I will. When your grandmother's funeral is over.'

Chapter Forty-three

It was a beautiful day.

'Your Gran will have ordered the sun especially,' Tubby said to Genevieve as he put his arm round Donna, steering her out of the church and into the sunshine. 'I bet she's looking down and wishing she was here with us.'

Almost everyone from the village had shown up at St Non's for Gran's funeral, and Genevieve was conscious that each and every one of them had something cheerful to say about Granny Baxter. But the best comment had been made by the vicar during the service. He'd said that Gran, who had never been slow in chiding him for the length of his sermons, was sure to be up there in heaven getting along like a house on fire with all the other saints.

In the graveyard, grouped around the hole in the ground where Gran's coffin was now lying, Genevieve thought of the instructions her grandmother had given them some time ago on how she wanted her remains to be dealt with. She'd made them all laugh by saying, 'Cremation? Over my dead body!' And just so that there could be no confusion on the matter, she'd left them a letter.

I've let you off lightly while I've been alive, but in death I'm determined to be a burden to you all. You'll have to tend my grave regularly and keep it nice with fresh flowers. None of those cheap plastic ones I've seen in graveyards these days. And I want an angel fixed to the stone, something with a bit of class. I've put some money by especially, so you'll not have to worry about the cost.

As if they'd have worried about the price of an angel, thought Genevieve, as she watched her father throw a handful of earth onto the coffin. His face was solemn, beaded with sweat from the warmth of the midday sun – he was wearing his only suit, a thick wool one. Her mother went next, then Nattie, helped by Lily-Rose, who was wearing her butterfly wing rucksack and looking appropriately angel-like. Then it was Genevieve's turn. She threw a sprinkling of dusty earth and willed her grandmother, wherever she was, to know how much she was loved and missed. Silently, eyes closed, she said, 'Life will never be the same without you, Gran. You were the one true constant in our lives.'

When the service was over, people began milling around, murmuring discreetly and admiring the many wreaths and bouquets. Some were blatantly inspecting the cards – who had given what? Had the florist got their order right? It seemed wrong, this undisguised act of curiosity, like snooping through someone's private letters. The scent of so many flowers filled the air and Genevieve was glad her grandmother hadn't specified there were to be none. As she used to say, 'You can't beat a bit of pomp and circumstance.'

A painful lump of grief rose in her throat. She wandered away from the main group of mourners and went to stand in the shade of a large yew tree that was supported on one side by a pair of sturdy oak props. She and Christian had sheltered here once from a sudden downpour. Disappointed that he hadn't been able to make it for the funeral – he'd emailed yesterday to say he was inundated with work – she thought how little contact there had been between them since Gran had died. She sensed something had changed between them, but couldn't put her finger on what it was. A distance had opened up, and not just a geographical one.

Standing under the tree, picking out the members of her family amongst the crowd of mourners, she had never felt so alone or isolated. She hadn't just lost a grandmother, she'd lost an irreplaceable life-long friend. And now, according to Nattie, Adam was thinking of moving away.

From across the graveyard, where he was standing on his own, Adam turned and caught her eye. He smiled and raised his eyebrows, as if to say, 'You okay?' She nodded, then stepped out of the shadows and into the sunlight to join him.

It was just as Gran would have wanted. Everyone, now that they had made a start on Genevieve's buffet, had loosened up and the wine was flowing freely. Not everyone who'd been in church had been invited, but those who had were pleased to see Serena back within the fold and were all making the assumption that she was here to stay. As she brushed Daddy Dean's collar – he'd managed to run a dirty finger round it at the graveside after throwing his handful of earth – she looked very much back for good. But from the way she'd spoken on the beach the day before yesterday, and the fact that she was insisting on sleeping at Angel Cottage, there was no knowing what the future held.

Genevieve had been desperate to talk to her father, to give him some kind of hint of what was expected of him, but her mother had made her promise, along with Polly, that they were not to say anything.

'It has to come from him,' Serena said. 'If there's to be any chance of us staying together, your father has to work things out for himself.'

But was it fair to test him in this way?

Most people were now retreating to the tables placed in the shade, but Genevieve was sitting on the steps of the conservatory, enjoying the sun. She was now onto her third glass of wine and prepared to drink a whole lot more before the day was out. She didn't normally drink so much – it was a control thing, like keeping everything tidy and in its place – but today was an exception.

'Room for a friend down there?' It was Adam, with a bottle of wine in his hand.

She moved along the step to make room for him.

'You look knackered,' he said, giving her glass a top-up.

'I'm fine.'

'You always say that.'

'Do I? Do I really?'

'Yes, and one day I might go the extra mile and believe you. But not today.' He put his arm round her. 'You need a holiday, Gen.'

She let her head rest on his shoulder. 'You might be right. Where shall I go? I hear New Zealand is particularly good for putting the spring back into one's step.'

'Wherever you want. Alaska or the Antipodes, you name it and I'll take you there.'

She lifted her head. 'Adam?'

'Yes?'

'You're always looking out for me, aren't you? Why?'

'Because I like you. In fact, I like you a lot.'

'How much a lot?'

He smiled. 'Is that a proper sentence?'

'You . . . you don't fancy me, do you?'

He laughed. 'Now what the hell made you ask a daft question like that?'

Sober enough to blush, she hid her face in his shoulder and mumbled something about being emotionally unstable just now. When she'd recovered, she said, 'So what's this I hear from Nattie about you abandoning us?'

'Ah. She told you.'

'Of course she did.'

'Do you Baxter girls tell each other everything?'

'Very little. That's half the problem with our family. Anyway, answer my question. I'm sick of people being so evasive.'

'Ooh, scary. Genevieve gets tough!'

She dug him in the ribs with her elbow, spilling some of her wine onto the step, but he just fastened his hold on her and pulled her closer, making her laugh.

'For heaven's sake, you two! Do you really think that's appropriate behaviour on a day like this?' Standing in front of them, hands on her hips, was Nattie, and she looked like thunder.

But all Genevieve could do was laugh even harder. How good it felt to let the tension of the last few days flow out of her.

Chapter Forty-four

Gran's will was very precise and, in the letter she'd written to accompany it, she was insistent that her wishes were to be respected. Money was not a subject she'd ever dwelt on, but everyone in the family was amazed at how much she'd squirreled away over the years. It was by no means a fortune, but it was more than they'd expected. She'd never been stingy, but she'd lived carefully and from what they could understand, had hardly touched the capital of what Grandad had left her in his will.

Instead of leaving everything to Daddy Dean, as they'd thought she would, she'd left it to Genevieve and her sisters. But whereas Genevieve and Polly were bequeathed an equal share of money, Nattie had been given Angel Cottage. The old lady had written:

This is to provide my granddaughter and great grand-daughter with a home. And to ensure that it can never be got hold of by some feckless man Nattie gets involved with, the house is to be put in Lily-Rose's name until her eighteenth birthday. Only then will it legally belong to Natalie, by which time she might have achieved the unthinkable and settled down with a reliable man she can trust.

Nattie's response was not to be outraged that Gran thought so little of her ability to pick a decent boyfriend, but to laugh out loud. 'Good on you, canny Gran!'

Later in the day, though, Genevieve found her in the orchard with Henry and Morwenna, tears streaming down her cheeks.

'Oh, Gen,' she sobbed, 'I don't deserve Gran's little house. She should have left it to you or Polly. You're both so much more deserving.'

'Nonsense. You have Lily-Rose to take care of. Angel Cottage gives the pair of you stability and security. Gran did exactly the right thing.'

Rubbing the heels of her hands into her eyes to stem the flow of tears, Nattie said, 'I wish she was here for me to thank her properly. I miss her so much.'

That had been a week ago and since then Nattie had undergone a dramatic change: she was talking about getting a job. It seemed that canny Gran had been exactly that. Now that she had a proper home of her own, Nattie was suddenly viewing life differently.

'It's like she's growing up at last,' Genevieve said to Adam. They were having a drink in the beer garden at the Salvation Arms. Mum and Dad were holding the fort together and she was enjoying a rare night off. She never did get the free day she'd bargained for with Nattie. Life had been too eventful since.

'You mean she's going to get off her bum and do a decent day's work?'

'She says she'll take the first job offer that comes her way, so long as it pays enough for a childminder for Lily-Rose, and then when Lily goes to school, she might go back to school herself and complete the degree she dipped out of.'

Adam nodded approvingly. 'Good for her. But I guess finding a reliable childminder for Lily won't be easy, or cheap.'

'It won't, but I'm sure I'll be able to help out now and again.'

Adam turned his beer glass round on the wooden

table. 'And what about *your* plans?'

'You mean, how are they going?'

'I mean, how do you think you'll have the time to take care of Lily-Rose if your own plans take off?'

She shrugged. 'Oh, these things have a way of sorting themselves out.'

He didn't look convinced, and after they'd finished their drinks, he went up to the bar for another round. She watched him chatting with Donna and thought about what he'd said. He was right, of course: babysitting Lily-Rose would be difficult, if not impossible. But as things stood, there was no knowing what was going to happen. She'd heard nothing back from the solicitors in Tenby who were handling the sale, despite ringing them several times, and was now concerned that something was wrong. Well, what else did she expect? These things seldom ran a straight course. They might for the likes of Adam, but not for her. She gave herself a mental rap on the knuckles. Adam had probably started out in business with exactly the same chance of making it as she did. And she wasn't doing anything as ambitious as buying acres and acres of run-down caravan park. All she wanted to do, with the help of a loan and the money George had left her, was buy a modest-sized property to convert into a teashop-cum-restaurant.

It had been Tubby who had unwittingly alerted her to the possibility, and the property stood right here in the village, two doors up from Angel Crafts. He had only told her about it in passing, as he did with any snatch of gossip. But she'd pounced on the opportunity at once, before anyone else could get there before her. For years the pretty little end of terrace house had been owned by a family in Cardiff who rented it out all year round, but now they wanted to sell up with the minimum of fuss and expense. Before they'd bought the house, it had been the village bakery, and one of the original bread ovens was still in place in what was now the kitchen. Planning permission to return the property to commercial use was a mere formality, so her solicitor had told her, but now Genevieve wasn't so sure. Perhaps this was proving to be the inevitable stumbling block.

Only two people knew about her plans, Adam and Christian, and they both kept telling her that she was worrying unnecessarily. Deep down she knew what was bothering her: irrationally she didn't believe she could be on the end of such good fortune. Just as Nattie had said she didn't deserve Angel Cottage, Genevieve thought she hadn't earned the right to this lucky break.

'You look glum,' Adam said, when he returned with their drinks. 'What's up? I leave you for five minutes and come back to a face like a mullet.'

She grinned inanely. 'That better?'

'Marginally.'

'So what's the latest news from the bar?'

He took a long sip of his beer. 'According to Donna, the talent contest next Saturday night is a total sell-out.'

'I know, she told me this morning. She also told me she's trying to persuade you to participate. Has she won you over? Adam?'

'Err . . . no comment.'

'She has, hasn't she? You're going to sing! Oh, now this I have to see. What will you sing? Or rather, who will you be?'

He winked. 'Again, no comment. But what about you? Are you going to throw your inhibitions to the wind and give us a song?'

'You must be joking. Polly's the only musical one in our family.'

'Who mentioned anything about me being musical? I'm just going to get up there and make an idiot of myself.' After another mouthful of beer, he said, 'How's everyone at Paradise House? What's the latest on your parents?'

'As you might expect, nothing's been decided.'

He frowned. 'I don't get it. Your mother seems genuinely glad to be back. I can't imagine her leaving again.'

'It's not as simple as that.' She told him what Serena had told her and Polly on the beach. 'It could only happen in my family,' she sighed. 'We just don't seem capable of acting normally. Mum's been home for nearly two weeks and as far as I know, she and Dad still haven't talked properly. They talk about everything else, like sorting out Gran's things, and the wallpaper that needs replacing in the guest sitting room, but they pussyfoot around the really important issue.'

'You'd think they'd both be desperate to clear the air and see how they stand. Especially your father.'

'I think Gran's death has taken precedence. And maybe they're both hiding behind it a little. Particularly Dad. He seems to be avoiding being alone with Mum. I think he's frightened she'll use the moment to destroy any hope he has.'

'It wouldn't do any harm to give your father a nudge in the right direction. Your mother need never know.'

'I could, but in a way I agree with her. She needs to know that Dad wants her home for the right reasons, not just because he can't function properly without her. She also wants to be sure that things are going to change.'

'If I know your Dad, he probably thinks by flying out to New Zealand he's already made the grand gesture to woo her back.'

'You could be right. Anyway, I know he's really upset about Gran, so we shouldn't be too hard on him. The sad thing is, Gran would have knocked their heads together by now and got them to see how committed to each other they really are.'

Adam gave a short, loud laugh. 'Commitment! Now that's a concept you and Nattie could do with familiarising yourselves with.'

'What do you mean? Nattie and I don't have a problem with commitment.'

'Sure you do. Look at Nattie. She deliberately chooses all the wrong boyfriends so she doesn't have to connect with them and get seriously involved. She's either terrified of being tied down or of being hurt.'

Genevieve had never thought of Nattie as vulnerable, but perhaps Adam had a point. And hadn't Serena more or less made the same observation? 'Okay,' she said, 'I'll give you that one. But how about this? Maybe you deliberately wanted Nattie because it saved *you* from having to make a commitment to a long-term girlfriend.'

'And why would I do that? Why wouldn't I want a proper relationship?'

'Mm . . . I don't know. You've got me there. Hey, perhaps you're gay and in denial?'

He nearly choked on his beer. He looked about him. 'A little louder, Gen. That way everyone in Angel Sands will know by the *Ten O'Clock News* that I'm a closet homosexual.'

She laughed and decided to wind him up. 'I notice you didn't answer me. So are you?'

'Am I what?'

'Gay?'

'*No!*'

'You could tell me if you were. It wouldn't make any difference. In fact, I think I'd like a gay friend. Mum seems to have benefited from having one.'

'Sorry to disappoint you, but I'm boringly straight. I wish now I'd proved it to you that night I had you in my bed.'

Now it was Genevieve's turn to see if anyone had overheard their conversation. 'Okay, now we're quits you can keep your voice down.'

He grinned. 'You started it. But before I let you off the

hook, what made you ask if I fancied you, the day of your Gran's funeral?'

She raised her glass of wine and did a poor job of hiding behind it. 'Trust you to remind me of that.'

'Well?'

'If you must know, in my drunken state, I was worried you might have transferred your affections from one loony Baxter to another.'

'And what gave you cause to think that?'

She squirmed in her seat, realising how silly she was about to sound. 'Because you're always being so nice to me,' she murmured.

He laughed. 'Nothing else for it, then. I'd better start being nasty to you. Now tell me about you and lover-boy. How's it going? I can't remember the last time you mentioned him.'

She sank back into her seat. 'Difficult to say.'

'In what way?'

'Something's changed between us. Maybe it's because he's there and I'm here.'

'Are you saying it's fizzling out between the two of you?'

'I don't know. I really don't. Perhaps if we could actually speak to each other it would help. The written word isn't my favourite form of communication; I can never say what I feel.' She drained her glass. 'Maybe long-distance relationships just aren't my thing,' she added gloomily. 'It doesn't seem to be enough for me.' She raised her eyes and looked at Adam. 'I sound selfish and greedy, don't I?'

'Not at all. There's nothing selfish in wanting to be with someone.'

Holding the stem of her empty wine glass, she twirled it round on her lap and thought of Polly and her long-distance relationship. Since coming back from Hong Kong, Jonjo had upped the ante in his bid to win Polly's heart. He called at least three times a day and continued to keep Rhys Williams, the florist, as busy as ever. Polly hadn't told their parents that Jonjo had proposed to her, and she'd asked Genevieve and Nattie to keep quiet about it until she'd made up her mind whether or not to accept. Genevieve had confided in Adam, but had made him promise not to breathe a word to anyone else.

'I wish I had what Polly's got,' she said suddenly. 'I don't mean I want Jonjo, nothing like that. I'd just like a bit more romance. Oh, God! I'm beginning to sound like my mother.'

He smiled. 'Do you think Polly will marry Jonjo?'

'You know, I have a feeling she just might. But in her own time. I've never known Polly to make a decision she's regretted, and I think it's because she won't be hurried into anything.'

'Or does she make the most of what happens as a result of simply making a decision, rather than wasting time and energy on procrastinating? It's what I've always guarded against in business. If you procrastinate it stops you from moving forward. You're always looking over your shoulder at what you can't change.'

After last orders had been called, Adam walked her home. Genevieve wondered if that's what she did too often: looked back. Then remembering what Adam had said about her and Nattie being afraid of commitment, she asked him what she was supposed to be too scared to connect with.

'That's easy. You're afraid to connect with yourself, Gen. And until you do, no one else will be able to get really close to you.'

She came to a stop. After he'd walked a few paces on his own, he turned round. 'Oh, Genevieve, don't tell me I've stunned you with my powers of deductive reasoning?'

'Just when did you get to be so smart, Adam Kellar?'

He slipped his arm through hers and made her walk on. 'I didn't make my first million by the age of twenty-six without being smart. People forget that about me sometimes.'

Chapter Forty-five

With the last of the breakfast guests gone, Nattie was helping Genevieve to clean the dining room. Two young boys – veritable demons from hell – had been allowed by their drippy, shoulder-shrugging, boys-will-be-boys parents to run amok during breakfast. They had left the area around their table a scene of war-torn devastation. The tablecloth was askew and covered in damp patches of milk and orange juice and revolting bits of half-chewed sausages dipped in ketchup; there was a smear of egg yolk on one of the chairs and some soggy Cheerios had found their way into the dish of raspberry jam. Everything Genevieve touched was sticky, including the carpet, which would need a thorough scrubbing in places. She felt sorry for the other guests, two of whom were year-in, year-out regulars: this was not what they came to Paradise House for. She would have to apologise to them later.

Mum had offered to stay and help, instead of going down to Angel Cottage with their father to carry on with the task of sorting through Gran's things, but Genevieve, eager to make her parents spend time alone together, had told her she and Nattie would soon have the dining room shipshape. Annoyingly, Dad had suggested, as he did every morning, that they take Lily-Rose with them. The little girl had jumped at the chance to play with Gran's old musical jewellery box again, so bang went another opportunity to resolve matters.

Maybe Adam was right, and someone would have to

have a word in her father's ear. If he went on avoiding being alone with Mum for much longer, he'd lose her for sure. Genevieve had hinted as much to him last night before going to bed, but he'd said, 'Genevieve, I know you think you're helping, but please, your mother and I need to take this gently. This isn't something we can rush. Slow and steady wins the race.' Exasperated, she'd given up and left him to his head-in-the-sand delusion. But she had then reminded herself that once again she was trying too hard to control what was going on around her.

Across the hall, where Polly and Donna were tidying the guest sitting room, Genevieve could hear Donna trying to press-gang her sister into lending a hand with the talent show; apparently the services of a musical director were now required.

'Everyone seems to be taking the talent show very seriously,' Genevieve remarked to Nattie as she shook out a clean white cloth and laid it over a table. 'I hope it's the success Donna and Tubby want it to be. They've put so much effort into it.'

'That's typical of you,' said Nattie. 'Always anxious on everyone else's behalf.'

'I just like things to go well. Anything wrong in that?'

'And if it's a disaster? What then?'

'Nothing, I suppose. But I don't like people to be disappointed.'

'But, Gen, it's *their* disappointment. Not yours. Oh, and talking of disappointments, Adam phoned to say he wanted to call in for a quick chat before going on to Tenby.'

'Did he say what he wanted?'

'No. And if you ask me he sounded distinctly furtive.'

Genevieve laughed and shook out another tablecloth. 'That's probably the nicest thing you've ever said about him.'

Nattie looked affronted. 'Hey, Adam and I are like this

these days.' She held up a hand, the first two fingers crossed. 'A closer pair of buddies you couldn't hope to find.'

'So why did you just refer to him as a disappointment?'

Nattie laughed. 'Because he's taking all the fun out of my life. What's he done to his clothes? They're so normal. And have you noticed he doesn't wear that tacky bracelet any more?'

Genevieve kept her face straight. 'Really? I can't say I've noticed. And frankly, I'm surprised you have. What's got into you?'

Nattie ignored the question and, clumsily folding a napkin, said, 'I reckon there's some new girl on the scene we don't know about. Whoever she is, she's obviously taking him in hand. Do you suppose we ought to keep an eye on him?'

'Whatever for?'

'Oh, come on, Gen. Adam's just ripe for the plucking. All that money's bound to attract the wrong sort of girl-friend.'

'And you care?'

'Now look, Gen, I'm getting sick of your cynicism. He saved Lily's life, so in my book, I owe him. Bottom line, I'm always going to be in his debt. Which means the least I can do is save him from some money-grabbing, high-maintenance madam who's going to take him for all she can get.'

Genevieve flicked a soggy Cheerio at her sister. 'Wow! He'll sleep easy from now on, knowing you're on the case.'

Nattie was out in the garden tidying up after Henry and Morwenna when Adam arrived. He was in full suit mode.

'Another business lunch in Tenby?' Genevieve asked.

'Another lunch, another dime.'

'Well, come on through to the kitchen and you can fill me in on what it is you want to talk about. Nattie said you were acting distinctly furtive on the phone. But then she'd say that about a newborn baby with wind. Sit yourself down. Coffee?'

'Actually it was Nattie I wanted to speak to. I thought I'd made that clear on the phone to her.'

'Oh. Oh, right. I'll go and find her. She's knee-deep in donkey doos, as Lily calls it.'

Adam smiled. 'I'll go and find her myself if you're busy.'

It had rained overnight and Genevieve looked at his expensive shoes. 'Dressed like that? I don't think so. Put the kettle on and I'll give her a shout.'

Nattie threw down the shovel and muttered crossly when Genevieve told her that it was her Adam wanted to talk to. 'Don't you dare leave me alone with him,' she said as she stomped back up to the house. 'I don't want him taking advantage of our newfound relationship.'

She kicked off her dirty boots on the doorstep, and went to the sink in the utility room to wash her hands. Seconds later she was in the kitchen with Genevieve and Adam, drying her hands on a towel, which she then slung over her shoulder.

'So what's this about, Adam? You've not come here to propose, have you? Because I must warn you, you should speak to my father first. It's a courtesy thing.'

Adam laughed good-humouredly. 'No, it's not a proposal of marriage, but it is a proposal of sorts.'

Putting their drinks down on the table, Genevieve said, 'You probably don't need me hanging round, I'll just go –'

'It's all right, Gen, there's no need to make yourself scarce. Unless, of course, Nattie would prefer it?' He turned to look at her.

Nattie shrugged. 'Always good to have a witness. Spit it out, then.'

'Right,' he said, 'first off, I hear you're looking for a job?'

She nodded.

'One that will provide you with the means to pay for a good childminder?'

'Spot on.'

'Excellent. Because *I* have a job for you.'

Nattie took the towel from her shoulder and straightened the straps of her dungarees. 'What kind of a job?'

'A nine-to-five kind of a job, working in the office of one of my caravan parks.'

She stopped what she was doing. 'In one of your caravan parks? You must be bloody joking! I'd rather shovel donkey shit all day than set foot in one of your tacky parks!'

He raised his eyebrows. 'I have it on good authority that you said you'd take the first job offer that came your way.'

Nattie threw Genevieve a look of disgust. 'Traitor,' she hissed. She turned back to Adam. 'There was a proviso attached. It has to pay enough for me to afford a reliable childminder for Lily-Rose.'

Reaching for his mug of coffee, his voice casual, Adam said, 'You're in luck. This job comes with a ready-made crèche for Lily; the one the holiday guests put their own children in. I only employ fully qualified girls, so you'd know Lily was being well looked after. What's more, it's free.'

Genevieve smiled to herself. He'd had his trump card up his sleeve all along. It was good to see Nattie being out-manoeuvred for a change.

Nattie chewed on the inside of her lip, then switched her gaze from Adam to Genevieve. 'Did you cook this up between the two of you at the pub last night?'

'No! This is the first I heard of it.'

'She's right,' said Adam. 'I only thought of it when I was having breakfast this morning.'

'I don't believe you.'

'Well, get over your disbelief and give me an answer.'

'How can I? I don't even know what sort of job it is.'

'I need someone to answer the phones and deal with guests' queries. It'd be a challenge for you, Nattie, because you'll have to be pleasant.' This last comment was said with a smile.

'Watch it mate, you push your luck at your peril. Anyway, I thought you were selling the parks?'

'I am, but these things take for ever. Meanwhile, I need someone to do the job for the rest of the season, or however long it takes. The girl who's been doing it for the last two years has just handed in her notice.'

'Why? Didn't she like the boss?'

'This might come as a surprise to you, but people generally like me. I'm a pretty fair employer, too.'

Nattie grunted. 'Okay then, when do you want me to start? But I'm warning you, one wisecrack about a perk of the job being that I get to sleep with the boss and I'll have you for sexual harassment.'

A smile twitched at his mouth. 'Don't flatter yourself, Nattie. Moreover, I never mix business with pleasure.'

Genevieve had to cough and clear her throat several times before she could speak without laughing. 'Adam, are you sure you know what you're doing? You're not worried she might sabotage your business?' She was thinking of the time Nattie had threatened to set fire to one of his caravan parks.

'Don't worry, I know exactly what I'm doing.' He finished his coffee and got to his feet. 'I'll be in touch with all the relevant details, Nattie. Presumably you have a P45?'

'The man's insufferable,' said Nattie, minutes later when Adam had left them.

'How can you say that when he's being so helpful?'

She smirked. 'I was going to add, he's insufferably generous. He'll be handing out blankets to the homeless next.'

Two days later Genevieve received bad news. The estate agent in Tenby who had been handling the sale of the property in Angel Sands wrote to say that the owners had received and accepted a higher offer. There was no hint that, were she to come in with a higher offer, she would be successful. Anyway, she didn't want to play that game. Though the letter knocked her back, she kept its contents to herself. Besides, everyone was preoccupied with their own affairs. Adam was away checking out his parks down in Cornwall; Polly was on a visit to Buckingham to stay with Jonjo and to meet his parents, and with Mum and Dad's help, Nattie was preparing to move in to Angel Cottage before taking up Adam's job offer.

Angel Cottage was almost unrecognisable. The bulky furniture Gran had squeezed into the little house had either been sold or moved up to Paradise House. The biggest transformation, so far, was the smallest bedroom at the back of the house, the one Gran had used as an apple store. Every year she would take the apples from the orchard at Paradise House and spend hours wrapping them in tissue paper, putting them to bed in the enormous mahogany chest of drawers that had dominated the little room. The chest had been put into one of the guest rooms at Paradise House and the apple room, as Lily-Rose called it, was now hers. Mum and Dad had completely redecorated it and had replaced the ancient swirly, head-spinning patterned carpet with a plain one. 'It's like the colour of the sea on a sunny day,' Lily-Rose told everyone, repeating Serena. She was thrilled with her new room, the pale blue gingham curtains Serena had made and the pretty seashells she had stencilled above the window. She was particularly excited about the desk and shelving unit that her grandfather had built for her at lightning speed.

But it was while Mum was up late one night, finishing off the stencilling in Lily-Rose's room, that she discovered what had made Gran think she had mice living with her.

'My first thought,' she told them the next morning, 'was that it sounded just like a mouse squeaking. I went all round the house looking for it, but when I listened closely, it sounded more like a gate in need of oil.'

It turned out not to be a gate, or indeed a mouse, but her neighbour Olwen Jenkins' rusting old weather vane that needed oiling, which Dad had since seen to. And the reason the noise had been intermittent was that it only squeaked when the wind blew from a certain direction. Poor Gran, driven to distraction because her neighbour's hearing wasn't as good as it used to be and she hadn't noticed what was going on up on her chimney pot.

It might have seemed that they were acting with indecent haste, doing up Angel Cottage so soon after Gran's death, but Genevieve felt sure her grandmother would approve. It did mean that while her parents were spending so much time down at Angel Cottage, they were continually in each other's company, which had to be a good thing. Watching their animated faces as they discussed the planned improvements, Genevieve began to have more confidence in her father, that slow and steady would win the race.

She had mentioned this to Christian in an email and he'd replied that maybe what her parents needed was a new project to interest them. 'It sounds like they've grown bored of Paradise House and not of each other,' he wrote.

It was the last message she'd had from Christian and

in the following days she'd steeled herself for what she now realised was inevitable; neither of them was suited to a long-distance relationship. She felt no regret that they'd tried to resurrect what they'd once felt for each other, and she knew she would always treasure the happy memories of this summer. Looking back, it now seemed an omen that they hadn't managed to sleep together. She recalled the scene of the two of them upstairs in her bedroom, and in particular the look on Christian's face when she'd said she could hear someone in the house. The memory made her smile. She would like it if they could remain friends.

Washing the mud from the potatoes she'd dug up from her father's vegetable patch, she thought how much better she was with friendships than love affairs. She thought of Adam and what he'd said about her being afraid to connect with herself. Until then, she hadn't realised that that was what she did. But it was true: time and time again she had withdrawn from a relationship not just because she wasn't able to trust the person, or because they didn't measure up in some way, but because, subconsciously, she didn't want that person to see the real her, the old Genevieve who had never gone away. The fat, ugly Genevieve who had convinced herself she didn't deserve a boyfriend like Christian.

Was she doing it all over again, then? Deliberately talking herself out of a chance of happiness in yet another act of self-destruction? Staring at the garden – it was raining again – and wondering if she would ever change, her attention was caught by a familiar song on the radio. It was Judy Garland singing 'Over the Rainbow'. Genevieve hoped that her parents had the radio on down at Angel Cottage – they were emulsioning the kitchen today. She pictured her mother on the stepladder, brush in hand, streaks of paint in her hair as she sang along, maybe even using the brush as a microphone, like she used to when they were little and she'd had one too many glasses of wine. Then very slowly a different picture appeared in Genevieve's head. It was a picture of her father. Holding her breath, frightened the faint glimmer of inspiration would fade, she held on to the image, right until the very last poignant note of the song.

Was it the answer?

Yes it was. It was the perfect answer.

But if so, would her father have the nerve to carry off her idea? And who would be the best person to persuade him?

Once again, Adam came to mind.

Chapter Forty-six

It was the afternoon of the talent contest and very nearly everyone in the village was participating in the event or helping with its organisation, including Genevieve. Overnight, though, the extent of her input had grown dramatically. Two members of the kitchen staff at the Salvation Arms had gone down with a nasty cold, so instead of just lending a hand in the kitchen, she was now in charge of cooking and serving a massive lamb and ham carvery with trifle and fresh strawberries to follow. If the menu had been left to her, she would have come up with something a little less traditional. As it was, she decided to throw in a vegetarian option just in case, a mushroom and aubergine lasagne.

In the kitchen at Paradise House, with Donna's help she was now getting to grips with the amount of food she had to prepare. The Lloyd-Morris brothers had supplied all the meat at a generous discount and Tubby had specially fetched the fruit and veg that morning, guaranteeing its freshness. Mum was also pitching in to help and was arriving later with Nattie and Lily-Rose; they had promised to be back from Tenby within the hour. In an effort to mollify Nattie, Mum had suggested they go clothes shopping for her new job. Cruelly, they were all putting bets on Nattie finding a reason between now and her first day next week, why she couldn't actually take up the job. Nobody believed her when she said she would prove them wrong.

'I'll work for Adam to spite you all,' she'd said.

Cynically, Genevieve would believe it when she saw it.

Something else she was having difficulty believing was Dad going through with her plan. She had Adam to thank, really. The two of them had cornered her father at Angel Cottage as he was jet-blasting the patio that Gran had never allowed him to do; she'd always claimed it would destroy the lived-in look of the place, never mind that it was as skiddy as an oil slick with the build-up of moss and algae.

'What have you got to lose?' Adam had asked, after Genevieve had outlined what she'd thought was a stroke of pure genius on her part.

'My self-respect?' her father had muttered.

'You don't want to think of a little thing like that,' Adam had said. 'No one will have an ounce of it left by the end of the night.'

'But I've never sung in public before.'

'Nor have I, but it's not stopping me.'

The prevarication had been astonishingly short-lived and, slowly coming round to the suggestion, Dad had said, 'You're sure it would work?'

'Yes, Dad. It's the perfect way to prove how much you love her. And because she knows you so well, she'll know exactly how much courage it took. Trust me; you have to do it.'

'But what shall I sing?'

This was when Genevieve told him what had given her the idea. 'You have to sing a big Judy Garland number,' she told him. 'One of Mum's favourites. She'll love it.'

But Adam shook his head. 'I've been thinking about that, Gen. Those songs are better coming from a woman. How about the King? Elvis.'

Daddy Dean looked doubtful. 'Would I have to dress up like him?'

'All the way or nothing,' Adam said.

'Yes,' agreed Genevieve. 'It's got to be a show-stopping

moment to bring a tear to Mum's eye.'

There were tears in Genevieve's eyes now: she was slicing onions for the vegetable lasagne. She slid them into the large frying pan on the gas hob, lowered the flame, added some crushed garlic and thought of her father, who should now be on his way home from Swansea with an Elvis outfit. There'd been nothing available locally, and with insufficient time to make one in secret, Adam had got on the phone and tracked down a costume hirer in Swansea.

'Where's your father gone?' Serena had asked earlier that morning.

'He's with Adam,' Genevieve had said.

'I know he's with Adam, but where have they gone?'

'For a walk, I think.'

'Then why hasn't he taken his walking boots with him?'

'Oh, hasn't he?'

'No, Gen, they're by the back door.'

'Perhaps it's not that kind of a walk. Just a leisurely stroll and a chat.'

Serena had looked at her suspiciously. 'Something's going on, isn't it? What's your father up to? And why does he always seem to be huddled in a corner with that woman?'

'Which woman?' Although, of course, Genevieve had known exactly who her mother was referring to.

'I'm talking about Donna,' Serena said impatiently. 'Has something been going on between those two while I've been away?'

Nattie had walked in at that moment. 'And what's it to you, Mum, what Dad gets up to? You didn't give a jam fig all those months you were away. Why be concerned now?'

There was no hostility in her voice, just a matter-of-fact tone that had made their mother drop her line of interrogation. 'Do you still want to go shopping in Tenby?' she'd asked.

Adding the salted and rinsed slices of aubergine, Genevieve stirred the pan and glanced across the kitchen to where Donna was peeling a mound of potatoes. It looked very much as though, without meaning to, their father had made his wife jealous. Serena's comment that he was always huddled up in a corner with Donna was an exaggeration, but it did contain an element of truth. The most professional singer in Angel Sands other than Polly, who was arriving home with Jonjo that afternoon, Donna was giving Dad singing lessons up at Adam's place. What Genevieve wouldn't give to be a fly on the wall during one of their sessions!

'Do you think that's enough potatoes?' asked Donna.

Knowing that Donna had a hundred and one things to do, Genevieve said, 'That's plenty. And thanks for your help. But feel free to disappear if you want. I've got it all under control here.'

'You sure?'

'Absolutely. Anyway, it's not fair of me to monopolise the star of the show.'

Donna smiled. 'I think you might change your opinion when you hear your father tonight.'

Having avoided asking the question till now, Genevieve said, 'He'll be okay, won't he?'

The smiled widened. 'He'll be fine, love. Beneath that reserve lurks a budding performer.'

Still worried and knowing she was responsible for putting her father through this ordeal, Genevieve said, 'People won't laugh at him, will they?'

'Trust me. He's got quite a decent voice on him. Shame he hasn't used it before. Mark my words, he'll knock everyone dead. Especially your Mum. I wouldn't be surprised if there was a drop or two of Welsh blood in him.' Washing her hands at the sink, she said, 'Now if you're sure there's nothing else I can do, I'll push off. I'll see you later.'

Encouraged by Donna's words, Genevieve thought of the others, apart from Donna, who knew about the surprise. Tubby and Adam, her sisters and Christian had all said the same when she'd told them about it. 'It's totally inspired, Genevieve,' Christian had replied to her email. 'I just wish I could be there with you to enjoy the moment.'

The disappointment that once again Christian couldn't spare the time to drive down hit Genevieve harder than she'd expected. There was no reason why he should want to witness an entire village making a fool of itself, but she'd invited him because, if nothing else, it would give them the opportunity to talk things through, face to face. Surprised how hurt she felt, she'd replied to his email with a businesslike update on everything, then told him how she'd been gazumped on the teashop. 'Turns out that my money just wasn't good enough,' she wrote.

'If it's any consolation, you did the right thing in not increasing your offer,' he answered. 'They could have strung you along trying to get even more out of you.'

It was exactly what Adam had said when Genevieve had shared her setback with him. He'd hugged her hard and said, 'And what will you do if the agent calls you because the current deal has fallen through?'

'I shall tell him to go to hell. Then offer slightly less than I did first time round.'

'Well done, Gen, you're learning fast.'

It didn't really feel like she was learning anything fast, but maybe Adam was right. He usually was.

Polly and Jonjo arrived home not long after Adam had dropped Dad at the front door, giving Serena no time to cross examine him on where he'd been or what he'd been doing. She was too busy anyway, what with meeting Jonjo for the first time and throwing all her energy into interrogating him.

Genevieve watched her mother assessing the man whom, in her own clichéd words, she'd heard so much about. They sat outside in the garden, a tray of drinks before them on the wooden table, where the not so subtle cross-examination was in full swing. Had she got it right that she ran a franchise of fitness centres? Jonjo took Serena's question, and those that followed, in his stride. Genevieve reckoned he'd met more than his fair share of protective mothers in the past, and had doubtless charmed each and every one of them. But of course, what Serena didn't know, and nor did their father, was that Jonjo was a serious contender for the role of son-in-law. Polly still hadn't mentioned anything to their parents about Jonjo's proposal and as far as Genevieve was aware, she still hadn't given him an answer.

Then the line of questioning took an unexpected turn.

'Genevieve tells me you're an old friend of Christian May,' Serena said.

Instantly Genevieve was on the alert and regretting she'd told her mother about seeing Christian again. Like Nattie and her father, she hadn't been exactly thrilled by the news.

'That's right,' Jonjo said, without looking Genevieve's way. 'I got to know Christian several years ago when he boasted he could have made a better job of designing my first fitness centre.'

'Really? That doesn't sound like the Christian we used to know. I don't recall him ever having a tendency to boast. Perhaps he's changed. Which might not be such a bad thing,' she added under her breath.

Genevieve cringed. But Jonjo, still not looking in Genevieve's direction, kept his tone even. 'I can't vouch for what he was like as a child. Apart from that one excusable blag he made to me, I'd say he's one of the most modest blokes I know. And completely reliable. Professionally as well as personally.' He put his glass down, before skilfully steering Serena off course. 'If you've got time, why don't I take you to look at the barn? The builders have made a start and I'm keen to see what they've done so far.'

Genevieve was grateful for his charm and quick thinking. 'That's a great idea, Jonjo,' she said. She shot her sister a glance, hoping for backup. 'Polly, why don't you go with Mum and Dad?'

Amidst the kerfuffle of decision making – could they really spare the time? – Genevieve leaned towards Jonjo and whispered her thanks.

'No problem,' he said. 'By the way, Christian sends his love. He said to be sure I got the message right. Not best wishes. Not regards. Not even fondest etceteras. But his *love*.'

Genevieve felt the colour rush to her cheeks. All she could think to say was, 'I was hoping he might make it down for the weekend.'

Everyone was on their feet now. Jonjo took Genevieve aside. 'Things are okay between you and Christian, aren't they?'

'We're fine,' she said brightly. But she suddenly heard the echo of the lie that had tripped so easily off her tongue. She remembered Adam saying that she always said she was fine. But she wasn't fine. She was confused. Christian seemed to be blowing hot and cold.

Keeping his voice low, Jonjo said, 'I got the feeling from Christian that he doesn't know where he stands with you. He hinted that he thought there was someone else in the background.'

'What? But that's absurd. He knows perfectly well there isn't. No, the trouble is we don't see –'

But there was no time to finish their conversation.

Serena was bearing down on them.

After waving them off, Genevieve hurried back to the kitchen to finish preparing the food for that evening.

Genevieve had often seen the Salvation Arms so crowded it took for ever to be served at the small bar, but tonight it was the busiest she'd ever seen. Anyone wanting a drink had better be patient, she thought as she looked through the gap in the door from the kitchen to the public lounge. Every chair, bar stool and table had been claimed (extras had been brought in specially) and people were queuing at the bar getting their drinks in, stockpiling a round or two if they had any sense. And it wasn't just locals who had bought tickets. Plenty of visitors to Angel Sands had shown up, and some were participating.

With half an hour to go before Tubby, acting as master of ceremonies, would be getting the proceedings underway, Genevieve closed the door and checked on the joints of meat in the ovens. The two part-timers from the pub's bar and kitchen staff, those who weren't off sick, would be here in ten minutes, along with Serena and Nattie, who were going to help serve. Back at Paradise House, Kelly was babysitting Lily-Rose and had promised to be on hand should any of the guests need something.

Dad was booked to do his slot towards the end of the evening, after Adam. Genevieve had spoken to him before leaving the house and he'd seemed extraordinarily calm and philosophical. 'What will be, will be, Gen,' he'd said. He wouldn't let on which particular Elvis song he was singing and he'd sworn Donna and Adam to secrecy. Mum was still completely in the dark about what he'd been up to, though she kept throwing Donna narrow-eyed, suspicious glances. Perhaps Polly's original idea of finding a girlfriend for their father hadn't been such a bad one after all.

*

There was only one person who could open the show and that was Donna. She looked as spectacular as she sounded – shoulder-length blonde hair backcombed to within an inch of its life, legs wrapped in the tightest jeans Genevieve had ever seen, and wearing her own body weight in lipgloss and eye make-up. She tottered around on the small makeshift stage on her six-inch, baby-pink stiletto heels, a death-defying act of pure bravery. She gave a magnificent, gutsy rendition of Bonnie Tyler singing 'Holding Out For a Hero' and had the place in an uproar when she finished. The crowd went mad, hands clapping, feet stamping. Tubby looked on proudly.

Watching from the steam-filled kitchen, with the door wedged open, Nattie said, 'Bloody hell! That's an awesome act to follow. Pity the poor devil who goes next. Anyone know who it is?'

Serena shook her head and said rather primly, 'Is she always as showy as that?'

Genevieve smiled. 'She's playing a part, Mum.'

With a sniff, Serena crossed her arms firmly over her chest.

The plan for the evening was an hour of performances followed by a break for supper and then a further hour of performances.

'Expect things to run over a bit,' both Tubby and Donna had warned Genevieve. 'We'll do our best to keep it on track, but once people get a whiff of the grease-paint, there's often no stopping them from hogging the stage.'

Standing with her mother and sister, Genevieve looked across the crowded pub to where the panel of judges – the vicar of St Non's, the Reverend David Trent, Stan from the mini-market and Ruth from Angel Crafts – sat with their pieces of paper. She didn't envy them their job. The obvious outright winner would be Donna, no question. But who would make second and third? Perhaps not the man currently on his feet doing an appalling impression of Tom Jones singing 'Sex Bomb'. Genevieve didn't recognise him, so assumed he was a visitor, but as awful as he was – a scrawny, middle-aged comb-over wearing a shirt slashed to his waist, revealing more sunburnt hairless chest than was decent – she had to admit the crowd loved him and was urging him on to thrust his hips out of their sockets.

Nattie groaned. 'I know this is for charity, but there are limits.'

'Gran would have loved all this,' Genevieve said.

Serena smiled. 'She would have done a turn herself.'

The next act was Jane Davies from the pottery. Done up as Shania Twain, wearing a fabulously raunchy leopardskin number, she threw herself into a slightly off-key version of 'Man! I Feel Like a Woman!'.

By the time Tubby called half-time and announced that supper was served, they'd witnessed a warbling Mariah Carey, two Frank Sinatras – one singing 'My Way' and the other stumbling through 'Strangers in the Night' – a leather-clad Ricky Martin, and a bursting-at-the-seams Dolly Parton. Queuing for their food everyone was in high spirits, talking and laughing about the performances. Judging from their comments, Donna was still way out in front to win first prize, with Ricky Martin close on her baby-pink stiletto heels. There was no sign of Daddy Dean. Or Adam. But then none of the singers, until they'd performed, were allowed to show themselves. Only when they'd sung could they sit with their friends and families. Those who had yet to sing were still upstairs, in either the dressing room or what Tubby jokingly referred to as the Green Room. Donna was currently ferrying trays of food up and down the stairs for them, which, Genevieve could see, was further annoying her mother. Serena had been amazed when Dad had told her he'd volunteered to help Debs get the performers down to the stage on time. Suspicious too.

'Let me take that for you,' Serena said to Donna now, as once more Donna came into the kitchen for a tray of food. 'You can't possibly manage the stairs in those shoes again.'

Gripping the tray of food, Donna laughed. 'That's okay Mrs Baxter, my feet are as tough as old coal scuttles.'

'Here, Mum,' Genevieve intervened – no way could they afford for Serena to go anywhere near the Green Room. 'Take this over to the judges. They look like they could do with a second helping of trifle.'

The first performer to take to the stage in the second half was Huw Davies. Dressed in a white singlet and ripped jeans, fake tattoos on his biceps, he got a massive cheer when Tubby introduced him as 'the cheeky lad from Stoke, Robbie Williams, singing "Let Me Entertain You".'

'Any time mate,' yelled out a woman from the back of the pub. But despite cries of 'Show us your bum!' he kept his trousers on right through to the end of his performance. 'I reckon he might knock Ricky Martin off the number two spot,' Serena commented.

'I had no idea Huw could sing so well,' Nattie agreed. 'It makes you look at these people in a whole new light, doesn't it?'

Genevieve knew that Adam was on next, and she wondered if Nattie might make the same observation of him afterwards. There was a short lull in the proceedings while Huw left the stage. Then Adam appeared – hair brushed back from his forehead, fake whiskers applied to his chin and a black leather jacket turned up at the collar. He stepped onto the small stage and exchanged a quick, nervous glance with Polly who was sitting at the piano to accompany him – everyone else had provided backing tracks to sing along to. Genevieve watched her sister closely, but Nattie's face was perfectly composed, giving nothing away.

Tubby introduced Adam. 'Put your hands together for none other than Mr Joe Cocker.'

A whistling, whooping round of applause went up, but when Adam leaned into the microphone and exchanged another look with Polly, the crowd fell quiet. The opening notes were Polly's and then Adam came in, his eyes closed, his voice low and husky.

'*You are so beautiful*,' he sang.

After all the raucous singing and booming backing tracks that had gone before, the audience was stunned into a pin drop silence.

'My God,' muttered Nattie, 'the bastard can actually sing.'

'And some,' whispered Genevieve.

'Ssh you two! You're spoiling it.'

'*You're everything I hoped for*,' Adam sang on, his voice cracking with a rich resonance.

Genevieve could hardly bear to listen. She felt weak all over, and all at once she realised that this was what she wanted from Christian. She wanted him to take her breath away, to make her feel she was everything he'd ever hoped for. She thought of what Jonjo had said. *Christian sends his love.* Did he? Did he really?

Adam's performance was mesmerising, and when he sang the words, '*You're my guiding light*,' he slowly opened his eyes and looked over to where Genevieve, her mother and Nattie were grouped in the doorway. For a heart-stopping moment Genevieve thought he was looking at her, but then she realised it was Nattie, standing just behind her, he was staring at. There was no mistaking that she was the whole focus of his gaze. G that he was singing to her, and for her alone. She risked a glance at Nattie and saw that she was transfixed.

Only when the audience leapt to its feet, whooping and yelling its appreciation, did Adam look away from Nattie and take his bow.

In the din of noise, Genevieve clearly heard her sister say, 'Oh, what the hell! In for a penny, in for a pound.'

Chapter Forty-seven

What happened next had the entire pub in an uproar of hysterical approval. Nattie pushed through the crowd, leapt up onto the stage and grabbed hold of Adam. She kissed him full on the mouth. He showed no sign of resisting – far from it – and just as Genevieve was wondering if she'd have to fetch a crowbar to prise them apart, Nattie pulled away. Grinning into the microphone, she said, 'Guess what folks, he kisses as well as he sings!'

Amidst more cheers and clapping, they stepped down from the stage, Adam leading the way to go back upstairs, but once again Nattie took matters into her own hands and propelled him towards the kitchen. As the door swung shut behind them, Genevieve caught a glimpse of Adam being pressed against the walk-in cold store.

'And about time too,' said Serena. 'That poor man' waited long enough for her to come to her senses. *Good God!* Is that your father? Oh, tell me it isn't!'

Despite the trademark Presley white fringed catsuit the black wig, the sideburns, and the silver-framed sun glasses, the man now up on stage was unmistakabl Daddy Dean. But what a transformation! He looked phe nomenal; lip curled, one hand held out to the side t show off the sleeve fringe, the other holding the micrc phone.

'Tell me he's not going to sing,' murmured Serena 'He's never sung in public before. Never!'

Hiding her own anxiety, reminding herself wha

Donna had said that afternoon, Genevieve said, 'Well, he's singing now, Mum.'

This time it wasn't Polly providing the musical accompaniment. The video CD up on the wall began with the backing track and 'Always On My Mind' started. Dad's eyes sought out Serena's face in the crowd. Her mother reached for Genevieve's hand, gripping it hard.

'*Maybe I didn't treat you quite as good as I should have . . . maybe I didn't love you quite as often as I could have.*'

He was singing from the heart and, amazingly, Donna hadn't exaggerated: he really could sing. But it was the sincerity in his voice that brought a lump to Genevieve's throat. That and the choice of song.

'*If I made you feel second best, girl, I'm so sorry I was blind . . . *'

Genevieve had never been more proud of her father. Had he known all along that this was how Mum had been feeling? When the music stopped and he took his bow to ear-splitting applause, she looked at her mother. Serena was openly sobbing, her face wet with tears. She tried to speak, but couldn't.

Genevieve put her arms around her mother. 'Now do you see how much he loves you, Mum?'

'But he only had to say.'

'It wouldn't have been enough, would it? You know as well as I do, you wanted something big from him. A grand, over-the-top romantic gesture. And they don't come much more romantic or dramatic than this.'

They both turned to look at the stage, to join in with the applause. Dad had already gone.

After Tubby had introduced the next act, Genevieve asked if he knew where her father was. 'I think Elvis has left the building,' Tubby joked. 'From the look of him, I'd say he went for some fresh air.'

Squeezing through the crowds, Genevieve and her

413

mother made it to the door and outside. It was still light and easy to spot him. Down on the beach, dressed in his white Elvis suit, he looked a lonely, incongruous figure as he hurled stone after stone into the sea. Genevieve nudged her mother.

'Go to him, Mum. Don't let him suffer any more.' She watched Serena walk away, and knowing she'd done as much as she could, Genevieve turned and went back inside the pub to make a start on the washing up.

That's if the kitchen wasn't still occupied by Adam and her sister. She had no idea what was going to become of them – one snog does not a relationship make – but she felt happy for Adam. Surprised too, that, despite his conviction to put Nattie out of his mind, his feelings for her had clearly never left him. She also felt a twinge of sadness. If anything did come of this evening, there would be no more cosy evenings for her and Adam. The close nature of their friendship would inevitably change, and she would be the poorer for it.

Genevieve stopped for a moment to watch the next performer, a shockingly awful Tina Turner lookalike, possibly a man in drag. Cautiously she opened the kitchen door, in case the kissing had progressed to something the health and safety inspector wouldn't approve of. There was no sign of her sister and Adam, or the part time kitchen staff who were supposed to be helping her. Instead, the unexpected sight of Jonjo brought a smile to her lips: he was standing at the sink up to his elbows in soapy water.

'Seeing as you've been abandoned, Polly thought you might like the extra help,' he said. 'There's a hell of a lot to get through, isn't there? Beats me why a pub of this size doesn't have a dishwasher.'

She picked up a tea-towel. 'There is one, but it's not working.'

'Oh, well, not to worry, you've got me instead. I'm

doing my bit to assure Polly I'm the domesticated modern man she needs in her life.'

Genevieve laughed. 'I don't think Polly would mind one way or the other.'

'You mean she's so in love with me she'd put up with coffee cups left in the sink?'

'No, I mean she's like Nattie, not in the least concerned how things get done. I would have thought you'd have realised that by now.'

Rinsing a plate under the tap and passing it to her, he tutted. 'Modern girls, I ask you. What's the world coming to?'

From the other side of the door, the music had changed tempo and an unknown woman's voice screeched out the theme to *Titanic*, 'My Heart Will Go On'.

'I'm glad we're this side of the door,' Jonjo said. 'The punters in there could end up with blood pouring out of their ears if they're not careful.'

'You shouldn't criticise what you're not prepared to have a go at yourself,' she said good-humouredly.

'Some of us aren't as fair-minded as you, Genevieve. I haven't known you long, but I can't recall you ever saying a harsh word about anyone.'

'You haven't seen me when I'm rattled. I can turn nasty when I want to.'

He laughed. 'Yeah, about as nasty as Polly. You're two of a kind. No, make that three of a kind; you're both like your father.'

'Leaving Nattie out in the cold?'

'I don't think she currently feels out in the cold. The last time I saw Nattie, she and Adam looked decidedly hot. But never mind them, tell me about you and Christian. What's the deal there? You have such an amazing history, you owe it to yourselves to work things out.'

She reached for a clean tea-towel. 'Who said we have anything to work out?'

Jonjo switched off the tap and stopped what he was doing. 'You need to talk to him. Talk to him properly. He needs your reassurance.'

'But how can we talk? We never get to spend any time together. Not like you and Polly.'

He frowned. 'It's never a good thing to make comparisons. Not when Christian isn't as lucky as me. I can take time off whenever I want, to be with Polly. Next to Christian, I'm a right lazy bugger. His problem is that he's bloody good at what he does and is in high demand. He's also lousy at delegating and saying no. Which leaves him sod-all free time.'

She looked away uncomfortably. 'Stop lecturing me, Jonjo. Or you really will see the nasty side of me.'

'All I'm saying is, go easy on him. Who knows, he might just surprise you one of these days. He's not entirely lacking in sensitivity. After all, some of my perfection must have rubbed off on him along the way.'

She smiled. 'There's only the cutlery left to do. Let's take a break and go and watch some of the acts.'

He glanced at the clock. 'The job's almost done. Ten minutes' more and then we'll venture back into the fray.'

Surprised at his willingness to stick it out, she found another dry tea-towel and scooped up a handful of knives and forks, grateful that in Nattie and Serena's absence she had him to help her. How typically thoughtful it had been of Polly to send Jonjo to her rescue. And how good of him to oblige.

Jonjo was true to his word, and exactly ten minutes later, when they could hear a squeaky-voiced Britney Spears singing 'Baby One More Time', he pulled the plug out from the bottom of the sink.

'That's it. We're done here for now. Let's see if we ca

mount an attack on the bar for a drink. We've definitely earned it. You especially.'

There was no chance of getting a drink, the bar was much too busy, but Genevieve didn't mind. She was just happy to be out of the kitchen; she was beginning to feel like hard-done-by Cinders again.

With Britney off the stage, Tubby bounced back onto it. 'Well, ladies and gentlemen,' he boomed, 'that was to be our last performance of the contest, but we've had a late entry, one we simply couldn't refuse. So, if you'd like to put your hands together and give a warm welcome to this act, I think you'll agree a very special person is in for a treat. Ladies and gentlemen, I give you the Angel Sands Choir!'

'Angel Sands Choir?' repeated Genevieve. 'Who's that?'

Jonjo shrugged. 'Who cares? Do as the man says and put your hands together.'

She did, and watched with interest to see who would emerge through the curtain of sparkly red tinsel. But before anyone appeared, the backing track started. Genevieve recognised it straight away. It was 'The Wonder of You'.

She turned to Jonjo to tell him how much she liked this particular song, that it was her all-time favourite. But he wasn't there. Mystified, she looked around for him, but he'd vanished into thin air. How very odd.

Back on the stage, the curtain moved and people began to appear, first . . . first Polly, and then . . . Nattie with Adam, his hand on her shoulder. Next came her parents, hand in hand, followed by Donna with a crowd of other performers. Including Jonjo! How on earth had he got there so quickly? He flashed her a grin and a wave. Then, with one fantastic voice that made the hairs on the back of her neck stand on end, they all looked at her and sang the words she knew by heart.

> *'When no one else can understand me,*
> *when everything I do is wrong,*
> *you give me hope and consolation,*
> *   you give me strength to carry on,*
> *and you're always there to lend a hand in*
> *   everything I do.*
> *That's the wonder . . . the wonder of you.'*

She knew who was behind this: Polly. Dear, sweet Polly. No one else would have been so thoughtful. No one else in her family would have known what the song meant to her. A flicker of sparkly red tinsel at the back of the stage caught her attention. As they began to sing the next line of the song – *And when you smile the world is brighter* – someone else appeared on the stage. Her heart leapt.

It was Christian.

He must have known where she would be standing because without hesitating, his eyes settled on her. And while everyone else swayed to the music and sang – '*You touch my hand and I'm a king, your kiss to me is worth a fortune,*' – they moved to let him through. And at '*your love for me is everything, I guess I'll never know the reason why you love me as you do,*' he stepped down from the stage and came slowly towards her. Again people made room for him to pass, and when he was standing right in front of her, he brought a hand forward and presented her with a single red rose.

'I couldn't serenade you in the way I'd have liked,' he said, leaning in to speak in her ear, 'so I roped in a few who could.'

She tilted her head back. 'You arranged all this yourself?'

'With a little help.'

The rest of the song was lost to her. Not minding that everyone was staring at them, she held the rose carefull between her fingers and threw her arms around his neck. She kissed him and kissed him. Then kissed him some more. Let them fetch a crowbar, she wasn't letting go of him for the rest of the night!

Chapter Forty-eight

Gran used to say that miracles happen every day of our lives. 'And the reason we don't realise it,' she would explain, 'is that most of the time we are in too much of a rush to notice the angels going about their business.' After what had happened at the Salvation Arms, and what was happening to her now, Genevieve was inclined to agree with her grandmother.

Catching their breath outside the pub, Christian told her he was kidnapping her for the rest of the night, that he had a failsafe way to avoid anyone disturbing them. He led her to his car, which was parked outside Gran's house, and told her he wouldn't answer a single question until the time was right.

'Am I allowed to ask where we're going?' she said.

'It'll be obvious,' he said enigmatically. She thought he was taking her to Tawelfan beach, but soon realised she was wrong when he turned off down the narrow track to Ralph's barn. Or rather, Jonjo's barn. Parking alongside a large skip and a cement mixer, he switched off the engine and got out. He was round to her side of the car before she'd put a foot on the ground. 'You have to close your eyes,' he said, his face close to hers so that he could see her clearly.

'But it's pitch black, I can't see a thing anyway.'

Producing a torch from the back of the car, he offered her his arm.

Giggling with nervous excitement, she allowed him to lead her. She heard a door scrape and guessed they were going inside the barn. But why? After a few steps, he said, 'Now turn round, put your hands over your ears and keep your eyes tightly closed.'

What seemed like for ever passed, but was probably only a couple of minutes. It was long enough to feel tempted to sneak just one tiny glance. But she didn't. Then feeling his hands on hers, he uncovered her ears and said, 'You can open your eyes and turn round now.'

There before her was a sight so out of this world, she could hardly believe what she was seeing. The far end of the barn looked like something out of the Arabian Nights. It was a Bedouin wonderland – a magical canopied palace strewn with sumptuous rugs and cushions. And everywhere there were candles sparkling like brightly polished jewels in the glowing stillness.

She turned to Christian. 'It's beautiful. But what's it doing here?'

'It's for you, Genevieve. Somewhere I can have you all to myself and not worry about being interrupted.' He took her hand. 'Come and sit down.'

In a daze, a little disorientated, she did as he said. Could the night get any better? Could anything more miraculous happen to her? When she was settled on a low stool, he poured her a glass of champagne from a bottle sticking out of a wine cooler.

'Care of Jonjo,' Christian said. 'He told me he'd never forgive me if I stinted on what we drank.'

She took the glass from him. 'Jonjo knew about this?'

He sat next to her. 'I thought it wise to seek his permission. It is his house after all.'

'He never said anything. Not a word.'

He clinked his glass against hers. 'That was the general idea. The surprise was meant to take your breath away.'

'Any more surprises on this scale and I shall die of asphyxiation. When did you get here and arrange all this?'

'Around lunchtime with Polly and Jonjo. I followed them down and they helped get the main structure up.'

'I don't believe it. My sister was in on it as well?'

'Your parents too. Jonjo brought them to see it this afternoon. It was also the perfect opportunity, after all these years, to meet your mother again, properly. And maybe convince her I'm not the bastard she remembers me as.'

Genevieve saw now how she'd been thoroughly tricked. Jonjo hadn't offered to show Serena the barn to silence her mother's questions, it had all been part of a much bigger picture. What a devious bunch her family turned out to be!

'Is there anything else I should know about? Do you have any other surprises up your sleeve?'

In the soft candlelight, he suddenly looked serious. 'I might. But first I have to ask you something. I want to know what your feelings are for Adam.'

'For Adam? What a strange question. What's he got to do with anything?'

'Genevieve, he has everything to do with it. Don't you see that?'

Confused, she said, 'No, I don't. He's a friend. A really good friend.'

'But you're so close to him. And it's him you always turn to, isn't it?'

She hesitated. 'Only because he's always there.'

'Like he was the day your grandmother died.'

'You were there, too.'

'Yes, but when we were in the conservatory at Paradise House, while he was saying goodbye, I saw the way the two of you connected. And believe me, I felt you didn't want or need me there.'

Genevieve thought back to that day and picked her way through the jumble of events and emotions – the relief that Lily-Rose was safe, but the devastation that

Gran was dead. With a flash of recall, she pictured the way Adam had touched her arm in the conservatory, and how she'd kissed him goodbye, and the moment shortly after when she had told Christian she wanted to be alone with Nattie. Shocked, she saw the conclusion Christian must have reached, and it was hardly surprising.

'Is that why your emails tailed off?'

'Yes. I couldn't work out how you really felt about me. You seemed distant in your emails, businesslike and beyond my reach, as though you weren't sure we were doing the right thing. I decided to back off and give you some space.'

'But why didn't you say something? Why didn't you just ask me what I felt?' Even as she spoke, she knew how hypocritical she sounded. Since when had *she* been able to come right out and lay her emotions on the line?

He put his glass down. 'You Baxters aren't the only ones afraid to open up, you know. I was worried that if I put you on the spot, I'd get the answer I didn't want to hear, and I'd lose you.' He paused. 'But I'm asking the question now. I need to know, Genevieve. I know Adam is mad about your sister, but are you secretly in love with him?'

She put her glass next to his. It was time to be completely honest with Christian. And with herself. She moved in close, so there could be no mistaking her words. 'I do love Adam, I admit that. But I love him affectionately, like a brother. The only man I've ever truly loved and desired is you. There's never been anyone else who made me feel the way you do. I loved you as a teenager and I probably started to love you all over again that day you showed up at Paradise House looking for somewhere to stay. There, is that clear enough for you?'

A slow smile lightened the solemn expression that had clouded his face for the last few minutes. 'Crystal clear,' he said. And when, with exquisite tenderness, he kissed her, she knew that whatever doubts he'd been feeling, had now passed. He moved her to the soft-carpeted ground and put a cushion under her head.

'Do you think I'm finally going to get my wish granted?'

'What wish would that be?'

But he didn't answer her.

They made love slowly, neither of them wanting to rush what they'd waited so long for. And all the while, Genevieve experienced a sense of déjà vu. It was as though their bodies were completely known to them, as though they knew exactly where to touch each other to give the most pleasure.

Afterwards, lying in his arms, bathed in the wash of golden candlelight, as he told her how beautiful she was, she did indeed feel beautiful.

And loved.

Chapter Forty-nine

In the weeks that followed, it was open season on the Baxter family. They had only themselves to blame, as Tubby was the first to say.

'If you must be so public in nailing your colours to the mast,' he teased Genevieve, 'what else do you expect, but for everyone to gossip about you?'

But for once, Genevieve wasn't bothered that her private life, a contradiction in terms these days, was being discussed so openly. Adam had just commented on this very point. They were up at St Non's; she was changing the flowers on Gran's grave and he, at Lily-Rose's request, was helping gather daisies to make a daisy chain to take home for Nattie.

'It wasn't long ago,' he said, 'that I recall a certain girl stamping her feet and throwing a tantrum when I dared to mention that folk were discussing her.'

Genevieve brushed away a fly that had landed on the angel of her grandmother's headstone. 'It all depends what people are saying. But luckily I'm not the only one they're talking about. I reckon you're of more interest to everyone.'

He went over to Lily-Rose, sitting cross-legged in the shade of the yew hedge in amongst the long grass, and gave her the daisies he'd picked. She was lost in her own little world, humming tunefully to herself as she laid out the flowers on her lap, lining them up like soldiers for inspection. Joining Genevieve again, Adam said, 'Any particular reason I'm the centre of attention?'

'Well, it's not every man who'd be brave enough to take on Natalie Baxter, is it?'

'At least they think I'm brave and not stupid.'

Genevieve smiled. 'So how's it going? Not regretting it, I hope.'

'No chance.' He hesitated. 'But how about Nattie? Has she said anything to you?'

'Oh, Adam, as if I'd repeat anything Nattie told me in confidence.'

'So there is something?'

Genevieve wished people wouldn't confide in her. She was hopeless when put under the spotlight. 'Look,' she said, 'it's not a big deal, and you must promise not to tell her I said anything, but . . . ' she paused to glance across to where Lily-Rose was still humming happily to herself, 'the thing is, she thinks you're holding out on her.'

He frowned. 'Holding what out on her?'

'You know.' Another glance across to Lily-Rose to check she wasn't listening. 'In the bedroom department. It's been three weeks since the talent contest and she's . . . well you know . . . wondering when it's going to happen.'

Adam's face suddenly broke into an enormous grin. But he said nothing.

'So, what's going on?'

'First off, it's no one's business but my own; second, it's unwise for her to go sleeping with the boss; and third . . .' the grin widened, 'and third, I'm making her wait the way she made me wait.'

It was Genevieve's turn to smile now. 'You're braver than we all thought.'

'And bloody frustrated into the bargain!'

'How long do you think you can keep it up?'

'An unfortunate choice of words, Gen, but I get your drift. But the way she makes me feel, I don't think I can hold out for much longer.' He suddenly looked serious. 'I don't want to hurry things. I'm not interested in an easy-come, easy-go fling with her, I want the real thing. Love.'

'Then you're doing exactly the right thing. I doubt any man's ever given her this much consideration. The fact that she's worrying why you haven't got her into bed yet means she cares. Something she hasn't had a lot of experience of doing in the past.'

Two days after the talent contest, after Christian had left to go back to work, Adam had called Genevieve to say he wanted to talk to her in private.

'You must have thought it very odd what I did,' he said to her, 'singing that song for Nattie after everything I'd shared with you.'

'Just a little. But only because you seemed to have got her out of your system.'

'I gave it my best shot, but in the end, I couldn't do it.'

'And what about selling up and moving away? Is that still going to happen?'

Shamefaced, he'd admitted that it had been a lie. 'I'm sorry, Gen, but I told you that because I was banking on you telling Nattie sooner or later. I hoped it would make her think what it would be like if I wasn't around any more. And then, what with all the business with Lily-Rose disappearing, things sort of escalated in a way I could never have foreseen. Do you forgive me?'

She'd pretended to be hurt for all of two seconds. 'I'll forgive you,' she'd said, 'if you make me a promise. One that's in both our interests.'

'Name it and it's yours.'

'You must never, ever tell a living soul what we very nearly did that night at your place.'

'You mean, when we very nearly –'

'Strike it from your memory,' she'd interrupted. 'For Nattie's sake, and Christian's, it must never be mentioned again. If Christian ever knew, I think it might eat away at him. And he doesn't deserve that.'

Breaking into her thoughts now, as she arranged the sweet peas Lily-Rose had specially picked for Gran's grave, Adam said, 'Nattie thinks you're avoiding me, Gen. Are you?'

'Yes,' she said, quite matter-of-factly. She didn't want to lie to Adam.

'Why?'

'Because you don't need an old chum like me hanging around and getting in the way.'

He'd looked at her sternly. 'You couldn't ever be in the way, Gen. I don't want things to change between us. And I don't think Nattie would want that either.'

Despite his words, Genevieve knew that their friendship had already begun to change. Today was the first time, since Adam had apologised for misleading her that they had been alone together. Well almost alone, they still, at Genevieve's contrivance had Lily-Rose with them to act as a chaperon. She'd had no idea that Christian had been feeling the way he had about Adam, and she would do anything to avoid hurting him.

With Lily-Rose wearing a daisy chain crown and carrying a matching one for her mother, Adam hoisted her onto his shoulders and they walked back down into the centre of the village.

After several days of grey skies and frequent showers, it was glorious again. The hot midday sun was high and bright in a flawless blue sky, and ahead of them the placid sea shimmered like an enormous blue jelly. The narrow streets were packed with smiling visitors – small, flush-faced children peering out from beneath sun-hats and waving fishing nets at one another, middle-aged couples strolling slowly arm in arm and groups of teenagers browsing the shops in search of trendy surfing gear. They passed Angel Cottage but didn't stop. Nattie, along with everyone else, would be waiting for them at Paradise House where Serena, having insisted that

Genevieve take the day off, was preparing a special lunch.

'What do you think this lunch is all about?' Adam asked as they waved at Debs through the open door of the crowded salon – it always amazed Genevieve that no matter what the weather, women of a certain age were always prepared to sit under the hot dryer to have their hair done.

'I've a feeling Mum and Dad are going to make an announcement.'

'Any idea what it is?'

'If you'd asked me that a month ago I'd have said their divorce, but since you and Donna did such a good job of turning Dad into Elvis, they've barely let each out of their sight. Mum got what she wanted from Dad that night, a grand gesture of love, and Dad got a surprise – the realisation that the limelight's no bad place to be now and then.'

They stopped to help a young mother negotiate the kerb with a pushchair laden with beach paraphernalia, then carried on.

'Everything your father did that night was his own work,' Adam said. 'Donna and I had very little to do with his performance. When it's from the heart, it needs no extra encouragement.'

'In that case, the same must apply to your own performance. I've said it before, but you were show-stoppingly brilliant. It was a shame you couldn't have won joint first prize with Donna instead of making do with second.' To her amusement, a faint hue of red coloured his face. 'I had no idea you had such a fantastic voice,' she said, further embarrassing him. 'Why have you never showed it off before?'

'Because, just as I do in business, I like to keep a few tricks up my sleeve. Take them unawares is my motto. It never fails.'

'Then perhaps you should have done that sooner with Nattie?'

Holding onto Lily-Rose's ankles as she started bouncing on his shoulders and telling him to giddy up, he smiled. 'But the wait's been worth every minute. I've no regrets.'

It was early days, but Genevieve hoped her sister wouldn't disappoint Adam. Nattie had been her usual self, of course, taking on the chin the flak dished out by Tubby and their father.

'So what if I've changed my mind about Adam,' she told them. 'I was merely biding my time. I was being selective.' She told Genevieve and Polly that she had no intention of changing, though. 'Just because I'm going out with him, it doesn't mean I'm going to turn into something I'm not.'

'I think he'd be upset if you did, Nats,' said Polly.

'Yes,' agreed Genevieve. 'Goodness knows why, but it's the headstrong, difficult, stroppy you he's worshipped all this time, not some shallow, pliable girl without a thought in her head.'

But what amazed them most was Nattie sticking to her word and working for Adam, something they had never truly believed she'd do.

'I'm a woman of principle,' she said, coming home after her first day of being nice to people she probably despised. 'I made a promise and I'll see it through. Even if the job is as boring as hell.'

Lily-Rose, on the other hand, had had a fantastic day and was full of all the fun things she'd got up to: playing on the climbing frames, winning several swimming races in the park pool, and having her face painted. As the days passed and she came home each afternoon with a different face – a tiger one day, a tortoiseshell cat another – it was obvious she was having the time of her life.

As was Polly. Much to Jonjo's delight, and considerable

relief, the night after the talent show, Polly had agreed to get engaged. Embellishing the story with infuriatingly little detail, Polly had told them the following morning, while he was upstairs in the shower, how he'd taken her down to the beach and, in the moonlight, had produced a ring he'd bought in Hong Kong. They'd all crowded round her hand to get a closer look at the cluster of diamonds, and had let out a collective whistle.

'It might have been nice for the young man to ask my permission first,' their father said when they'd run out of superlatives, and Nattie and Mum had stopped trying to squeeze it on their own much larger fingers.

'Oh, Daddy,' said Polly, genuinely upset. 'I'm sure he would have if the right moment had arisen, but –'

'It's okay, Poll, I'm only joking.' He hugged her warmly. 'I suppose this means you'll be moving to Buckingham?' Genevieve could see he was trying to be brave, that he hated the idea of losing her.

'Not for a while,' Polly said. 'And anyway, Jonjo and I will be here as often as possible staying in his new house.'

Even now, as Genevieve led the way round to the back door, she couldn't imagine Paradise House without her youngest sister's benign presence in it.

Lunch was an alfresco affair. Dad had set up two tables end to end in the dappled shade of the orchard. Mum had covered them with a couple of large white cloths, and then had artfully flung handfuls of rose petals in between the plates and glasses. It bore all the hallmarks of a grand Baxter celebration. But what exactly were they celebrating?

Luckily there were no guests hanging around. With the answerphone switched on so lunch wouldn't be spoiled by having to run to the phone every five minutes, Mum instructed them to sit down.

'Adam and Nattie, you sit with Lily-Rose between the two of you. Jonjo, you sit opposite Polly and next to Nattie, and Genevieve, you go at the top of the table, next to your father, and, well, Christian, I think it's fairly obvious where you should go, next to Genevieve. There now, that's everyone sorted. Well, Daddy Dean, what are you waiting for? Let's get these glasses filled!'

Looking happier than Genevieve could ever remember seeing him, her father moved slowly round the table, pouring out their wine. Sitting here with her family, each one of them hugging their own newfound happiness, it was once again easy for Genevieve to believe in her grandmother's theory, that while no one was looking, the angels had been meddling in the nicest possible way. If it had been left to us Baxters, she thought, it would have all ended in tears.

Across the table, she caught Nattie's eye as Adam showed Lily-Rose how to turn her paper napkin into a swan, another of his hidden talents. Nattie smiled at Genevieve and rolled her eyes in Adam's direction. But there was no scorn or malice to the gesture, just a look of happy indulgence. Had the inconceivable happened? Had Nattie been tamed? Had she come to realise that Adam would make the most wonderful father for Lily-Rose? And a devoted husband into the bargain. Even Nattie must have figured that one out for herself. Not that Genevieve could talk. Look how she'd totally misread Christian's feelings towards her.

She still couldn't get over the wonderful double surprise he'd pulled the night of the talent contest. Apparently, when Polly had been staying with Jonjo, and they'd had dinner with Christian, she'd seen how miserable he was and had encouraged him to come back with them so he could talk to Genevieve properly.

'Will it do any good?' he'd asked.

'You'll never know unless you try,' she'd told him.

A slight squeeze on her leg under the table had her turning to Christian. 'You okay?' he mouthed.

She reached for his hand and mouthed back, 'I'm fine.' There it was again. *I'm fine*. Yes, but this time she really was.

'Hey, you two!' said Nattie from across the table, 'no secret conversations. We had enough of that when we were children. The pair of you were always leaving the rest of us out.'

Christian missed what she'd said, so Genevieve repeated it for him.

'Perhaps you ought to learn to lipread, Nattie,' he said.

Adam burst out laughing. 'Steady on, Christian, she's got enough to do learning to be nice to me.'

Again Christian missed what had been said and after Genevieve had put him right, Serena raised her glass. She waited for them all to follow suit. She looked down the length of the table to where her husband was sitting.

'Here's to us all and what lies ahead.'

They responded to the toast and Lily-Rose, gulping down her apple juice too fast, let out an enormous burp and made them all laugh.

'Do you think we ought to tell them what does lie ahead?' asked Daddy Dean.

'I suppose we ought to,' Serena said, 'seeing as it affects them so directly.'

'Come on you two,' demanded Nattie. 'We've played along enough. It's time to hit the newsflash button and tell us what this lunch is all about.'

Serena looked at their father. 'Go on, then. You do the honours.'

With all eyes on him, Daddy Dean said, 'Your mother and I have decided we need some time away together and . . . and if it's okay with all of you, we want to go on an extended second honeymoon.'

'What a wonderful idea,' said Polly. 'For how long?'

'Um . . . We haven't decided exactly. But it'll definitely be longer than our first.'

'Perhaps a month, maybe two,' Serena added more assuredly.

Nattie whistled. 'Now that's some second honeymoon.'

'Where are you thinking of going?' asked Genevieve.

'New Zealand. Your mother wants to show me where she's been staying and then we'll go exploring somewhere new. Australia seems a likely bet. I've always been fascinated by the idea of Alice Springs.'

'Then perhaps you'd better make it two to three months,' suggested Jonjo.

'But what about us? And Paradise House?' Nattie's voice had taken a turn for the worse, like a child who didn't want to be left behind.

Serena said, 'You'll be fine without us, Nattie. You have a lovely new house to live in, a job, a gorgeous daughter and,' she cast a look in Adam's direction, 'a man who adores you. I'd say you have everything a girl could wish for. And as to Paradise House, well, that's slightly more complicated.'

She turned to Genevieve, and with a sinking heart Genevieve braced herself to hear the words she didn't want to hear. If there was one thing she was sure of, she didn't want to go on running Paradise House as it was. It was too exhausting. Too chaotic. With five guest suites, she needed regular help she could rely on.

'Genevieve,' her father said, 'your mother and I owe you a huge debt of gratitude for all the hard work you've put in since you came home, so before I say anything else, I just want to thank you. I, personally, don't know what I would have done without you.' Clearing his throat, he carried on. 'It's entirely up to you, but w wondered if you would want to take on the full responsibility of running Paradise House, but not as it is. So, we've come up with an idea we want you to consider. It would mean a total revamp of the place, someone to help oversee the work, and more importantly, someone special to put it on the map. And we think that special someone is you.'

Still holding Christian's hand beneath the table, Genevieve took a gulp of her wine and listened to what her parents had to say.

Genevieve was banned from going anywhere near the kitchen for the rest of the day. Not even to help with the washing up.

'Christian, I order you to take her for a very long walk,' Serena said. 'As far away from here as possible.'

'You don't have to do everything my family says,' Genevieve said, once they were away from Paradise House and standing outside the Salvation Arms, looking down onto the beach. It was early evening, the sun was dropping in the pale sky and most of the people on the beach had gathered together their belongings and gone. Only a handful of Power Boat People were left, as usual making their noisy exit, winching boats onto trailers, yelling and slamming car doors.

'Don't you mean *our* family? According to your mother I'm now an honorary member.'

She turned to face him. 'You're joking?'

'I'm not. Your mother said that now I don't have a family of my own, I'm to treat yours as mine.'

Genevieve cringed. 'Tell me she wasn't as insensitive as that.'

'Her exact words. So how do you feel about me being part of the family?'

'Outraged. She'll be handing over the priceless family silver next.'

'I'd rather have the best prize of all. You. OK, I know that was the cheesiest line ever uttered, but give me a break, I'm learning from the master, Jonjo.'

'Then stop it. Stop it right now. One charmer in the family is quite enough. Do you fancy a drink in the pub, or a walk?'

'Let's walk to Tawelfan.'

They walked hand in hand along the coastal path, in an easy, comfortable silence. Genevieve knew that Christian was tired from the strain of trying to keep up with so much hectic conversation during lunch.

Taking the steep path down to Tawelfan, they found they had the beach to themselves. The dunes were also deserted, and they sat on the warm, dry sand, staring out at the horizon. What little breeze there had been blowing in off the sea all day had now dwindled to nothing. Faint strands of clouds had formed in the sky around the setting sun and a chain of gulls flew along the shore, their wings hardly moving as they glided elegantly into the distance. In the perfect quiet of the moment, Genevieve thought of all that had been discussed that afternoon. Her parents going away for a second honeymoon; Jonjo saying he didn't want a long engagement – 'If I give Polly too much time to think about it, she might change her mind,' he'd said – and Polly admitting that she'd already applied for several teaching jobs in and around Buckingham so she could be with Jonjo. And lastly, there was her parents' idea to turn Paradise House into a smart upmarket country house hotel, with a restaurant offering fine gourmet food. 'It's the way a lot of B & Bs are going these days,' they said.

They'd clearly put a lot of thought into it and had even been to the bank to see about a loan. 'We want to semi-retire,' her father said. 'We'll help as much as you want us to, but we want officially to sign over Paradise House to you three girls.'

What they had in mind was for Genevieve to have the marginally larger share, because she would be the one responsible for making it work. Initially, Genevieve was unsure. Would this be her dream? Or would it still be her parents'? She decided that the only way she could take it on would be if she had a full say in how things were run. She would need the right kind of help too, proper full or part-time staff. Donna, who'd already proved herself so invaluable, and had now moved in with Tubby, was the ideal candidate to be in charge of housekeeping. With someone so reliable on hand, Genevieve would be left to do what she enjoyed most – cooking. She might even go on a few courses, get a few fancy badges to her name.

The more she thought about it, the more excited she began to feel. She pictured the dining room having undergone a much-needed facelift. There would be candlelit dinners, with cocktails beforehand on the terrace if the weather was warm, and roaring log fires to cosy up to in the winter.

But to achieve any of that, there would have to be a great deal of upheaval. As her father had said during lunch, 'The worst bit will be living here while the work is being carried out. The layout will have to be improved; rooms knocked about, walls taken down, walls put up. For instance, you'll need a much larger kitchen. An extension's the answer. And if you got rid of the private sitting room you could turn it into a games room.'

'But where would we have our own private space? We can't lose that altogether.' Genevieve had said.

'You're forgetting the extension.'

'Sounds to me like you need an architect,' said Jonjo. 'A decent architect who comes with impeccable references. I wonder if anyone knows of one?'

*

Turning from the sea and looking at Christian, Genevieve said, 'You know that architect I might be in need of?'

'Yes.'

'Do you suppose he might be too busy with all his other commitments to help at Paradise House?'

'He might be. But on the other hand, he might not.' He shifted round so they were face to face, and reaching for her hands, he entwined his fingers through hers. 'I've come to an important decision, one that requires your approval before I take it any further. How would you feel if I lived more locally?'

'How locally?'

'Here in Angel Sands.'

'That's quite a commute. You'd have to be up early to be in the office for nine each morning.'

'True. Although it would depend where the office was. If, say, I worked for myself, I could work wherever I wanted.'

'Are you saying what I think you're saying?'

He stroked her cheek, traced her lips with a finger. 'I love you Genevieve, and more than anything I want to give *us* a real chance of working. We can't do that if we live so far apart.'

'You'd really do that?'

'In the blink of an eye. All I need to know is that you feel the same; that it's worth a go. But I'll warn you now I've got it all planned. For the time being, I'm going to rent out my parents' house in Shropshire, sell my flat and rent a small cottage near you. That way we won't be rushing things. Oh, and as to work, to begin with I reckon I can make a living from all the barns in the area that are ripe for conversion. Tubby's already put me onto several further along the coast. And there are always holiday homes to create or renovate. So what do you think? Will it work?'

A euphoric surge of happiness filled her. 'I think it will work *fine*, Christian. But just to be sure, this isn't a double bluff, is it? You're not threatening commitment in the hope I'll do a runner?'

He laughed out loud. 'You're not running anywhere. In fact, you're staying right here.' He pushed her back onto the warm sand and kissed her.

As Genevieve closed her eyes, she caught sight of a faint ghost of a cloud floating directly above their heads. She was probably imagining it, but it looked just like one of Gran's angels gazing down on her.

Acknowledgements

I'm indebted to many people who helped with the writing of this book, but any errors are all down to me!

Thanks to everyone at the Dyslexia Institute in Wilmslow and to Caroline Aspin for being kind enough to share her experiences.

Thanks to everyone at the Deaf Centre in Northwich, especially Linda Gill who was so generous with her time.

Thanks to all those in Pembrokeshire who unwittingly helped by allowing me to strike up conversation with them. And I apologise for fiddling with the geography and making room for Angel Sands.

Thanks to John and Celia Lea for the guided tour – sorry I missed the bluebells.

Thanks to Val and Barry of Congleton Farm for the helpful insight.

Thanks to Paul and Amanda for allowing me to pinch Paradise House.

Thanks to my ol' mate Welsh John for his insider knowledge.

Thanks to the real Christian May who, of course, bears no relation to the fictional character – just in case he's thinking of suing!

Thanks to my Cranage Buddies – Sheila and Kath – for their warmth and friendliness and for not laughing (too much) at my fake tan!

And lastly grateful thanks to Jonathan Lloyd and everyone at Orion.